TO BURN ALL BELIEF

SECOND DANCE OF THE
SIBLING SUNS

JOSHUA SCOTT EDWARDS

ARCHEFIRE
PUBLISHING

PRAISE FOR
DANCE OF THE SIBLING SUNS

"A hell of a lot of fun"
—**Fantasy-Faction**

"My favorite read of 2023"
—**Rob Leigh**, author of *Pathlighter*

"Exceptionally satisfying"
—**E.L. Lyons**, author of *Starlight Jewel*

"The prose is excellent"
—**Timothy Wolff**, author of *Platinum Tinted Darkness*

"Edwards writes with a clear voice"
—**Mark Timmony**, author of *The Blood of the Spear*

"Had me hooked within the first couple of chapters"
—**Craig Bookwyrm**

"A fun, enjoyable romp which also delves into some dark places"
—**Nick Procter**

"Unique and outside the box"
—**Quinn Guigere**

"An incredibly solid debut"
—**bunnyreads**

Archefire Publishing LLC
Lansdale, PA 19446
www.archefire.com

Editing by Stacey Kucharik
Cover art by Felix Ortiz
Cover design by Shawn T. King
Bright Empire map by Keir Scott-Schrueder
Liwokin map by Dewi Hargreaves

To Burn All Belief / Joshua Scott Edwards. -- 1st ed.
ISBN 979-8-9856162-2-4 (ebook)
979-8-9856162-3-1 (paperback)

*For Brielle, who
persevered through the
dark to shine so bright*

Contents

PART THREE: BEACON

APPENDICES

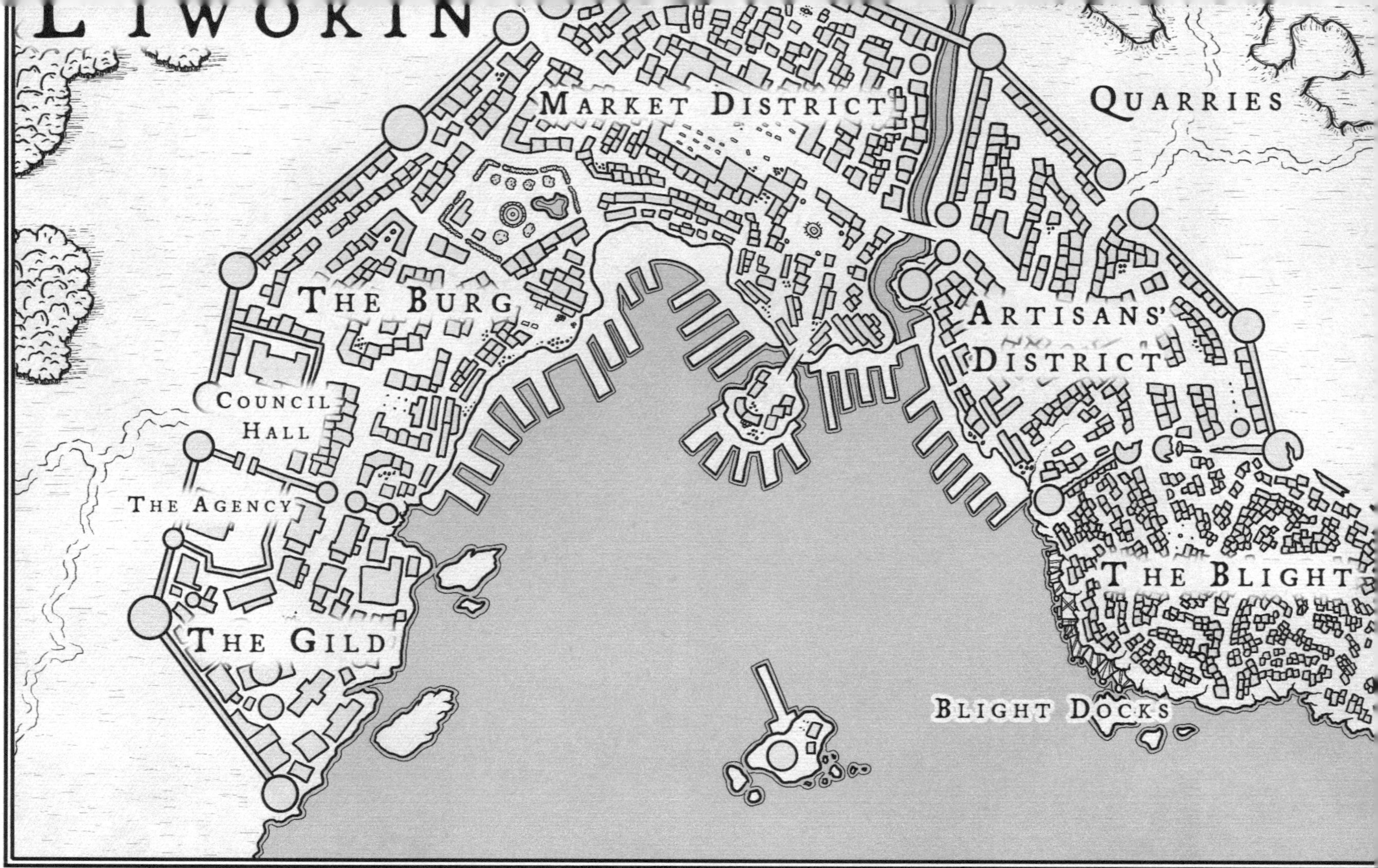

LIWOKIN
QUARRIES
MARKET DISTRICT
THE BURG
ARTISANS' DISTRICT
COUNCIL HALL
THE AGENCY
THE GILD
THE BLIGHT
BLIGHT DOCKS

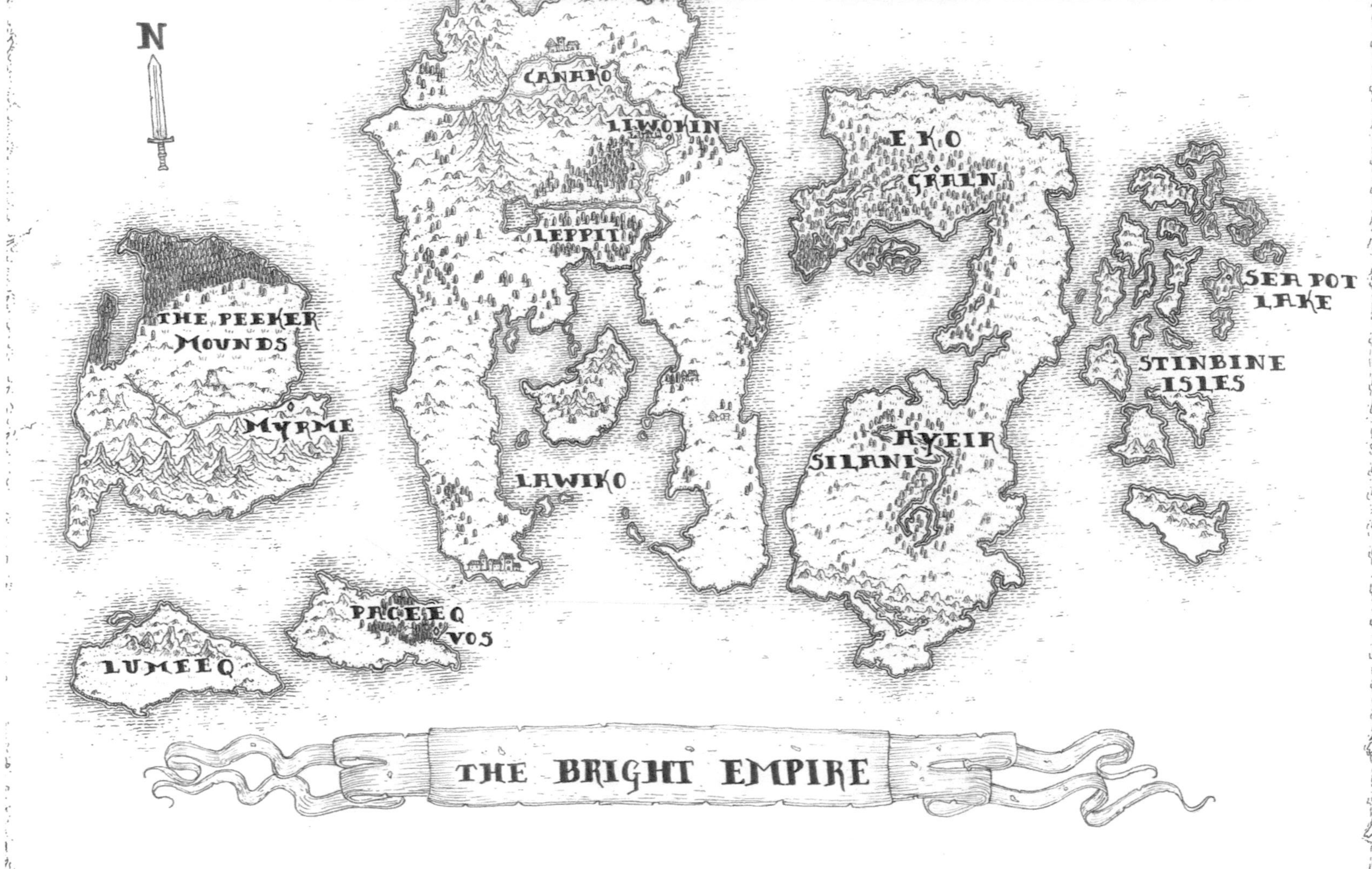

N
CANARO
LIWOKIN
EKO
GRALN
LEPPIT
SEA POT LAKE
THE PEEKER MOUNDS
STINBINE ISLES
MYRME
AYEIR
SILANI
LAWIKO
PROEEQ VOS
LUMEEQ
THE BRIGHT EMPIRE

The Story So Far

Thank you for returning to the Dance of the Sibling Suns series! It has been some time since the release of An Ocean of Others — certainly a bit longer than I anticipated — so for those of you who have been waiting, this section should serve to refresh your memory for the story to come. I'll include only what is necessary to enjoy To Burn All Belief. More info can be found in the Glossary and Character List at the back of the book, but beware of spoilers.

CONCEPTS:

• **Benefactors** are parasites infesting the brain of many characters, including Grim. They exist in an Incubating state until the host dies, upon which they take over the host's body and transform them into an Emergent Benefactor. These monsters emit Auras that cause nearby people to experience sensory illusions and emotions. These are linked to memories and experiences of the infested host before they died. Those infested with Incubating Benefactors are subject to experiencing Deluges that force the victim to relive the memory of a Benefactor they came in contact with.

• **The Agency** is an organization founded, on paper, to eliminate the Benefactors. In truth, the original Head of the Agency, Ulken, worked with his advisor to spread Benefactors as a means to gain control over the city of Liwokin. The organization has several classes of employee, listed below:

—**The Head,** leader with full control over the Agency.

—**Nerves,** couriers who relay messages from the Head.

—**Eyes,** reconnaissance officers who discern Benefactor activity.

—**Fingers,** field agents who carry out the Head's commands.

—**Hands,** groups of five Fingers dispatched to hunt Benefactors.

—**Organs,** administrators for specific Agency operations, such as Logistics or Evidence.

—**Heels,** low-level workers who perform menial labor.

• **Archemagic** is practiced throughout the Bright Empire, mainly in the form of Archefire but sometimes as forbidden Archedark. The prefix Arche- is applied to many professions that employ magic in their craft (e.g. Archesmith, Archehealer, etc.). Archemetal is a metal imbued with the Fire, making it exceedingly durable and unburnable.

• **The Church of Light** is the dominant religion in the Bright Empire, with a pantheon of two opposed gods, the Lightmother and the Darkfather, and personifications of the Sibling Suns.

• **The Sibling Suns** are the Brightdaughter in the northern hemisphere and the Shadowson in the southern hemisphere. Both have unpredictable orbits leading to varying lengths of day. Time is marked in the Bright Empire by the Rhythm of Time, bells rung by mathemelodians who calculate the Brightdaughter's movement through the sky.

SETTING:

• **The Bright Empire** is the hegemonic empire of the northern hemisphere. Its capital, Vos, is located on the island of Paceeq. Led by a Bright Empress with a religious mandate and enforced by an Order of Paladins. Elzia, the latest empress recently passed away.

• **Liwokin** is the capital city of Lawiko and a main trading hub of the Bright Empire. Divided into five districts:

—**The Gild,** name given to both the financial district and the cabal of wealthy financiers that runs it.

—**The Burg,** residential area where many Liwo own homes.

—**The Market,** where merchants live and sell their wares.

—**The Artisans,** where artists and craftspeople set up shop.

—**The Blight,** common name for the run-down old city where Liwokin originated.

• **Arza**, a promising technician who replaced lead mortician Tak after his death at the hands of a Benefactor.

• **Oltrov**, Gildmember who worked with Reed to overthrow Ulken.

• **Bello**, an elevator operator from the Blight.

• **Raylen**, an enterprising smuggler who sold Druid's Tears from the Enclave; however, the Enclave now refuses to do business with the Agency.

• **Cavern**, Sentyx's brother and the second Skardwarf in the north.

• **Tunnel**, Peeker rescued by Garret, Grim, and Sentyx from the Mental Ward.

STORY:

At the end of An Ocean of Others, Grim and the rest of Hand Sixty-Four defeat Ulken, who they discovered worked to spread the Benefactors with his advisor, Prost. In the process, Grim is nearly killed but rescued by Reed, who bestows him with the power Ulken had been seeking—the knowledge of ten thousand lives and more, the ability to see through eyes not his own, and the power to shape reality as he sees fit.

Within that ocean of others is Reed's memory, which allows Grim to become an entirely new type of Benefactor. One that is human in form, not monstrous, and in Grim's control. Benefactors evolve and learn, and by spreading through Peekers, the new type of Benefactor Grim inherited has much further reach and strength. The fact of Benefactors reaching the Peeker Mounds leads Grim to believe Prost is there as well.

Grim's wounds are healed as his Benefactor Emerges along with a torrent of memories from everyone infested by the organism. Grim kills Ulken and becomes Head of the Agency, vowing to his friends that he'll reform the Agency as a force for good so it can ensure humanity survives the Benefactors scourge.

TO BURN ALL BELIEF

In kindred Light find thee solace on Darkening shores,
when this land grants us shelter and Brightness no more

—Second Proverb of the Book of Light

PART ONE
DISSOLUTION

Prologue

In darkness, her memories came to me.

The classroom's nauseating smell of ammonia and saltpeter cloyed at my nostrils, disturbed by a waft of mint that accompanied the slow meandering of a rotund man. My husband had eyes only for Prost now. They were locked onto his accomplice, who lectured at me, slapping down worthless plans and diagrams on the desk I sat behind.

"...unique opportunity for Ulken to regain control of the city," he advised. "Perhaps far more than that."

Ulken's eyes flicked to me as if to gauge my reaction to Prost's insane ramblings.

But I was hardly listening. I had been forced here against my will, only acquiescing to come with the assurance that Ulken would take my opinion seriously if I dissented with the "plan."

Plan? No. These are delusions.

The more I listened, the greater my certainty grew that the decision had already been made. I kept a firm grip on my long coat, wrapping it tight.

Why drag me *to this fetid classroom, then, husband?*

"...and believe me, your husband will serve Liwokin to the best of his abilities. He is quite a remarkable pupil. Only one other listened better than him. Alas—"

Ulken bristled at being talked about as a subordinate. Only bristled. Once, he would have shown this fool how much of a man he was. I mourned for those lost days, traveling the Bright Empire together, marveling at its wonders. But there was no bringing them back.

Some choices cannot be unmade.

"Is there a point to my being here?" I demanded.

"Don't interrupt, my love," Ulken said. "It's unbecoming of a lady."

I squeezed my fists, fingernails digging into my palms. That man knew how to make a woman's blood boil. Had he always been such a pig? Had I been blind to his true colors? There was no missing them now. They showed themselves in his obeisance to Prost.

The man's footsteps and clacking cane stopped right beside me. He leaned forward on the desk, far too close for comfort, breathing heavily, even though ambling around the classroom was the only way he exerted himself. He grinned as though I were a prime cut of meat he looked forward to devouring.

If Ulken didn't have the good sense to fire his advisor after that disastrous Council Chair selection, I would have to put an end to this myself, lest he do something that got him arrested by the militia and hanged.

"It's quite all right," Prost said, licking his lips. "She simply needs more convincing. I have just the thing."

"No." I stood. The chair's feet screeched against the floor, and Ulken's mouth twisted in rage.

It almost cowed me...I almost sat back down...but I was his *wife*. *Let him face the rage of a woman, and we'll see if he doesn't wither beneath my gaze.*

"I've heard more than my fill of this prattling. One more sentence from you," I warned, poking my husband's handler in his considerable flab, "and you'll be begging the Lightmother for mercy. On and on about the Peeker Mounds, Paceeq, Eko. Skardwarves and immortality. Children's stories! What about the people of Liwokin?" I asked Ulken, praying that he might finally see reason. "The Liwo whom you tried to become Council Chair to *help*. Have you forgotten *us*?"

"Yezna...I haven't—" Ulken started.

"Becoming Council Chair was always unnecessary," the heavy man said with a waggle of his hand. "I tried to tell you how the selection would turn out. That insufferable hag couldn't be beaten." He chuckled, a short, choked-off sound. "Not like that, anyway."

I noticed that Ulken dared not scold *him* for interrupting. As much as my husband believed himself powerful and in control, this worm in his ear held the real power. I had held that sway once. He had listened to *me*.

Are those days truly gone?

"But what need for mere *political* influence," he said 'political' like it tasted of rotten fish, "when Ulken could see through the eyes of his enemies? Know their minds as clearly as they themselves know them. Better, even."

I sniffed loudly. "Why don't you crawl back into the mortuary where you belong, rather than filling my husband's head with...with..." Ulken cut me off with a laugh, as though I'd said something funny. He wasn't the only one with an infuriating grin on his face. "Or should I take you there myself and lay you out on a slab for your own dissection? Your students would learn much with such an *ample* specimen."

"Oh ho," he laughed, and slapped his rippling belly. "I'm certain they would. I taught them well. Sadly, they're all preoccupied with, what did you call it? 'Our little experiment.'" He had that hungry look again, that same look a circling gull casts down upon the bay.

At that moment, two figures entered, both wearing colorful hoods and elongated masks that made them look like flightless terrorbeaks from the stormjungles of Eko, where Ulken and I honeymooned. Both carried supplies that they placed on a table beside Ulken—worn leather straps, a dirty spoon, a wooden stick covered with bite marks, and a glass vial of bubbly, greenish-brown fluid.

My breathing quickened with each item they laid down, but it was the last that made my mouth go dry. One of the hooded men pulled from his pocket a syringe with a needle as long as my finger. When he began spooning the viscous liquid into the back of the syringe, I straightened my back and turned to my husband.

"What is this? You think I'm some animal? A rat to scurry around in this madman's maze?"

Ulken had the decency to look abashed. He tried to look at the syringe, now laying full on the desk beside him, but I pulled his gaze back to my own. Over his shoulder, the three other men loomed. Motionless. Waiting for my husband to make a decision.

He can't go through with this. He'll listen to me. He must.

I held his hands in mine. "Do you remember the oaths we swore to each other when we married?" He didn't pull his hands free. That was good. Maybe there was still a chance to convince him. "To follow the Lightmother's guidance, to walk her path together..."

"To protect each other from harm," Ulken continued, and I squeezed his hands with a smile.

"Until the Darkfather consumes the world," we finished together, just as we had all those years ago at sunrise with Reed and the others watching on. This bloated man who so enamored Ulken hadn't been there. He was nothing, a foreigner from an unknown land, a passing shadow in the Brightdaughter's light.

"That's just it, my love," Ulken said, and all the softness in his eyes faded. "The Darkfather *has* come. Only we can stop it."

I jerked my hands free of his grasp, stared up at him. He wore a face I had come to loathe, so cold, an expression that bespoke his suppression of what he *felt* for the benefit of what he *wanted*. He wanted to do this. He believed he must. He was wrong, but he'd never see it.

Breaking your vows, subjecting your wife to this? *You're no husband of mine, Ulken. No longer.* My eyes filled with tears as my mind conjured an image of the one man I could think of who could help. Reed. Not for the first time, I wondered if I had chosen wrong. It was a pointless question. Ulken might break his vows, but I wouldn't. *I was only trying to protect you. From him.*

I glared at Prost, disgusted by the look on his face that told me he was *enjoying* watching this. Without wasting another word, I whirled and strode out the door.

Two steps down the long hallway, and it creaked open again. I rounded on Ulken as he stepped out of the classroom. When he closed the door behind him, a gust of air struck me, carrying that same acrid scent. Ammonia and saltpeter. I nearly gagged.

"*What?*" I snarled.

"Yezna," he said, "please, just listen to what Prost has to say."

* * *

I had seen enough. I knew what happened next in Yezna's memory, and it sickened me too much to watch it unfold again. Ulken taking his wife painfully by the arm, injecting her with the Benefactor organism against her will. It was unthinkable, and all for some delusion that he could save the world from the Darkfather. How many people had died because of Ulken's madness?

Yezna's memory faded, replaced by another.

* * *

I ran down a shadowy street paved with gravel, a bundle of signs slipping from underarm. Counting the number of turns—one left, two left, one right, three left—down a dirt alleyway I went, with the Gild towers looming overhead and the bells of the nearby church somberly chiming. Sixty paces until the door—I didn't need an address, but where I was going wasn't listed in the official registers anyhow.

"Eight, nine, forty, forty-one, two, three..." I counted aloud, the thrill of what we were doing drawing my excited energy out. "...six, seven—"

My foot hit a rock, and I hit the stone ground, hard. The signs scattered before me, unreadable in the dim light. The Brightdaughter had arced high today, but dusk was fast approaching. I still whipped my head around, left, right, to make sure no one could see. Left again.

Boots stood not a pace away. The man wearing them scoffed, then placed down a crate. Dust swirled and metal clacked as the wooden box settled into the dirt. My tongue felt swollen inside my mouth.

"You imbecile." Strong hands gripped my collar and lifted me to my feet.

He slapped me softly on the cheek and smiled.

It was *him*. None of us used names—too risky, and risk was for the Gild—but we all knew who he was.

Dark blue eyes, the color of the bay before dawn. A scruffy beard and bushy eyebrows were the only hair on his bald head. He wore a plain brown coat that hung to his ankles, a match for the worn leather of his boots. He carried no sword, though he had the strength to use one, certainly, judging by those thick arms of his. Probably couldn't afford one, no different from the rest of us.

Light knows what I would give for the coin to buy a sword. Thirty stars in the Artisans, no great sum and not far from home. But I haven't enough even for a proper meal no more.

He helped me collect my signs, but his words were not so kind as his actions. "Do you realize what would happen if a Finger saw you carrying those? A Heel, even? The rest of us would lose our heads, but not before you lost as many body parts as the Agency could name while they tortured you to give us up."

I gulped, tried to say anything, but my drunk tongue still disobeyed.

Darkfather, I shouldn't o' been drinking. Only, I'd needed the courage. You had to be a complete fool or a brave man to paint what I'd painted on those signs. *Or a brave fool. A drunk, brave fool.*

"That's right. You understand. I couldn't watch that happen. I care about you. *We* care about you. And the moment we're drawn out of the shadows, our time to prepare is over. You don't believe me?"

"I-I-I believe you."

"Good," the man said, shoving the six signs he'd collected back into my hands, making a total of eleven. A good number. Two ones. "Because the rest of this city doesn't. We ask for so little and get nothing in return. Our cries have gone unanswered for too long." He hefted the crate, revealing a deep impression in the dirt beneath. It must have weighed sixty pounds, but he lifted it with no strain whatsoever. "Well, the Old Hill has been trod on long enough. Now come. I didn't lug these across the city for nothing."

I followed him to a door barred with planks, watched with glee as he knocked one, two, three times, then three more in quick succession. In response, six locks clacked, and the door opened, revealing the desolate front for the ruse it was. Together, we walked down fourteen steps into a basement bursting with people.

Setting my signs down on a table lit with a steam-powered light—there must have been an Archemage in the crowd—I admired my handiwork. The handwriting was unsteady, but the message was clear enough.

'Justice for the dead.'

'Off with his Head!'

Perfect. I smiled in satisfaction, then turned to see how many people were in the room. Filling the space from wall to wall, there were too many of us to count.

CHAPTER ONE

Madman

The organism has reached the Peeker Mounds. As this has developed just as foreseen, might I suggest you finally rid yourself of the First? It must be done eventually. Better to inflict the wound quickly to grant it time to heal.

—Unsigned letter to the Head of the Agency

"Grim, you are again doing it," Inac said. My friend flicked a switch on the wall with his left hand, and the lights in Ulken's office whirred on.

No. Not Ulken's office. Mine.

I sighed, preferring to keep the lights off. That way I didn't have to look at the mess the prior Head left behind. A collection of broken seals from the letters I'd opened. A drawer full of keys to unknown doors, presumably all around the city. Ulken had come and gone where he pleased. Not that he needed to leave the tower much after gaining the ability to steal the memories of those he met, using Yezna's Benefactor to abet his crimes. He'd turned his office into a nest of treasures, and he treasured nothing so much as evidence that incriminated his enemies.

Inac sat in the chair at the side of my desk, then carefully slid a stack of documents to the side so he could see me. "Anything new this time?"

My friend gave me a sympathetic, questioning smile. 'Are you well?' it asked, the same question I wanted to ask him. Dark bags framed his green eyes. His sandy mop of curly hair had grown beyond unkempt, well into disheveled. He kept the hood of that tattered blue robe up to hide it, most times. Always the blue robe, and his arm beneath it, at his side. My friend looked travel-worn.

Travel-worn and tired. As weary as me and more.

I shook my head. "Nothing useful. Preparations for some protest against Ulken. Besides that, the same memory I always see. Ulken and Prost infesting Yezna."

Creating the first Benefactor, though I doubted they knew it at the time. It was Yezna's Emergence that caused the Great Riot, and even Ulken wouldn't wish that upon the city.

Then again...

A memory surfaced of Ulken's hand gripping my arm so tightly, I turned, expecting him to be in the room with me. Here in the office of the Head of the Agency. An office that wouldn't exist if not for the Riot. Had the chaos of that day been his plan from the very start? Or had his advisor masterminded the misdeed?

Ulken and Prost. Madmen, the both of them.

Yet I was the one jumping at old memories. Reed had called it a gift, his last act. To bequeath me the power of the Benefactors, the ability to see through the eyes of others and know their thoughts. The dead First Eye had made it seem a grand thing.

In reality, it meant my days were plagued by intrusive memories as thoroughly as my brain was infested by the tiny organisms responsible for them. It meant carrying the lives of ten thousand dead within my mind. It meant *I* was responsible for stopping the scourge from consuming us all.

With a wry laugh, I threw down the pen I had been chewing on. It bounced off a stack of papers on my desk, rolled off, and clattered on the floor.

Nicely done, Reed. The fate of the Bright Empire rests on the shoulders of a madman brought back from the dead who can't even make sense of these snuffing tax documents.

And that was only one of the piles of forms.

I bent to pick up the pen. "How did he do it, Inac?"

Inac had been talking, though I hadn't been listening, absorbed by my thoughts as usual. He bore the interruption gracefully—exactly opposite from Ulken's tendencies.

"Do what, my friend?"

"This." I gestured at the paperwork covering every flat surface in the room. A bounty hunter prepared for all possibilities, but ten thousand lifetimes of memories hadn't prepared me for this. "All of this, while afflicted by Yezna's memories. Everyone's memories. How was he in such control?" I was pacing, and nearly kicked over an open inkwell on the floor.

"Ulken always believed himself to be in control." Inac scowled. "Right up to the moment you rose from death and stabbed him in the heart.

"The Lightmother knows, he was confident."

Otherwise, he would have had some contingency to destroy the evidence of his corruption. But it was precisely that evidence that revealed how darkly competent Ulken truly was.

I gestured at a stack of letters by Inac's feet. "Do you know what those are? City officials. Gildmembers. Archemakers. Darkfather, even some abyss-damned Clerics. The whole of Liwokin is in here, and Ulken had blackmail on them all. But it gets worse."

"Worse how?"

"Now *I* have blackmail on them all. And I sure as shadow don't *want* it."

"So get rid of it. There are for you more important matters to attend."

I paused, taking a moment to level a look at my right-hand man. "Come on. Do you think I wouldn't have done that if it were so simple?" I would have restored the militia and bounty hunters to the city with a pen stroke, if I could. Except both required cooperation from the Liwokin Council, who refused to answer my correspondence.

Taking a handful of letters from the pile on the ground, I poked my pen at an open leather book filled with illegible scribbling. "Ulken's ledger. He didn't even try to hide it. Do you know why the Agency never charges commission?"

Inac's lips twitched in a grin. "Because Ulken loved the common Liwo?"

I threw down the first letter. "Because Ulken found out *this* man skims coin from the Gild's investments." The Agency charged no coin—people paid instead in their secrets, stolen by Ulken's control of Yezna's Benefactor. The next letter was to a mage now operating our boilers. "He found out *this* woman paid an Archemage to burn down a competing smith's practice." Another. "Murder." Another. "Slavery. Blasphemy."

Inac's face grew more disturbed with each revelation.

I couldn't help but laugh at the absurdity. "A portion of a Cleric's stolen tithes pay for our lunches. The whole city is rotting from the inside, and the Agency is feeding on its corpse. Some days it seems best to ask you to burn this tower to the ground."

Inac had been sullenly studying the floorboards. He winced when I mentioned the Fire.

"I—" I reached out with my right hand to grab his shoulder. He looked sidelong at it, and I hastily lowered it. "I'm sorry. I didn't think—"

Best stop peeling back the skin when it starts to bleed.

I changed the subject. "Believe it or not, it gets even worse than that."

"I know..." He drew a breath and pulled his tattered robe tighter. Inac had a way of reading my mind. Maybe it was the infestation in his head talking to mine, or maybe he was simply a close enough friend. "We will figure it out."

We had to. Because worst of all was that we couldn't tear down the sinister machine Ulken built. The Agency was our best tool for stopping the Benefactors.

If I could just figure out how to run the damned place. My eye landed on a letter describing an outstanding debt to the Gild. *Before we run out of money, would be nice.*

"This place is all we have," I said. "What I *wish* we had was someone good with numbers. Ulken's plotting will be easy enough to unravel. What'll be hard is how figuring out how many stars we *really* have in our coffers. How much time we have left."

Inac began scrawling on a notepad pulled from his inner coat pocket. He had been leading the efforts to hire more Fingers, though he was having trouble making up for those we'd lost fighting Benefactors under Ulken's command. Big surprise, no one existed in Liwokin who wanted to fight indescribable monsters.

"Oh!" An idea surfaced, a chance perhaps to put my curse to some good use. "That memory of the protest against Ulken. It came from some guy in the Burg, obsessed with numbers. He had it out for Ulken, too. Maybe we could find him, if he's still there." What had his sign said? Justice for the dead, off with his Head? I would have laughed if not for the sign reminding me of the thousands of Liwo the Great Riot killed. "If he hated Ulken as much as I think, he might be willing to help."

Inac had stopped scribbling notes. "From how long ago was this memory?"

I opened my mouth, then shut it again. I had no idea, really. After the Great Riot, of course. But the man could have been killed in Reed's Woods. Far too many Liwo had lost their lives that day, assimilated into the Benefactor's twisted tower.

"Right. Numbers. I will think of someone. You should focus on more important tasks, such as—"

"Fighting the Benefactors."

Inac glowered at me and stood abruptly. The lights dimmed, and the room grew colder. "You told to me these jobs would be done before I returned." He lifted an unlit lantern from a scattering of handwritten requests. "Reports of crime in the Burg. Crumbling infrastructure in the Blight. Arson in the Artisans. This is serious. These are from the people of Liwokin. The people you *promised* to me the Agency would serve."

"The Agency *will* serve them," I said, slamming a fist on my desk.

As soon as I can make it run.

"In the only way that matters."

The only way I know how.

"By stopping the Benefactor plague from spreading." I relaxed my posture and softened. "It's just taken longer than I'd hoped to adjust." With a smile, I added, "And you haven't been long away, friend. Four or five days—"

"Thirty-three," Inac interjected. "I was away thirty-three days." He no longer sounded angry. Concern colored his voice now.

Darkfather... How much time slips away while I hunt for answers in old memories?

The stacks of neglected work on my desk, floor, and side tables seemed answer enough. Too much. But no matter how pressing the tasks brought to me by Fingers and Nerves, none of them superseded the hunt. I needed to find the man responsible for spreading the Benefactors.

We needed to find Prost.

Sentyx volunteered to search the Peeker Mounds for the elusive man, and Garret had followed along. Those two were inseparable. If Prost was there, I had no doubt they would find him.

But if Ulken's advisor remained in Liwokin, there might be some clue to his whereabouts in the ocean of others that filled my head. Failing that, might some of these memories contain the expertise to unravel this bureaucratic tangle I found myself in? Even that seemed too much to hope for.

The people of Liwokin would have to wait. Until I halted the spread of the scourge in Liwokin, none of their requests mattered. Crime. Repairs. What were those compared to an all-consuming plague that turned the dead into monsters?

Monsters like me.

As if he could read my thoughts, Inac's expression shifted to one of greater worry. What did he see in my own? Pain? Pity?

Maybe a bit of self-loathing.

I had killed the monster that threatened Liwokin to get here—Ulken. But in doing so, became the very thing I was trying to destroy. A Benefactor. As maddening as it was, allowing another to break loose was the last thing I would allow. Not while I was Head of the Agency.

My friend tentatively reached out with his left hand, offering a comforting touch. I would have let him. Lightmother knew I needed some bond to keep me grounded in my humanity.

A Nerve burst in through the door instead. Cold, flickering light poured in and outlined his silhouette. He wore a long, white coat with gold trim lining every edge and matching white gloves with golden tree-like patterns opposite the palms. Those gloves creaked as he balled his fists and gave a sharp salute across the chest.

"Sir."

I had never seen one salute like that before. Nor had I ever seen a Nerve look quite so...nervous. He was breathing hard and trembling. Blood stained his white coat.

Must be a new hire. "What's wrong, er..." *Damn. What's his name?* With the memories of ten thousand lives in my head, each face was too easily forgettable. "Out with it. Before I decide you'd serve better as a Heel."

I winced at the outburst and stole a glance at Inac. It was obvious he shared my thoughts. Threatening the man with demotion purely out of impatience.

I sounded no different from Ulken.

Abyss take him for naming them Heels. This Agency can be so much better.

When the Nerve delivered his news, it became clear just how far we had to go.

CHAPTER TWO

Ceaseless Flow

You might work for free, but the Artisans is starving for stars already. The thieves took a quarter-measure's worth of Archevials and ran off. I ain't fool enough to chase after them myself. Send one of your Dark-loving greencoats after them, afore we have another Blight fire to contend with.

—Form G-11b, Request for Agency Services,
submitted by an Archemaker

Say what you would about the Blight, the engineers who designed their elevators were geniuses. That was never clearer than when rushing down twenty-seven floors of stairs to reach the Agency courtyard, which gave ample time to reflect on the last time I used those elevators on the Blight docks. That had been back before joining the Agency. Ten thousand lifetimes ago, and with that many memories stuffed into my head, some things were bound to be forgotten to make room.

I really ought to have repaid that elevator operator. What was his name again?

A bellow came from below, growing louder the lower we got.

"Maybe," Inac shouted, "you should move your office to the bottom floor."

"I really like the view," I said between heaving breaths as we reached the fourth floor and the crowd obstructing our way.

The discordant chorus of voices were tinged primarily with confusion, spiced with anger, worry, and disbelief. A healthy blend of emotions, so at least there was no Benefactor involved.

Still, I had to push and shove my way down the stairs. Heels chatted with each other, speculating about the incident. Two Organs, administrators in bronze uniforms, called me rude when I squeezed between them. Mostly, everyone was doing the same thing I was, trying to squeeze outside as if the building were on fire. Which it wasn't.

I hope.

In short order, all downward movement came to a standstill, everyone pressing into the back of someone on the stair below them. I wasn't the only one grunting in frustration. Everyone had always been focused and compliant under Ulken's leadership.

And then I got here. What am I doing wrong?

As if in answer to my question, I felt it. A sharp tug, more akin to what an Archemage feels when manipulating the Fire than to any physical sensation. A presence, fighting for my attention. Or perhaps trying to avoid it. Like a crackle at the base of my skull.

A death knell.

The host of an Incubating Benefactor somewhere in the city had died. Somewhere close by, if the strength of the pull was indicative. I clamped down on it with scarcely an effort, felt it wither into nothing.

A stronger Benefactor would have put up a better fight, but most Incubating were new. Young. The infestation was spreading rapidly. Several times a day now, I prevented a new Benefactor's Emergence, and the rate was slowly climbing. The memories of the newly-dead spilled into my mind—not their whole life, only the moment of death. Never a pleasant experience, this death knell was particularly bad.

My weapon had no effect. The demon's stone fist struck faster than I could react. A crushed skull, then emptiness.

Each time, it felt like dying myself.

Sooner or later, I was going to break.

It must have been obvious to those around me. I shook my head to clear the dying memory and found myself being lifted to my feet, having fallen into an Organ on the stair below me.

"What are we standing around for?" I muttered, then cringed as I remembered what we were doing. Seeing a leader stumbling around confused and talking to himself in his madness wasn't exactly confidence inspiring.

"Er, come with me, sir." The Nerve who had originally delivered the bad news pulled me by the arm back up to the fourth floor, where Inac was already waiting.

"This way," Inac said, gesturing with an arm sticking out from his robe. As I passed him, he eyed me, wordlessly asking if I was okay. I nodded, but he surely knew it to be a lie.

The Nerve led the way through the floor, past the offices of several Organs whose functions I had never heard of. I only had cause, not to mention time, to visit three or four floors of the tower, most often the very top, which I didn't often leave since Heels brought me everything I needed. The rest of the Agency was a labyrinth as easy to understand as the web of threats and corruption spun by the old Head.

Which was to say, not easy at all.

"Do I even want to know what the Organ of Fluid Intake does?"

"Oh yes," Inac said, hurrying behind me. "Nyna is a very sweet girl. You should meet her."

The Nerve arrived at a thin darkwood door in a corner where the Brightdaughter's waning light didn't reach. He opened it and gestured for me to enter. "After you, sir. These stairs lead right to the courtyard."

I was beginning to like this fellow. *I really should get his name.*

"Aren't you new here?" I asked him. "How do you both know about this?" I looked at Inac.

Inac shrugged one shoulder. "I explore."

The Nerve hesitated. I really needed to break him of that habit before it settled in. "New here?" He whispered, then looked at me with concern. "You attended my wife's funeral, sir…"

"Oh, er…" I had attended so many funerals lately. Dunnax's was but the first. The rest of those trampled by Ulken's ambitions came next. "Which one was…" I wiped a hand across my face, weary. "Sorry."

Darkfather, isn't there anyone better suited to this role?

The stairs beckoned. Facing what I knew awaited at the bottom was better than wiggling my way out of the accidental insult to the man. I hurried down, taking the steps two at a time. Outside to my left, the crowd spilled from the tower's front doors and coalesced around something at the center of the courtyard. It had begun drawing on-lookers in from the Burg.

"Close that gate!" I shouted at the Heels who were eying the commotion rather than doing their jobs. No time to oversee it done. I shoved through the crowd to reach the center. "Back it up! Move! Give us some room!"

My underlings were far less eager to jump at my commands than I liked. Heels, Nerves, and the new lead mortician's technicians all knelt around a man in a green coat stained red.

Recognition surfaced with a sick feeling in my gut. Not a coat. A robe, heavy and woolen. And not just a Finger, but an Archemage, lay dying before us. Some of that sticky-wet red that marred his wear flowed between the cobblestones he lay on. I didn't remember the mage's name but seeing him there brought to mind the sight of his unconscious brother, bleeding from the stump of a leg severed by a daggerclaw.

Not again.

"Enough!" I screamed, and a flare of Archefire bloomed in the air above the mage. Its light illuminated faces cloaked in the shadows of dusk.

The crowd jumped back at that. One Heel tore off his smoldering hat and stomped it underfoot. My lip curled as I glanced at Inac, who wore a disapproving look. Reed's gift had given me the ability to sense the flows of Archemagic, but they slipped through my fingers whenever I tried to grasp them. I hadn't even intended the Fire this time; I needed to better control it.

It produced the effect I wanted, however. A space opened for me to kneel beside the Archemage, press my hand against his wound. The Finger shuddered. He was alive. It wasn't too late.

My fingers felt his belly. Stabbed in the gut.

"We need an Archehealer!" I looked around at the crowd, but none stepped forward. Bengard had been right—the Agency really did need more Archemages.

A moment later, Inac arrived beside me. "Who dealt to him this wound?"

I gritted my teeth in frustration. Neither of us could use the Fire properly. I was liable to burn myself up, and Inac... Without his hand... It pained me to think about what he had given to protect me.

A Lawi Finger stepped forth, broad in the face and dark of hair. This man, I remembered. Nill. He had fought the daggerclaw with us in Reed's Woods and saved his people from Ulken.

"Rebels," Nill said, his voice hoarse like he had been yelling. "They been taken care of."

The mention of rebels threatened to surface the memory I had seen in my office, but I shook it off. A man was dying under my watch. I needed to stay focused on the present.

Beside Nill, a Skardwarf stood motionless as members of the Agency jostled around him like a river flowing around a boulder. I had only met two Skardwarves in the Agency, and I knew for certain Sentyx was not here. This was the other, then. Cavern. His hands were balled into huge fists.

And one was covered in blood.

Over his shoulder, another crowd of Heels gathered around the body of a man dressed in rags, arguing over who would be the one to transport him. I thought they might be squeamish about touching a dirty Blightdweller...until I saw the viscera and gray matter covering those rags. The Blightdweller's head was smashed to pulp.

The demon's stone fist struck faster than I could react.

The remembered death knell left me feeling dizzy as it faded. I glared at Cavern, who shrugged, then at Nill. "How could you allow this to happen?"

"What did you say?" Nill furrowed his bushy black brows and wrinkled his flat nose. "We were attacked by those thugs. Caught us a prisoner, but..."

"Pulled a knife on me," Cavern said and had the gall to laugh. He spun to show off a broken-off blade poking from his back.

"Self-defense," Nill said with a nod. "Ain't a problem, is there?"

"There is a problem," I fired back. "I don't like that tone, Finger. You're speaking to the Head, and I *commanded* that no one be killed within the city. We will *not* allow a Benefactor to Emerge within Liwokin's walls."

"The brain was destroyed," Cavern said with a slow shrug.

"I don't care," I snapped. Justice in Liwokin was always swift and cruel. That saying had been true since before the Bright Empire invaded.

It isn't right. And it's going to get us killed. Kill every Incubating Benefactor and sooner or later one will slip through the cracks. I won't be able to stop it.

"You take the assailants *captive*. All of them. There are five of you. Is that so difficult?"

Useless snuffing Fingers.

"Not one of you is a Dark-loving healer?" I shouted at the hovering members of the Agency, growing desperate as the mage's life seeped away.

I shook that thought away. That was Ulken talking again. If any-thing, I was the useless one here.

I knew all he needed was Archehealing. The Fire could seal his open wounds. It would be trivial to an Archemage.

Any Archemage but me.

There was another way, though. I had survived a wound just like this. Ulken had given it to me himself. When Reed's Deluge began, the Benefactor used its power to heal my body. A power based not in Archefire, but Archedark.

It had healed me from the brink of death. Why couldn't I use it to save one of my own Fingers? I closed my eyes and began concentrating.

"The guy came out of nowhere," Nill said. "Got a shot off from his pistol and bolted. Right into Cavern here, and...well, you know what happened."

I was hardly listening. A cold seeped into my hand pressed against the mage's skin. Even with eyes closed, I could see a swirling cloud of Archemagic forming around me. I was the eye of a storm, its energy pouring through my hands and into the dying man. In moments, the tips of my fingers felt frostbitten. The mage's body shuddered beneath my touch.

"No, Grim!" Inac pried my hand up. All that uncontrolled energy siphoned into his body, and I stopped with a shivering gasp. Inac's face clenched, and his body curled momentarily, then he relaxed, the storm taken inside, under control. "You must not use Dark without the Fire to balance it."

"Then you do it!" I told him. "I won't just let him die."

He was my responsibility. All of these people were. Fingers, Heels, Nerves, Organs, and most of all my old Hand Sixty-Four. My friends. They were my responsibility, and I had to use them. Each of them played a role in surviving the Benefactors.

Inac looked ashamed. He performed no healing, and one of the few Archemages in the Agency perished.

When he died, I suppressed his Benefactor's Emergence and absorbed his death knell into the ocean of others.

Grasping my belly, tensing in agony. Looking up at my friends. All of us, scared. Vision faded. Cold.

It was far from the worst I had seen. At least he was surrounded by friends. That made it no easier.

I was able to heal myself *after* death. Why couldn't I heal a single Finger?

Two more people had pushed their way to the front row, just in time for the gruesome conclusion to the show. Ulken's First Eye, Jacquin, accompanied a man in blue mage's robes, identical to the dead man's save for the color. His brother, Yesk. He walked with a crutch, which he threw to the ground as he fell to one knee, then toppled forward, sobbing.

Yesk wailed into his brother's corpse. A man's lived a good life if someone cries that loudly over his body.

"Would you like the corpse to be disposed of, sir?" Jacquin quietly asked me.

I grimaced at the man. Something about him made my suspicions burn. He had always been so loyal to Ulken, never questioning anything.

I could order that man to commit atrocities, and he'd bite his lip and do it.

He did good work though, and as tragic as this was, the body was infested by Benefactors. The longer we all crowded around it, the greater chance they had of spreading. My suppression of their Emergence might have been enough, but I wasn't taking any chances.

"To the mortuary," I confirmed. "Have Arza look at him first." I doubted she would learn anything from the thousand and first corpse that she hadn't already learned from the last thousand, but she had to try, all the same.

Tragic.

All of us are doing what we can, and none of it ever helps.

The matching mage's death was the entire situation in microcosm. Needless death. All because I couldn't make anything work the way I needed it to.

Standing as Jacquin ordered two technicians to carry the corpse, I turned to Nill, the Hand Captain, and commanded him, "Next time, keep your eyes open, and—"

I cut off as that same invisible tug from in my office pulled at my skin, sharp as a fish hook. An Emergence began in the city. Lightning exploded in my skull. It knocked me back to my knees, and it felt like I had fallen a great distance. The death knell appeared.

Splintering wood. Screaming. Screaming and falling.

The Benefactor was a pitiful thing, weak as a newborn, easy to suppress. But as it dwindled to nothing, another hook caught my flesh, and another. Their death memories intertwined.

Sharp crack. Deep rumble. Shoved from behind. Water rushing up. Head crushed, then nothing. Crushing cold, then nothing.

I blinked to clear the gruesome images from my eyes. Grasping my head, I suppressed the first, the next.

Another dozen Benefactors began Emerging. All young, easy to end. Or, they should have been, if not for the Deluge of chaotic, mass death assaulting my mind.

Falling. Falling. Wood. Panic. Screaming. Wood. Rocks. Wood. Falling. Water. Breaking. Crashing. Screaming. Gasping. Sinking.

Dying, dying, dying. Death in such magnitude it overwhelmed me. I was screaming with the ghosts inside my head. A hand grabbed my shoulder, and a voice spoke my name. But they were one of many. Dozens. No, hundreds of dead Liwo now fought for my attention. Those hooks covered every scrap of skin, all demanding to be torn out.

These Benefactors were young, one and all. Even so, it took every last strand of concentration to root them out before they completed their transformation. One Emergent Benefactor in the city would be a disaster. Dozens loose with unknown changes, Benefactors whose kind we had never before seen...

We would have to flee to Paceeq to escape the carnage. Liwokin would be lost, and it would be my fault. I drove my fists into the ground, clenching my entire body equally hard as I suppressed each Emergence.

Abyss take you, Reed, and your snuffing "gift".

I scoffed. Gift. In all his notes, Ulken never once explained why he decided to name the organism a Benefactor. If he expected this power Reed stuck me with to be a blessing, he would have been disappointed. It was nothing but an abyss-damned curse, and the sooner I was rid of it, the better off I would be.

The myriad visions passed, and I was beginning to catch my breath.

Inac squeezed my shoulder again. "I too felt it."

"Lightmother..." Sweat dripped from the tip of my nose, landed in the drying blood between cobbles. "What was that?" My heart rate slowed. It was over.

A final Benefactor Emerged, one unlike the others. Its death knell was different.

A knife in the back. Utter surprise. Rope burn. The knife sliding in again.

The man's shock and pain had lasted only a heartbeat before the end. A better death than the others, if more treacherous. A knife in the back... I sighed and put an end to the Benefactor.

It dwindled, getting smaller, smaller. Then, it was as though it just refused to be stomped down anymore. It fought back, resisted me. No matter how hard I squeezed, the bug wouldn't pop. It began gaining ground. Drawing energy from somewhere outside itself, using it to grow more capacious. I sensed this change as surely as I felt my fingernails digging into stone. I hated this infestation in my head, but I trusted its senses as if they were my own.

Maybe they were, in a way. The organism was so deeply rooted in my brain, what would happen if it died? The prospect of this Emerging monster growing powerful enough to pop my own Benefactors…

Terror gripped me by the back of the skull, and I screamed at the ground just a hand's width from my face. The veins bulged on the back of my hands, and my fingertips were scrawling bloody lines on the gray stone.

I poured all the energy I could muster into squashing this new competition, screamed my lungs ragged with exertion. And it worked. The creature shrank before me, wisping away. A rush of pride filled me as I watched the routed enemy cower and break. I was the master of this city. While I served as the Agency's Head, Liwokin was protected.

And Inac thinks I'm not doing enough to help.

My limbs were suddenly bone wearing. I had yelled my throat raw, and it felt as if scorched by fire. My vision wavered. The Emerging Benefactor shrank down to an infinitesimal speck, too insignificant to sense.

My strength gave out, and I collapsed to the ground.

It's finally over.

I let the darkness take me.

Over. For now.

CHAPTER THREE

Home

Yearning for connection, a cursed predilection
Forever reaching out, our hearts we never doubt

No Light, O night, and the Darkness reaches in
No night, O Light, merest chance, a lover's whim

—Verses from Shadowson's Lament,
First Song of Half-Dusk

Lorelay believed it impossible to remain miserable for such a long journey. Up the river to Canako, through the canal, down the coast to the island of Paceeq, her memories haunted her all the way.

Shows what I know. She took another swig of warm ale.

She was sitting with her legs hanging off the side of the ship's bulwark, in her usual spot toward the front of the vessel. The first time the sailors had seen her there, they rushed to her in a panic, afraid she was preparing to jump overboard. The thought had crossed her mind, she had to admit.

One last sad tune, *The Lament of Lorelay*, she would call it. Then a quick drop into the rough black sea, and that was that. There was no need to fear drowning. The ship would plow over her and knock her senseless as soon as the current dragged her under. Easy. Not painless, true, but the pain would be short-lived. Unlike the pain she currently felt, heavy enough to drag her to the bottom of the harbor.

She never could bring herself to take the plunge. Not that she particularly felt she had anything to live for—her mother and father were probably tortured to death by the Empress' Paladins, and her brother had...had... Lorelay sniffled and shook her head until she was dizzy enough to rid herself of the thought. All of this was her fault. The world would be far better off with her dead, she decided, but there was just one problem.

She had promised Grim she would win the Bright Throne as an ally, and Lorelay was no liar... Except for the lies she had told her families to get out of church service when she was young. And the lies she had told the Paladins questioning her about a heretical lyricist in the capital. Oh, and lest she forget, there were the lies even she herself believed about starting a new life in Lawiko. Her eyes squeezed shut on their own and threatened to bring up tears if she continued down that line of thinking.

She drank instead.

All right, so Lorelay *was* a liar. But she was trying to be better! Singing the songs of the Book of Light for so many years made her lips curl at the idea of saying anything that she did not believe. Her whole life, she had aspired to being a silver-tongued devil, paying only a nod to truth but ignoring it completely when something better sounded good.

And look where that got me.

She glanced at the Radiant Palace looming over the city, a preposterously indulgent construction of white marble and glimmering Archemetal. All those snooty nobles up on their hilltop palace thought they were so bright and virtuous. Meanwhile, children starved in the capital's streets. Her eyes drew down to a bustling road leading into the heart of Vos, divided into two avenues by a line of olive trees. Shadows fell on painted religious statues, buildings fronted by thick columns, and homeless people gathered around public wells, begging for stars.

The Brightdaughter was setting on that sad sight, dipping behind domed roofs of red and gold, ushering in the end of Lorelay's dismal journey. Or was it only the start of a new misery? She never thought she would return, but now?

Right back where I started.

Well, however she had gotten here, she was smart enough not to make the same mistake twice...or a third, no...fourth time. She had made a promise. Lorelay was going to win the Bright Empire's armies as allies for the Agency.

Sure, she had only given her word to Inac, not Grim, but the mage was obviously the clearer thinker of the two anyway. Despite his own command, Grim had probably yet to realize she had left, so absorbed was he in his Benefactor visions up in his dark office.

Lorelay could relate—too little ale existed in this world for her to forget the monsters she had seen. She could hardly blame Grim for wanting to be someone else after the ordeal they had survived. She just wished that other person was a bit more unlike the last Head of the Agency.

Inac, on the other hand, was quite caring toward Lorelay. In fact, she had grown rather fond of him during the journey up to Canako. When she needed a drink, he was there with ale, or better yet, rum from the Stinbine Isles. He could toss the stuff back faster than she could, and he needed no excuse to do so. His wrist shamed him, she saw that much in his body language, but the man found a coping mechanism in his work with the Agency.

She should have asked him how he did it—Lorelay had kept all her body parts, but it felt as though a vital piece of herself had been ripped away.

Right on cue, a memory from Reed's Woods split her heart in half. Coming out of her stupor only to find Hand Sixty-Four was missing a member. Grim had told her what happened. *Why did you have to go and do something so stupid, you big lummox?*

Drink.

Finishing the ale, she tossed the empty tankard into the harbor. Alas, Inac was gone and so was his rum—he had left the liquor with her, but it had been drained by the time the ship exited the Canako Canal. The next day's voyage had been on a choppy sea, each crash of the waves sounding like the crash of cymbals behind her eyeballs.

It was a lucky thing she hardly remembered that. The drink worked just as she hoped. Maybe with a bit more, it would start erasing all the difficult memories from before this journey started. Where would they have to begin?

Sometime around the beginning of my whole life.

Drink—

The tankard was gone. She groaned, remembering the captain told her she was cut off. He used different words—actions really. The last time he found her sitting on the railing, he slapped the mug from her hand and glared at her. Then he and the other sailors had hauled their "wares that she was wasting" down the gangplank and into the city.

"It's not like I didn't *offer* to pay," she muttered to herself. She mocked the captain's Ekoan accent, repeating what he had said when she first boarded. "Ladies drink for free on this vessel, or I don't be a true sailor." She rolled her eyes. "Idiot."

Lorelay sighed and looked away from the sea, finally confronting what she had been putting off. The ship had arrived in Paceeq's capital several spans ago. Vos. Her home, the one city in which she never again expected to set foot. Once, Lorelay had read in a forbidden book that true art can only be produced by a tortured soul. Given all that occurred since she had been exiled from Paceeq and the nascent emptiness within her, Lorelay's songs would be works of art unattainable by any other musician.

Of course, she could never *play* those songs, not within the confines of the Bright Empire. As soon as a Paladin heard her blasphemous tunes, she would be thrown from a high window somewhere in the Radiant Palace.

Lorelay laughed bitterly. "They would never allow one such as me to set foot in their hallowed halls, their pure palace, their sacred, solemn, stupid, snuffing—" She burped, and a bit of vomit made its way up her throat into her mouth. She spat it out. "Hate this place..."

Why had Grim sent her of all people here? He *must* have known she was exiled. For all she knew, the Paladins were still searching for the girl who plastered rebellious posters around the city and spread heresy with her songs. Lorelay protested the command, of course, but she was pretty sure Grim was lost in his thoughts, mindlessly muttering about how much sense it made.

She knew the culture of Paceeq—Lightmother help her, but she did—and she knew Vinlin, the Bright Prince. Some rotten luck that was, running into the insufferable son of Elzia during Hand Sixty-Four's *very first* command. As if more evidence was needed that Lorelay was cursed, the man specifically *requested* her to escort him back to his ship, awaiting in Canako.

For the briefest moment, she had thought a stroke of uncharacteristic luck had swept him out of the carriage when they fled the plague-spreading Benefactor. Of course not. He made it into the back with all his precious treasures for his dead mother. The abyss only knew what she *needed* all that junk for.

But Vinlin could not have been more pleased with Lorelay—even though all she did was snap the reins and let the horses do the rest. He even extended her an invitation to accompany him back to Paceeq with him, where he could court her as his lady. When she laughed at him, he said he was serious. When she laughed again, he only laughed with her, and told her that sooner or later she would have to return home.

Well...he was right. She had no idea why he wanted her to come back, but evidently, he was going to get his wish.

"Maybe he likes my songs," she mused, plucking her lyre from her belt clip.

Her fingers tightened around the grooves where her grip had worn down the wood over the years. Her sole source of comfort in this world, she held the horseshoe-shaped instrument close to her chest and swept her calloused fingers across its strings.

They responded with an unmelodious hum, and Lorelay winced. She picked at the high string. It sounded like a cat in heat. Out of tune. She would need to string the instrument with fresh horsehair before she gave any performances. She snorted. Performances. Right. Not in the heart of the Empire. But no one was around now, save a few stragglers who, like her, had yet to disembark. With the wind blowing in from the south, they would be out of earshot anyway.

Conscious to avoid the foul note, Lorelay played a melody, humming quietly. A sad melody it was, but *The Lament of Lorelay* it was not. She played no wrong notes, even with the sour string, but the song was ugly to her ears, and her rhythm was shaky under the influence of the drink.

"Right, that settles it," she said, spinning and hopping off the railing.

The composition of her next opus would have to wait. There was only one thing to be done.

Before the Brightdaughter could fully set, she stumbled down the gangplank and into the streets of Vos.

Lorelay was home.

Heretic

Fuck the Empress, First of Her Name
Her eponymous talent, a world-renowned fame
Burn the Empress, turn back her lust
Reduce the white palace to ashes and dust

—*Early work of the Veiled Songstress.*
Scrapped. Too brash.

"I'm back!" Lorelay announced, bursting through the doors.

The patrons of the Blueflame Tavern's common room—Paceeqi, one and all—turned their heads at the noise with little interest, then went back to wallowing in their cups and listening to the droning flute rendition of *The Darkness Gazes*. The air inside the tavern called to mind the stench of Liwokin on a rainy day—the odor of bodies and the stink of sweat mixing with the old, sour ale to form a truly rank concoction. Blue fires flickered in wall-mounted braziers, providing the establishment with its namesake and the bare minimum of light to see by. Everyone kept to themselves, keeping the room free of lively chatter.

The mood of the Blueflame was amplified by the musician's absolutely awful performance. Every note was correct, but wavered as if the man was unsure of the correct fingering. That was impossible—everyone in the city knew the same Twelve Songs—so perhaps the man was as drunk as Lorelay. Or he might have been out of breath, fearing the Paladins punishing him for his musical butchery. For his part, the Empire-mandated Paladin in his gleaming silver armor just leaned against the wall in the corner, either bored with his posting or sneaking a standing nap.

Lorelay grinned. This place was perfect. She had no recollection of her feet carrying her through the streets of Vos, nor how she wound up at this tavern of all places. Well...it was no surprise she ended up in a tavern, but *this* one?

This was where she debuted her first song, all those years ago. Officially, it was blasphemy, and it had caused an uproar, drunkards shouting and Paladins drawing steel. Unofficially, she knew the people had loved it. *She* had loved it. For the first time in her life, she had done something she was *meant* to do. No one wanted to hear the same stodgy songs of the Book of Light over and over for the rest of their lives.

All right, maybe some people do. Lorelay's mother existed, after all.

But still, most people were a bit more exotic in their tastes. Not a difficult feat, to be sure. Only listening to Twelve Songs, a full nine of which were in a minor key, was about as exotic as spicing your food with salt. Lorelay had no difficulty imagining a world where tastes were so confined—enforced by the Empress—but she had endless difficulty putting herself in the shoes of people who tolerated, or worse, *defended* it.

People like the Paladins. People like her... Tears welled in her eyes the moment her brother came to mind.

Don't you dare think about him.

Lorelay had staggered her way through the city to reach this tavern. Past Paladins, boys wrestling, and a group of stray cats that brought her dangerously close to tears. What she lacked was strong enough liquor to keep her head hazy enough to persist. That was it, she realized. Her throat was dry with thirst. An easy fix in such a fine tavern as this.

She dragged herself to an empty table, plopped into a chair, put her head down, and waggled a finger in the air until a server arrived. When footsteps and a curt "Whaddaya want?" drew her gaze upward, she nearly fell out of her seat.

The server backed up a step, eyes popping out of his skull. "Lorelay?"

"Jenx?" She smiled at her old friend.

He grimaced, eyes sliding toward the Paladin, whose head lolled to the side before he jerked upright. Definitely napping.

"You shouldn't be here," Jenx said.

"Why not?" Lorelay crossed her arms. "Don't tell me they brainwashed you too."

The man before her resembled the boy she had grown up with, who had taught her to wield her knives despite the role of women in Paceeq. He had a streak of rebelliousness almost on par with Lorelay's own. She grinned, remembering the time he had almost been caught painting 'the Church of Dark rules Vos' on a building in the middle of the night.

"You know they killed Gravis because of your song?" Jenx asked, glowering. "Took him below the palace, and we never saw him again."

"What?" Lorelay's eyes scanned the bar, but the old man who had booked her first half-dusk performance was nowhere to be seen. She expected the man to spread the word to other taverns, blacklisting Lorelay, not for him to be punished. "He didn't know I was going to play that song!"

"Yeah, well once the mob you incited attacked the Paladins, the Bright Empress figured the place was in need of more pious management."

Lorelay pouted. It was just like the Bright Throne to punish the innocent and the guilty indiscriminately. Everyone was guilty according to the Book of Light. The Empress only needed a pretense to crack down. "All the more reason for us to fight them. The Throne can't throw all of us in prison."

Jenx jerked his head wildly. "Keep your voice down! We're not children anymore, Lorelay. I have a family."

She smiled "You do? I want to meet—"

"All this talk of fighting back needs to stop." He gestured at the sullen tavern goers. The musician had just concluded his song, and no one applauded. "Take a look at this crowd. Does it *look* like anyone here wants to be part of your grand rebellion?"

"It looks like they're all sleeping. If someone woke them up..."

Lorelay had considered that her duty once, rousing the people from their slumber. Could she go back to that life? It would be an escape from the void within her, but as duties went, few were more dangerous. The truth of that had never been clearer than when the Paladins learned she was the one spreading what they called Dark Verses.

Sing a song they don't like, and they'll rip out your throat. What a kind and just society we live in.

Lorelay reached for her drink, only to find she had yet to order one.

"You haven't changed at all," Jenx said.

To which Lorelay smiled and replied, "Thank you." His dour face told her it was not intended as a compliment.

"Now, are you going to drink anything? If Hep sees me jabber-mouthing, she'll have me by the hide." He glanced at a woman with sagging jowls grumpily scrubbing stains from a nearby table.

"So that's it?" It had been years since she had seen her old friend, her best friend, and he was treating her like some ordinary customer. The betrayal of it made Lorelay's head hurt. Or maybe that was the hangover starting early. "You changed."

"I grew up, Lorelay. It's time you did too."

Nope, not the hangover. Definitely the betrayal. Lorelay squeezed her fists to stop herself from slamming the table. "Your strongest," she said. "And keep it coming."

The man had the nerve to hold his hand out, expecting payment.

Lorelay slapped the coins into his open palm. "Take your snuffing stars. And don't talk to me again."

He was more than happy to oblige that demand. Returning, he left a mug in front of her containing dark brown liquid, thick as blood. It smelled of rotten fruit and tasted worse. She downed it in one gulp, banged it on the table, and called for another.

She had no idea how much time had passed, but by the time it arrived, her head was already spinning. When she looked up at the new drink, she found there were three mugs before her. When had those gotten there? And why were they empty? No matter. Lorelay reached for the new one, only they split into two and she had to guess which one was right. She must have guessed wrong, because her knuckles banged into the side of the mug and knocked it over.

With a frustrated snarl, she swept it off the table. It shattered on the floor, spilling the vile fluid across the floor's planks. Lightwood, of course—even the abyss-damned *wood* was mandated by the Throne. She hoped the ale would soak in and stain, leaving a mar on the oh-so-perfect—

Rough hands grabbed her by the shoulders. "I think you've had enough," a gruff woman's voice said.

The world lurched as Lorelay was pulled backward. Her combat instincts kicked in. She dropped into a crouch, spinning, and reaching for her knives. Lorelay turned on the balls of her feet, expertly balanced, and—

She crashed into a table, waking up a snoring old codger and falling into the puddle of ale. More hands grabbed at her coat, but she scrambled away between table legs and peoples' legs and found her own feet near the front of the stage. The flautist had stopped, staring at her with wide eyes.

"Play on, man! Let's hear *Shine! Noon Eternal.*" That was the sprightliest of the Twelve Songs. Almost fun, even! It required nimble fingers and a nimbler tongue. Lorelay's tongue was numb. Looking down cross-eyed, she found it was bleeding. She spat red onto the ground and urged the musician. "The show must go on! Never let them stop you."

The show did not go on. The man ran off-stage, his ridiculous multicolored coat billowing behind him. But the show *must* go on. Not the show *should* go on. *Must!*

Lorelay climbed on-stage before Hep or Jenx or anyone else could reach her through the press of drunks who, she had to admit, were much livelier now. She was always good at getting people on their feet.

With her lyre in hand, her fingers automatically plucked a tune, darker than she expected, but then, her music was always a fit for her mood. And once it began, all else faded away. There was no crowd, no clinking of glasses, no chatter to interrupt. It was her and her music. The lyrics came effortlessly. If you had to force the words to come, they were hardly worth saying. Only what flowed from your innermost soul truly had any meaning. She sang, her voice not missing a note, her fingers plucking not one bad string.

Dark is the world we inhabit this day
When threats of false justice keep mercy at bay
And if Lightmother's mercy for gold stars is sold
Then who from the shadows turns Empires cold?

A brother, a sister, a family long torn,
To hide their dark hearts is bright armor worn
The brightness we savor is no longer warm,
When soldiers cast innocents into the storm

Where has the light gone—

Something struck Lorelay hard, and she hit the ground, head bouncing and sending the already spinning world into a chaotic tumble. Cracking her eyes open, they landed on her lyre, just out of reach. She stretched her hand toward it.

A silver boot stomped down and smashed the instrument. Lorelay choked on a strangled gasp. She had carved that lyre herself, wound the horsehair strings in her own fingers. It was the only possession she had that she truly cared about. Nothing but a heap of splinters now.

She opened her mouth to utter the worst curse she could imagine at the man who had done that, but all that came out was a wracking sob. Someone hauled her to her feet, but she went limp. The golden gleam of firelight in steel caught her eye, along with the sound of a weapon sliding out from its leather scabbard and the gasp of a crowd.

"Don't any of you look away," a voice growled beside Lorelay's ear. The Paladin held her upright with ease, though all Lorelay wanted to do was slide back down to the floor. "This is what awaits all dark-loving heretics."

With great effort, Lorelay crooked her neck and looked upon the crowd. Many were pushing their way to the exit before this got worse for everybody. Some watched with eager eyes, as though a girl who sang songs deserved death. Maybe Lorelay did deserve that. For everything else she had done, but not this.

The majority of the crowd were cowards though. They studied their cups, not saying a word in favor of the girl about to be executed before them.

The majority, but not all.

"Mercy!" Jenx shouted. "Mercy, please Paladin."

"You speak for the heretic?" The Paladin jerked Lorelay's arm roughly.

The crowd parted around Jenx, and he stammered. "I...no...but—"

A woman's gravelly voice cut him off. "What he means to say is that this is no place to make an example of her. Not on my stage, here in front of a bunch of drunks." Hep dropped a rag on the floor, pushed it around with her foot. Another, she tossed to Jenx. "She's already made enough mess in the Blueflame. Mercy for us is what the boy means. We're the ones who'd have to scrub her tainted blood from the floors. For her..." Hep shrugged indifferently. "A public execution would serve the Throne better."

The Paladin considered. A low, throaty laugh rumbled. "Very well. It's been too long since the city has had a good show. For such a flagrant blasphemer, the Bright Prince will be pleased."

Lorelay's head drooped, spittle dribbling from her lips. She closed her eyes and put up no fight as the man dragged her out of the tavern into the darkness of the night.

CHAPTER FIVE

Betrayer

In larger numbers, Pairs of Pairs are relatively common as well; however, no further grouping beyond four Pairs has ever been observed. The unsophisticated mind of the creature is hypothesized to only allow sixteen Peekers to work in unison, though some theorize the limit may be thirty-two.

—Page 2, Institute of Biotism Peeker Compendium, Vol. I

There's a traitor in Hand Sixty-Four. Garret's grip tightened. *And he's close.*

His back tensed, pulling the bowstring taut. Could make this shot without looking, easy. Twenty paces out. The ranger's eyes tracked the target, a silhouette in the fog gliding overhead in lazy arcs. Garret breathed in, tasted the humid sea air.

Steady breaths, steady feet. He felt the rhythm of the waves shifting the deck. These Peeker ships didn't move like human galleys or steamships. More like rickety canoes, always on the verge of tipping if you leaned too far over.

The ship rocked violently, and something solid thumped him on the back. Garret stuffed down his annoyance, concentrated on the shot.

Loosed.

The bow twanged, the gull crowed its final squawk, and lunch plunged into the ocean.

Garret turned to find Sentyx behind him. Standing *way* too close. "You gonna get that?" he asked with some bite.

The Skardwarf grunted.

'Keep a Peeker close', the saying went, 'but keep a Skardwarf closer.'

Whoever said that has never smelled a Skardwarf's breath.

Suppressing a gag, Garret questioned his wisdom in volunteering to follow Sentyx to the Peeker Mounds. He could have been back home in Eko, trying to make another ally for the Agency. But his time was better spent keeping a watch on the Skardwarf. Eko's rangers had given up on everything outside preserving Graln long ago. Trying to broaden their narrow minds sounded even worse than boarding this dark-loving, sorry excuse for a ship.

At the time, anyway.

It was too cramped and narrow, and freezing water constantly splashed over the sides. Soaked right into the pulpy material that made up the whole vessel, so his boots always squelched with each step. Every so often, hurrying out of the way of the score of Peekers on board, he'd sink down into the hull. Made him feel like he was going to fall right through, into the water.

Not sure how Sentyx hasn't already fallen in. The thought of the Skardwarf sinking right down to the sea floor made him laugh to himself. Not that it would hurt Sentyx, of course. He'd probably walk all the way to shore. That was what he'd done when he thought he was in the Brightcalm Bay, under Reed's illusion. Walked. Backwards.

The Skardwarf might've gotten to the Peeker Mounds faster that way than sailing with Garret. 'Sailing' was the wrong word for it. The Peeker ship didn't *have* sails. Oh, no. Nor a rudder, a helm, a prow, a keel, gunwales, an anchor—nothing. Pretty sure it wasn't even a real ship, thinking about it, no matter what the Peekers insisted. More like a misshapen lump of hardened slime that he and Sentyx had to take up *oars* to propel into the winds down Lawiko's coast.

Didn't bother Sentyx, naturally. Cold didn't matter a wit to Peekers or Skardwarves. *He* was the one freezing off his b—

Water struck Garret in the face and soaked his hood. Got in his mouth too. "Augh!"

He spat salty seawater at the Peekers who had jumped into the ocean to fetch the dead gull he'd skewered. Half a dozen of them chittered endlessly as the bristly almond hairs covering their bodies went stiff as a stergoderm in heat. Was that a physiological response to protect from the cold? And what were they chattering about? Probably debating whether to give the bird back to Garret or hoard it for themselves.

Sentyx rumbled with laughter behind him.

Garret didn't see what was so funny. He lowered his hood and squeezed the water from his knotted hair. "Surprised you haven't started *eroding away* yet."

Of course, water's no way to hunt a Skardwarf. He wished it were that easy. *Snuffing impervious to* everything.

Sentyx grunted again, his dark pupils shifting toward the Peekers.

Lightmother help me, but I'm starting to understand him.

"What do you mean, 'what are they doing?' They're fetching my lunch. Didn't even have to *ask* them. More than I could say for you."

"They know thoughts," Sentyx said. "Two brains. One mind."

"They can't read *my* mind!" Although, watching them, Garret reconsidered.

Two brains in one mind, aye, Peekers were called that. They always worked in Pairs. Darkfather, they were practically braindead without another around. The Institute of Biotism claimed the foremost knowledge of Peeker behavior, but their biotists wouldn't leave the canopy of Graln to perform a real study if the entire treetop city was on fire. Observing the creatures on the way to the Peeker Mounds, Garret decided the biotist literature about Peekers was complete, all right.

Complete azear shit. He spat, though this dead Peeker ship had no thirst for his body's water. The Peekers had constructed it of some sticky material they excreted from a hole where their bellybutton would be if they were human. Resin, Garret named it, since the Institute's writing never mentioned the foul stuff. Almost felt like a real discovery. Like he was some real biotist.

The strange insect-like creatures were using now resin to adhere their bodies together in a line that extended from the ship. It came out of holes on their abdomens, and they took it up in their long-fingered hands, rubbed it all over each other with glee. At least, that's how Garret interpreted their clicking noises and vibrating antennae.

Other Peekers hurriedly trampled over the bridge of bodies to reach Garret's meal, three-toed feet on stick-thin legs stomping right on the heads of their companions. None ever complained. They worked in perfect coordination as though they were a single living organism. The cluster of Peekers reached out like a tentacle, grabbed the bobbing gull, then retracted back to the ship.

Garret shook his head in disbelief. No books described anything close to that level of sophistication among Peekers. Then again, no writer had ever been so close to this many Peekers at once. It was almost enough to rcignite Garret's childhood ambitions. Traveling the world, advancing humankind's understanding of nature. He itched to document his observations.

He snorted. Nothing but fantasy. Garret couldn't even *write*.

Besides, I'm in the middle of a hunt. One that resembled no other in his experience. Which made it all the more dangerous. This would test his survival skills like nothing else could. Not the rangers' rite of endurance. Not even the Benefactors.

Garret liked to put his abilities to the test. He'd hunted three daggerclaws, though never more successfully than in Reed's Woods. Took that as a sign he was improving. One arrow right in the eye, and the beast went down on the burning log.

That's all it took, a good strike to a weak spot. For daggerclaws, the eye. For Benefactors, their skull.

What about Skardwarves?

No clue, but he'd be on the lookout once they arrived in the Peeker homeland.

Until then, he had to stay sharp. It was why he packed no rations. Not before leaving Eko to reach Liwokin, and not before venturing to the Mounds. He'd hunted his meal every day, though admittedly he was getting sick of fish and doubted seagull would taste much better.

The Peeker who had plucked Garret's lunch from the water skittered toward him. "The human never misses," it said. "This one is most impressed."

Garret grimaced, thinking of the two arrows that failed to skewer Ulken in Reed's tower. *I only miss when it matters.*

He forced himself to grin. "Wouldn't be the greatest ranger in the Empire otherwise, now would I, Tunnel?" Garret took the gull from him and passed it over his shoulder to Sentyx. "Here, gut this." Turning back to Tunnel, "You sure—"

With a pop, a squish, and a grunt, Sentyx handed a pulverized bird back to Garret.

Last time I ever ask you for help. But what did he expect?

"Do I even want to know what just hit my boots?" Garret asked.

No answer.

"Worry not," Tunnel said, unfazed. "These ones will clean up. Please, enjoy your meat."

Going to be hard to do that when half is still in the cracks of Sentyx's fingers. Garret eyed the pulp in his palms. He dropped it with the rest of the carcass. "You sure Myrme will have food I can eat?"

Tunnel nodded vigorously. "Oh yes, yes. Many humans visit the Collective. All reside in the mountain of Myrme. Few prefer the food from the Feeder Hollows. Still, it is available in the Human Aerie, should you wish to ingest it. A delicacy." The Peeker clicked its pincers together, and its eyes rolled up in their sockets.

"Think I'll stick to the imports," Garret said, then turned to Sentyx. Considered. Could Peeker slop be their weakness? "You might like it."

"No."

"Suit yourself." He could always slip it into Sentyx's meal to see the effects. The thought gave rise to another idea, perhaps a faster way to learn how Peekers and Skardwarves interacted. "Tunnel, are there any other Skardwarves living in the Mounds?"

"This one is aware of no other Skardwarves, though these ones do not call ones like Sentyx by that name."

Garret leaned forward, interested. "You don't?"

"Ones like this are called Burners."

He blew out a laugh. "Him? Can't even start a fire, this one. Believe me, I've seen him try. What do you call humans? Let me guess. Bonebags?"

"Soft," Sentyx added.

"Screamers," Tunnel said. "But the humans do not wish to be called this. Screamers and Burners, both are very dangerous to the Collective."

That sucked all the fun out of the air. "We're not here to hurt any Peekers," Garret assured. "Only looking for Prost."

Garret wasn't sure Prost was going to be in the Peeker Mounds, but no one he or Grim had interrogated knew anything about Ulken's advisor. Most had never even heard the name. The last word they had about him was from Oltrov, reporting to Reed that he was in the homeland of the Peekers. Trusting a Gildmember was ludicrous, or so Garret believed. Until he and Grim had stolen Pinch from the Mental Ward and discovered he was an Incubating Benefactor, not to mention nastier than a terrorbeak's bite. The Peeker and his bandit brothers, Benefactors all...Whatever awaited them in the Peeker Mounds, it seemed they were as good a place as any to begin the hunt.

The Peeker clapped its hands together. "This one knows these two are friends. They saved this one from being Unpaired in Liwokin." Tunnel perked up. "This one is recalled. Can you feel it? The Queen is close." Abruptly, the Peeker scurried to the front of the ship.

Truly an enigma, that species. At least Tunnel seemed grateful he, Grim, and Sentyx had broken it out of the Mental Ward. Maybe that would earn them some good favor with the Collective.

Sentyx turned southward just in time to weather a burst of cold wind.

Garret cringed as the gust cut right through his cloak, leeching the heat from his bones. "You better not say it." He was already covering his ears.

The Skardwarf opened his mouth and bellowed, "I face into the wind."

"Just can't bleeding help yourself, can you?" Garret muttered.

The impenetrable fog surrounding the ship rolled away over choppy waves, carried off by the gust. The Brightdaughter warmed Garret's skin as he looked up and closed his eyes. Inhaled deeply. Savored the fresh air in his nose. The equatorial winds calmed to a chill breeze that rattled the bones in his hair.

"Say what you will about this ship, at least we're out among nature."

"Ship smells bad. Hurts head."

"I didn't mean to *literally*—" Garret threw his hands up. The more time he spent around Sentyx, the more he was coming to think of the Skardwarf as something of a moron. "You know what? I'm going to take a nap. Wake me when we're there." Garret unstrung his bow, turned toward the ship's sleeping hutch, and started up the steps.

"We are there," Sentyx intoned, obviously confused.

"Yes," he explained, turning back. "When we're—" Garret's eyes widened as he peered over Sentyx's head. "Here."

Steep, jagged mountains rose from the horizon, connecting sea to sky, fast-moving clouds shielding several of the tallest crests from view. Greenery covered their north faces like moss on a rock. The two largest mountains, directly ahead, looked like one single lump of rock split in two with an axe. The wide bay that formed in that wound housed a harbor that brimmed with Peeker ships. Only those vessels provided Garret with a sense of scale.

Sentyx gave an unimpressed grunt. "Tiny."

Garret squeezed his eyes shut. *They're not tiny, they're far away, you big dense lump of—* He opened his mouth, then decided it was best to just let the Skardwarf learn on his own. "What do you say we pack up? We still need to figure out our first steps."

They entered the sleeping hutch together. Despite sharing the qualities of a cave with oozing walls, this section of the ship had become oddly comfortable. It was perfectly dark, and he slept like he was in the thick of a brightwood giant's canopy. His belongings never moved. His supply pack was secured to the wall with the same viscous resin Peekers excreted to stick themselves to walls, ceilings, floors, everything. Not to mention each other.

Since the entire ship was made out of the material, in his boredom Garret had found himself scraping samples from the walls to later study. It was brittle and attracted sharks and other fish that nipped at the vessel and tore gouges in its hull. The Peekers had made so many repairs, he wasn't sure it was even the same ship they'd disembarked on. The sleeping hutch, likewise, was often attacked by birds. Didn't bother the sailors though. They just slimed over the damage and went about their business.

Garret was too fascinated by the behavior to be disgusted. He'd learned so much about the creatures, their feeding habits, how they solved problems, their sleep cycle. Several slept in the hutch at that very moment, their snores vibrating the air like a mosquito in his ear. If they weren't the most pleasant noises, well, Garret could sleep surrounded by any animal sounds. It was the dreadful silence of a Skardwarf that unnerved him at night.

He dug into his pack and found a ration of dried rabbit meat, tossed it to Sentyx, then found another for himself. Garret didn't know if the Skardwarf even needed food. He gnashed the meat between teeth of stone, but more seemed to land on the ground than stay in his mouth.

Where would it even go? he wondered. *Do they have stomachs?*

Garret sighed, sat down, and munched on the jerky while he thought. All this time since spotting Sentyx in Liwokin, hardly ever leaving his side, and he'd learned so little about him. All he had to go on was what the Institute taught. Little difference between those lectures and sermons in the Church. Called them demons and prattled on about them being servants of the Darkfather. Foolishness. Garret wouldn't lend credence to those tales. He had two eyes, and he'd use them to form his own understanding of nature. That was his specialty: the wilderness and what it took to survive.

The only thing he knew more intimately was betrayal.

Grim would never understand treachery the way Garret did. Just like Ulken, the new Head didn't even see it when it was right in front of his eyes. Garret *remembered* the Deluge in the mortician Tak's apartment. Feigned ignorance when Hand Sixty-Four were shackled and at each other's throats.

Their light blinds them. Sentyx's thoughts surfaced in Garret's mind as he recalled a legion of Skardwarves preparing for war. *They will never see us coming.*

But Garret had spotted them. The Skardwarf could have said something when they were all airing their dark pasts, courtesy of the monster in Grim's head. Instead, he said nothing. That memory wasn't something he was trying to move past, like Inac killing his brother or Dunnax slaying another Paladin. Or Garret...he grimaced, recalling the sticky feel of blood on his hands, and instinctively wiped them on his cloak.

No, Sentyx wanted his purpose to remain hidden. What was it? Why had he joined the Agency? Clearly not to warn them of a coming Skardwarf invasion.

He eyed the Skardwarf, his silhouette blackening the doorway. One of these monsters was bad enough. An entire invading force? How could the Bright Empire fight back against that?

It began with learning the enemy's weakness. When a ranger stalked his target, he never let the quarry out of sight. Doubly so when that prey was a vicious beast that could rip your arms off. No doubt Sentyx could.

Seen him punch a snuffing hole right through a Benefactor. If this mission went wrong, no one could save him. He had to be careful. Watchful. Survive long enough to learn how to kill a Skardwarf before Sentyx saw fit to give up on his friendly act.

Garret grinned. "You and me are going to be spending a lot of time together." His smile faded when the ship rocked and he had to steady himself on Sentyx. "At least we won't be in quarters as cramped as this."

CHAPTER SIX

Screamers

Can only say one good thing about the Institute's work on Peekers: they actually sent a guy to live with them in the Aerie for a time. Guess he didn't tell them what they wanted to hear, because none of that experience made it into the compendium.

—From the first oral history of Ekohold

Tunnel and his Pair led Garret and Sentyx to their room in the Human Aerie. The Peeker opened the door and gestured inside. "A suite for the Colony's esteemed guests from the Agency."

Suite? Looked more like a storage closet. Tiny, smoothly chiseled out of the mountain's stone in the shape of a cube. That was what Peekers believed humans liked, Tunnel explained, since they always built boxy houses. Ten paces from side to side, and that wasn't accounting for the beds taking up most of the space. In what little remained, Garret was always in arm's reach of Sentyx. Tunnel too.

Pretty sure the door won't close with all four of us in here.

"Are the human accommodations to your liking?" the Peeker asked.

Garret had some ideas to improve them.

"Yes," Sentyx said.

Tunnel clapped. Sounded like knocking two sticks together. "Excellent. This one is most pleased." Its head twitched as it continued speaking to itself. "Human accommodations suit a Skardwarf as well. Fascinating. The Collective will learn from this knowledge."

Garret studied the Peeker. It seemed pleased with itself. Calm, showing no signs of anxiety. Not worried about bringing a Burner into its home? Then again, Screamers didn't sound any better, and there were plenty of them here.

"Where are the common areas?" Garret asked. "Places with lots of foot traffic."

"Many humans gather at the Nectar Hall." Tunnel chittered, its head cocking to one side then the other. "This one can direct the guests to a map. The Cartographers have marked all the walls in the Colony's complex."

"Don't need a map, thanks," Garret said. "We'll find our way around."

Tunnel stood straight up. Still. Body language for alarm, Garret guessed.

"This one must insist—" the Peeker started.

Garret cut it off. "Don't worry about us. Worry about finding Prost. You know what he looks like, aye?"

It nodded vigorously. "This one understands. If Prost is found in the Colony, this one will return. These one must obey the Queen's directive, however. The winds change. A new generation approaches. There is much to be done."

Garret peered both ways outside the door when the Peeker left. Shut it only when sure no one had followed or was listening too closely.

Let the hunts begin. Garret took a slow breath to steady his pulse. An Ekoan ranger must remain calm, give no signs of fear. Animals can always smell fear.

Garret smiled broadly at Sentyx. Only a bioluminescent pod provided light to see. Slimed to the ceiling, of course. Dim and pale green. He had seen similar fungus in a cave beneath the stormjungles. Felt like he was in a cave now, for that matter. That notion was only strengthened when he jumped onto the bed and bruised his tailbone.

Wincing, Garret arched his back, digging his shoulder blades into the pillow. He rubbed the tender spot and rolled onto his side. "Harder than the beds Ulken gave us."

Sentyx sat on his slab and cracked it.

Garret snorted. "I'm not paying for that."

The Skardwarf's mouth widened in a grim pantomime of a smile. "Human accommodations."

"Listen, let's make something absolutely clear. Under no circumstances, and I mean *no* circumstances, are you to say the name Prost out loud. With your lungs"—*Does he have lungs?*—"it would echo through these caverns and Prost would know we're looking for him. Understand?"

Sentyx grunted a yes.

"Good. Another thing. Grim's going to want reports." Garret spat at the thought of his past commanders. Always wanted bleeding reports. "I need you to do it."

"Why?"

Garret chuckled. "Pains me to admit, but I can't write. Can't hardly read either. I'll make it up to you. You write 'em out, I'll take 'em to the post."

Wherever that is. Should've asked Tunnel. But if he got lost on the way, it'd be no bother. More time for him to read the reports. He grinned inwardly. If he caught Sentyx in a lie to Grim, it could tell a great deal about the Skardwarf's fears and motivations.

Sentyx agreed. "We split up. Look for..." Another soft grunt.

Garret waited. Realized no more was coming and sighed, shaking his head.

At least it bleeding worked this time. Didn't say the name.

"No, we stick together. Can't have you sneaking off to your Skardwarf pals." Garret chuckled, as though it were a joke.

"I will not sneak."

"Don't think you could if you wanted to," Garret agreed. "And that's just it. We don't want you to. Word of a Skardwarf in the Mounds. That'll spread. Make it back to Prost, if he's here."

"I do not understand."

What was so hard about this? If Prost knew they were hunting for them, he'd be gone faster than a hare fleeing its warren. But an unrelated Skardwarf searching in the Mounds? If Prost learned another enemy of the Empire was here, he might see an opportunity to gain Sentyx as an ally. And when they made contact, Garret would have them both right where he wanted them.

Couldn't have asked for better bait. He grinned, pleased with himself for his ingenious plan.

"You don't have to," he said. "Let me do the thinking. You just follow my lead. Do what's..." Natural, he was going to say, then pictured Sentyx wandering off following some inscrutable Skardwarf instinct. "Just stay close."

Garret was up and out the door before Sentyx could even grunt. He looked left. Right. Nearly identical either way. Only difference was a group of men and women ambling down the dim, rocky corridor one way. Garret shrugged. Might as well follow everyone else. Nectar Hall must be in that direction.

On the way up to their rooms, Tunnel had explained this Human Aerie. It was a special project, taken on by cartographer Peekers to provide a living area for humans. Driven by trade, of course. There was money to be made in mixing. Only, Garret didn't know if the Peekers were exploiting humans, or the other way 'round.

Maybe some sort of symbiotic relationship. He considered the line of thought, trailing the group ahead of him.

Like the azears picking bugs from their sticky fur, relying on the rock turtles whose dung attracted those insects. All connected, part of an intricate cycle. The Cycle of Light, religious sorts called it, but it seemed to Garret no god was needed for nature to deserve worship. He could admire it for its intricacy. The appearance of simplicity with endless facets that only appeared when probed.

All the more reason he distrusted Skardwarves, same as he distrusted most people. They thought themselves above the natural order. Existing outside of nature, unaffected by its touch. Sentyx was proud of that, called it resilience. Garret recognized it for what it was. Flattening forests into stone. An all-too-human impulse.

Even the construction of the Human Aerie reeked of human design. Peekers might have carved these tunnels, but they were made solely for humans. All straight lines and hard edges. It stank like a cave, but Garret wasn't fooled. Humans, Peekers, Skardwarves... couldn't trust any of them not to ruin the natural world. For Light's sake, they came across a *balcony* when they turned the corner. Rectangular doorways led out to a vista of real beauty: nature.

The Brightdaughter was low on the horizon, copper rays peeking through the darkened clouds. The light landed on the side of the mountains, highlighting their edges with a glow that drew the eye downward. There, white-crested waves lapped at the mouth of the harbor, rocking moored ships. Peekers scrambled over their ships, each one a differently formed mass of resin, designs brilliantly adapted for their tasks.

Wide lateral wings were attached to the hull of one Peeker vessel, providing ample room for harvested shellfish. Another sported a resin-constructed container that swarms of Peekers were emptying of mail from another country in the Bright Empire. Garret suddenly realized how wide and squat the ship he'd arrived in was. Must have been necessary to keep it afloat with a Skardwarf aboard.

The man-made ships, by contrast, would have been indistinguishable if not for the gaudy flags they flew. Bright Throne sigils, Liwokin trading companies, the Ayeiri desert sun. None that gave any hint at Prost's presence.

Garret wasn't the only one studying the view. Rather, other people *had been*. Until Sentyx showed up and drew everyone's gazes to him. Aghast, the people of lesser constitution fled into the tunnels.

To those frozen in fear, the Ekoan bared his teeth. "What're you looking at? Never seen a Skardwarf before?" Scaring them, making them understand what they were looking at. Garret figured he'd encourage them to blabber. Word would spread fast.

As fast as they all cleared out when the word *'Skardwarf'* left Garret's lips.

"Scared," Sentyx said, his voice rumbling beneath the wind.

Almost sounded like the Skardwarf was...sad. An unwanted knot of pity stirred in Garret's stomach.

"Some people," Garret said, and spat over the railing. "Just don't take well to seeing something new."

He recognized that knot inside of him as something that had been plaguing him since they'd fought Lomin in the Shaded Grounds. A tangle inside his guts that he'd had starting when the Skardwarf saved him from the Hunter's snares. Made him feel guilty for being so suspicious. Like he was unduly scrutinizing a friend rather than a traitor.

His stomach churned. Garret figured it must be his hunger, and he strolled back inside, following those fleeing the Skardwarf. Humans were typical animals, always gathering around food. Safety in numbers and all that.

"Map," Sentyx grumbled.

"I don't need no bleeding—"

And then Garret saw it.

The most beautiful map that had ever been put to paper. Or rather, to stone. It was etched into the wall, a complex tangle of lines and chambers filling out the rough shape of a triangle. An image formed in Garret's mind as he studied the carving. Mountains filled with tunnels. Perfectly lifelike and teeming with millions of Peekers. And in the corner, relegated to a small cube with straight, crisscrossing lines...

"We are here." Sentyx gestured at a black gem of hardened slime, but pulled his hand back before he touched it. Like a person putting his hand in fire and flinching at the lick of flames. Strange.

"The Human Aerie. How sad." Garret's eyes returned to the vast tunnel system. What secrets did the Peekers hide from humankind? What might he learn with but a peek beneath the mountain? He yearned to explore the complex...

Stopped when he caught himself daydreaming again. The Peekers were irrelevant. Prost and the Skardwarf. They were his targets.

"Don't need no map," Garret muttered. *Don't need anybody's help. Only one who cares about me surviving is myself.*

Sentyx's lumbering footsteps trailed behind him as he stalked the tunnels to the Nectar Hall. Thump. Thump. Thump. Sounded like a daggerclaw closing on its prey, and it unnerved Garret, put him on edge. They were soon drowned out by a rumbling din that grew louder as they walked.

Around the next corner, the tunnel opened up into a cavern roaring with the sound of the ocean. To the right, the stone wall appeared blown open, and the stormy sky peered through. Four Peekers that looked uncanny to Garret's eye crawled on the wall near that opening. Crawled on all fours rather than walking, and their body was more elongated than normal Peekers. Some sort of variant? They filled the opening with slime like four spiders spinning one web. Garret decided to name them—Builders.

Garret could have watched them work for a full span, but escalating shouts drew his attention the other way. The feeding area was a wide avenue with shop signs lining both walls into the distance. Between them was a whole lot of tables and benches. He was assuming—couldn't see anything amidst the seething mass of people. Crammed together like fish in a net. Garret reflexively grimaced in disgust.

"I thought Liwokin was bad. But what would I expect from people who choose to live in the Mounds? Crazier than city folk, even."

"Many humans." Sentyx grunted.

"Too many. Easy to see why they call us Screamers."

"No," Sentyx disagreed.

"I'm waiting," Garret realized. "Why would I ever wait for explanation? You never tell me anything going on behind that thick skull of yours."

Not that I can blame you. Keeping secrets keeps you alive.

"Now, before we get lost in there," Garret said, voice nearly lost beneath the human wind, "you remember what Grim told us?"

Prost. A man as round and wide as he was tall. Thick, dark glasses perched above an upturned nose that seemed almost comically pig-like when paired with his receding hairline. Garret could picture the target easily. Even more easily imagine chasing him down. Darkfather, he might not even have to run.

Sentyx grunted a yes. "Big man."

"That's right. Let's keep an eye out while I get some food. That sign wouldn't look out of place in Graln." Garret's mouth began to water at the thought of authentic Ekoan food. It had been years...

Garret and Sentyx walked out of the shadows.

And the Screamers began to scream.

CHAPTER SEVEN

Rope Burn

Remind me why you insist we need the Skardwarves? The old man you left me with tells me they're uncivilized, and nothing I've seen disputes with that fact.

—Unsent letter discovered in the Head's office

In my dreams, the memories of others still haunted me. Nightly, I suffered their visions. Death knells more often than late, but even the most pleasant of them was tinged with some grief. Dreams mirrored waking life, it seemed. For tonight, the memory was my own.

Theirs were faces I would never forget, no matter how many deaths I witnessed. Had I sent them to their own? Lorelay's tears flowed as she and Inac departed for Canako, as they had every day since her brother's death. Was she weeping for Dunnax, or for my sending her back to her homeland? I wept as well, because the world waits not for grief. It only piles more upon you.

I don't want to send you away, I was thinking when I issued the command. *I have to. We need help.*

But she needed our help too. No one should have to go through what she did alone.

The next pair of faces appeared. A mountain of stone on a strange ship, a hooded figure beside him. It departed in the night. They were on the hunt, and justice would be done.

I watched it sail into the darkness, unsure whether I would ever see them again in the light.

One by one, I was losing them, and it was my fault. It wasn't just my sending them away. I was using them, like they weren't my friends, only tools. I should have kept them close.

But I was doing what I had to do.

The dream contorted to another memory, surfacing from the dark horizon of the ocean's waters. A memory not my own. A memory belonging to the first of the Benefactors. Yezna.

I'm doing what I have to do.

Ulken's thoughts filtered into my mind. Husband and wife were connected. Empath and Benefactor.

Ulken was transporting me somewhere. I observed this with equanimity. He was strong, and his flesh was warm. He carried me close to his chest, walking with surety under cover of night from my usual location below his office to a newly constructed room he had prepared for me. I sensed his thoughts as though they were my own. The line between us blurred. The thing sharing my mind wanted flesh to meld as well, but it did not know how.

We descended two dozen flights of stairs, all the while Ulken pondered his coming confrontation with Reed. Once he claimed his power, what would happen to him? To me? He looked down into my eyes and felt nothing—the only thing anyone ever felt around me. Thoughts of how to use the power he had been seeking for so long occupied his mind. The ability to amplify his will. To make others see as he sees, and to see through the eyes of others without my help. He remembered what drove him to this moment—a love no longer felt but still remembered. How could he forget the flood of memories that assaulted him upon discovering his wife murdered? He had witnessed the storm of bloodshed and primeval vengeance that came from the eyes of countless Liwo. They were a perfect match for the hateful rage that bubbled inside him.

But that was long ago. He felt none of that rage as he killed the Heels who finished the construction of the secret room he now brought me to. He was simply doing what he needed to do, as he always did when we were together. Ulken wanted me kept safe while he was away, so he could return to claim me after his victory.

And if he still wanted me out of sight, ashamed by my disfigured appearance, I would not protest his locking me up in the dark. I didn't judge him. Felt no fear or sadness. I only witnessed the experience itself. Witnessed and remembered.

What my husband did to me, I would never forget.

There were only objective facts: Ulken would always try to control me, and I would continue to give him Nothing. *Because that's all I am. To him, and to myself.*

Another memory attached itself to the end of this one. Like attracted like.

Nothing. That's what we are to them.

My arms strained. Some gluttonous Gilder making the ascent, most like. But that was the job. Lifting up those who'd be happy to squash us down. Oh, what I wouldn't give to wear the boots myself. From our hill they looked like insects in their golden streets, ripe for the stomping. I hauled, fist over fist—

And the rope snapped. A loud crash came, then screaming.

Before I could look over the edge, pain exploded in my back. The rope slipped from my hands as my limbs went cold. My eyes bulged, and I opened my mouth to scream but couldn't draw any air into my lungs. I turned, already curling my fist to strike back, and the knife went in again. I crumpled to the ground, unable to move. A boot pushed me over the edge, and I was falling.

Falling, into darkness.

I started awake as though someone had thrown a bucket of water on me. My hands frantically darted over my chest, until I realized there was no pain. I looked at my palms; they were unburned. Weariness still threatened to send me back into slumber, as it did every morning. Nightmare-plagued sleep wasn't quite what my body needed.

Certainly not when those nightmares contained visions of Ulken. I was trying to distinguish myself from him, to free the Agency from the corrupt foundations he laid…but so far, I hadn't even been able to grasp the true depths of his scheming. Apart from sorting through endless pieces of blackmail, what had I really accomplished as Head?

For one, I had stopped the use of the haze throughout the Agency Headquarters. Ulken called it "incense", but it really turned out to be burning seedlings extracted from the brains of the dead, supplied in bulk by the mortuary. Disgusting. Whatever it was called, Ulken only used it to counteract the effects of Yezna's dulling Aura and to keep his workers productive.

But Ulken's wife was gone. Even without the haze, her Aura couldn't be felt. Maybe she had died with Ulken, her Empath, the link between them severed.

The way things seemed to slip further from my grasp every day, I wondered if Yezna hadn't been the only thing keeping the Agency functional from the start. That thought made me want to curl up and command someone else to solve my problems while my body recovered from whatever in the Darkfather's name happened last night.

But if I let my weary bones decide what to do, nothing would ever get done. I followed my head instead and threw my feet over the sides of the bed onto the cold stone floor, then paused.

How did I get to my room? Looking down, some heat flushed into my face. *And who undressed me?*

Before the siren song of warm blankets beckoned me back, I forced myself out of bed and threw open the window. The Bright-daughter was well above the horizon—I was no mathemelodian, but from her height, I knew this going to be a long day.

What *was* that Emergence? What damage had it done? I scanned the city, tense as I waited to see any sign of a disturbance, but it all looked just as I expected. The smoke of the Market and Artisan's Districts rising steadily into the windless blue sky. The crescent shaped

Docks spanning from the Gild to the base of the Blight hill, ships of every color sail—and some with no sails at all—crowding the harbor. In the distance, the Old District, called the Blight by most, appeared quiet.

Appeared, but I knew better. Most of the bounties I'd hunted led me into the heart of that rat's nest, a warren of tight alleys, squelching mud, and any number of cold-blooded murderers hiding in the burned-out shanty town. The Blight may appear nascent from afar, but the signs of activity were there if you knew them. A crack of gunfire echoing across the Brightcalm Bay. The scaffolding they called the Docks overcrowded with Blightdwellers long-line fishing or trading their meager supplies.

From my quarters near the pinnacle of the Agency, those people looked like insects crawling across the cliff face. It was no wonder the Gild thought of them that way. I couldn't see the Financial District from my window, but I knew their Archemetal towers must have been glistening in the Brightdaughter's light. The Gild was foolish to dismiss the Blightdwellers. No matter what they looked like from this distance, up close, they wouldn't hesitate to put a knife in your back.

Or your front, for that matter.

Something was going on in the Old District. I hadn't sensed carnage like that since...the only thing that came to mind was the Great Riot, but I *hadn't* sensed that. I had no memory of that day, no Liwo did. Yet, imagined scenes of that violence played in my mind even now, as though beckoned by a sibling to come out of hiding.

Hateful slaughter, seen through the eyes of many. In their eyes and behind them there was rage. His rage. I watched this and felt Nothing—it simply happened.

I rubbed my eyes, trying to clear the memory—another of Yezna's, no doubt—and returned to my private quarters in the tower. The window pane swung in a light breeze carrying the same scent of saltwater I had always known. In the next gust, it shifted to the same fetid waste odor that I was unfortunately even more familiar with. It was still Liwokin out there, no matter how quickly things were changing.

The same Liwokin, and the same Liwo. My kin. How many had perished last night? As many as the Great Riot? It didn't seem possible... Surely, there would be some sign of the destruction through my window. There was nothing but those death knells.

Frantic footsteps had just registered in my ear when the door crashed open behind me.

"Sir." A woman's stern voice accompanied a hissing of fabric that could only be a Nerve snapping to a sharp salute.

I nearly turned. Then, I remembered I was entirely naked and settled for looking over my shoulder instead. Impossibly, she wasn't blushing at all, and stared me directly in the eyes. How could that be when my own crimson face felt hot enough to boil water? It was starting to become clear why Ulken had given them that name. Their surprise visits were starting to get on my nerves.

"There's a problem," the Nerve said.

"Will the day ever come when you barge into my quarters and tell me there *isn't* a problem?"

It had been one thing after another ever since becoming Head, and none of them ever seemed to get solved. How did Ulken do it? Was I incompetent, or had things always been unraveling beneath the surface?

The Nerve's eye twitched, and her lips pursed for just a beat. I noticed her sharp salute had slipped a touch lower. "I was on my way here to remind you of the meetings with the Gild and Council you scheduled for today, sir." She hesitated before adding that last.

If it was making her uncomfortable, me standing here in the raw, well then, all the better. Maybe next time she would knock before intruding. And for a reminder of my schedule? I had been preparing for these meetings for days. I needed no reminder.

Then again, I did sleep nearly until noon.

"Surely, you could have waited outside for me to get dressed."

The poor girl seemed on the brink of tears, suddenly. Still, she kept her gaze high. "I couldn't, sir—"

"And stop calling me sir," I said, grimacing. "It creeps me out." *Reminds me of Jacquin, that lickspittle.*

"I can't, sir."

"Why not?"

"It's in a Nerve's control agreement. We agreed to behave this way."

I blinked. "You're following a rule that says you *must* barge in?"

The girl squeaked agreement, suddenly making sense of why the doors to neither my office nor my quarters had locks. I squeezed my fists. *Ulken.*

"Well, stop following them!" She flinched back as if I were going to strike her, but still never looked away. "There's Agency has a different Head, now. Things are going to be different."

"'A Nerve's eyes must never leave the Head,'" she recited, "'until the command is given. Then, it must be executed exactly and without delay.'"

I groaned. "Forget that. Just tell me what news you have like I'm a person, not some...tyrant."

"You cannot just change the rules, sir."

"I can," I told her, "and I will. Now, if you don't avert your eyes so I can cover myself with a sheet, Lightmother help me..."

"I must not, sir."

What has Ulken done to you? Too much time in Yezna's nullifying Aura, and their minds had been molded into tools shaped for the Head's hands. Those weren't my hands. I wasn't going to repeat the mistakes of my predecessor.

"Here is my command," I said. "Leave me and go figure out which Organ has the authority to change control agreements. When you find that person, you tell them the Head wants the agreements changed. Have the Organ send them to my office. Now go." I hoped that would keep her occupied for some time. In truth, the last thing I needed was more paperwork added to my desks. But these rules Ulken enforced were becoming ridiculous.

The Nerve didn't go.

"You *just* said—"

"I haven't yet told you what the problem is."

Of course.

CHAPTER EIGHT

Repeating History

...over a timespan long enough for their Patterns to grow increasingly similar, such as when humans domesticated dogs. However, by chance, even the Patterns of seemingly unrelated creatures align. One wonders if in the past these animals had a closer relationship to one another, an influence that survived the ages.

—Excerpt from 'On animal affinities',
filed with the Organ of Understanding

Moments later, I was hurrying down countless stairs en route to the mortuary. A chill crept into the air as I descended the final, tight, spiral staircase. The dark stone walls closed in, the candles housed in recessed nooks coming ever closer to scorching my arms. At the bottom, I had to duck beneath the door frame to reach the dark corridor that led to the morticians' domain.

Beneath a crooked sign reading *'Mortuary'*, the iron-banded doors hung askew from one hinge. The lock had been smashed, and whatever did it had left a gash in the stone door frame.

I hesitated before stepping past the buckled door. Any number of creatures strong enough to break in came to mind, but how many of them could fit down here?

"I haven't touched anything." Arza, the lead mortician strode toward me holding a lantern. "Everything you see is exactly as I found it when I arrived just after dawn."

Chunks of stone and concrete littered the ground so thoroughly, walking among the rubble was likely to inflict a twisted ankle. Shelves of lab equipment had been destroyed, shattered glass and wood mixed with broken ceramics that had spilled their ashen contents. The lid of a lockbox in the corner of the mortuary was torn from its hinges; whatever lay inside was gone along with the one who ransacked the place.

"Dawn? Arza, it must be almost half-noon. Why am I just hearing of this now?"

"I had to check on my parents, make sure they weren't targeted too. They're old, they can't protect themselves."

Arza flashed a grin that seemed unsuitable for the situation until I adjusted for the fact that she practically lived down here among the dead. She had been the only technician who volunteered to take Tak's place following his death. All the better that she was his most accomplished pupil; after the many deaths in Reed's Woods, she had produced a wealth of new knowledge about the Benefactors, building on the old lead mortician's discovery that it was a tiny organism infesting the brain. She even claimed her latest theory explained why Sentyx and his brother had been so heavily affected by Reed's Aura—though sadly, it was one of many documents I had yet to find time to read. I would have to do so soon. The Ayeiri woman was exceedingly good at her job.

Tak was good at his job too, right up until it got him killed.

Was I leading Arza down a path that ended inevitably in her demise? Was I leading all of us down that path? Until I figured out how to fix the Agency, I was hardly leading at all.

Right now, it was like an unaligned crossbow. Powerful, but whatever I aimed at, I was sure to miss the target. And I didn't need to align only the Agency, but the rest of Liwokin's squabbling factions as well. Instead, it felt like I was only reacting to one disaster after another. When would I be able to get my footing?

"I'm glad you weren't here when it happened," I said.

"I'm not." She put her hands on her hips, then raised one, palm to the ceiling. "I could have stopped them. No Ayeiri woman is defenseless." A strand of Archefire emerged from her palm, rising and twisting in accordance with her fine finger movements. Arza flung her hand to the side and released a bolt of Fire that lit the crematory on the far wall. A body lay on the slab at the mouth of the flames.

A body, but no head.

Judging by the bloody green robes beside the pile, it was the mage I failed to save. I started to turn away, then stopped. This was an attack on my Agency. On *my* people. I couldn't shy away. "Who did this?"

"I do not know," Arza said, crossing her arms. "But they stole Taktus' notes. *My* notes. Who would want those?"

I approached the body, got a better look at the fleshy pulp that had once been a human head. Whoever had broken in here had stolen Tak's notes and smashed in the skull of the dead man. Why do that to a corpse? Unless something living remained...but I had already suppressed the Emergence of the dead mage's Benefactor. His death knell came to me, a disorienting shift of my perception to the last moments of the corpse I was looking down upon. *Looking up at my friends. All of us, scared.*

In the mage's final memory, one of those in his Hand he considered a friend had been the Skardwarf, Cavern. He appeared indifferent to me, not scared, the blood of one of the mage's attackers dripping from his fist. Another skull smashed in. Slowly, I was piecing it together. The Skardwarf clearly had knowledge of Benefactors. But then why steal Tak's notes?

I would put that question to him myself. He needed to be detained, brought to justice for what he did to this Finger. And for disobeying my commands.

"What notes were stolen?" I asked.

Arza blew out an exasperated breath. "All of Taktus' originals. His journal entries as he discovered the organism in Pinch's head. His observations on differences between human and Peeker Patterns. The notes he took while serving as technician. Everything...and I was so far from completing my transcription. It was slow work. Taktus' handwriting is harder to decipher than finding an oasis in the Ayeiri wastes."

So, we were looking for someone inside the Agency with knowledge of Benefactors and the strength to break down a locked, iron-banded door.

Not to mention a history of bashing skulls in.

"You've had time to look around," I said to Arza. "Best guess as to who did this?"

She chewed her lip while she thought. "I rushed home to my parents because I have my own notes there, and if whoever did this knew that, they also know that my parents are likely to be infested with Benefactors because of my job. As I ran up those stairs, I know what I was afraid I'd run into when I got home: a Skardwarf."

"Then we're in agreement. The Skardwarf Cavern must be arrested for questioning. And I don't care how valuable a Finger he is, if he did this..."

This was a human no longer. On the slab before me was only meat. His brother cried over his body, and the Skardwarf had reduced him to meat. A pulverized mess at the end of a naked body. Fit only for the fire. Disgusting.

A memory assaulted me, made me woozy. I had to catch my balance on the stone.

It surfaced from the Pool of Andya, the plague-ridden Benefactor. My body was withered, covered in pustules. Oozing. Shrinking. In terrible pain from this curse that afflicted me. But no matter how terribly my body ached, my mind was broken further still. I looked down upon myself.

Disgusting.

Surfaced memories never came alone anymore. Always, another followed, as though they had been conjoined all along, one experience. This time it came from Ulken. Or Yezna. With those two, it was often hard to differentiate, they were so deeply intertwined.

The loathing I felt entering her chamber was second only to the loathing of leaving her behind. I felt her pull like a lover urging me to bed. Perhaps it felt that way because of the love we had shared once, as husband and wife. No longer. Now, we were only Empath and Benefactor. Now, we both did what we had to do. Liwokin needed me, and I needed her. A perfect balance of duties.

Reaching the top, I closed the lid of the chest behind me and made my way up from the treasury to my dark office. I didn't bother lighting the incense as I sat behind my desk, cherishing her touch on my mind perhaps for the last time.

When I returned, everything would change.

The Organ of Treasure assigned to guard our empty vault always complained about how little he had to do. Well, I had given him what he desired, a role of utmost importance. He couldn't know the real treasure was in the promises I'd extracted, the oaths sworn to me, sealed in blood and ink. The Agency's wealth lay in that power.

And in her.

All of this functioned only because of her. They executed my will because of her. She gave me vision I lacked. Such insight. The experiment had borne even greater fruits than I expected. And this was only the beginning. Prost had found the tool we truly needed to save the city from falling to chaos. The city, and then beyond.

I pulled from my pocket a silver key decorated with a single garnet and placed it in my drawer beneath a false bottom.

"Rest now, my darling," I gently whispered. "Soon we will be reunited for good."

Ulken's memory faded as he left his office, thoughts of the Chimera swirling in his mind.

A sense of vertigo overcame me as I realized my feet weren't on the ground. The rest of me was, however. I hardly noticed. I drew a breath in, realizing what I had just witnessed through Ulken's eyes.

Arza knelt over me. "What is happening to you, Grim?" Her voice held real concern, not like that of a worker to the Head, but of someone witnessing their friend in pain. Though I had a long way to go before believing Arza considered me a friend.

I'll settle for her thinking of me as someone who hasn't gotten her killed, as the previous Head did to her predecessor.

I would not make the same mistakes as Ulken.

But I was making different ones. The Benefactor in my head was interfering with my duties. I couldn't keep waking up and finding myself on the ground or learning that several days had passed unnoticed.

"It's fine...just a dizzy spell, seeing the body."

Arza crossed her arms, seeing right through the lie. "I heard about your incident last night."

"Great," I muttered. Arza literally lived under a rock. Several hundred tons of it—the Agency was nearly as deep as it was tall. If she had heard about the news, everyone in the Agency must know what happened. Or even... "Has it gotten outside of the Agency? The last thing I need is the Council or the Gild thinking me weak."

"Your reputation is not what matters," Arza urged. "Your health is what is important. I was trained by Ayeiri Archehealers, the best in the world. I can help you. It would be a better use of my time than studying another corpse."

I sighed. She didn't know my secret. Only a handful did. The members of Hand Sixty-Four and Jacquin, and I regretted that last. I didn't trust him. The others, I trusted my life to them. They were the only people in the Agency who saw things as I do. They had been put through Ulken's gauntlet the same as I had. They were reliable.

Always reliable.

I looked up. So was Arza. She knew what she was doing. She wanted to help.

"Learning everything you can about Benefactors *is* helping me, Arza. I promise..."

I trailed off, narrowing my eyes in thought. Two threads tied themselves together in my mind. Yezna and Arza. Perhaps it was time to expand my circle of trust. I wasn't certain anything would come of it, but we had to check what I saw through Ulken's eyes.

"Come with me."

Her technicians would be perplexed when they came down to discover this mess, but she wasn't going to need them if she agreed to this plan. They could handle the grunt work on their own. The lead mortician had a more important task to do.

I left Arza on the fourteenth floor and climbed the tower to my office. Ulken's key, silver and garnet, had been sitting in his desk since I took over. I had discovered the drawer's false bottom that hid it, but simply never found its lock. Until now. Clutching the key hopefully, I rushed down to the treasury.

"—feel as empty inside as this vault," the Organ of Treasure said. He laughed wistfully, shaking his head.

Arza was sitting on his desk and patted him on the back. "She doesn't know what she gave up."

I cleared my throat, and they both jumped at my appearance. "Am I interrupting?"

The Organ shot to his feet and coughed as he awkwardly saluted. "No, uh, sir. Everything is in order. Kept it locked up tight like the last Head commanded. No intruders."

I cocked an eyebrow. "Didn't think there would be."

"He wants to know if he's going to get paid soon," Arza said. "His girlfriend left him because he couldn't afford to buy her a new necklace."

The Organ squeaked in embarrassment. "Arza!"

"What? I'm helping." She turned to me. "Well?"

"Oh...uh, isn't that the responsibility of the treasury?" Blank stares met me. "I'll put in a word with Jacquin." Surely, he would know, but I couldn't be bothered with it at the moment. I gestured at the vault door, darkwood and iron with a heavy crank in the center. "Can you open this for us?"

The Organ jumped into action, unlocking and spinning the crank until a dull thud sounded from the other side and the heavy door swung open.

I felt her as soon as I stepped over the threshold. Beyond the unlocked door, past the sad sacks of gold stars that sagged like rotten potatoes, in the shadowy recesses of the trove, a thick layer of dust coated the top of an ample chest. Plain brightwood with bronze banding across the lid. I unlocked it and found it filled with neither gold nor jewels. Only a ladder. Summoning the courage to climb down, I told Arza, "Follow me."

Yezna's Aura dulled my emotions as I descended. Strange that it should only affect me in such close proximity when before it shrouded the whole tower. Perhaps my Benefactor granted me some immunity to her influence, but it was welcome now. Like seeing an old friend after a long absence. I feared not the darkness that steeped the room at the bottom. Nor did I feel the elation I should have that she even remained within the tower. I thought she was dead until now.

Arza followed. Fortunate because I had no way to make light. Without needing to be told the lead mortician summoned a mote of Archefire and kept it hovering above her shoulders to serve as a torch. Her Archemagic illuminated a spacious, half-finished room with no windows and cobwebs in every corner. Pipes dripped steaming water onto muddy stone. The whole space had a musty smell with a sour undercurrent. That smell grew stronger as we approached the lone door opposite the ladder.

Pushing it open, the odor amplified tenfold. I gagged. The only thing that ever smelled worse was Andya's cart. Not even Liwokin after a heavy rain.

Arza strolled right in, undeterred.

"That doesn't bother you?" I regretted opening my mouth. Now I *tasted* that odious fume.

"There's something...pleasantly pungent about it," Arza said. "Other technicians pack flowers and other sweetly-scented things in their masks, but I never felt the need. I like the smells of death. I think my brain must be broken in some way." She smiled. Then all the color drained from her face, and she froze, turning the corner.

Her shock didn't prepare me for what I saw. All the blackmail and corruption, none of it compared to this. Yezna was a brown-haired woman, face sunken in, eyes covered by lids sealed permanently shut. Her arms were scarred flesh clinging directly to bone, no room even for ligaments or tendons. The iron-barred cage that held her hung from the ceiling, softly creaking in time with the motion of her exaggerated breathing.

Ulken had dressed his wife in a silky-translucent white dress with a neckline that came right up to the scar across her mangled throat.

My jaw clenched, grinding my teeth back and forth. Of everything Ulken had done, this was surely the worst. She was a living person, his *wife*, caged and malnourished. Kept alive only by Archedark— it emanated from her as surely as the patterns of Archefire around Arza's flame. Being an Archemage herself, I knew she could feel the Dark as well.

The look of horror on her face, even in the presence of the nullifying Aura, told me the rest of what I needed to know.

"Help me with this." The lock on Yezna's cage yielded to the same key as the chest. Arza helped me move her to a chair in the corner. Ulken must have sat there when he tended to her. "I have a new command for you."

"This..." she sputtered. "I have seen many things, but *this—*"

"This is Yezna, Ulken's wife. She is the first Benefactor," I said. "Help her. However you can. Learn from her, but remember, she's *alive.* She's a person." I hoped that was true, for my own sake. "Don't harm her. We're trying to *cure* the Incubating, not kill them. If we can cure Yezna, we can cure anybody."

Once again, I found myself using someone like a tool, setting them down a dangerous path.

"You know how Tak died." I myself knew all too well; I possessed the memory of the Peeker who killed him. Reading Jacquin's report on the Emergence had been the first task Arza had set for herself as lead mortician. She took that disaster to heart, I knew. "Don't make the same mistakes he did."

Perhaps with the assistance of Yezna's Aura, Arza overcame her stupefaction. Now, there was something else in her eyes as she looked at the Benefactor. Hunger?

"I understand," she said. "But this is an Emergent Benefactor, yes? It cannot be discovered we are keeping an Emergent in the tower."

She was right. One Head had been toppled by a conspiracy fomented by the use of Benefactors in the Agency already. A conspiracy that resulted in my own ascension to the role.

Let's not repeat history so soon, shall we?

"I take it you're okay with working in the dark?"

CHAPTER NINE

A Surprise Visitor

They come for Her flame, She gives them Her Fire
Speak ill of Her name, let burn Her bright pyre
Disgrace leaves us cold in Her flickering flames
While the Dark lover dances, Her influence wanes

—Verse from Burn! Flame of Her People,
Second Song of Noon

Lorelay opened her eyes to darkness, tried to sit up, and groaned. Her body ached. Her shoulder was bruised. Her neck creaked as she turned her head looking for...anything. Even with nothing to see, her vision spun, and she had to suppress the urge to vomit. Again...judging by the stench and the sour taste in her mouth.

A cold stone ground was about the only thing she could discern. Around her there was a dark void and the weak moaning of tortured souls. By the abyss, where was she? She dared not feel around for fear of her hand landing in her own vomit...or something worse. Standing was not happening, so Lorelay slowly slid backward, trying not to hit her head. A throbbing pain kept beating a rhythm in her head. The last thing she needed was to crack her skull on a wall.

She did avoid the wall, but only because she went the wrong way and cracked her head on iron bars instead. She yelped, and a voice in the darkness spoke.

"Awake, girl?" a man asked.

Lorelay was so startled by not being alone, she screamed. Another person beyond the iron bars screamed back. A third person shouted, "Keep it down!" But by then it was too late. Her first outburst had set off a cascade of noise that did nothing to help her aching head. So, she was in a prison. A very dark prison, probably the Radiant Palace's dungeon.

Her mission to gain the Bright Throne as an ally was not off to an auspicious start.

Judging by the cacophony—not to mention the fact that she was *sharing* a cell—the Bright Empire was imprisoning a great many people. She wondered how many of them were in here for harmless crimes like she was. And for that matter, what exactly *her* crime had been. Trying to remember was like dancing a jig while plucking *Sing for the Dawn*. The raucous prisoners only made it harder to concentrate.

Thankfully, a guard had arrived to set things right. With a flare of torchlight that made Lorelay's eyes water and a squeaking hinge that burrowed into her skull, a tall man—even for a Paceeqi—hunched through a newly open doorway just long enough to shout, "Any man who doesn't shut up, I'll find your mother and gut her before tossing her corpse in with you!" The door slammed, the lock clunked, and to the man's credit, the noise ceased.

"He seems friendly," Lorelay muttered. "Definitely no underlying mental issues there."

The man in Lorelay's cell chuckled. It iced her skin to know that he was just waiting there in the dark. "That's the Sugarman. He's not so bad. Keeps us fed and watered. Nothing healthy, mind, and it'll take a few days before you'll work up the courage to suck on the same wet sponge as all these other dark-lovers. But the man's honest, so you'd best take him at his word." He gave a rueful laugh when Lorelay gasped. "Might not have your teeth in a few decades, but you'll get used to him."

"Don't think I'll have time to." She remembered why she was here. The song she sang was hazy, much hazier than the Paladin's gloves digging into her arm and the new tavern owner convincing him to spare her life only to save herself a bit of cleaning. Lorelay hated this place. Why had she ever agreed to come home? She rubbed her eyes, trying to make the pounding go away. "Pretty sure I'm supposed to be public executed tomorrow."

Or was it today? Lorelay had no notion of how much time had passed, and it was unlikely the Sugarman was going to be playing the Rhythm of Time for the prisoners.

"That's what they told me too."

"Really?"

The man grunted. "Three years ago, or thereabouts."

Lorelay gasped again, and this time the man found no humor in the situation. Nor did Lorelay, for that matter. Could she really be stuck in this dark cell for years? It was unthinkable. No music, no light. Stuck with little more to occupy her thoughts than her regrets, her failures... She shook her head. "You can't be serious."

"Do I sound like I'm joking, girl? I'm doing you a favor. Better set your expectations right now, otherwise you'll be begging for death before long."

The darkness, already claustrophobic, seemed to press in even tighter. It was so cold. Lorelay hugged herself and shivered.

"What did they pinch you for, anyway?" her cellmate asked.

Lorelay ignored him, rocking back and forth, trying—failing—to think straight. She had to get out of here. She wanted to call for help, but even beyond these walls, there would be no one listening. She was all alone here. All alone in the world. A brief remembrance of Reed's Woods entered her mind, but Lorelay slammed her head back against the iron bars before it developed into a full thought. She groaned, spittle bubbling from her mouth as she began to cry. The pain in her head was great, but it was nothing compared to the mountain of sorrow inside her.

"Oh, don't tell me you've broken already. It was a simple question. Me? I didn't do anything. Nothing at all, and I'm here for three years."

I'm sure you're entirely innocent. The bitter thought surfaced as the man answered a question she had no interest in asking. Her palms pressed at her temples.

"Nothing...just bad luck. Never had good luck, true, but never thought my life would be confined to this dark box because some fool girl started singing some Dark-loving song in my inn."

Lorelay's eyes popped wide open. She saw nothing, but she faced the shadowy spot from which those words emanated. Gravis, the Blueflame's old owner...could it be him? There was no way it was him. But how many other heretical musicians were out singing their songs in Vos' taverns?

"For me to be stuck in here while she's out there denouncing the Book of Light...where's the justice in that?"

"There is none." Lorelay found her voice unexpectedly shaky.

She had expected the man to blacklist her from Vos' inns, not for him to be punished for her actions. Lorelay should have known the Bright Throne would be so unreasonable. Too many people suffered for her mistakes, yet she seemed only to dig herself into deeper pits.

Unless...now that Lorelay knew the damage she had caused, perhaps she could make amends.

"You don't deserve to be here," she muttered, wishing she could direct her anger at the one who truly deserved it. The Bright Prince. "I'm sorry."

A long sigh came from the darkness. "No sense apologizing. Won't change a thing. Besides, it's not your fault our laws are so strict. We're all bound to find ourselves on the wrong side of them eventually. That's the price for keeping the Light alive."

"Price?" Lorelay snapped.

Hearing him talk about the value of the Bright Empire's tyranny from inside a cell was too much to abide. She had to speak up. What was the worst that could happen? She was already imprisoned.

"What kind of price is that? Forcing everyone to live in fear so the Bright Throne can maintain its power? Executing people for singing songs? Leaving good men like you to rot in prison for crimes you didn't commit? They claim they want to keep the Dark Era at bay but condemn us to the darkness to rot. We're not paying to keep the Light alive, we're paying for its funeral."

"She's right," someone whispered from a nearby cell, but someone else shushed them. Lorelay almost smiled. She had finally found an attentive audience. A captive audience, but still...

"You're a good man," Lorelay told Gravis, "and I'm sorry you're here. If I had known they would imprison you, I never would have played at the Blueflame. But it shows how important it is to fight—"

"You," Gravis growled.

Lorelay flinched, eying the darkness as though it contained a wild wolf.

"You...are you really here?" His throaty laugh contained no humor, only malice. "All that's kept me alive these years, the *only* thing, are thoughts of what I'd do to you if I got my hands around your throat. The Darkfather's justice, it'd be."

It dawned on her what her stupid tongue had let slip. Her boots scraped the ground as she instinctively tried to flee, succeeding only in pressing her back harder into the iron bars. She tried swallowing, only to find her throat was parched. "I'm sorry." Lorelay's words were a whimper, a plea, and she knew they might be her last. "For everything. I'm sorry."

"Sorry isn't good enough," Gravis said. "Not when I've waited this long."

The rustle of clothes was all the warning she had. The man had lunged for her. Lorelay rolled to the side, heard a grunt as he hit the bars, and tried to steady her spinning vision. Lightmother, she was practically still drunk. Still, she somehow found her way to her feet. Not for long, however.

Hands grabbed her ankle, and Lorelay yelped as she fell to the ground. Pain blossomed in her lower back. She was kicking at her invisible assailant, landing her blows. Other than earning a slew of curses, they had no effect. His hands grabbed at her thighs, then her wrists, working their way toward her throat.

When his breath gusted into her face, she jabbed at the side of his head. She remembered Gravis being a burly man, but her punches were as effective as if she had hit a Skardwarf. He was implacable. The prisoners were in an uproar again, some yelling at him to stop, others goading him on. She barely heard them over the pounding of her heart in her own ears.

His hands found her throat, and Lorelay was lifted off the ground. Slammed back down. A flash of light behind her eyes lit the darkness. Stars twinkled overhead, the last light she would ever see. She tried gasping in air, but Gravis had her in a vice grip. All of her struggling, her fighting back...it amounted to nothing.

Lorelay thrashed, heels sliding uselessly on the ground, elbows scraping cold stone. Her body fought, but in her mind, she had already given in. Warm, golden light flooded the cell, enough for her to see the hatred in Gravis' eyes. It told her what she already knew.

She was going to die here.

For what she had done, the abyss was what she deserved. Tears streamed down her cheeks as hands choked the life from her. Everyone she loved was dead. Because of her.

This is my punishment. Guilt and grief were a potent mix, poison for the soul. She drank it down and let her fate be decided.

And then someone shouted above the din. "Get him off of her!"

A silver-gauntleted fist connected with the side of Gravis' head and sent him sprawling.

Lorelay sucked in the air, coughing on it, flaring the pain in her head and ragged throat. The stars still danced in her vision. She lay there, thoughts swirling. The cell was lit. Lorelay blinked, reached up to feel the back of her head for blood. The tenderness of the spot she touched produced a wince, but her hand came away dry.

A face appeared, a man leaning over her. His jewelry and the golden adornments on his coat caught the light, glimmering. They had no right being in a cell as dingy as this. More surprising than those, however, was the genuine concern on the man's face as he studied Lorelay. His eyes slid from the stained, green tunic she wore to the bruise that must already be coloring her neck. When they finished their journey and met her eyes, Lorelay's breath caught as recognition dawned on her.

"Vinlin?" she asked weakly.

A sad smile spread across his face. "My dear, what has he done to you?" Vinlin's hands were gentle as they slid to her middle back and lifted her to a seated position. That his regal coat dragged through Lorelay's vomit, he either did not notice or did not care.

Gravis gaped, wide-eyed at Vinlin while on his hands and knees. The man looked exactly like Lorelay expected of someone sentenced to rot in prison for two years—plus some extra blood trickling down his face, a bit of which also adorned the Sugarman's gauntlet.

Lorelay's assailant collected himself, got to just one knee, and bowed his head. "Bright Prince Vinlin. Please forgive—"

The Sugarman yanked him by the collar of his soiled shirt up to his feet. "What should I do with him, Your Radiance?"

But Vinlin was too busy examining Lorelay for more damage to notice. "How badly did he hurt you? Are you able to stand?"

Lorelay wanted to nod, but the world was still spinning from when he sat her up. In any case, words tumbled from the Bright Prince's mouth as they did only for a man feeling great relief and prevented her from getting a word in edgewise.

"I rushed down as soon as I saw your name on the prisoner intake list. A mistake that will not go unpunished, I assure you. Your brother is not here, is he? Your crime may be pardonable, but—"

Lorelay stopped listening as soon as Vinlin mentioned her brother. He never should have gone with her to Lawiko. If he did, maybe he would still be... The tears flowed freely, as they always did whenever bitter thoughts of Dunnax's demise intruded on her thoughts.

"Oh, my darling, do not let this cretin see you cry." Vinlin stood with angry zeal and stomped toward her attacker. "What is your name?"

"G-Gravis, Your Radiance."

"Gravis, for laying hands on Brightness Lorelay, you are sentenced to public execution before the Brightdaughter wanes this day."

Lorelay choked on her sobs and coughed. Her mouth filled with the taste of blood. Her throat still ached. But the light of her soul had been tarnished enough. "No! He didn't do anything," she rasped.

Gravis wavered and had nearly fainted, but the Sugarman kept him on his feet. The Paladin watched Lorelay impassively, until Gravis tried to speak up in his own defense, which the Sugarman rewarded with a backhanded slap. Teeth clattered on the cell floor.

Vinlin knelt beside Lorelay. He tried to caress her neck, but she pulled away. "He had his hands around your throat."

"I attacked him first," she lied. "He shouldn't even be here."

Vinlin considered, then shook his head, chuckling. "You must be confused, Lorelay. Of course he belongs here. The Bright Throne makes no mistakes when it comes to justice." The words sounded rote coming from the man, as though they had been ingrained in him from birth. He helped Lorelay to her feet, placed her arm over his shoulder, and walked her out of the cell. The Sugarman locked the bars behind them with Gravis still inside. They left him there weeping in the dark.

Ascending from the dungeon, Vinlin sighed with pleasure. "I had not even heard of your arrival in the city, Lorelay. Were you hiding from me?" Lorelay stiffened, and he laughed, thinking it a clever joke. "I am so pleased you decided to accept my invitation, after all."

Invitation? Lorelay wondered, but her mind was still back in the dark cells. Gravis was an innocent man. She had done too little to attempt freeing him. How many other innocents were stuck down there while she was rescued? What had she done to deserve her freedom?

She stopped in her tracks, suddenly remembering the invitation that Vinlin was referring to. The Bright Throne makes no mistakes when it comes to justice, Vinlin had said. But if he thought she was here to be courted by him, he could not be more mistaken.

CHAPTER TEN

Continuity

Of course, your husband need never learn of your indiscretions with the Lumeeqi girl. One stroke of your pen on the enclosed document, is that so much to ask?

—On display in the office of Gildmember Alyse

The gate to the Financial District stood as a reminder of how everyone on this side of it didn't belong on the other side. Well, I figured most gates were built to serve that purpose, but the Gild's was particularly effective at making its message clear.

They had their own guards, Archecloaks, they called them, so named for the Archemetal-trimmed capes they wore buckled to their heavy plate smithed from the same precious metal. They looked like the Empress' Paladins, only richer. Even their title seemed to suggest they were somehow better than other guards. Seemed no different to me, save their fancy suit of armor.

Just like the Gild. Same scoundrels as the Blight, but with a shiny veneer.

Two Archecloaks stood looking bored with tilted spears, glaring at me through their slit visors and preventing access to the door beside the portcullis, the only open way through. It wasn't designed for much foot traffic, but foot traffic was the last thing the Gild wanted anyway. The huge Archemetal gate opened only on occasion, to let protected wagons of stars in or out—almost always in.

That, or some other exotic animal for the menagerie.

89

Apprehension grew in me as I approached the Archecloaks. The gate must have been open when the daggerclaw that killed Dunnax had escaped. I had no desire to see another such beast today—Lightmother willing, they only had the one. It broke free in the confusion of Reed's Aura, and my Hand killed it. Right outside the illusion of a gilded inn.

The Glisten Inn, a fine establishment to squander all your gold.

As I had done upon sneaking past this very gate the night Garret and I broke two Peekers out of the mental ward. Thankfully, now I had no need to sneak—I was welcome in the Gild, no matter the convulsions it would give the snooty Liwo inside. Their reaction was predictable.

Approaching the Archecloaks, my own reaction was less sure. What would I feel once inside? The last time I'd believed myself in the Gild was under the effects of the Emergent Reed. Those cobble-paved roads would always remind me of the dead in Reed's Woods. A slaughtered Hand beneath an Archeflare. Countless Liwo assimilated into a twisted tower.

Dunnax.

His loss wounded me most deeply. My first command as Hand Captain, and I got someone killed. A Finger whose life was my responsibility. My friend.

My thoughts drifted to Lorelay. She must blame me. Would she ever forgive me for what I allowed to happen to her brother?

"Ahh, Finger Grimley," a man said, emerging from the door behind the guards. He wore the type of Archemetal-trimmed coat only a Gildmember dared to wear outside the district and walked with the swagger of a man who never worried where he was walking, as though everything he stepped on was already owned by him. Oltrov—the prime conspirator who worked with Reed to overthrow Ulken—stopped uncomfortably close to me and smiled a devilish grin. "I was worried you would not make it."

I tried not to scowl when he blew his warm, mint-scented breath in my face. "I told you I was coming. Do you not believe me a man of my word?"

He put an arm around my shoulder and guided me past the guards. "There's always a risk when it comes to...continuity, shall we call it?"

"Call it whatever you want." I didn't much like his familiarity. If he thought I owed him anything because of his schemes with Reed... But I did owe him something. Just not for his actions against Ulken. What I owed him for was far more dire than that. An inordinate sum of money flowed from the Gild's coffers to our own.

They're your problem, now.

Ulken's last words echoed in my mind as my jaw started to ache from clenching it so often. I still didn't know to what, precisely, he was referring. His tangled web of corruption? The members of the Agency? All of Liwokin? The spreading Benefactor scourge? Ulken never thought of the Benefactors as a problem, only as a tool, so that ruled out the last. The rest were as good an answer as any.

Maybe it's all of them, taken together.

The Head had prepared a perfect mess for his successor. Whatever Ulken had his hands in, I wanted nothing to do with. Hence this meeting, to which we were strolling much too slowly for my tastes. Better to get this over with.

A commotion at the gate stopped us in our tracks. I turned around to find a man in a blue Eye's coat waving through the dim doorway, papers flailing in his hands. Not just any Eye; Ulken's First Eye.

Jacquin couldn't get past the Archecloaks barring his way. As much as I would have preferred that remain the case, I recognized the incriminating documents he was waving around and cursed myself for not hiding them somewhere safer.

With a sigh, I shouted, regretfully, "He's with me!"

The Archecloaks' spears snapped to vertical, and Jacquin sprinted toward me, his sky-blue cloak billowing behind him. As soon as he reached me and Oltrov—the Gildmember observed the whole thing with wry amusement—the Eye held out the papers with apparent reverence, bowing slightly.

"You forgot these, sir."

I narrowed my eyes at him. I hadn't *forgotten* them at all. The last thing I wanted was Oltrov or any other Gildmember getting even a glance at the documents before I could present my argument. With my luck, they were probably looking for the first good reason to pull their support from the Agency. Without the Gild's funding, the Agency would die.

In a flight of fancy, I wondered if bounty hunters would return. Fondly, I recalled the conversation with Inac that led to us joining the Agency. Maybe we should have gone back to our so-called lives of luxury. The thought put a grimace on my face. It wouldn't have lasted. The city would fall, Benefactors destroying everything we loved. The Bright Empire itself would soon follow.

We had to unite Liwokin. It would start today by convincing the Gild to continue their generosity.

"You've come prepared, I see," Oltrov said, his voice too dry to be anything but sarcastic. He was tilting his head, trying to read the letter on top.

"Thank you, Jacquin." I pushed the Eye's hand back. "You keep a tight grip on those, and don't get too far behind." Then I turned and put my arm around Oltrov in the same manner as he had done to me earlier to distract him from the documents. "After you, my friend."

He led on, me walking half a step behind him, and Jacquin another dozen steps behind us. Two problems solved—keeping the blackmail hidden and keeping Jacquin from talking to me—but both solutions were only temporary. I didn't trust Jacquin but kept him close. At least that way, he was following my orders rather than doing Darkfather-knows-what out of some residual loyalty to Ulken. As for the rest...

I began rehearsing what I was going to say at the meeting.

'*Ulken has been blackmailing you and the Council, but I vow to put an end to it. A gesture of goodwill for your funding.*'

Maybe that was too brash.

'*I'm not the old Head. Under my guidance, the Agency will end its practice of—*'

I didn't want to mention the blackmail. It would do nothing but agitate potential allies. But I had no choice. If the Agency was going to change, it couldn't keep relying on its dark foundations. I had to be honest.

Oltrov continued at his slow, meandering pace, as though he knew I was a cauldron of bubbling water ready to boil over. Despite my fears outside the gate, the most prominent emotion was annoyance.

Can't he walk any faster?

We passed casinos with ladies in fine silk and gentlemen in velvet suits stumbling drunk through the front door. The menagerie was still closed, judging by the collapsed perimeter fence surrounding the striped tents. Somehow, a steam carriage snuck up on us and blew an ear-shattering whistle—I practically dove out of the way just as it clattered past, bouncing on the uneven cobblestones. Jacquin rushed to my side to help me up, but I waved him away as Oltrov looked on, laughing.

"Here we are," the Gildmember finally announced as we came to a curving tower that seemed to defy all the natural laws as I stared up at its apex. Its white core seemed to be a tower of similar shape to the Agency, but the ribs of Archemetal that curled up the structure like frozen flames made it appear as though it was going to fall in three different directions. "The meeting will be on the top floor."

The blood drained from my face. My legs still ached from journeying up and down the Agency's twenty-seven floors all day, and these Financial District towers were even taller. I was pleasantly surprised, however, by what Oltrov shared in the building's lobby, a shimmering room of gold covering every gaudy surface save the crystal chandeliers.

"The elevator will get us to forty-fourth floor suite. From there, we will need to climb two flights of stairs. Apologies for the inconvenience." He grinned, and I couldn't help but return it. He knew where my office was.

Both our grins disappeared when three of us jammed ourselves into an elevator designed for two. More accurately, when Jacquin insisted he could fit and made the rest of the ride rather uncomfortable for the trio of us.

And we're not the only ones cursing him for it, I'm sure.

The elevator lurched upward in a familiar rhythm. "I see you've used the same design as they do in the Blight." Very little design at all, that was—someone pulling a rope with a cage on one end and a counterweight on the other. Jacquin had just made his job exceedingly difficult, and they had a long ride to go.

I felt Oltrov's grimace—he was packed too close for me to see it. "Is that so?"

When we exited into the top-floor suite, the elevator operator was nowhere to be seen. Evidently, his employer preferred him out of sight and out of mind. At least in the Blight, they had the decency to thank the fellow who had just lifted them to the top of the cliff. I recalled a wiry bald man who had last done the job for me. His face, anyway. His name, I couldn't remember.

Didn't I owe him for something?

There was no time to worry about that now. Jacquin opened the door for me to enter a sunlit room with a ceiling made of glass and six men and women with faces made of stone. They wore suits and dresses lined with Archemetal, as expected. What was unexpected was that Oltrov took his place at the head of the table.

He gestured at the seat opposite his, then folded his hands and waited.

You? You're in charge here?

I took the seat, trying to hide the surprise on my face. Better to let them think I knew all along. If they realized how little I *really* knew, I was in serious trouble.

As soon as I settled in, Jacquin standing beside me like a personal protector, Oltrov cleared his throat.

"Now that we're all here, let us begin." Six notebooks snapped open in front of all the Gildmembers lining the tables. I blinked, startled by their synchronization. They readied their pens. "Grimley, you requested this meeting. Why don't you go first?"

I took a deep breath and tried to steady my nerves. I had been preparing for this, but if I misspoke, overlooked anything, or worst of all, had another episode like last night's...it could mean the end of the Agency. The end of our best chance at stopping Benefactors from spreading. The end of the Bright Empire and everyone.

Silently rehearsing my opening argument one last time, something nagged at the back of my mind. Something I remembered. And I threw out what I had been preparing to say.

"Continuity," I said. "What did you mean by that, Oltrov?"

Six pens started scribbling in response.

CHAPTER ELEVEN

Eevoq

In Hoggens' account of his travels to the Peeker Mounds, he reported creatures of varying morphology living among humans. No such mutant Peeker has ever been observed in Eko, leading many to doubt the veracity of the formerly preeminent biotist's claims, in this matter and many more beyond.

—Page 4, Institute of Biotism Peeker Compendium, Vol. I

"Demon!"

"Monster!"

The words were a roar in Garret's ears, coming from all directions and repeated at every frequency human vocal cords could produce. Those were the minority of the screams. The majority were wordless shrieks of terror. The people moments ago enjoying a loud but peaceful meal were up and scrambling over one another to flee the Skardwarf. Panic looked the same in every species, Garret reflected. The herd forgotten; each animal transfixed with survival. Trampling each other. No coordination, just chaos.

Garret leaned on Sentyx, as solid as leaning on the mountain itself. Figured he'd just wait it out. No one was approaching them—most couldn't get far enough away.

"They really haven't seen a Skardwarf before, have they?" Garret spat. No other Skardwarves in the Mound. All the better. The panic ought to attract Prost's attention even faster.

"Up." Sentyx straightened from a slouch, throwing Garret off-balance; he caught himself on the Skardwarf's shoulder.

Four Builders dropped to surround Sentyx and Garret. In place of hands and feet, their reverse-jointed limbs possessed claws covered in spurs that dripped a sticky fluid. *An adaptation for climbing the walls.* Garret admired the Peeker morphology. *Also good for threatening people.*

"Explain, human," four Peekers demanded as one.

"I..." Garret was still holding onto Sentyx. He didn't let go.

Because over the strange Peeker's spiked shoulder, a rotund man had just glanced toward Sentyx and turned a corner.

Garret's eyes focused like a wolf's pupils upon spotting a deer. It was *him*. The advisor.

"I...have apprehended the Skardwarf," Garret hurried to say. His quarry was escaping. "He won't resist, will he?" Garret didn't know how to interpret the grunt he got back from the Skardwarf. "I'm a Finger of the Agency, Tunnel will tell you. Look, I've got a green coat and all."

"Who is Tunnel?" the two Peeker Pairs asked, then turned all four at once toward Sentyx. "Is this one Tunnel?"

"Talk to the Skardwarf about it." Garret pushed past the Peekers. To his surprise, they didn't offer any resistance. Only started asking Sentyx questions. Garret snorted. *Good luck getting anything from 'this one'.*

The immensity of the crowd made slipping into the mass easy. Like the migration of the terrorbeaks each Ekoan decade, Garret just had to flow with the current. Easy. Only a handful of Ekoan boys died at each running.

His ankle rolled as his foot landed on the arm of a motionless woman. Garret grimaced. Why should he feel like her death was his fault? He didn't know the crowd would act like a bunch of dark-loving idiots. Why should he feel bad? But he did.

Keep moving, he urged himself. *If I lose track of this target, I deserve to have my nocking hand removed.*

He pushed forward, grabbing at shoulders and elbows to drag himself through the crowd. Few followed him into the tunnel where the big man had turned, and Garret sucked in a grateful breath of air. Worst part about being in a crowd like that was the stench of sweat and body odor. Not enough air for that many people, makes them all act crazy.

Garret ran down the tunnel, no target in sight. He made a left into the dark, following his intuition that Prost would take the shadowed path. In the span of a heartbeat, Garret had discerned no sign either way. He would just have to get lucky. After a few more turns, he did.

Slowing to a stop, Garret ducked back behind the corner when he spotted his target waddling away. No, waddling wasn't the right term for it. It was more a self-assured gait than that, as if the man was unshakably in control. Was this Ulken's advisor? He didn't seem to be fleeing or know he was being tailed.

As soon as the man reached his dwelling, Garret rushed forward from the darkness and jammed his boot into the gap of the closing door. He hoped his momentum would carry him right in, but it was like a Skardwarf stood on the other side of the wall. Garret nearly bounced off and lost his foothold.

"Go away," a deep voice drawled.

Talks as slow as a Skardwarf too. "I just want to come in and talk," Garret assured him.

"I said—"

"Look, my name is Prost," Garret said, donning the name of the advisor himself.

"Never heard of you."

Garret's foot was squeezed harder in the door, and he winced. *Darkfather.* He believed him. "Then you're not the one I'm looking for. But you can help me find him."

The pressure on his foot relaxed. "Why should I help you?"

Garret laughed. "Because I'll pay you. Everyone needs gold."

And Grim, after all, didn't *explicitly* bar Garret from taking some gold from the treasury. It was only implied. Something about Ulken's debts that Garret didn't worry about. He knew he could put it to good use, and the daft Organ boy didn't even notice him appropriating the key.

The door edged open, just enough for Garret to squeeze through, bones rattling in his hair. Once inside, Garret found himself looking up past the belly of a huge man with enough beard hair to make up for his bald scalp. He slammed the door and crossed his arms, stood close to Garret as if to intimidate him.

But Garret had fought two daggerclaws and lived. He wasn't scared of some human. "Move."

"Make me."

Garret smiled. Slapped the man's belly and watched it ripple. Admired that the man reacted as stoically as a Skardwarf would, nodding his head. "All right."

He wrapped his hand around the short bow strapped inside his cloak. Before the man could blink, Garret clubbed him in the jaw with it, then vaulted over his shoulder and slid the curved bow around his neck. Garret pulled, and the man stumbled backward gasping for breath. He couldn't reach the ranger clinging to his back, nor the metal cane leaning against the wall.

Garret kicked off the wall to propel the man away from his weapon. When the man fell on his ass, Garret flung himself away to avoid being toppled on. He got to his feet and stood over his target. "Much better. Now, you ready to talk?"

The growl Garret received was convincingly Skardwarf-like.

His boots found the fingers of a fat hand, and with a little pressure...

That growl died in place of a howl.

"Let's make this easy. Tell me who you are and where you're from, and I won't kill you." Garret replaced his short bow, opting for a knife instead. To clean his fingernails.

"Light's disgrace, Southerner. I should have your head for—"

Garret dropped the knife, listened in satisfaction as the words cut off in a strangled panic. He caught the blade just before it reached the big man's eye.

"Clumsy me." Garret tossed the knife up spinning, caught it by the handle, then knelt. Teased the man's ear with his blade. "Thought I spoke pretty clearly. There some dirt that needs digging out of your ear?"

"N-n-no," he spluttered, chins trembling. "No, no. My n-name is Helman. I'm Eevoqian."

Now, that was interesting. Garret stood and stepped away, eying the Eevoqian skeptically. "As in the lost country of Eevoq?" It was absurd, but Garret found himself considering.

Many Lawi liked to eat, but this Eevoqian was far more bulbous than any man Garret had seen. His girth seemed unnatural. Then again, he didn't know what Eevoq was like. Perhaps heavy weight was a natural result of that environment.

"Are all Eevoqians this fat?"

"Are all Ekoans such arseholes?" the Eevoqian retorted, sitting up with great effort. "Of course we're not all so large. Only those with enough talent can achieve this physique."

"Right." Garret rubbed his face. "I'm looking for another Eevoqian." Prost had to share the nationality—this man matched his description too closely. "Prost. Know him?"

"I had lunch yesterday with an Ekoan named Naffin. Know him?" The Eevoqian attained his feet and rubbed his bruised jaw. "I've decided I don't want your gold. You were with that Burner. If you're helping him, I want nothing to do with you."

"What makes you think I'm helping him, not using him?"

"Bah. A Burner has no use. They should all be buried in the dirt they came from."

"Agreed. You've encountered one before?"

"One?" The Eevoqian snorted. "There are thousands in the Old Country. I sailed south to escape them, as soon as the seas were willing. Didn't expect them to reach these lands first."

Garret raised an eyebrow. Could he learn anything about the legions of Skardwarves from this man? "The sea is uncrossable."

"Believe what you want. Leave me out of it."

"Afraid I can't," Garret said regretfully. "You're the only lead I've got on my target."

"I told you I don't know any Prost."

"Other Eevoqians, then. Who did you sail here with?"

Helman crossed the small room, sat on his cracked bed. "No one. I came alone."

"You crossed the sea by yourself."

"I said so, didn't I?"

Garret scraped his knife across the stone wall. "You're lying."

"I told you. Believe what you want."

"Why, then? Why go through all the effort to cross the endless waters?"

"Good question." Helman showed an ugly, toothy smile and grunted. Sounded exactly like a Skardwarf, that deep rumble from his belly. "This journey has done naught but disappoint. Liwokin is minuscule beside our capital. The Peekers call their hill a mountain. Tell me, are Eko's giant trees taller than Myrme, or shall I expect further disappointment?"

"Our trees are tall enough."

"I see." Helman's jowls flopped as he shook his head. "This worthless Empire has withered under your star's light. Still, your food provides great nourishment. I'll enjoy it while I can."

"What's that supposed to mean?" Garret gripped his knife more tightly.

The Eevoqian shifted his mass in a great, heaving shrug. "Burners are not easily resisted. My people have had thousands of years to learn that lesson. What will you do given a fraction of that time without our help?"

Garret pursed his lips. He already knew the Skardwarf legions were going to invade. That fact was as good as confirmed when Sentyx tried hiding memories from the Hand. Garret hated when people withheld information from him. "I don't need your help. I only need one thing."

"What's that?" the Eevoqian asked with a bored expression.

Garret lunged across the room and sank his knife into the man's blubbery hand. The bored expression didn't survive. "I need you to stop fucking around and tell me what I want to know."

"I told you! I don't know anything!" He was on his knees beside the bed, grasping his wrist below the hand bleeding onto his blankets.

Garret bared his teeth. "Pretty sure you know plenty."

"Please! What's it going to take for you to believe me?" the Eevoqian whined.

"I guess we're going to find out."

Garret twisted the knife.

CHAPTER TWELVE

Cloaked

Your presence is required at the top of Financial Tower 4. Our elevator is out of order—we decided to give poor Timothy the day off.

—Crumpled notice recovered from the Head's garbage

The Gildmembers hadn't stopped scribbling until the meeting ended. They recorded everything for posterity, a shocking fact, considering the admissions they made. The real shock came upon realizing how this was yet another brazen demonstration of the power they wielded.

They had known from the beginning that I had come to discuss blackmail, and they were demonstrating that they could not be coerced. I grew angry at first. Someone had leaked the information to the Gild— it was reasonable to assume I had traitors within my ranks. But in truth, they knew because that was the only reason they ever received visits from Ulken. They called it "giving him his marching orders."

I had marched straight through the door when they tried to insist we should continue this arrangement, "between friends." They even had ideas about how we could "develop our relationship," which meant using my connections to get even more incriminating information about the Seats of the Hall.

Storming through the front door of the tower with Jacquin in tow, I scoffed again.

Friends. No. Tools to be used.

"Relaxing their regulations, Jacquin?" The Eye scurried up to my side. "Do they take me for some obedient dog? To be taught the tricks that got their old hound killed?"

"If they think the Head of the Agency is a dog, sir," Jacquin replied. "They'll soon find out you're a wolf. Do not allow them to tame you."

"Let me guess. You gave Ulken the same advice?"

"Oh no, sir. The Gild wanted nothing to do with Ulken by the time I replaced First Eye Reed. He had already shown them he was a wolf. With that mane he had, maybe a lion."

The admiration in his eyes as he spoke of the mass murderer Ulken disgusted me. I turned aside, lest he see me looking at him in the same way Andya's husband looked at her.

I muttered, "I think that reluctance may be exactly why the Gild's leader was working with Reed."

Jacquin nodded in agreement, then spoke quietly. "We can't trust them, sir."

No, we couldn't. Suddenly, I felt uneasy. Exposed. Oltrov had told me he'd give me time to reconsider, which he strongly encouraged me to do. Was that a trick to get me to lower my guard? I was adamant about not helping them overturn the laws that kept them in check. What would Inac think if I told him I folded under the Gild's pressure? It would only hurt Liwo, and I was here to serve *them*.

But the Gild never cared about the common Liwo. Everything they did only served to trim their own cloaks in Archemetal.

They wouldn't strike me in broad daylight, would they? And yet, everyone who witnessed it would be glad to see me gone. The last words I'd ever hear would be, "Good riddance!"

I ran, keeping distance from the wealthy Liwo who watched me with contempt. Any one of them could be concealing a weapon.

"Running? A splendid idea, sir! We mustn't tarry. The Council is waiting." Jacquin kept up, his documents flapping in the wind.

By the time we reached the gate to exit the Gild, it was with the haste of two people running for their lives. I couldn't shake the memory of the death knell, and my nightmare.

A knife in the back. Rope burn.

Betrayal haunted my mind. That murder was senseless violence in the Blight, but it seemed like if I didn't escape the Gild quickly enough, the vision might become premonition.

When we made it back to the Burg without having to survive an assassination attempt, I began to breathe easier.

Jacquin was thrilled by the action. He hopped from one foot to another, smiling childishly. "An excellent pace, sir. If we do that again, we might even make it to the Council on time."

I narrowed my eyes at the Eye. He had no idea what was going on in my mind.

"We'll walk," I said, and began doing just that. If we didn't arrive before half-dusk, they would wait for us. And I needed time to think, to unravel the web Ulken had spun. As infuriating as the meeting was, it made sense of some of the documents in Ulken's office I was having trouble deciphering.

The Gild *knew* about the Head's extortion—in fact, Ulken tried to blackmail both the Council Hall *and* the Gild. While it worked on the Seats of the Hall, the Gildmembers were shameless. They laughed about the lascivious charges brought against them, those contained in the documents Jacquin brought. Instead, they proposed a different arrangement. The Gild would happily pay for the Agency's expenses in return for leniency toward the Financial District.

This evolved into the Agency doing the Gild's bidding, twisting the Council's arm to skew Liwokin law in favor of the rich. Ulken played along for a time but grew more intolerant toward the end of his reign. Oltrov told me we would continue this arrangement. The risk, however, was that they didn't know how Ulken discovered their secrets in the first place. Now that he was dead, could I continue to exploit the Council's lecherous tendencies for them?

What truly sickened me was how for a brief moment, I actually considered it. I had the ability. Ulken used Yezna to spy on his victim's memories, and I could do that far more effectively than him. Maintaining the status quo would have been so easy. It would have ensured the Agency's longevity.

But at what cost?

My gut churned. I had promised my Hand there would be no more secrets. It was my first act as Head, a private act made among friends. That so few knew of the promise only made it the more important to keep. If I broke it, if I took the easy path of running the Agency with coercion and lies...I would be no better than Ulken.

I can't repeat his mistakes.

I would not continue spreading his corruption, and the only reason I was allowed to walk out of the Gild alive was they believed I was going to change my mind.

In the distance, church bells intoned half-dusk. Their soft call pulled me from my thoughts. We were approaching the square where the Agency Headquarters loomed over the squat Council Hall opposite. The tower's eerie white lights shone from the shadowed face of stone. I was admiring the Brightdaughter's halo of light around the Agency when a man screamed.

"For the Resistance!"

A sharp crack exploded in my ears.

I flung myself aside in animalistic terror. My ears rang, but I felt no pain. Wait, there it was. Something had cut my cheek. It stung, but it was nothing serious.

"What *was that?*" I shouted.

Jacquin and two other men had reacted to the sound, but most people continued walking as if nothing was awry.

A man scrambled backward on the ground, grasping his bleeding hand, his mouth wide open. Something smoldered near his feet. Now that I saw him, I discerned his pained screams through the noisy ringing in my ears. He saw me looking at him and redoubled his efforts with wide eyes, pushing himself to his feet, and turning to run.

"Jacquin! Stop that ma—"

He was gone. There was no crowd to conceal him. No alley for him to sprint down. No way for him to disappear. He simply...disappeared.

Words from the hunter Lomin surfaced in my mind. *It's what you don't see that kills you.*

"Who, sir?" Jacquin asked. "What was that?"

"I don't know."

A man vanishing. A sudden sound without a source. Most Liwo going about their business, ignoring the commotion.

Ignoring it, or they're not conscious of it.

Only one thing caused behavior this strange. An Aura.

I was ready for this. Reed told me that Benefactors as we knew them were finished. The new had come in to replace the old. The variety of Benefactor in *my* head, that was the new. I must have missed one in the storm of Emergences. But if I was only a man, so were the monsters I hunted.

"There's a Benefactor in the city," I said. "Alert the Agency. Get them ready."

Jacquin eyed me warily. "And what are you going to do, sir?"

"I'm going after that man. It could be him."

The Eye cleared his throat. "Sir, is it not a bit undignified to do that sort of work yourself? Send a Hand to do it. That's what they're for."

So, the man wasn't a footstool after all. He had advice to give, and if anyone knew the Agency's rules, it was him.

I'm sure he knows exactly *which rules Ulken broke, down to the sub-clause.*

"He's getting away, Jacquin." I turned to follow the Benefactor's path.

"But sir, I don't sense an Aura. And you're unarmed."

He was wrong about that. I had told Oltrov I had no weapon, but I always kept a knife hidden on my person.

"And if there really *is* a powerful Benefactor, we would need the Council's help evacuating people, right?"

Abyss take me, he was right. I wasn't some ordinary Finger anymore, on the front lines fighting monsters. If I was going to end this threat, I needed to use the tool fit for the job. The Agency.

I rubbed the cut on my cheek, and my fingers came away bloodied. "Point taken. I'll continue to the meeting. You go inform the right Organ about the need for a Hand."

"They'll be given their command post-haste, thank you sir," Jacquin said. Then, he bolted for the open courtyard gate, nearly bowling over a Heel as he turned the corner.

I smiled. Post-haste, indeed.

No. Don't forget who he served. The atrocities he idly witnessed.

The Agency had to be better than that. Even I had to admit it was a low bar. But it would start tonight, by ending this coercion, showing the Council how things would differ under my leadership.

CHAPTER THIRTEEN

Seats of the Hall

I'm perfectly happy rolling the dice to learn what Maise thinks of working with an embezzler. Maybe we could involve your friends in the gambling house, eh? But then, what fun is it placing bets when the outcome is predetermined?

—Sent to a Seat who tried calling a bluff

I stood before the Council Hall, a building that once looked grand before being overshadowed by the Gild's and Agency's towers. At four floors in height, it was large enough to house not only the Seats of the Hall but all of their serving staff. It wasn't often Liwo were invited inside, leading many to make up stories about what went on behind the silver-carved doors. Occult rituals to the Darkfather and private parties with Artisan's courtesans were among the tamer ideas. The former was ridiculous. The latter, well, that turned out to be mostly true, given what Ulken discovered.

More mundane activities occupied the bureaucracy's day-to-day. A simple clerk welcomed me inside. She smoked an odious cigar, which she threw to the ground to let burn as I approached the shallow stairs. Without a word, she turned and walked in. I took it as a sign to follow.

The door creaked shut behind me.

"You're late," the clerk said in a voice gravelly enough to mistake her for a Skardwarf. "Down the hall, third glass door on your left, cross the water garden, take the first door straight ahead, then up the stairs. Got it?"

I nodded and started forward, not at all sure I had it.

"Good. Once upstairs, it's two right turns, you can't miss them, and the door will be open for you. Wouldn't be surprised if Maise is out in the hallway tapping her foot." She chortled, and I darted off before the directions left my head.

She was wrong, though. Maise wasn't waiting impatiently outside the door. Instead, she was shouting at me from the moment I poked my nose in.

"Just who do you think you are, mercenary?"

I pulled back. Was this the wrong room?

"Head of the Agency," she scoffed.

Guess I'm in the right place.

Entering the room proper, the Council Chair didn't wait for me to find a seat before unleashing a tirade against me. Her eyes were hawkish with brows that cut across her face like knife edges. Her black hair, streaked lightly with gray, she kept in a tight bun. Though as she ranted, she was so animated her hairpins failed to keep it all contained, and she had to keep tucking it behind her ears.

"That title was nonexistent just three years ago. I'm the fifty-sixth Council Chair, the latest in a lineage of servants to the city of Liwokin that dates back to our founding, four-hundred forty-seven years ago. I thought I would give you an education, because standing before me is not the man whose place you've stolen, but an upjumped boy from the Blight—

"My orphanage was in the Burg, Madam Chair." It took everything in me to keep the anger from my voice. I hadn't come here to make enemies, but to make amends.

"You think you can keep *us* waiting? You're a schoolyard bully, is what you are. But this isn't your orphanage anymore. This is not a game. Your Agency—if it truly is yours—exists only at our discretion. Your predecessor tried to keep us under his thumb, but—"

"*Wait,*" I interrupted, which she didn't take very kindly to. But she stayed quiet. I looked across the faces in the room, seated around the table. None of them would make eye contact with me, and all of them noticed the others were doing it. "Do you *all* know already?"

A few grumbles accompanied more uncomfortable squirming.

"Darkfather's balls... Look, *that's* why I'm here, why I requested this meeting. Any dirt *Ulken* was holding over you, consider it gone."

"I don't know what you're talking about," a man said, unconvincingly.

"You know exactly what I'm talking about." *Evidently, I was the last to find out.* "I just came from the Gild, where I met with Oltrov and—"

"You throw his name in our face!" shouted a woman with more than a touch of gray hair.

"I don't appreciate your thinly veiled threats," Maise said in a warning tone.

Which I completely ignored, slamming my hand down on the table. "If I was *threatening* you, you would know it. That was not a threat." I wasn't in good spirits when I came here, and these people had been rubbing me the wrong way since I'd entered the dusty, smoke-filled Hall.

If they knew what I truly was, if they knew of the monster inside me, what I can do...

Seats of the Hall they called these people. I called them antiquated. Each of them was more concerned with history and their legacy than with the future and the people that would inhabit it. It was an ancient institution, not built to solve new problems. The Agency, on the other hand, was created specifically to solve this problem.

And I'll be doomed to the abyss if I let these dark-lovers get in my way.

"I am not here to provoke old feuds between you and the Gild. Whatever enmities you have with one another, leave me out. If you have grievances with the Agency, we can settle them. We can't afford to squabble among ourselves with the threat of the Benefactors looming over us. We need to be united, and I want to make the first gesture in return for you giving the Agency the resources we need to protect our city."

Maise scoffed. "Resources to protect Liwokin. We've heard that before. Honesty, however, is something we've found sorely lacking from the Agency." She leaned forward and fixed me with a penetrating stare. "Tell me, do you and your Fingers and your Toes, even know the meaning of the word?"

"Toes?" I shook my head. "I *am* being—"

"Yes, of course. How else to explain the lies growing in your tower like the fungus between Lesch's toes?"

The old man beside Maise grumbled and slunk down in his chair. "Why'd you go and—"

"I *said* let me do the talking." The Council Chair continued to berate me before I could slip a word in. "You see, this is the problem with you lot. You claim you want to end our *squabbling*. As though we're a flock of gulls pecking at a dying crab. But this goes beyond squabbling, far beyond."

"If you'd let me expl—"

"Quiet, boy. Ulken never understood this, but perhaps I can drill it into your brain while it's still young and impressionable: The only way to succeed in Liwokin is with the truth."

The four Seats of the Hall flanking Maise bobbed their heads in agreement. Lightmother have mercy, this woman was infuriating. If she would just *listen*, she'd hear the truth I was trying to speak. With a huff, I decided to sit back and wait until she deemed it my turn.

"For eight years I've been privileged to serve in this institution because Liwo *know* that a promise I make is a promise I keep. Every single one. Until Ulken. I promised our city they would be safer at night without the militia or bounty hunters because the Head of the Agency *assured* me he would provide the resources to protect Liwokin with no need for taxpayer support.

"Should have known it was a lie. As was his promise to rebuild the Old District. Instead, what did we get out of our agreements?"

Maise gave a bitter laugh. "Bronze numbers on every house and an eyesore of a building outside my office window."

"We're agreed on that," I blurted when she paused to take a drink of water.

"Is that so?"

"Ulken was a liar. I may not have been on the receiving end of it as often as you, but his lies got my friends killed by Benefactors."

"What is that?" Maise fixed her hair that had come loose. "Benefactors. Twice now you've said it. Is that what you call those funding you in the Gild?"

"No. And I don't *want* their funding." Not after what they revealed about our prior arrangements. "Benefactors are monsters. Organisms that infest people, then take over their minds when they die. Ulken worked with Prost to—"

"Spare me the details of your fantasy stories."

My teeth clenched. "It's *not* a story. They've killed thousands of Liwo, going back to the Great Riot."

Lesch laughed. "Everyone knows what started the Great Riot."

By the abyss, if the Seat of the Hall said, *'Nothing'*, I might not have been able to hold myself back from assaulting him. Luckily, Maise intervened with a venomous look that had him slink down even further.

This is one of the men who'd run Liwokin all my life?

No wonder Ulken was able to step in so easily.

Maise, however, was a woman of a different sort. Annoyingly rude, yes, but confident in her power. In her eyes was skepticism, but she didn't dismiss my claims about the Riot outright.

Sensing an opportunity to convince her, I spoke up. "Even the Great Riot was nothing compared to what happened at the end of Ulken's reign. Thousands more died in the woods outside the city."

"Yet the city thrives," Maise said, "does it not? Have you any evidence for your claims, or am I supposed to accept the word of a liar's successor? One who collapsed after raving like a madman in front of all his employees..."

It took a great force of will to remain calm. I wanted to shout that I killed Ulken for his lies. But how would that make me look? If they thought me a murderer and a madman, there would be no working with them. "Did none of you find yourselves inexplicably before a burning tower, surrounded by thousands of other Liwo?"

Blank stares.

Really? None of them were in Reed's Woods?

I sighed. "Listen, I know you don't trust me. That's why I want to make the first gesture, like I said. All your agreements with Ulken, consider them void. They're all skewed in the Agency's favor anyway. I want this to be a fair partnership. We'll destroy the blackmail we have, and next time we meet, we can renegotiate our terms."

It would be a start, but the problem of the Gild still remained. Somehow, I'd need to get us all together in a room to sort out our differences. But that was a problem for later. For now, I straightened and waited to gauge their reaction, sure that I had never done a finer job at petitioning an ally.

CHAPTER FOURTEEN

Fire Gardens

There once was a goddess of Light
Who suffered no humor or slight
But the jest best of all
Is the Darkfather's balls
Hung free in her chambers at night

—*Scrawled on a napkin left at The Light's Faithful,*
subsequently burned

Daintily treading the white gravel path, an abundance of crystalline jewelry tinkling with each step, Lorelay tried not to notice all of the stares she drew from the ladies of the court. She avoided eye contact and ignored their whispers, their tittering, their scoffs as a commoner made her way past. A firm jaw might hide her discomfort, but nothing could hide the *ridiculousness* of her outfit.

Some women found purpose in putting themselves together come dawn. Lorelay felt no less empty than before, and ten times the fool. The pink velvet dress flowed around her legs, and Lorelay hiked up her skirt enough to prevent tripping on it. The bodice was already cut too low. Stepping on the hem might cause an international incident. Or perhaps Vinlin would welcome it since this preposterous getup was his idea in the first place.

Lorelay had refused to wear it at first, sending out the ladies' maids who had ambushed her in her guest chambers. Only, her clothes were soiled from the dungeon, and she had a role to play in the Radiant Palace. A dirt-stained lowborn would have no chance of convincing the Empire to send aid to Liwokin. So, Lorelay had swallowed her pride and called back those maids.

It's not like I had a choice. No one could get into this costume without help. She *had* tried, though...with admittedly disastrous results. Turning her wrist to cover the torn stitching that traced her forearm, she kept her eyes up and kept walking. Very, very carefully, lest a stray rock dig into her heels right through her paper-thin slipper.

This was the first she had ever stepped foot in the palace's gardens, and she could see why they were named the Fire Gardens. Huge red and gold banners bearing the flaming sigil of the Empire hung from the pure white walls enclosing three sides of the courtyard. The open side abutted the Ember River that flowed down a waterfall to the sea, and on either side of the watery expanse were twisting spires of Archemetal that scattered the Brightdaughter's light in every direction. Tulips red and yellow, roses white and blue, lilies, hydrangeas, irises, and orchids—all were carefully arranged to convince the eye there were fires made of flowers. Scattered amid the flora, Archejugglers seemed liable to set them alight in truth. They performed to delighted crowds of nobility, drawing cheers and laughter tossing dozens of Archefire balls back and forth—no one even minded that the jesters' coats were singed.

It was almost too much for Lorelay, opulence in a sickening degree. People on the streets of Vos were begging, starving, scraping by in their miserable lives. Yet, ask any one of them, and they would tell you how thrilled they are with the royal family, how sad they were to hear of Empress Elzia's passing. The truly sad thing was that so many Paceeqi had already had their free spirits crushed.

Not for the first time since waking up in her plush bed, Lorelay's thoughts went to Gravis whimpering in the dungeon. He convinced himself his imprisonment was a fair price to pay to make sure Paceeq lives in the Light. What would he think if he knew what was happening right over his head? All these sneering nobles sipping tea and giving less than no thought to the suffering in their city.

They won't win me over with luxuries, Lorelay promised herself. All she had to do was look in any direction, and a Paladin would be standing guard keeping his ears open and his sword loose in his scabbard. At any moment, someone might open their mouth and say some terrible, dangerous *words* that these poor nobles needed their sensitive ears protected from. *Sensitive ears and sensitive minds.*

Lorelay snorted, then realized where she was and collected herself. Still, she glanced at a nearby Paladin, as though he could hear her thoughts. He paid her no mind. In fact, he looked positively *bored*. Lorelay bit her lip in annoyance. Patrolling the gardens was supposed to be a Paladin's highest calling. It was Dunnax's dream...a dream he would never... She bit her lip harder, averted her eyes from the silver-armored man, and winced, tasting blood.

An arm wrapped around her waist, and she flinched. "Come, Lorelay!" Vinlin squeezed her tighter. "I have prepared a private table for us with the most magnificent view of the Ember."

"You mean you ordered your servants to set out some tea?" Lorelay tried wriggling free to no avail. She let herself be guided toward through the gardens, cheeks heating from embarrassment. *Everyone* was looking at her now, like she was some courtesan to the Emperor.

Vinlin chuckled as he whisked her under an archway of roses. "Well, yes, of course. My servants are an extension of my will, as all citizens are extensions of the Empire. All we do is for the good of the Light."

Lorelay tried not to let him see her scowl—he made it sound like the Empire was a Benefactor, a mindless amalgamation of bodies—but she need not have hidden it. He was focused on the grandiose table on a balcony overlooking the river. Far too big for two people, the lace tablecloth was nonetheless entirely covered by plates of strudel and biscuits, along with bowls overflowing with fruits. Servants poured steaming tea into cups on saucers set out with sugar and milk beside them. Two high-backed chairs awaited, not situated at opposite ends of the table but side-by-side.

The Bright Prince made a big show of pulling Lorelay's chair out for her. She took a seat, still aware of the countless eyes on her back. This was his idea of privacy? They were on a dais, practically on display for all to see. Not to mention the servants, half a dozen of them waiting to take orders, in earshot of everything Vinlin and Lorelay might say. What if they found out about the Benefactors? Would she cause a panic in the capital?

One of the servants, a young boy dressed in red livery, set the full teacups before them and asked, "Would you like sugar in your tea, Your Radiance?"

When Vinlin remained quiet, Lorelay realized the question was addressed to *her*. "Your Radiance? Me? I...uh—"

"I think that is a no, Chrys, and I will abstain as well." Vinlin patted his belly, not ample by any means—he was in fine health, by all appearances. And Lorelay had seen him in combat, the muscles of his arms, the strength of the man. A little sugar would do him no harm. "The Bright Prince must maintain his physique, after all."

"Of course, Your Radiance." With a deep bow, Chrys retreated, taking the bowl of sugar with him.

"It will take some getting used to," Vinlin said. "The titles, I mean."

"But...'Your Radiance?'" Lorelay said. "I'm no Empress."

"And I am no Emperor." His eyes drew down, tightening. "Not yet." He looked up and smiled, dimples forming behind the blond stubble on his cheeks. "The boy is young. He can be forgiven for erring on the side of caution. Best not to offend the Prince's lady."

Lorelay nearly choked on the tea she was sipping. "I'm—" She was going to correct his mistake about her interests in him, but if she did...might he send her away? She needed to use this opportunity to win Vinlin's alliance. "Do you remember the gate to Canako Canal?"

"Of course. I would never forget that."

It might be easier to convince him than I thought. Lorelay almost believed that, until she noticed he was grinning stupidly.

"Our time together on the road from the city," he continued, leaning close to speak furtively. "Your songs were so...ribald! I see you ignored my advice not to recount them in the capital, however. I truly am sorry you wound up in that awful place, but the people of Vos have a different sensibility than those abroad." Vinlin shrugged. "Nothing can be done about that."

Lorelay was far from convinced about that, but she let the point fall to the side. "I meant, do you remember the monster that attacked us." His only reaction to that was a cocked head and a raised brow. "Green clouds, swarms of insects, any of that ringing a bell?"

"Oh! Right, I do remember that. To be perfectly honest, I had no idea what to make of it. A monster, you say? That, I do not recall. What did it look like?"

"Well..." Lorelay worked her jaw. "I'm not sure, actually. The Hand guarding the gate killed it after we escaped."

Just the mention of Hand Sixty-Four formed a knot in Lorelay's stomach. She swallowed bitter tea to calm herself.

"The point is, the Agency is fighting those beasts in Liwokin. Monsters that project Auras to make people see things like those flies or smell rotting flesh."

She distinctly remembered that smell. Even after reaching Canako, it seemed to linger.

"And that wasn't even the worst one. I fought a creature with huge tentacles whose Aura confused and disoriented us. It turned two Fingers in my Hand against each, brothers fighting until the thing snuck up and killed them both. They're called Benefactors, and—"

Vinlin was nodding along, smiling and staring into her eyes.

"Are you listening to what I'm saying?"

"I am rapt with attention, my dear. Only," Vinlin said this completely unabashedly, "you are just so adorably fierce when you get worked up."

Lorelay clenched her jaw to keep it from falling open.

"We really should spend more time together, you and I," he continued. "There is a view from the top of the palace that you simply must see." Vinlin considered, then added, "When the time is right, of course."

Men. Lorelay glared at him. *It would be nice if they did at least some of their thinking with their heads.* She was describing a threat to the Bright Empire, and all he could think was that she looked *cute.*

Vinlin was at least wise enough to recognize what her look meant. "I apologize, my lady. That was too forward of me. How can I make it up to you?"

"For one, you could actually listen to what I'm telling you. These Benefactors aren't just going to stay in Lawiko. In fact, we know they're beyond it already—Grim told me they found some in the Peeker Mounds." He was sulking, now. Lorelay leveled a flat look at him. "Do you know what that means?"

"Grim...I wish you would not mention that brigand's name over such a lovely breakfast."

Lorelay's eyes widened. She shook her head, earrings clattering, frustrations rising. "He's the Head of the Agency! Not just some brigand. And I'm his ambassador, not some...mistress!"

Vinlin looked away. "What has the Agency ever done for the Bright Empire?"

Petulance, now? Lorelay should have known the royal family were a bunch of big babies.

"You mean besides saving our central trading hub? Making sure you still get enough of your precious taxes to pay for these silks and rubies? They're only thing currently standing between those monsters and the shores of Paceeq." She crossed her arms. "Are you just going to let them fight alone while you cower here behind palace walls?"

"Well...I suppose the Agency isn't all bad." He smiled at her, and Lorelay almost felt her own scowl fade. Almost, but she kept it firm. She would *not* give him the satisfaction. "After all, they sent you here."

When she stood with a disgusted groan, the Bright Prince's eyes looked about wildly. Evidently, he was used to always getting his way. Well, not from her. Lorelay had her dignity.

"I think I've had quite enough of the riverside view," She pushed her chair aside and turned to go.

"Wait," Vinlin spluttered, and grabbed her by the sleeve. The torn stitching ripped all the way up her arm, sequins popped off and launched into the air, and Lorelay's was completely free of the fabric. The ruined dress was one thing, but already the ladies of the court were snickering.

Well, snuff them. Lorelay shook with rage. *They can go straight to the abyss for all I care.* She ripped the torn sleeve free at the shoulder, letting it fall limp in the stunned prince's hand. "You can keep that," she snarled, then stomped off toward the garden's gates.

Lorelay would keep her composure. She would *not* give the laughing lords and ladies the pleasure of watching her fall apart. She would *not,* abyss damn them.

But before she knew what she was doing, tears were stinging her eyes, and she was running.

CHAPTER FIFTEEN

A Choice of Dress

Lovers entwined
Finality crystallized
A cold, sharp sea
Reflects the night sky
Fly, fly, Her end is nigh

—Verse from To Dance the Night,
Second Song of Dusk

Lorelay stormed back to her private chamber, crying. *Why am I crying over such a stupid man?*

She slammed the door behind her, slumped against it, and banged the back of her head several times on the lightwood.

I can't do snuffing anything right.

All her life, she had fought against the strictures of Paceeqi religion. And for what? Her grand uprising was ignored. Nobody wanted to hear her songs. Nobody wanted to hear *anything* from her. She failed even to win an ally in someone who clearly already favored her.

A frustrated growl broke from her throat, and she pushed herself to her feet, wiping her eyes with the forearm no longer covered by her torn dress. She stalked to a desk and began a letter to Grim. She failed. His command was impossible.

Maybe if he were less of a stubborn fool, the Bright Prince would harbor less ire for him. She could hardly blame him after Grim insulted him upon their first meeting and accused him of being a smuggler at their second. Why did Grim have such a bone to pick with Vinlin? He lived in Liwokin, far from the grasp of throne and Church.

Her pen nib pressed into the paper, pooling black ink. What was she going to do, ask him to apologize?

Hand Sixty-Four. Useless! Not least because she was one of its members. She threw down the pen and slammed a fist on the desk.

When did everything fall apart? There were good memories too, were there not? They had saved Leppit village together, gave those people their lives back. And Grim's heart set him on the right course. He sent her to Paceeq because he was trying to help his people. By extension, hers as well. He stopped Ulken in Reed's Woods...

But not everyone made it out of that dark forest. Dunnax... She had no chance even to say goodbye. All she saw of him was a pile of charred armor. If she saw through Ulken's lies, stayed with her brother...

My fault. This is all my fault!

Tears fell onto the paper, mixing with the ink. Black streaks trickled down the page, and Lorelay screamed, tearing the letter to scraps. She stomped to the door. Lightmother help her, but she needed a drink.

As soon as she opened the way out, however, the old servant who helped her dress stood in front of her with hands on hips. Despite being stooped, she managed to appear imperious.

"Where does you think you're going?"

What was she, Lorelay's mother? "The tavern." She tried to push past but was stopped with a firm hand on her wrist.

"Not dressed like that, you're not." She looked at the shoulder where Lorelay had torn off the sleeve, shaking her head in dismay. "Come here, girl. Sit down. Before you ruin the dress further."

Lorelay scoffed, letting the serving woman lead her to a chair before the wardrobe. "Ruin it further? It's already beyond ruined."

"Nothing I can't fix up with the right fabric and a few stitches."

"Why bother?"

"Guess he didn't tell you. This was one of his mother's dresses."

Lorelay's eyes shot open, and the old woman chuckled.

"That's right, the Empress Elzia, blessed Lightmother cradle her," she said bitterly. "I bet you got all sorts of jealous stares when you showed up in that."

"I'm not sure jealous is the word I'd use."

"I'm entirely sure I would. I've been around these hens long enough to know exactly what's going through their minds anytime a pretty young girl like you shows up on the scene. Likely the same thing that was going through Vinlin's head. Nothing good."

Lorelay's lips quirked up in a smile. Should she be worrying about listeners at the door? Such sentiments would see this old woman thrown into the dungeons.

"Now go on, tell me what possessed you to rip the sleeve off like that." Her face suddenly went stern. "I swear by the Darkfather, if that boy mistreated you, the Church won't have to lash him. I'll do it myself."

Lorelay gasped. "You can't say that!" She was unsure whether she meant swearing by the Darkfather or threatening the Bright Prince, but... a giddy thrill ran through her. She was going to get along with this woman.

"You bet your pretty behind I can. I've been alive this long, and the Lightmother hasn't seen fit to punish me yet." Except for giving me two princes and a princess as squealing whelps to take care of. They were easier as babies."

"Vinlin has siblings?" Lorelay asked, surprised.

The way he acts, he seems more like a spoiled only child.

The servant waved that line of discussion away. "Enough about me, are you going to answer my question? What happened?"

Lorelay considered how much she wanted to tell the servant. They just met, after all. But she seemed trustworthy. And she was easy to talk to. How different would her life have been if she had this woman for a mother? Guilt stabbed at Lorelay. As vile as her mother could be at times, she wished she was around to tell her everything that happened.

Her family was gone. She was alone. And she found herself spilling every little detail to this stranger.

That she was here as an ambassador for the Agency. That there were monsters threatening the Bright Empire. That Vinlin only seemed interested in taking her as a lover. If she imagined even so little as kissing the Bright Prince and her lips curled. She would prefer to remain alone than endure such a romance. She needed no one else in her life to lose.

The woman listened attentively as she unlaced and removed Lorelay's dress, then nodded in understanding when Lorelay's rant finished. "I don't know anything about the Agency, or these monsters. But I know the Bright Prince. If I had to guess, he's somewhere licking his wounds trying to figure out what went wrong. He was so excited last night after he returned to his private chambers."

"He was?"

"Practically giddy." She smiled wistfully, folding Elzia's garment. "Something I haven't seen in a long time."

"He didn't seem that way to me. Just...wool-headed."

The serving woman snorted with laughter. "Sure, sure, he can be sometimes. What man isn't? But there's a lot to admire about him too. The weight he's holding on his shoulders is enough to crush most men."

Lorelay's eyes narrowed, and she crossed her arms, covering her exposed body. Suddenly it seemed the servant was trying to sell her on the idea of romance. "I just told you I wasn't interested in him. Whose side are you on here?"

"Side?" Without complaint, the serving woman cleaned Lorelay's mess at the writing desk with a wet rag. "Lightmother, but people only think of two sides." She held up the stained paper. "Light or dark. Brightdaughter or Shadowson. Bah. It's a sickness of the mind, I say. The only 'side' I'm on is wanting the Prince to be happy." Lorelay opened her mouth to say that she had chosen a side, then. "Don't go interrupting now. I know what you're going to say, and I want *you* to be happy too. Fool I am, thinking two people can be happy and both get their way."

Lorelay smiled, recognizing a bit of her own thinking in there. But the chances of her being happy died in Lawiko. "Tall order."

"Well...more fanciful things have happened. Like bugs that turn people into monsters when they die, say?"

Lorelay snorted. When put that way, it did seem silly. "You don't believe me?"

"I do! But I'm not surprised Vinlin doesn't want to hear about it. He's got enough problems, I told you."

She was tempted to dismiss those outright as the problems of nobility. Those that came with the power they wielded over others. Instead, Lorelay wanted to extend her time with this serving woman now that her duties appeared to be complete. "What sorts of problems?"

"Oh, girl, where do I begin? Perhaps with the Church not considering him a legitimate heir? The Church of Light and the Bright Throne have been inseparable since the Era of Dark, but he has few friends in those cathedral walls."

That sounded fine to Lorelay. It was about time the Church lost some control. She was curious about the rift, however. "Why not?"

"For one, he's the first man to ascend the throne in...well, ever, if our songs are to be believed."

That was a big if, in Lorelay's mind. Songs were far from the most reliable form of record keeping. Especially when the histories were all thousands of years old. "What's wrong with a male Bright Emperor?"

"Tradition, girl. I saw your clothes last night. Don't tell me you aren't aware how strongly Paceeq keeps to tradition."

Strongly enough to throw a girl in prison for the wrong word.

"All right, I'll give you that. But is it *really* that bad? What difference does it truly make if we have an Emperor or an Empress?

The woman sighed. "You know, if the wrong ears heard that, you might end up back in a cell."

Lorelay tensed. This stranger's kindness had loosened her tongue to a dangerous degree.

Rather than alerting the Paladins, the woman tightened the sheets on Lorelay's four-post bed. She was like a whirlwind moving about the room, tidying all the mess Lorelay made in the short time she had been living in these quarters.

"You're right," the servant said quietly. "Elzia was beloved. They say she embodied the Lightmother's grace even more than her mother, the Empress before her. To some people, a man on the throne is no different than the Darkfather himself sitting the throne. As though it's a sign of the Dark Era's return. Bah. Superstition is all that is. Vinlin will make a fine Emperor, but it's his duty to prove himself. And one sure way to frighten the daylight out of everyone is telling them there are monsters threatening our borders."

"But there *are* monsters threatening our borders."

"Well, that's your job to convince him. Not mine."

Lorelay sighed. "I know. It just feels so...impossible. I tried explaining it to him, but he wouldn't believe me."

"And everyone succeeds on their first try, do they?" The servant opened the wardrobe and rifled through it.

Lorelay sat in the chair, naked, exposed, observing herself in the wardrobe's mirror. She looked so small. And she had just told *everything* to this woman. Was she going to regret that? One more slip of the tongue to land her in a mess. That would be just like her.

"You can call me Minny, by the way," the servant said, laying out two outfits on Lorelay's bed.

One, a beige tunic and wine-colored vest with matching drawers, appropriate for Lorelay to go to the tavern. The other, a navy dress of high cut and no sleeves, trimmed with gold thread. What a noblewoman would wear to entreat the Bright Prince.

"So, what's it going to be? Will you give up? Or do you believe in your mission enough to try again?"

CHAPTER SIXTEEN

The Eye

Explorers sped off as soon as the Queen's hold on them failed. Strange variant, that one. Peeker I knew told me Explorers planted the first giants' seeds themselves. Don't tell me you're not impressed.

—From the first oral history of Ekohold

The Eevoqian had said nothing more of value.

All Garret had come away from that encounter knowing was that Prost had come across the seas from a country called Eevoq. Probably with the two Skardwarves, proving he was right not to trust them. For that information—and an assurance he'd keep quiet—Garret let Helman keep all his fingers. While Garret was cleaning blood off his knife, the Eevoqian swore he'd be leaving the south as soon as the winds allowed.

Strange man, that one. The south? Something must be wrong with his head. Garret reached his conclusion as he reached the door to his dwelling. Pushed it open to find Sentyx standing in the middle of the room.

"Speaking of strange ones," Garret muttered.

"You left."

"Nothing gets past you." He laid on the bed, closed his eyes to sleep. The vision of Eevoqian blood on his hands filled the darkness behind Garret's eyes, reminded him too much of Ekoan blood on his hands. He lay wide awake staring at the bioluminescent bulb on the wall for a time. "On second thought, why don't you tell me what happened with those Peekers?"

"They reported to Queen," Sentyx said.

Word of the Skardwarf is spreading. Should reach Prost's ears in no time.

"Good. Maybe she can keep everyone from freaking out next time you show up."

Sentyx grunted. "Not me. Us."

Garret sat bolt upright. "Me? Why would they include me?"

"We are Fingers. Queen will meet us." A low rumble emanated from Sentyx's chest. "Soon."

Soon, as it turned out, was by Skardwarf standards. For several days, Garret and Sentyx searched for Prost with no word of an invite from the Peeker Queen. Garret was anxious to get on with it. Not meeting the Queen—he didn't give a damn about that—but venturing into the true tunnels of the Peekers' hive.

Garret was ready to leave the Human Aerie. The squared off caves had become more drab and discomfiting with each passing day. Reminded him of the Agency before Grim destroyed the incense that made Ulken's mind-numbing haze. He still didn't fully understand how that worked, but it seemed to be going on here too. Without any haze, though. Only an overly docile crowd of people.

"Like they forgot all about you," he told Sentyx, passing through a queue of Lawi waiting for steaming crabs served over rice.

"Calm," the Skardwarf said. "Smell?"

"Does smell good," Garret agreed. "But they're not this calm just for fresh crab."

Sentyx gave a drawn out grunt.

Garret ignored it, scanning the area for anomalies. Nothing he could see. Just people eating and Builders working on the walls, excreting their slimy resin. Everything seemed normal, that was the strange thing.

Whatever was happening, people living in the Aerie were much more cooperative for the hunt. Or at least, they didn't run from the Skardwarf anymore. Barely answered any of Garret's snuffing questions, though. Felt like he was running a bleeding campaign to improve Sentyx's public relations. All anybody wanted to know about was the Skardwarf, the Burner, the demon.

So, Garret waited, impatiently bouncing on the balls of his feet, while Sentyx answered whatever inane questions they had for him.

"Are all demons so nice?" a young Paceeqi boy asked.

"No."

"How old are you?" A brown-robed Ayeiri insisted he must know, for his private calculations.

Sentyx gave him a noncommittal grunt and lumbered away to the next person. People were excited for the chance to speak to the Skardwarf.

Even though he hardly answers anything. Bleeding waste of time. Garret brooded over the Skardwarf's useless responses. Didn't even give him a hint about their weakness.

"Why do our hosts call you Burners?" a woman inquired. A promising question, for once.

"We have fire inside." Sentyx bared his flat stone teeth. A grin?

Garret raised an eyebrow. Was he *enjoying* this attention? The woman nodded vigorously, muttering something about metaphors and how brave Sentyx must be.

When a Lawi man with a plate of cracked crab legs and butter dribbling down his chin asked how Sentyx defecates, Garret could take no more.

"All right, I think we've learned enough today." He tried pulling Sentyx away, but moving the Skardwarf was as futile as lifting a snoutbear.

Sentyx grabbed a crab leg and crushed it in his palm. Ground it right down to tiny orange splinters. He held his hand over the plate, loosened his fist, and crab dust sprinkled down, blowing onto the Lawi's shirt with an errant gust of wind.

Garret looked around for the metaphor lady. She would be *thrilled* with this, he was sure. "Can we go now?"

Sentyx finally relented and let Garret pull him aside to a private nook between shops.

"What are we doing here?" Garret wondered. "This is clearly getting us nowhere."

"They see Skardwarf." Sentyx grunted. "You said."

Garret wiped a hand down his face. "I know what I said. Didn't think you'd be parading yourself around like some Liwo courtesan." He looked at the fading light though the Nectar Hall's cavernous hole. No storms brewing, it would be a calm night. "You keep talking to people. Maybe try to find out if *they* know something, aye?"

Sentyx agreed.

"I'll find you later," Garret said, and began retracing his steps to the harbor.

Ninety-degree turn after ninety-degree turn, it was making him sick. He needed to get out of these artificial caves, find some semblance of the untouched outdoors. The further from the Human Aerie, the better he felt. Like some hand had stopped squeezing his mind. Almost as if a Benefactor were in the Mounds.

Garret touched his face, considering the possibility. Ran a finger along the rough vertical scar on his temple. He wouldn't forget his first encounter with a Benefactor. Almost lost his eye to the witch under its control. But this time there was no Aura. No panic. Least, now that they were used to Sentyx.

Just need some fresh air. It's been too long.

Along the way, he passed a tunnel glowing phosphorescent blue at the far end. He would've investigated, but the two Peekers standing guard might have had a few words for him. Then again, the way they were built, all upper body and thick necks, these two didn't seem the talking type. Another variant. Soldiers. Garret strolled away. Didn't even pay them a second glance, though he paid them a second thought.

Outside the Mounds, Peekers all looked the same. Traveled as a Pair. Kept to themselves, mostly. Always soft-spoken and quick with their chittering laughter. Those two guards, though...looked more like Pinch after assimilating that Cleric. Like flesh was stolen to transform their bodies. Struck Garret as odd, but none of the normal-looking Peekers the Soldiers let scurry past ever made a peep about it.

Another mystery of the Mounds, then. Garret couldn't write, but he could keep a record in his mind. All the strange happenings he'd come across, and those he was sure to encounter. Was it a biotist's fancy, naming all the Peeker variants and learning how they lived? 'Course not. A ranger needed to know his environment. Had to stay aware to survive.

Right then, Garret was aware of his need to escape for some time to think. Kept his hood up and marched against the current of people. Outside, under blessed clear skies, he spotted a newly arrived ship, people disembarking. He found a spot to slip aside, clambered up a hill with no path and a good vantage to glance at each face, then waited.

None of the visitors looked like Prost. No one he recognized, neither enemy nor friend. Just nameless people of no consequence.

He sat, watching the ships rock in the harbor. Feeling the breeze on his skin. The hood stayed up. Didn't want anyone noticing him, getting curious. He wanted to be alone. Always alone.

Soon he found himself pondering better days. But that was just it. There were no better days. Every single day of his bleeding life was a fight for survival. Bandits, monsters, even his friends. All wanted him dead at some point.

Better to be alone than to have friends who betray you.

No, there were no better days. Not in the past, not in the future. They only existed in his useless snuffing dreams.

"Remember what's real," Garret said with disdain. He spat.

Then held back his reaction at the crunch of a stick behind him.

In one fluid motion, Garret was up with his knife at the man's throat. "Following me? What do you want?"

"Easy now, friend," the man said, licking his lips. He held his hands aloft. No threat.

Garret was happy leaving the knife right where it was, friend or not. "If you're looking for a good time, you're barking up the wrong tree."

The man chuckled, then winced as the knife nicked him. "You're with the Skardwarf, aren't you?"

"The last man who didn't answer my questions found out how good I am with this knife. How little compunction I have in using it. Now, want to rethink your answer?"

"I'm a friend of the Agency. And I'm unarmed."

Garret looked him up and down in the long-faded sunlight. He had a Paceeqi build. Donned a blue coat, calf-length, as long as the man was tall. "I know a deserter when I see one. You were an Eye."

Still, he was unarmed. Unarmored too. Even had an eye-patch. This Eye was half-blind. Garret could kill him in a heartbeat. He put away the knife.

The Paceeqi showed no relief. His jaw muscles clenched. "I was a friend of the *Agency*. Not of Ulken. The men and women working to keep Lawiko safe. Like you. I know a Finger when I see one. Despite the unconventional uniform."

An enemy of Ulken should be a friend to Grim's Agency, but this was a man who'd proved himself a turncloak. "I suppose now you're going to tell me what Ulken did to you?"

"It's what he did to *us*. Started mixing untrained recruits with veterans and sending the Hands out to face…" He looked around and confirmed no one was around. "Them." His expression twisted. "You were one of them, I remember. Don't think I'll forget when Ulken brought those demons into the Agency. Put us *all* at risk. And he paired you up with one of them."

Garret spat. The Eye was right, but that did nothing to stop the tangle inside him from tightening. It was a good thing he'd stuck close to Sentyx. Might not have made it out of the Shaded Grounds otherwise. "I survived. Now are you going to whine until dusk breaks, or are you going to answer my question? What do you *want* with me?"

"I want to *help* you. You're stuck here with that demon. I get it, Ulken gave you his command. A Finger being here can only mean one thing. Those monsters are dangerous. If a tragic accident were to befall your companion...well." The Eye shrugged.

Garret laughed. "Is that what you think? I'm stuck under Ulken's thumb? Head of the Agency is dead. Killed by a Benefactor."

The Eye had good instincts. The word made him flinch and check the path both ways for listeners. Then they struck home. "Dead? But then, the Agency...is it...?"

"The Agency is fine. Under new management. Might even be better than Ulken."

If Inac keeps him in line.

White teeth showed in the man's dark smile. "Good riddance."

"Aye."

The Eye ran the fabric of his coat through his hands. "Well...I can't go back. They'll have me on file as a deserter. I'll be hanged." He looked Garret in the eyes. "My offer stands. The Mounds aren't safe. Not with a Benefactor and two Skardwarves around."

"What did you say?" *Finally, something interesting.* "Two Skardwarves?"

The man's eyepatch wrinkled when he furrowed his brow. "You don't know? There's a Skardwarf working with another human. Word in the Aerie is he has the ear of the Queen."

"Have you seen him?"

"No, but anyone with their ear to Peeker politics knows what he looks like."

When Garret heard him describe an Eevoqian, his lips split in a wide grin. He hurried down the hill without another word.

"But wait, what about the—"

His words were lost to the wind, but Garret didn't care. The half-blind Eye had spotted his target.

CHAPTER SEVENTEEN

From Every Shadow

A clear mind is crucial for controlling the Fire. Your time is limited, I know this, but a span spent in meditation saves a full day of practice. When I return from Canako, we will continue our sessions.

—Signed by a friend and Sage

"And how from you did they take it?" Inac asked. We met in Inac's quarters so my friend—and Sage—could resume his Archemagical instruction.

"About as poorly as I could have imagined." The Darkfather's own luck. I was sure I would have convinced them.

Maybe I shouldn't have mentioned blackmail explicitly.

"They thought it was an underhanded tactic to leverage my power over them."

"Yes," Inac said, "your immense power." He held out a hand, palm up, holding a candle. "Now, light this. And you had better not scorch my fingers."

I closed my eyes. It was easier to see them that way. The patterns of Archefire surrounded me, waiting for me to notice them, to tug them in some direction away from their natural state. The strands were slippery, sliding off each of my attempts to grasp it.

Remembering that I had only started seeing the subtle hints of the Fire recently—after returning to life as a Benefactor—did little to squash my frustrations. They were a faint sensation, vibrating clouds of movement clinging to anything flammable—so nearly everything.

To discern them required all my focus. Trying to wield them was like navigating the Agency with my eyes closed.

"Delicate, my friend," Inac patiently instructed. "You are not trying to stomp your foot on a bug, you are trying to sway your body with the trees in the wind. Feel inside yourself the flow. Move with it. You do not want for it to fight you."

An intrusive memory of an Archemage glowing in the dark of the night appeared in my mind. My skin sloughed from flaming bones. My eyes turned to Fire in their sockets. The vision released me, and I was sweating. Burning up was a bad way to go. I suddenly felt wary of touching strands of Fire at all.

Everything ends in fire.

"Do not cower before it," Inac warned. "That is for yourself as sure a way to be consumed as by rushing into it."

"That's what you said last time," I muttered, still trying to focus. "I still have the burn scars from trying to follow that advice."

"Then you did not follow it properly. You did not move with the Fire. When it leaned itself in a direction you did not want for it to go, you pushed it. You should not be surprised when it against you fights back."

I half-opened one eye, then snapped it shut when I saw Inac studying his twisted stump of a wrist. "You talk about it like it's alive." *And like it's a friend you lost contact with.*

"It *is* alive," Inac said. Observing the arrhythmic movements of the Fire, it was hard to disagree with him. "And like a wild animal, it must by us be respected. Like any other, it is training *you* as much as you are training *it*. You should listen for yourself to what it is teaching you. And to your Sage."

I didn't need to open my eyes to know Inac was smirking at that last.

All right, Sage. I'll take your advice. Move with the flows. Delicate.

Relaxing my shoulders, sitting as comfortably as I could, I slowed my breathing. The vibrating strands pushed at me while moving through me, as though I sat at the bottom of the Brightcalm, swaying in the currents. But none of it interacted with my body; it was all happening mentally.

Reed once told me, all of everything happens inside our heads.

Only once my body was tuned out could my mind truly focus on the dancing Fire around me. They seemed to cling to the objects in the room, outlining the shape of everything in my mind. Where the light glowed on the ceiling, the Fire flickered only dimly. Where the lantern burned on my desk, the Fire jumped and sparked as if excited to be alive.

The flow *wanted* to be alight, all of it. To bring warmth and light to the world. I just had to bring about the conditions to let them ignite.

I reached out with my mind toward the strands on the wick of Inac's candle. My hand moved as if of its own accord, fingers moving—no, moved by the unseen currents. Like throwing stones into a brook, my hands moved just so to create turbulence downstream. I felt the twists of Fire starting to dance.

Inac's candle melted in a burst of Fire that evaporated the top half of the wax. The flames surged back toward my hand, the source of the turbulence in the current. Grunting, I pulled my hand back, but the stones in the brook stayed in place. When the Fire reached them, my hands felt the heat of the inferno as the blockages were incinerated and the natural flow was restored.

"You drew to yourself its ire," Inac said as I grasped my burning hand. A line of blisters traced from the end of my long finger to the base of my wrist, with red scorch marks spreading from that main trunk like the branches of a tree.

"I was only doing what you said!" I couldn't clench my fist all the way, not without breaking open those blisters.

"You did exactly opposite of what I said. I watched it happen."

"Then why didn't you stop me?" I shot back. "Or better yet, why don't you show me what you mean? Because I have no idea."

"You know I cannot." There was fire in his voice, for someone who couldn't summon the Fire.

"And why not?" I demanded. "You told me yourself that you don't need your hands to control Archemagic, only your mind."

I needed him to get past this mental block. He was the most powerful Archemage I knew, and the Agency needed his help. Not just fighting, but learning. We knew Benefactors were closely tied to Archemagic, and only Inac and Arza had the expertise to discover if they had any vulnerabilities to it. Working together, our progress might just be fast enough.

A young Finger who had been killed in Reed's Woods called Inac an Archemaster, once. He had been right. But the Inac sitting before me could not control the Fire. It didn't make sense to me what had happened when Ulken severed his hand. It had changed Inac, stolen the vigor from his eyes.

I needed him to teach me to control this power, but more importantly, I needed him to be okay. He was my friend, and I pained me to see him with his head held so low.

"I do myself not understand it either, Grim. It is as if to me like he cut off that part of my mind when he cut off my hand. I feel outside me the Fire, but I cannot touch it." He pulled back his robe and revealed his severed limb.

My lips tightened, but I did not look away. At the end of his forearm, the flesh transitioned from smooth to wrinkled to lumpy and malformed. Inac's hand had been severed by Ulken's blade. With no Fire, he had one choice to not bleed out.

Archedark. Some called it Archedeath, but Inac would have skewered me for using that name.

"And the Dark?" I asked, tentatively. He was exposing himself here, and I didn't want to probe too strongly.

I've already pushed too many friends away.

"To stir it without using Archefire to navigate..." Inac shook his head. Looking closely, I saw he was using the motion to disguise some emotion in his eyes. "Too dangerous. You must not do it again."

I groaned. "We don't have *time* to teach me the *right* way to do things. We need to take some risks. I need to understand Archedark too."

Being able to sense the fields of Archemagic... This part of Reed's so-called gift truly was a blessing. I couldn't let it go to waste.

"Do you know what to you happens if such a risk does not pay off? If your flip of the coin lands for you on the wrong side?"

A shiver ran through me. What was the equivalent of burning up with the Dark?

It didn't matter. I wasn't backing down. "We're all risking our lives, here. Why should I do any less than what I'm asking of everyone else? I should be doing *more* than everyone else."

"You should be making better decisions than everyone else," Inac said, pointing at his mop of sandy hair. "Using your head, as your position implies. Exposing yourself to danger with no need is unwise." I opened my mouth to make my case again, but Inac cut me off with a gesture. "However...I will consider it."

He stood, and I stood with him.

"I am disappointed in you, Grim."

"What did I do now?"

"You did not ask to me even once how Lorelay's departure went."

Darkfather's balls. I hardly noticed he left. It didn't feel like he had just come back from anywhere.

I had been so absorbed in my own problems of running the Agency—and the intruding memories from the numberless dead—I never stopped to think about my friends.

He gave a sad smile. "It was for both of us bittersweet. But otherwise uneventful. You did the right thing, you know. We need for ourselves the support of Paceeq."

The logic had never changed. The number of infested in Liwokin alone attested to how quickly the scourge spread. If Benefactors were on the Peeker Mounds, as Pinch proved, they were everywhere. Paceeq and the Peeker Mounds were home to two of the most densely populated capital cities in the Bright Empire. Plenty of new host minds for the organism to infest.

Paceeq's leadership needed to be warned of what was coming, but more critically, they needed to fight beside us. We didn't know what the next phase of the war against Benefactors would look like—they were always changing and adapting—but the devastation of the last one was reason enough to start preparing.

Tens of thousands dead. All living inside my mind, driving me mad.

Put that way, the world seems destined to fall to these monsters.

I touched the cut on my cheek. They were already here in the city. Had Jacquin sent a Hand to search for that Emergent? How long ago had that been? The days and all the problems they brought blended together like memories of the dead.

"I'm sorry, friend," I said to Inac. "You deserve better from me. I am grateful for the things you do for me. You're the last person left in this place I feel I can truly trust. You, and maybe one other." My mind stumbled to a halt when I noticed Inac grimacing. "What I'm trying to say, is thank you."

He gave a short chuckle. "We may civilize you yet, Grim, up-jumped boy from the Blight."

That drew a laugh from my gut. "Hope so because we need the Seats of the Council to come around. Can I ask you a favor?"

"Of course."

"Start planning a meeting, no...a summit. Make it official, whatever paperwork and scheduling you need to do. To bring Liwokin's leaders together. The Agency, the Gild, and the Council. If we're to unite against the Benefactors, we need to get everyone in a room together talking to each other."

He chewed his lip thinking, then nodded and stood to leave. "How will we convince them to attend?"

I have no idea.

"Leave that to me." If anyone could peer through my veil of confidence, it was Inac, but he said nothing as he made for the door. "Oh, and send Jacquin up here if you see him. I need to know what he's got on that Benefactor we saw in the Burg."

"As long as you continue responding to those requests," he said, reminding me of the stack on my desk. Shorter than before, but still considerable. "Like you promised to me."

"I got through a bunch of them before our training!"

He left smiling and shaking his head.

It had taken the entire span from dawn to half-noon, but it felt good to keep a promise. More paperwork, however, was not what I had planned for this half-dusk. I climbed the stairs to my office, kept the lights off and sat in my chair. If Jacquin hadn't found that Benefactor yet, perhaps I could. It was easier to focus on memories in the dark, and the hunt was on.

Like attracted like. I pictured the moment we stumbled across the Emergent. That loud bang that nearly sent me to my knees. His bloody hands. Most of all, I tried to focus on the man's face.

Difficult, considering a never got a good look before he disappeared. Clutching his hand, scrambling away, then...gone. My sanity was already cracked. Was he just a Benefactor's illusion, another event similar to Reed's Woods? Or was he really there?

The blood on my fingers seemed real enough to me. But the mind was easily deceived. Even the sharp pain could have been an illusion. Maybe even now, I was under the influence of the Benefactor's Aura. How would I even know?

Remember what's real.

Reed had told me that once when he was not a Benefactor but a man. Bengard had told me the same. I clenched my fists at the residual guilt *his* name summoned. Both of them were dead. Their advice was old—did it even still apply? How could I remember what was real when the Benefactors' Auras seemed to change reality itself?

They permeated through everything, unfazed by walls of stone or metal, spreading to the minds of everyone infested. I felt them out there, as faint as the currents of Archefire, tugging at my consciousness nonetheless. So many infested, and these were only the ones within my reach, inside Liwokin. The more time I spent sinking into this dark ocean, the more clearly I felt their minds. Felt *where* they were, albeit imprecisely, as though looking down from a great height.

In this landscape, my attention traveled from the Agency tower, down across the Burg, over the Market and into the Artisans' District, where I reached the limits of my senses at the edge of the Blight. Beyond that, I felt nothing, as though running up against an invisible wall.

I searched the memories of everyone my Benefactor touched. But I didn't even know what I was looking for. An ear-ringing crack? A man disappearing? I tried to picture the scene again to determine if there was anything I might be missing. I saw him kicking to get away from me, the fear in his eyes a match for the confusion that must be in my own. He had kicked something toward me. Something smoking, a lump of blue-gray metal in a shape that resembled...

A flintlock pistol? But the sound was wrong, more of a sudden bang than the sizzling crackle that accompanied the pull of a flintlock's trigger. And yet.

My imagination faded as my mind opened to accept the memory of another. Rather, it felt as though my Benefactor was siphoning the memory away from someone. Sitting in the dark with my eyes closed, I had no control over what happened among Benefactors. I was simply a passive observer, watching. Learning what I can.

If anything at all.

Most of the memories were useless. What flooded my mind were contextless fragments of time from the life of some nobody. A random Liwo, someone with no bearing on what befell the city as a result of the Gild, the Council, or the Agency.

The memory I pried from an unsuspecting Liwo this time, however, was far from useless.

I looked down upon a crate full of pistols wrought from blue-gray metal.

Worthless junk.

Grumbling, I packed the last one away and started hammering nails into the lid to keep it shut. Sixty-seven pistols. Sixteen nails. Lightmother help us, we'd be better off never opening this crate again.

When I finished, a woman joined me. I wanted to ask her name—she was strong—but we weren't allowed. Too dangerous, he'd said, and we had a job to do. One thing you can say about us Blightdwellers, when there's work to be done, it'll get done.

She took the crate by the handle opposite mine, and we hauled it up fourteen stairs. She was breathing hard by the time they exited out into the Burg. So was I. At least it was cool. A breeze blew in from the bay, and the Brightdaughter was nowhere to be seen overhead.

"Can't believe he carried this across the city by himself," the woman said.

"Could've saved himself the effort. Heard about what happened to the guy who stole one?"

"He saw his chance and took it. Could have been a hero."

"Yeah, and instead he's got three less fingers than yesterday."

And if we're lucky, one less head. Can't have no thieves scurrying about. Then again, after losing thirty-eight of our people in the collapse...

"Fewer."

"What?" This lady wasn't making any sense.

My wife, Lightmother preserve her, always said my brain was my smallest muscle, and that's how she liked it. Only did one thing good, she'd say, and that's counting. Always said that before complaining she'd rather we had coin to count than grains of rice. I eyed my partner's big arms.

Maybe muscles and brains don't go together in women, neither.

"Forget it," she said. "Now lift. And don't gimme any of that grumbling. Last thing we need is a guard hearing us."

"Better worry about the Head hisself," I said. "I hear he's got eyes watching from every shadow of the city."

"Nonsense. Now quiet. He's counting on us. Don't mess this up for me."

The memory vanished, leaving me alone in the dark with my own thoughts. Frustrated thoughts, since the strange man whose memories I witnessed were barely coherent. If I could better control these visions, I could have seen where they were transporting those weapons. I recognized the crate they were stored in from somewhere, and something in my mind dimly connected them to resistance against Ulken.

How had the disappearing man gotten his hands on one? Perhaps once Ulken died, the Liwo who had been working against him abandoned their resources, and he stumbled across it.

Somewhere in the Blight, no doubt.

If those weapons were still out there, they represented a danger that needed to be stopped. I slammed my fist on the desk, toppling a pile of request forms.

I can barely control the Agency, let alone the monsters in my head.

The lights on the ceiling buzzed to life, glowing a ghostly white that stung my eyes. How long had I been sitting in the dark?

Jacquin stood in the doorway, as expected, twisting the valve that controlled the lights. He approached my desk wordlessly.

"Good," I said, "Inac sent you. What have you learned about the Benefactor we felt in the square?"

"In the square?" the Eye opened his mouth, but the voice did not belong to Jacquin. It belonged to an Ayeiri woman. "No, she has not left her...chamber."

My face scrunched up in confusion, and I rubbed at my eyes. When I opened them, the lights were still on, and standing before me was the lead mortician.

"Arza? Where's Jacquin?"

"Jacquin? I have stayed far away from him, as you said. What is going on, Grim?" She sounded genuinely concerned. "Are you all right?"

Sitting here in the dark, losing my mind. Everything is snuffing wonderful.

For a moment, I considered spilling everything to her. If anyone was qualified to help, it was the lead mortician. But controlling the powers inside my head had to remain my own problem for now. She couldn't know what I truly was, and it would only distract her. I needed *her* to help everyone else.

Lightmother willing, she'll find a way to help me too.

I hoped she didn't see my desperation as I waved her concern aside. "I take it you're here to report the latest on Yezna? What have you got?"

CHAPTER EIGHTEEN

Man of the People

You're still thinking too small. We need to light a fire so big, the damn Bright Empress herself can see it on the horizon.

—Nameless note

A cure for Incubating Benefactors. I could hardly believe it. Arza was doing *exactly* what I hoped. Hearing of her progress lit a fire under me, made me certain I had to act quickly, otherwise she'd have a solution and be stuck waiting for me to unite Liwokin's factions.

Of the many efforts I had set in motion, only Arza's experiments with Yezna seemed to be progressing. Even without Inac's help, she was able to use her own Archemagic to test ideas and had discovered that Benefactors react in minute ways to Archefire. She was confident given more time she could eliminate them from the brains of the Incubating before they ever became Emergent.

Meanwhile, as for my friends...I heard nothing from them. Garret and Sentyx's hunt for Prost, Lorelay's mission to seek the Bright Throne as an ally—I had nothing but my dark imagination to fill in the void of information.

Maybe I'll never hear from them again.

The nagging fear persisted, the voice that told me I had ordered them all to their deaths. But they had to succeed, accomplish what I had sent them to do. If *any* of us failed, the odds of us surviving this infestation would rapidly vanish.

Any of us. I couldn't worry about their commands. I could only worry about the problems directly before me. Walking across the square to the Council Hall with all of Ulken's blackmail, there was much to be worried about. How would the Gild react to this? By working to replace me, like Oltrov plotted with Reed? With a quick assassination?

A knife in the back. Rope burn.

The Gild would have no reason to murder a Blightdweller, but an unruly Head of the Agency? My shoulder blades itched as I expected to feel a blade plunging in.

I picked up my pace toward the Council Hall. How would the Seats of the Hall perceive what I planned? If I learned one thing from my first meetings with both groups, it was that I was a terrible judge of what to expect from them. I was no politician. I was a bounty hunter.

Give me a problem I can solve with my sword, and you won't be disappointed.

But I was a Finger no longer. I was the Head, and Inac was right. My head was exactly what I needed to use.

"Try to talk me out of it one more time," I told Inac, clenching the incriminating documents more tightly.

Inac sighed. "One last time. I do not know what you expect. You did not reconsider for yourself when I argued against it the third time. Or the fourth."

"Just..." I hesitated. "I want to make sure."

"Good. Because if we are about this wrong, it will certainly make matters worse. It is not too late to turn around, my friend. Or perhaps to share with me a pint at the Wistwicker." Inac grinned. "For the sake of old times."

Sighing, I shook my head. "I wish we could. This would be easier with a shot of Stinbine rum in me."

The strong liquor had burned my nose and throat going down. This day, something else would burn. Only, how could I be sure it wouldn't lead to them burning me at the stake?

"If everyone *knows* they aren't alone in being blackmailed, then we no longer have a tool to control them, right?" I asked. "They can ignore whatever we held and know I'm serious about working together. They should all thank me for this."

"I am not sure they will agree," Inac said. "I *am* sure they will not like you flaring the Fire in their faces. If you can control it..." He muttered the last.

"I can do it," I said firmly, as much to myself as to my friend. Despite practice, I remained incapable of anything but the simplest controls. Still, this would work. Archefire had been used to heal wounds for ages. I could use it to heal this rift. The Agency and the Council had to work together if Liwokin was going to survive.

And if they can help me deal with the Gild, all the better.

I didn't have an appointment with the Council, and they didn't know I was coming. I got their attention by banging on the door until a clerk yelled at me to go away. I yelled back that the Head of the Agency wouldn't be turned away, and that got me inside.

"Have them meet me in the same room as last time," I told her. "I can wait."

As Inac and I sat there in silence, death knells from the infested pulled at me from all throughout the city. The Council *must* accept this gesture. Couldn't they see how big of a problem we had on our hands?

Except, they *couldn't* see it. It was invisible, unfelt to all but a Benefactor. That was the problem. It wasn't a matter of whether *I* recognized the problem, but whether everyone else did. How could I make them understand without letting them know my own secret?

Without revealing the monster I am.

It hadn't come to that yet. The best plan I had was to show them how seriously I took the problem myself. Making myself vulnerable to them, convincing them I didn't intend to be a threat.

A risky gamble—I was exposing myself in order to sway them—but I didn't have time to reconsider. Inac and I stood as the door was practically kicked in. Five Seats of the Hall strode in through the open door, one behind another. Last among them was the Council Chair herself, Maise, wearing a much more informal outfit than our last meeting.

And a considerably redder face.

Before she started steaming from the ears, I held up the documents. "Here it is. All of it."

"Do you take this for some whore house you can come barging into?" Maise ignored what was in my hand. Her paralyzing gaze never left my own eyes.

My eyes met hers with the same fire in them. "None of you were alone in being blackmailed by Ulken." That brought the mutterings and denials I expected, but before I could be derailed, I put an end to the chatter. "Enough. Your secrets are of no importance to me."

I narrowed my eyes and focused. Strands of Archefire danced expectantly around the stack of sworn oaths and incriminating letters in my hand. With a twist of my hand, the Fire sparked to life and incinerated all of the documents. When it began to fight back, I expected it and moved with the flows to put the Archemagic back to rest.

When I opened my eyes, five stunned faces greeted me, and I took the chance to explain. "We all make mistakes, often painful ones. Painful for ourselves and for others." Their faces weren't exactly fonts of hope, but I pressed on. "I urge you not to make the mistake of confusing me with my predecessor, the man who did this to you. I am not Ulken. And I will not make the mistake of treating you as my enemy. We only have one enemy, Benefactors, and we need to fight them together."

"*Benefactors,*" one man scoffed.

Another eyed him quizzically. "What's that? I'm quite sure I've never heard the word in my life."

My jaw clenched. I had explained the Benefactors in our last meeting. These stodgy old men refused to take me seriously.

"You are right," Maise said, her voice a cold dagger in my ribs. "We all make mistakes, and you've just made a grave one."

By the abyss, woman. What will it take to convince you?

"I'm doing this," I said, "because I know the arrangements the Gild has used to keep your hands tied. Their mistake is underestimating the people of Liwokin, the people *you* represent. The same people I'm trying to protect. Do what's right for them, for *all Liwo.*"

Maise hesitated, then laughed. A sharp, cutting laugh. "Oh, we shall, as we always have. And that begins with asking you to leave before I have you placed in the stockades. Don't look so indignant. You put on a good show, but I see you for what you are. You claim to be some savior of the people, but you're a would-be tyrant. You don't look the same as the man who came before you, but you act like him. Now begone, *boy,* or—"

"It is *not* too late to heal this divide," I said through clenched teeth. I tried to remain civil, but this Council Chair was testing my patience. "If we don't, Liwokin may not surv—"

The door slammed against the wall, and a clerk came running into the room, out of breath. "Fire! In the Council Square!"

My anger had been about to boil over before the alarm. *Boy?* My fists were white-knuckled, ready for a brawl. That rage cooled not a degree as I rushed outside with Inac and the five Seats of the Hall. In the square, it only heated further. There was an entire mob of Liwo shouting and waving wooden signs and holding torches aloft. They directed their display not at the Council Hall, but at the Agency.

Where did they come from?

I sensed no Aura, no Benefactor and looked to Inac instead. Was this because I hadn't prioritized the requests made by common Liwo?

My friend's face held no answers, only showed his worry. But this didn't seem to be about that. I listened to the shouting voices, the angry cries from what must have been three-hundred people.

"Justice for the dead!"

"Murderer!"

"Kill the killer!"

"Off with his head!"

My eyes widened.

Justice for the dead. Off with his Head.

"How are you going to handle this, man of the people?" Maise called from the bottom of the steps to the Hall. I hardly heard her over the shouts of the mob.

No...it can't be.

Inac put a hand on my shoulder to slow my approach. "Grim, we *must* be careful."

My feet carried me forward as though they had a mind of their own. Those signs. They faced the Agency, but from the back they looked familiar. I recalled the sight of them scattered in the dirt of an alley. Painted on a table in a dingy basement.

Those signs were about Ulken...

Had those signs been abandoned and rediscovered, along with the strange pistols?

I kept my hand on the knife concealed beneath my coat as I reached the edge of the protest. They had their backs turned to me. One woman with a sign painted to read 'Ass of the Agency' stood apart from the rest. I expected no great deal of them would notice if I talked to her, so I tapped her shoulder. She turned away as if I was being impolite, looked at me over her shoulders, then rapidly spun to face me.

A Blightdweller, her skin unwashed and her clothes stained. The woman regarded me with wide eyes. I didn't recognize her, but she must have recognized me. The shock in her expression turned to anger, and she swung the sign at me. I dodged backward just in time to avoid a wooden swipe to the head.

"You're him!" she shouted at me, pointed a crooked finger.

And reality hit me.

Their anger...it was directed at...

"Me?"

Inac was tugging at my coat. "This is bad, Grim. We must go."

Go where? The only way to the tower was through this crowd, and the gate was closed, as expected. Otherwise, they would have stormed into our headquarters by now, I was sure. And I had to know the truth. How had this happened?

"These people aren't our enemies." They were Liwo. My responsibility. "This must be a mistake." I pulled my sleeve from Inac's grasp and turned to the woman. "Why are you doing this?" Though I was trying to keep my voice level, it wavered a bit from the anger still roiling inside me. I was conscious of Maise and the other Seats still watching me from afar. They wanted nothing to do with this.

"You killed him!" she screamed.

My heart palpitated. Many had died by my hand, and more than a few I wasn't proud of. Who was she talking about?

Other protesters turned around, drawn to her outrage like bear-sharks to blood.

"You are a killer!" The woman's face was turning red as she screamed at the top of her lungs for all to hear. "Ulken was the Hero of the Riot, and you murdered him in cold blood!"

"Murderer!"

"Kill the killer!"

The shouts were taken up again, though no longer directed at the Agency. Now they were all aimed directly at me.

My stomach clenched in fear and regret. This was my own doing. In the shadow of Reed's twisted tower, I confessed my crime to the world. Now, the time of judgment was here. Far too soon for my liking.

"Grim?" Inac's voice was a panicked whisper.

Both of us were backing away as the crowd seemed to press closer and closer. If we ran now, this mob would catch us and tear us apart. But what else was I to do, get up on a podium and try to calm them down? They wouldn't listen to reason; they were driven by emotion. If emotion was what it took to reach them, I had plenty to channel.

Fear. Confusion. But more than anything else, anger.

The strands of Archefire danced.

"Enough!" my voice boomed, and I pulled on the strings of Fire. A burst of flame erupted from the surface of my skin with the force of a shock wave. It pushed the crowd back, and for an instant I shined like the Brightdaughter.

That got their attention.

The entire crowd had gone quiet, still and stunned, as if in a fugue state. It unsettled me, reminding me of the mass of senseless Liwo in Reed's Woods. I glanced at Inac—his expression matched theirs. For that matter, I was sure mine did as well. But now was the time to act. I looked from stunned face to stunned face. I licked my lips.

Lightmother, what do I say?

"You think Ulken was your hero?" That produced some grumbling, but I pressed on. "He *caused* the Great Riot. *He* was responsible for all the dead. Justice for them, yes! Every last one of them. I gave them their justice." I put on a firm face, and looked out upon the crowd, trying not to hyperventilate. And I waited.

And waited.

And...

By the abyss, did that actually work?

The majority of the crowd seemed mollified. Faces turned toward each other and talked in uncertain tones. Relief accompanied the sight of signs calling for my execution lowered or tossed down. Someone smiled, shoved another person aside, and made her way toward me. A representative coming to talk?

I narrowed my eyes at the woman. She wore a ragged leather vest over a filthy blouse with the sleeves torn off. She was muscular.

My eyes popped open. I recognized her.

And the weapon in her hand.

Blue-gray metal caught the Brightdaughter's light, then chaos erupted.

Inac shouted my name. A loud bang knocked the sound from the world. My ears rang, and my stomach had a hot iron poker digging into it. The crowd scattered. Screams reached my ears as if from a great distance. The strength faded from my left leg, and my knee buckled. When it hit the ground, I hardly felt the pain.

Even in my shock, I knew what happened. My assailant could hardly believe it; she stood there gaping at me, the pistol trembling in her hand. Then her hand steadied. Her expression firmed. She took aim at my head.

I gritted my teeth, and the strands of Archefire danced. The pain in my stomach spread upward and threatened to plunge me into dark unawareness. I growled, a guttural thing from deep within, fighting to stay awake. A yell erupted my from throat, and the Archefire vibrated with urgency. They lay on the silhouette of the pistol pointed at me. With the mere intention of a thought, those strands bunched together and ignited into a brilliant nova of Fire.

The assassin shrieked, and I opened my eyes. She knelt in the dirt, eyes wild with pain. The pistol had exploded in her hand, mangling skin and bone. Crying out for her mother, the woman toppled to her side, started wriggling and kicking up dirt. I felt no pity for her, my murderer.

I summoned the strength to find my feet, stumbled toward her squirming body. One step, two steps, then I toppled. And as I fell, I drove the point of my knife into her ribs. She grunted and gasped, and I drove the blade deeper. Twisted, and pulled it free. The woman's life spilled from her, and she stopped moving.

Collapsing atop her, my thoughts slowed.

I'm dead...

A tear rolled down the side of my face.

Inac...I'm sorry...

A familiar tug at the back of my mind kept me from drifting beyond the brink of awareness. The woman had been infested by Benefactors. I could help one last time. Focusing my wavering attention on the Emergence, I attempted to suppress it.

My own Benefactor had other plans, however.

Weakened as I was, the monster exerted its power over me. Rather than squash the Emergence, it amplified it. Fed on it. Patterns of Archefire warped in the space around me and the Emerging Benefactor. Glowing hot gold cooled to an orange with no vibrancy.

A memory surfaced, dredged up by my Benefactor's instinctual actions. In my right hand, strands of Archefire obeyed my delicate touch, cooled by the Archedark that I controlled in my left. The Dark was invisible, but its effect on the Fire was unmistakable.

Flaring pain ripped me from the memory. Muscles seized. All around me and the dead woman, the cloud of Archemagic strands remained unperturbed. Between our bodies, Fire and Dark melded together, the vibrations slowing as if near to freezing.

The Emergence grew. A man's memories began flickering into my mind—marching from the Burg to the Blight with weapons concealed, a culmination of so much planning, a chance to seize justice—then the Benefactor somehow inverted the flows of Archemagic, and they abruptly stopped.

With no moment of relief, cold pain radiated from my stomach. It intensified with each beat of my heart, which in turn quickened its rhythm. I opened my mouth to scream, but instead sucked in the biggest gasp in my entire life.

The last time I remembered gasping like that was...when I returned from the dead.

My hands pressed against the wound, where it should have been. It was gone. Wet blood coated my hands, the only thing convincing me of what just happened.

Pushing myself from the dead woman, I—

I froze. I was atop a dead *man*. His thick beard evidently hadn't been combed for several years, judging by the debris tangled in it. He was muscular, but no. No, there was no way I had mistaken this man for the woman who approached me. She had blonde hair, wore a ratty leather vest. This man's beard was reddish-brown, but he was bald beneath the cap that had fallen from his head, and he wore a torn shirt stained with sweat, and soiled by both our blood.

But his hand was mangled from the weapon that exploded.

I scrambled to my feet as Inac arrived. He opened his mouth and began to say something, then rapidly cut off as he looked upon the same thing I did.

"You saw that?" I asked, voice shaking nearly as violently as my limbs.

"Yes," Inac confirmed. "A Paceeqi woman attacked you. You fought back with Archefire and finished her with a knife." My friend sounded morose recounting the events, as though it were *my* corpse emptying itself of blood at our feet. But he confirmed that what I saw had really happened. I wasn't insane.

At least, not completely.

"Changing appearance like that..." I looked to Inac searching for an answer. "Can that be done with Archefire?"

The mage managed a forced chuckle but couldn't be bothered to add any humor to it. "No, I think not. I sensed no perturbations of the Fire around the woman."

I was running out of explanations, so my mind grasped for even the most improbable. We discerned no Benefactors, the obvious possibility, and the next best thing was the Fire. It had astounded me in many ways lately, and there might be things even Inac didn't know about. Did he feel the siphoning of life from the dead man into my own body? *That* had touched the Fire, in subtle ways I couldn't begin to describe. What Archemagic was that?

"Inac, what does the Dark feel like?"

"Now, you want to discuss this?" Inac glanced at the Council Hall, where all five Seats of the Hall stood watching the spectacle in the full light of the Brightdaughter's noon. I set my jaw.

Let them see I'm not so easily disposed of.

I grabbed Inac's arm, and his attention. "When the Dark is used, how do the threads of Fire change?"

My Sage pursed his lips. "Now is not the time for us to speak of this. We must get inside before any of that mob return."

Return and see this mess.

The entire crowd had fled at the sound of gunfire, leaving Inac standing beside me in the middle of an empty square with a dead man at our feet. A dead man whose blood covered my front and who had been disguised by a Benefactor's Aura. An Aura that neither Inac nor I could sense.

If there was any light in this dark moment, it was that I discovered I had a way to heal myself from the brink of death.

I just had to murder someone to do it.

I wiped a hand over my face and shouted over my shoulder, "Open the gate!"

"Sir." Someone tapped me on the shoulder, and I spun in alarm, only to find a Nerve waiting with stiff-backed posture. Over his shoulder, the gate was already open, though I hadn't heard its creak.

"What's your message?" I asked.

"No message. Just awaiting your command, sir."

I blinked. In some ways, Ulken had them trained well. "Get this body to the mortuary. Send word to Arza to meet us there immediately."

The Nerve took off at a run back toward the Agency, and shortly afterward, two crimson-coated technicians rushed out to retrieve the body. Inac and I followed them inside, all the while I could feel the judging eyes of the Council Hall on my back.

CHAPTER NINETEEN

Without Hesitation

Lightmother's tits and Darkfather's balls
Slapping reverberations fill these halls
Entwined in the sheets, my ear at the door
"O Father, O Father, please give me some more"

—*Verse from It Takes Two*

Standing with her fist raised, ready to knock on the ornate door in the center of the Radiant Palace, Lorelay hesitated.

She had already spent several days garnering strange looks in the palace, trying to play nice with the ladies of the court, and, Lightmother help her, attempting some politicking. All her efforts had done little more than confirm she was swimming in waters too deep for her to comprehend. A lyre to pass the time would have been welcome but for her proximity to Vos' nobility limiting her repertoire to only the Twelve Songs. Yet, without musical outlet, the waiting for Vinlin's summons quickly became unbearable.

Standing at the door to the Bright Prince's private audience chamber, she wondered whether she was merely dooming herself to sink even further into her troubles.

Oh Lightmother, what am I doing?

The colors of the Church of Light coated the door red and gold against a backdrop of lightwood brown. Swirling flame patterns were carved into the paneling, giving the door a depth that caught the Brightdaughter's light streaming in from the northeast through stained-glass windows. For all that, it looked more imposing than inviting, not the least because it was flanked by two Paladins staring straight ahead, pretending as if she were not there

Lorelay had come here at Minny's insistence. It was either this or give up and go back to Liwokin, let Grim know she had failed, and wallow in misery until the Benefactors overran the Bright Empire. Put that way, the choice seemed simple. Still, she hesitated before knocking. Simple did not mean easy.

When she finally gathered the courage to knock, one of the Paladins announced the name she had provided. "Lorelay, Your Radiance. Ambassador for the Agency in Liwokin."

A scramble of noise ushered from opposite the heavy lightwood door, then the door slowly creaked open, and Vinlin's face poked through the crack. When his eyes landed on her, they took her in from toe to top, and a smile spread across the Bright Prince's face. It lasted only a moment before turned to a look of chagrin, but Vinlin still bid Lorelay enter.

Checking both Paladins to ensure they would not stop her, she entered.

Once inside, Vinlin closed the door behind her, kept his back turned and his head hung low for a moment's breath while Lorelay scanned the chamber. The royal garb Vinlin had worn to the Fire Gardens was strewn on a bench beside a window overlooking the city. The Bright Prince evidently could wait no longer to don more comfortable clothing than she had. His slacks and tunic made Lorelay feel overdressed for...whatever she had come to do.

Truth be told, she still had yet to quite figure it out. Something about Minny's words echoed in her head. The weight Vinlin was holding on his shoulders was enough to crush most men. Eying his weary posture as he braced against the door, Lorelay could believe it.

The Bright Prince straightened his back and turned. "Brightness, I must apologize for my behavior in the Fire Gardens. It was...unbecoming of an emperor."

That...was not what Lorelay had been expecting. *Wool-headed the prince may be, but evidently he can rise to the role of a gentleman.* She remained quiet, a slight quirk to her lips, waiting to see how he would proceed.

He met her silence with his own and took her by the hand instead. She shivered, which she could only assume was a shiver of disgust at having her hand held by the man who was emblematic of the authority she had spent her life fighting. It took every bit of her will not to yank her hand free, but she would not embarrass the man.

Like he embarrassed me. The bitterness in her thoughts subsided with a sigh. *But I need his help.*

And so she let him guide her to the benches by the window. From the plateau upon which the palace rested, all of Vos spread out before them. Buildings of white marble topped with red domes, countless Archemetal spires from which mathemelodians called the faithful to prayer, boulevards full of greenery where young couples read in the shade, busy squares with crowds admiring towering statues of the Lightmother and Brightdaughter. Her home was beautiful to look at.

If only it were as beautiful to live in.

"A stunning view, is it not?" Vinlin asked, gesturing for her to sit.

She turned her back to the city and took a seat on the bench. "The city is stifled. Your people are suffering. They won't be able to survive the Benefactors when they come."

Vinlin pulled his hand free of hers and scoffed. "This again? I've given you—"

"I know," Lorelay interrupted. "I know your thoughts on the matter." She had always been someone who confronted her problems head on, but with the Bright Prince she needed to try a different tack.

"I'm not asking you to change your mind. I...know you're burdened with too many problems already."

"You don't know the half of it." Vinlin crossed his arms, twisting to look out the window, eyes traveling to the harbor overcrowded with ships. A breeze blew in from the south, tousling the wavy auburn hair that fell below his garnet-crested crown. "But I won't bore you with the details. Why have you come to my private chambers, if not to convince me to add more problems to my plate?"

Lorelay gazed out the window to buy time. To add more problems to his plate was exactly why she had come, but after the fiasco in the gardens and the Bright Prince's display of stubbornness, she needed to think of something else. She had promised herself she would not lie, but avoiding the question was not a lie...was it?

"I'm sorry I ruined your mother's dress. It was..." *Not beautiful. Gaudy and ridiculous.* She kept her lips shut tight. "I didn't know it was hers."

"Yes, well..." Vinlin waved an uncaring hand. "It was only a dress. She won't miss it."

Lorelay could tell his throat tightened at that. His eyes glistened, he looked away, and she knew he was trying to hide his tears. Lorelay may have had no sympathy for the Bright Throne, but for the man sitting on it...her nurturing instincts took over. She squeezed his shoulder. "I know what it's like to lose a parent."

She neglected to say that her relationship with her parents was as cold as the abyss, and that she had only lost them because of the Empire's tyrannical, ancient laws. But...that was untrue. She had lost them because of her own actions. She had lost everything, and it was all her fault. Before she knew it, tears filled her own eyes, and she sniffled.

Vinlin's head whipped around at the sound. He opened his mouth, but evidently was at a loss for words. Then his shoulders slumped. "Look what I've done now. Twice I've driven you to tears. Not exactly the image of princely chivalry, am I?"

"No, it's okay." Lorelay wiped a sleeve across her eyes. She tried to steel herself. Sitting here crying about the past was no way to solve their problems. "It's not your fault. I know it must be hard for you dealing with the Church and the succession at the same time."

"The Church? Minny has been wagging her tongue again, has she?"

Lorelay shrugged.

Vinlin chuckled. "Then she must have told you about their insistence that I produce a female heir and abdicate the Throne immediately. No doubt so High Cleric Namravi can guide the throne '*as befits the voice of the Lightmother.*'" His voice took on a mocking tone at the title that drew an unwilling smile from Lorelay.

Minny had mentioned nothing of the Church's demands, but Lorelay was unsurprised. They placed unreasonable demands on the Paceeqi. It only made sense they placed unreasonable demands on Paceeqi royalty as well, the pompous asses they were. They really believed themselves above *everybody.* "The High Cleric isn't even willing to give you a chance?"

"No." The Bright Prince sighed. "And the truth is, I'm not sure she's wrong. I wasn't meant to be the Emperor. My mother should have lived another fifty years. My..." He shook his head. "I haven't been trained for this."

Lorelay snorted. "Do you think anyone is really prepared to become the leader of an empire?"

The prince's flat look told Lorelay she really knew nothing. "From the moment my... mother could speak, the proper words were put in her mouth. From the moment she could read, she was instructed from the Book of Light. She was born to lead the Empire. I was born to...I don't know. Watch from the parapets."

To live a life of luxury. Pampered. Never wanting for anything. Somehow, he made that sound like such a miserable existence.

"Saying what they demand you say, reading only what they allow," she said. "Does that really sound like a good life?"

"No, which only further proves I'm unsuited for this role."

Lorelay sprung to her feet, suppressing a groan. "It proves that you're *perfect*. Look, I already told you Paceeq is withering under the old ways that your mother, and her mother, every mother before her had to uphold. But the world is changing."

She looked out the window, searching for something she had seen upon arriving in the city. When she found it, she pointed. A moving plume of light-gray smoke dissipated above the conjoined Vosian residences at the foot of the plateau.

"See that? A steam carriage. Something that didn't even exist before I left the country. I had never even seen one until I got to Liwokin. Their harbor is *full* of steam-powered boats. Archemages are using the holy Fire to carry barrels of stinking *fish* across the Empire."

"Feeding those in need is a tenet of the Book of Light," Vinlin recited as if that were an argument. She had hardly known the man existed until bumping into him in Lawiko, but she knew for certain he was the most stubborn person she had ever met. He had no idea what he was even arguing *against*.

"My point is that the Church needs reforms."

"As I am painfully aware...but how am I supposed to reform an ancient institution on my own?"

Lorelay grinned. She had him. "You don't have to do it alone. I can help." The Agency was all about solving problems, and Vinlin had more problems than she knew what to do with. If she could prove that she was a useful ally, perhaps she could win his support against the Benefactors. It was genius!

"You would do that?" Vinlin said, wide-eyed. He looked like his dreams had just come true.

"Without hesitation," Lorelay declared, full of pride at how deftly she had navigated the situation. She even got a strange urge to tell *Minny* of all people. She barely knew the old woman, but Lorelay knew she would be pleased to hear what she had accomplished.

Things are finally going my way.

Right up until Vinlin wrapped his hands around the small of her back and leaned in for a full-lipped kiss. Lorelay practically broke her back she leaned away so hard, and she wriggled free of the Bright Prince's grasp.

"What are you doing?" she demanded.

Vinlin's face with the image of shock. "I don't understand. You said you would help me. With someone as strong-willed as you for my Empress, we can take on the Church toge—"

"*Empress?*" Lorelay gaped. "What makes you think I *want* to be Empress?"

She fumed. He was simply trying to *court* her once more.

Darkfather, I'm such an idiot! was the mildest of self-disparagements that passed through her mind. As always, she had royally screwed up. She had completely misread the situation. Vinlin had only one thing on his mind, only one purpose she could serve. One problem she could solve for him: producing heirs. That was all she was good for. Lorelay even believed it—nothing else in her life had ever gone well. Vinlin was destined to be an awful Emperor, but Lorelay was destined to be an awful *person*.

The thought of it was too much to bear, and the idea birthing children for the Bright Throne filled her with such disgust she ran from the room before...before she what? Before she vomited in his royal chamber? Before she punched him square in the face? She just had to get out of there.

Storming away from the Bright Prince was becoming a habit for Lorelay, but it was a habit she intended to snuff out quickly. She could stay in the Radiant Palace no longer.

Benefactors, Vos, the whole Bright Empire be damned to the abyss. Lorelay had had enough of this. She was *done*.

CHAPTER TWENTY

Which Fire

...demonstrated that the organism responds very differently to Fire and Dark. How did the Head's mage come to possess what Silani's guilds so closely guard?

—Note scribbled in a secret chamber

The body on the slab was only the body of a man. A man who I had killed. He had attacked me, but it wasn't a fair fight. He was only a man, and he didn't know he was fighting a monster.

If it were fair, I would be dead.

Instead, I was looking down on his blood-drained face less than a span after recovering from a shot to the gut. That pistol of blue-gray metal lay beside the assassin's body. Even with Reed's gift, his efforts had almost been enough. If he had aimed higher, at my head, I would be the one laid out in the mortuary. There was no coming back from that. I looked down at the blood on my hands, covering my shirt and coat.

"Liwo from the Blight." My voice croaked wretchedly. "Head of the Agency." *Benefactor,* I reserved for myself. "Our blood is the same."

I laid a finger on the pistol, resurfacing a memory where I looked down upon a crate full of the mysterious weapons. It was clear to me what that memory was. Not a memory at all. What I had seen was the preparation for this protest, *as it was happening.* It made no sense to me. Such a thing wasn't possible.

Once again, I reached a vantage point from which I could look back and say, "I truly knew nothing." Benefactors were a continuous source of these surprising viewpoint shifts. Changes in perspective that showed me how far I had to go. That was a familiar feeling from my days as a bounty hunter. Rather recent days, I reflected, no matter how distant they might seem.

Every time I received a bounty, the hunt began in the same way. Asking questions. Which direction did he travel after robbing you? Had you seen the bounty in your district before the incident? Have you seen him since? Learning enough to establish a baseline, probing at the deeper questions. What districts was the target known to frequent? Who were the target's associates? Who was this person, really?

Always questioning, trying to learn about the target. The bounty dictated what streets I staked out, what innkeeps I questioned. But leads were rare. Days could pass without a hint of the bounty's location. When I got one, I had to pounce on the opportunity before it washed away.

The Benefactor in my head had just given me a lead, a chance to better understand it. It had changed its behavior, or rather, expanded it.

Seeing through the eyes of other Liwo as the events are happening... Darkfather...

Ulken would have used that power to spy on the Council and the Gild, tying his sickening knot of corruption ever tighter. I could use it for nobler purposes. Searching for Prost within the city, to bring him to account. Watching for clues about the Benefactor that disguised the assassin in the square.

But should those visions be used at all?

It came from a Benefactor, the very monster I fought to eradicate from the world. I never asked for Reed's power. I wanted to let it die with me. It was driving me to the brink of madness. Tempting me to be more like Ulken. Tak's words surfaced unbidden.

Ulken is much like you, I should think.

Hearing those words raised my blood pressure. Tak spoke the truth. Like Ulken, I recognized the benefits inherent to Reed's gift.

It had just saved my life. Again. And I was the only one capable of preventing Emergences within Liwokin from spreading out of control. Since I was stuck with the power, it made sense to use it while I could. Then maybe, one day, Arza would discover a way to rid me of the monster in my head.

"I am glad you see it this way, Grim," Inac said.

"See what? What way?" Lightmother, was I distracted again?

Arza tromped in through the open door, two technicians trailing behind her. "I was about to ask the same thing. What are you two whispering about here in the dark?" She lifted a palm and the crematorium ignited, bathing the mortuary in golden light and skin-wrinkling heat. Broken concrete, shattered glass, and chunks of wood still lay scattered across the floor from Cavern's break-in. "Never mind. What did you call me down to this mess for? Waking a slumbering Ayeiri woman is not done lightly."

"Sorry," I said, and gestured at the dead assassin. "I wouldn't have called for you immediately if it wasn't important. This man may have a new type of Benefactor in him."

Arza eyed me skeptically through spectacles, then turned to the body. "What makes you say this?"

"It showed a behavior we haven't seen before. This man tried to assassinate me, disguised as one of the protesters."

"Protest?" Arza asked, bleary-eyed. "I could sleep through a howling sandstorm back home. What were they protesting?"

I raised an eyebrow. She was more interested in the protesters than the fact that I had narrowly avoided assassination? "Me," I said, and sighed. If Arza was going to be able to help, she couldn't be kept in the dark. I could trust her. Couldn't I? The words were in my throat, but desperately tried to crawl back down.

Start with the easy bit. The part everybody already knows.

"You know I killed the last Head, right?"

"Of course. It is the only way to become Head, it says it right in our bylaws."

I breathed a laugh. If I could ever get rid of Jacquin, all his expertise was matched right here.

"You don't know everything though," I said. "And you need to. If you don't know the whole story, you'll never solve this problem."

You'll never cure me of this madness.

Inac gave me a questioning look. "Are you sure about this?" it asked.

You already know I am.

The lead mortician studied me, pursed her lips. She gestured to the two technicians behind her, waved them out of the room. "Leave us." Only when they had gone did she hop up to sit on the slab beside the assassin's body. She took up the pistol and examined it, checked the ammunition scattered on the table—one of those casings had been spent, the one that emerged from my body after the Dark healing. "Strange...these patterns in the Fire...may I take this to study?"

"Keep it. Better load it, too," I told her. "By the end of this, you might want to use it."

Then I told her the whole story. How Ulken turned his wife into the first Benefactor. How she tried to take her own life when she felt the organism warping her mind, changing her. Reed had been witness to that, and she put everything she'd gone through in a letter addressed to him. He read it every day as he worked to stop Ulken from using the Agency as a tool to search for the power he was promised by Prost.

When Arza asked, "What was the power he was promised?" I knew I had to tell her the truth. She had to be let in, to know what I had become.

"The power to see through the eyes of others, viewing their memories as if they were my own. To shape reality as you see fit, Reed told me." I sighed. Best to get it over with. "The power that is now mine." I waited for her reaction. And waited. Inac coughed, and I could tell he was eager to say something. But I shook my head.

Let her process this. It must be a great shock.

"This explains some things," Arza said. "Such as your episode in the courtyard."

I nodded numbly. "I felt the Emergence of a new Benefactor. Had to be."

That was it? *This explains some things?*

"How he became an Archemage," Inac put in.

"And how you found Yezna's chamber," Arza finished.

"Yezna's chamber?" Inac asked. "She is alive?"

"Oh, you did not know this?" Arza looked from Inac to me, made an apologetic gesture.

"No," I said, "this is good. We shouldn't be keeping secrets from one another. Yes, Yezna is alive. Arza is studying her to find a cure for the Benefactors."

"You speak of it like an illness," Inac said, then scrunched his mouth in consideration. "A cure for Benefactors... A cure for the madness in your head."

"Well, I don't know if *madness*—" I spluttered.

Darkfather. It's like he knows my thoughts.

"I suppose so, yes..."

"Good," Arza said, "because you need help. Even Archehealing is useless here. I've tried to use it to eliminate the Benefactors on a sample of Yezna's flesh."

"You're taking her *flesh*?" She told me her experiments would be humane.

"Only small samples. She feels nothing, no pain."

"No," I said as soon as the words were out of her mouth. No pain? Tak had thought the infested Peeker called Pinch felt no pain during his probing. He had been torturing the thing. "Don't make that mistake. Don't assume anything. How can you be sure she feels no pain?"

"I can show you."

I rubbed my eyes. "Tomorrow. Focus on this now."

Arza nodded, hopping off the table and attending to the body. "It is fine, really. Her flesh is replenished and reinfested each time. Brand new, like nothing happened."

"Replenished...how?" Inac asked. He stood beside the assassin's body on the opposite side of the table from me and the lead mortician.

Arza nodded down at the corpse, then to a bloody hatchet on an adjacent slab. "He will serve."

Inac looked like he was going to be ill.

"We need you to study his Benefactors," I said.

"Most of his body is not infested. Only the head. The rest can be put to better use."

She started patting the body down like she'd done it a thousand times, then pointed at Inac. "Help me, will you?" She grinned and added, "You are my technician now, yes?"

"Umm," Inac mumbled, but with Arza's persistence, he had no choice but to help her turn the body over. A new spurt of blood pumped from the wound I'd dealt him, and Inac jumped backward. He still ended up with a red spatter on the fringe of his blue robe. That set him mumbling even more. But when Arza told him to start undressing the body, he followed her lead.

"What is this?" she said, followed by two tiny glass clinks. She held a razor thin needle, shattered in two. Within the crystalline sticks sat a glass teardrop with a wispy tail, thin as spider's web.

My eyes nearly popped from my head. "Druid's Tears?" Inac said it at the same time, and we looked at each other with mirrored shock.

"How did an assassin come to possess one of those?" Inac asked.

How can we come to possess more?

Those toxics would prove invaluable in combating the Benefactors. "I need you to find the answer to that question, my friend. You know what they could mean."

Inac gave an affirmative grunt, then turned to leave. Arza's voice pulled him back.

"Look here." She pointed at the tip of one broken needle. A few specks of faint red dotted the last finger's width of the Tear. "And this." She held up the man's bloody arm—mostly from the mortal wound I dealt him. Almost lost in that sticky scarlet coating was a soaked-through bandage, crudely tied. "He already used one."

"What does that mean?" I mused. A strange Aura we couldn't discern, and Druid's Tears, meant to suppress Auras... I suddenly felt very weary. All of these threads. It was too much to manage.

"I do not know, but it could be significant."

It was *all* significant. That was the problem. There was no way to narrow down the most important, to decide which fire needed putting out first. How had Ulken done it? A flash of his memory appeared in my mind.

This functioned only because of her.

Ulken used her to dampen the spirits of the Agents, to control us. I would have to find a way to run the Agency without her. She was not a tool. She was alive. I wouldn't become like Ulken.

Even if I wanted to, her Aura had disappeared.

Something about that touched another thought in my mind. Her Aura had disappeared... The Aura that cloaked the assassin could not be detected. Was Yezna's Aura influencing the infested outside the Agency tower? I had seen the first man, whose gun exploded in his hand, nearby to the headquarters as well.

I sucked in a breath. That was another assassination attempt. *Two in a row. Will I be so lucky as to survive a third?*

Anger flared, and I slammed my fist on the stone slab. *Why* did they want me dead so badly? I only wanted to help them. Darkfather, I *accepted* this role only because I wanted to do some good for Liwokin, the Blight included. Lightmother knows I didn't need the headache.

"Are you well, Grim?" Arza asked. It was a perfunctory question, as though she just needed the information to update her records. Inac, on the other hand, conveyed the exact opposite in nothing but a look.

"I'm...fine, yes. Just tired. Arza, there may be some connection between this man and Yezna."

"A connection of what sort?"

I shook my head. "I don't know. Just keep it in mind." I furrowed my brows looking at the assassin. Why? Or perhaps the better question was...who?

Who sent you?

A difficult question to answer given how many factions had cause to kill me.

The broken iron door squeaked on its hinges as a man rushed into the room. I started, but it was only a Nerve in neat white and gold.

The moment his lips moved, I interrupted, "Don't even tell me you have news. I'm going to bed, it'll wait until tomorrow."

"I'm afraid it can't wait, sir." The Nerve held out a letter sealed with the stamp of the Liwokin Council.

CHAPTER TWENTY-ONE

New Generation

The Queen of the Peeker Colony possesses no name; she is simply known as the Queen. As was the Queen preceding her, who birthed her in an egg much in the way of a common swallow.

—Page 9, Institute of Biotism Peeker Compendium, Vol. I

"Human friends of the Aerie!" eight Peeker criers shouted in unison. "The Queen has summoned thee, one and all, to witness the coming generation. Gather thyselves in the Audience Chamber 'ere the mountains shadow the harbor and hear the Collective speak."

With that, the Peekers dispersed and left the human denizens of the Aerie to discuss among themselves. About time. Garret had been sitting on the Half-Blind Eye's information about a second Skardwarf in the Mounds too long. No way past the Soldiers guarding the mountain tunnels but a summons from the Queen, which Sentyx told him was coming soon. Since then, they'd waited and continued increasing Sentyx's profile in the Human Aerie.

"Thought we'd get a personal invite, at least," Garret said to Sentyx.

"Strange words," Sentyx said.

Garret nodded in agreement. "Not half so strange as the reaction."

"No reaction."

"Exactly." Garret turned to a Lawi family. Husband, wife, and daughter, all just sipping soup quietly at the table next to theirs. "Does the Queen make pronouncements often?"

"Don't reckon she does," the man said, and slurped his soup loudly. "I remember one other time. Back when I was a boy. Why?"

The fact he's lived here his whole life explains at least half the strangeness.

"Where's the commotion?" Garret asked. "The uproar? A once-in-a-lifetime invitation to hear the Queen, and it seems no one has any interest in going."

The husband and wife shared a glance, then shrugged. "Figure we'll go. See what all the fuss is about."

"What fuss?" Sentyx asked.

The girl had to be no more than eight or nine years of age. She beamed at Sentyx. "You're a funny Peeker."

"I am no—"

"Aye, he sure is," Garret interjected. "And he has to go to bed now. Say good night, Sentyx."

Sentyx's chest rumbled for a long while. Probably struggling to understand that Garret didn't want him scaring this little girl. He got there eventually. "Good night."

Garret started for the Nectar Hall's exit. "You've got a lot to learn about kids."

"Yes."

"Rule number one: Don't traumatize them saying you're a monster from their nightmares."

"I am no monster," Sentyx said in as close to a whisper as Garret had ever heard from a Skardwarf.

"Aye, I know."

Most so-called monsters were just animals. Big, scary, but simple to understand. Trust them to do what they must to survive. No compunction about killing, eating babies. Cubs and chicks eaten by the thousands. Garret first started studying the beasts of the stormjungle to avoid sliding down their gullets. Only afterward did he begin to understand the complex beauty of nature.

But people, well...they were worse than monsters. They'd kill babies just as quick but come up with a reason why *you* were wrong trying to stop them. Turn on you after you helped them, just so they could have a bigger slice of meat. A person was practically defined by betrayal. Life's nothing more than a list of broken promises. Either hunt or be hunted.

There's more subtlety to this world than just predators and prey. The voice in Garret's head came out of nowhere. Made his neck ache, until he cracked it. He narrowed his eyes at the familiar voice. Wasn't his own.

"You're not a monster," he told Sentyx, and even half believed it. "The real monsters are the ones infesting everyone's head. Including our Agency's."

Including my own. Garret's thought was filled with dread. He had as much an idea how to get out of that bind than an azear cub in the jaws of a daggerclaw.

After a long silence making their way from the Human Aerie to the Peeker tunnels proper, Sentyx added, "And Peekers."

"What's that?" Garret had forgotten what they were talking about, too occupied with thoughts of organisms squirming around in his brain. Something about monsters? "Peekers aren't so bad." He eyed a Pair that strolled past in the tunnels chittering to themselves.

As animals went, Peekers ranked among Garret's favorite. The more time they spent here discovering how they behaved, the more he liked them. Once, he would've said he never met a Peeker he didn't like. Until Pinch came around. Bleeding Benefactors ruined everything.

"Weren't so bad," he corrected as they reached the two Soldiers barring their way forward.

Beyond them lay the Peeker Queendom, the Colony. The Mounds in all their glory. Garret's mind filled with questions. So many answers lay inside. He could recite an entire dissertation for the Institute.

He spat, and the Peeker guards cocked their heads. The Institute had already betrayed him. They didn't care about biotism anymore, only pleasing the Empire's lackeys. Garret didn't give a Darkfather's wee dick about the Empire or the Institute. He would keep what he learned of the Peekers to himself. Use it to stay alive. Use it to catch his prey.

He's here. Garret affirmed the knowledge to himself, letting it settle like a weight in his chest. He'd been sharpening his knives each night. The time for killing was near.

"Audience Chamber," Sentyx said, and the guards cocked their heads again, like confused wolf cubs. They looked at each other, then back to Sentyx, clicking their mandibles. "Where?"

"No need." Garret didn't slow. The Peekers paid him no mind, still studying the Skardwarf before them. "I know my way around. That map..."

When he pictured the chaotic carving, an expansive hazy image flooded his mind. He couldn't have drawn it, couldn't have explained it. But Garret understood how to follow it.

"Hurry up, Sentyx. Brightdaughter rides low today."

The Skardwarf worked his way up to a run as though rushing into battle. Garret had seen the same in the Shaded Grounds. He kept ahead of Sentyx with a light jog. Unstoppable once they got going, but at least he could keep away from a Skardwarf if it ever came to that.

The tunnels wound their way through the mountain in natural curves, lit only by phosphorescent green fungus and spores. Peekers poured out of each intersection in droves, all heading the same direction as Garret. A blind man could have followed the commotion, mental map or not. The tunnels were wide and tall, allowing for ample Peeker traffic, widening further as they approached the Audience Chamber.

Ahead, a Pair of Peekers spotted Sentyx and Garret, and started against the current. Navigated through the press of bodies effortlessly. Garret raised his eyebrows, impressed. Felt to him like the walls were closing in, so many abyss-damned Peekers were on the march. They were fast, too. Overtaking him and Sentyx like the Skardwarf was a rock in a raging river.

The Pair reached him and matched Sentyx's pace. Speaking as one, they chimed, "Garret! Sentyx! This one is called Tunnel."

Garret craned his neck. Genuinely couldn't tell them apart. "Which one?"

"This one," they both said. Then one spoke alone, antennae fluttering. "This is the flesh that traveled with you from Liwokin."

"And what's your name?" Garret asked the other.

"This one, humans have called Tunnel," it responded. "The human's questions are strange. It traveled with this one on a Colony ship."

"Right..." Garret didn't understand yet, but he would. Was language a branch of biotism? He supposed so. Like a terrorbeak's mating cry, it gave insight into the animal's behavior.

"Garret and Sentyx almost missed the proclamation," the Tunnels said. "Where are the other humans?"

"Eating soup," he said with a grimace. "What's this all about?"

Tunnels shook their heads in synchrony. "This one cannot speak the words of the Queen without command. Garret must wait to satiate its curiosity."

"Fine. But what do you mean we almost missed it? We came as soon as you called. Sentyx isn't *that* slow."

If Garret thought they were beating the rush, he was wrong. The Audience Chamber was a vast cave centered on a podium of rock that rose ten paces from the ground. The size of the space impressed Garret by itself. But he was in awe. The chamber *swarmed* with Peekers.

Not just on the floors, gathered in a seething crowd of chittering chitin. On the ceilings and walls too. Stuck on with their resin or dangling from thick, gooey strings. The clicking that comprised their conversation was bad enough, nearly deafening. But the squishy, oozing squelches of Peeker resin being newly excreted was too much for Garret. Disgusting.

But he couldn't look away. He had never seen so many of the creatures. Suspected no one alive ever had. Certainly not the Institute which claimed their population at ten thousand. He was witness to twice that many, easily. In their multitude, he spied no other humans.

And the only Skardwarf around is breathing his foul air down my neck.

"By the abyss," he muttered, and Sentyx grunted in return. "Prost would have an easy silhouette to spot in *any* other place. If you see him, tell me."

He put his Ekoan ranger training to work scanning for targets, set his eyes to searching every crevice cloaked in shadow. Ulken's advisor would want to stay out of sight. Working behind the scenes, as usual. It's what Garret would do.

And so he did. Found a little nook where the phosphorescent blues and greens didn't reach, and a tall wedge of stone gave him a vantage over the crowd. Sentyx stood near the wall and blended in.

He's bleeding camouflaged and doesn't even know it. Lucky bastard.

Even with his keen sight, he'd never spot the Skardwarf he was warned about. How by the abyss had that half-blind deserter managed it? Worse, how was *Sentyx* going to see him? Garret had only told his fellow Finger he got a tip about Prost, including no details about a second Skardwarf. That plan fell apart quickly. He would have learned a lot watching Sentyx's reaction to another of his kind.

Oh well. Time to focus on Prost and the Queen anyway. In fact, Garret was growing impatient waiting for the Queen's address. He was growing bleary eyed scanning thousands of Peekers.

Most were the Workers seen throughout the Bright Empire. Quite a few others were Builders, and he spotted several dozen Soldiers in the mix. Beyond that, however, were variants in Peeker morphology he never would have dreamed of. Eight-legged Peekers. A handful with horns jutting from their wide, flattened heads.

Across the chamber, a particularly brutish set of eight stood facing outward from the stone podium, like Soldiers but with even more exaggerated proportions. An honor guard for the Queen? They had four arms. Two up top that would give the strongest Paceeqi a good arm wrestle, while the two below jutted from their torsos and ended in sharpened blades.

Suddenly, all twenty thousand of the animals turned toward the podium. Silence fell, eerie in a cavern so crowded. Garret's gaped as the Queen of the Peekers descended from the ceiling. She was thrice the size of the soldiers guarding the tunnels. Four Peekers clung to the four uselessly small legs on her inflated abdomen, excreting a great stretching bulk of resin lowering her down.

The material grew thin and snapped just as she reached the podium rock, and she fell. The Queen struck the rock with a thud, pulverizing those who had borne her weight. Their guts launched over the Queensguards and splashed the front row to the spectacle, but neither the crushed nor the splattered reacted in any way.

At once the din of chittering rose to a crescendo, and Garret spat. Bleeding disgusting. Sounded like applause for the gruesome scene. But as quickly as the thought passed, the quiet resumed.

The Peeker Queen spoke. "The sky patterns herald the Turn. The stars call thee home." Her words rang understanding in Garret's mind, but his ear could comprehend none of it. "This duty is thine: to seed the new generation."

Forty thousand mandibles snapped together in a rhythmic pattern. *Clack. Clack. Clack.*

The pounding beat continued as the address went on, the voice in Garret's head taking on a fanatical fervor.

"She comes. She comes. The new Queen awaits the ceremony. With thy bodies shalt thou give her succor."

The clacking grew louder. Louder. Until with the next words, it ceased all at once.

"But our eternity shan't end," the Peeker Queen declared. "Ere the end, we discovered salvation."

Garret tensed. Something was wrong. A wave of confusion spread through the masses, he could practically smell it. He eyed the exit, started sliding toward it in case they needed a quick escape. Then froze as he caught more movement above the podium.

Two more Peekers descended on their stringy resin. They carried a corpulent man with a dark velvet coat that hung past his waist, giving his shape the impression of a squat mountain. Oddly similar to Skardwarves, Garret noted. Bald as a Skardwarf too, as seen when the man doffed his wide-brimmed cap to wipe his forehead with a handkerchief.

The description was a fit. Prost was here.

Chittering erupted once more. Not the calm cadence of reverence toward the Queen. No, this was the verge of panic.

"The Eye was right," Sentyx rumbled.

"Aye." Garret regretted leaving his bow in his quarters. From so close, he could have put an arrow through the big man's eyes and ended this whole ordeal. Instead, he slid back into the shadows. The prey must never know of the hunter's presence.

Prost dismounted the Pair of Peekers and stood by the Queen's side. Looking as smug as Garret always pictured him. Calm too, leaning casually on a bluish metal cane. He lit a cigar, puffed on it and blew out gray clouds as he surveyed the crowd. Nodded to himself in some private satisfaction.

"This Colony shall weather the Dark storm," the Queen said. "Lent aid by humans. And Burners."

A boulder fell from the ceiling and slammed into the podium at full speed. Struck like a hammer on an anvil. A cloud of dust billowed out. Shards of stone rained on Peekers.

Then the boulder stood up. A Skardwarf.

Sentyx let out a prolonged growl. "Cavern."

"The one from Reed's Woods?" A Finger. And Sentyx's brother. Garret edged a step farther from the Skardwarf beside him.

Sentyx grunted a yes.

Garret's eyebrow raised. He'd expected denial, not honesty. He was surprised.

Not half as surprised as the Peekers. They were pushed into full-blown panic with the Burner's arrival next to the Queen. Until a pulse of soothing passed through Garret's mind, and all quieted down. He almost gave in to the calm himself, let his guard down. But he knew what he just felt.

An Aura.

"You too?" he asked Sentyx.

Sentyx didn't respond. His eyes were locked on Cavern like a wolf hound.

"Persist in the crossing as tradition demands," the Queen continued, talking in Garret's mind like a Benefactor, "In an era to come, two Colonies shall Pair. This too becomes thy duty. Now witness. The egg of life comes."

"You might want to step back," Prost's voice reached Garret. He was talking to the Skardwarf.

Cavern was staring at the Queen. "I face into—"

The Peeker Queen screamed. A wail to make a man's ears bleed. She laid back, and her abdomen began to distend. Growing, growing until it looked ready to burst. The whole Colony trembled and writhed, sharing in her agony. Then burst it did. Guts showered a dozen Peekers before her, and they began shoveling it between their mandibles.

Garret put his hand to his mouth and gagged. But the display was far from finished.

The Peeker Queen folded her torso forward, digging into her own gaping wound with scissoring mandibles. Her head delved deeper into her own body, until she emerged, slime-covered and gripping a spherical, translucent-red egg. It dripped with viscera until the Queen gently placed it down in a pool of resin pumped out by the Peekers who ate her innards. The egg safely ensconced, the Peeker Queen collapsed onto her back. Her legs curled up, twitching.

"She's dying," Garret said. Despite proving herself so grotesque, he felt sorry for her. A one-of-a-kind creature, life draining before him. A light extinguished.

Prost dropped his cigar and put it out under his boot. Stepped closer to the fading Queen and held his hand out, palm down. His fingers flexed, and the room went cold. The steady phosphorescence flickered, and slowly, the Queen's ruined abdomen came together like sludge. Folded in on itself until she was back to normal size.

Her thin legs flexed, their claws squeezing closed. "We live. This Colony shall sur...vive..."

Taking that as their dismissal, thousands of Peekers poured out of the cavern's many exits. Garret heard quiet words whispered. Preparation. New generation. Princess. The Turn. He couldn't make dark or light of it.

Prost tapped his cane twice on the rock then took a deep breath, a satisfied grin spreading wide across his face "As sure as the freezing winds. All too easy. Grab her."

Cavern grunted and stomped toward the Queen. Took her by the arms and hefted.

The Eevoqian took one last look at the egg of the Princess, chuckled, then waddled out of the chamber. With little apparent effort, the Skardwarf dragged the Queen's near-corpse behind him.

Human, Skardwarf, Peeker. All together on the stage. Garret looked at Sentyx to gauge his reaction.

When he saw none, Garret shook his head. "What in the bleeding dark did we just witness?"

PART TWO

DEMONS

CHAPTER TWENTY-TWO

Swift and Cruel

I sent the remaining test subjects back to their homes as you suggested. Informants will keep an eye on their development, but it would be easier if you told me what you're expecting to see. All we've achieved so far are fragile bodies with broken minds.

—Unanswered letter

I had never seen the Council move so swiftly in my life. I didn't think they had it in them. When trying to schedule that first meeting with them, it had taken days for them to decide which *clerk* to assign to me. Sending messages through the clerk was about as slow as two-way correspondence between Liwokin and the Capital in Paceeq.

I wonder if they were doing it just to screw with me.

I wouldn't have put it past them, now that I saw how vicious they were.

The dawn bells rang, and I hadn't slept a wink. All night I had stared at the letter, or paced to rid myself of nervous energy, or ruminated about how this was all coming crashing to an end. Knowing that all hopes of reconciliation between the Agency, the Gild, and the Council were dashed.

Here I was, staring at the letter in my office again. Waiting. Desperately hoping and waiting for help. For the one man who might get us out of this.

Darkfather, where was he? It wasn't like Jacquin to make me wait. I had dispatched a Nerve telling him to be in my office at dawn. The Eye had never disobeyed a command before. And on today of all days.

Damn it, I can hardly stand to be around the man. But I need his help.

When he finally arrived, he looked positively morose. His shoulders slumped, his uniform was wrinkled, he hadn't even shaved this morning. Simultaneously, he looked puzzled as he studied the letters in his hand.

"You heard the news?" I asked.

Jacquin looked up at me with sad, round eyes. I took that for a yes.

"How could you have possibly heard the news? I haven't told anyone."

"It's the talk all around the city, sir. They say the Agency's finished, the Council pulled their support." He flinched, evidently at his own thought, because I hadn't moved a muscle. My bones felt cold as ice, keeping me frozen in place. "They say, sir... They said you murdered a protester right in front of the Council Hall, and you're to be hanged."

I slumped down, sank deeper into my chair, and tried to go deeper still. Memories surfaced from the ocean of others inhabiting my mind with me. A boy with his sister's needle mending his broken neck, punished for wanting to prove his worth. A woman disgusted with her husband for letting her children die, for letting them get close to her. A hunter collapsing atop his kills, carcasses he had collected in a single night of revelrous insanity.

Their memories were among the strongest I possessed. The first Benefactors I had encountered and had killed. I could never forget their names. Wyran, Andya, Lomin. They were like close friends. Friends who I had to put down to end their suffering. Their suffering always began with the death of the host when the Emergence transformed them into monsters. Each of them prepared for death in their own way.

How would I prepare for mine? Walking to the gallows, what would be running through my head? I had been so worried about preventing my friends from getting killed, I had condemned myself to death. I suddenly wanted Inac by my side, my oldest friend. His council would be most welcome.

Because I could not go willingly. I *would* not. Not when it risked unleashing new Benefactors on the city. Without me here to squash Emergences as they began, Liwokin would soon suffer the full extent of the scourge. As an already Emergent Benefactor, a rope around my neck might not be enough to kill me, but that wasn't an experiment I was willing to run.

"Is it true, Grim?" Jacquin asked quietly. My eyebrows twitched upward in surprise. Grim? That was the first time he had called me by name. Dropping the title, as though depending on my answer to his question, the Agency already *was* over in his mind. For Jacquin, a man with no purpose but to serve, that would be too much to bear.

"Of course not." I slapped the Council's missive down on my desk. A curl of dust wisped away on the rush of air. "It was in self-defense, Jacquin. An assassin disguised by a Benefactor's Aura shot me, would have killed me too, except..." I looked Jacquin up and down. I couldn't trust him, I knew that. But he did know my secret, and he hadn't told anyone. "Except that my Benefactor healed me...when I killed him."

Jacquin considered that, then gave a sigh of relief. "I believe you, sir."

"Thank you, Jacquin. And you know, I prefer if you call me Grim." I figured a gesture of goodwill wouldn't hurt in keeping the man's loyalty. And if it meant dropping the constant formality, all the better.

"I know, sir," he replied. "But it's in the bylaws. I have to use your title when directly addressing you."

"The damned bylaws again?" I groaned. "Enough with all these rules. This place is about to fall apart, and the bylaws are just hampering us."

"Is that a command, sir? To change the rules? Because they're the only thing keeping this place functioning. I think changing them is likely to do more harm than good. And overseeing the changes are an unneeded distraction."

I wiped a hand over my face. "You're right, of course. What I really need you to do is look into the Council regulations, the laws they recognize for Liwokin. If there's any provision that can get me out of this because my actions were in self-defense, and I can prove that they were, then you need to find it."

Until then, I was going to have to buy us some time, even if that meant putting up a fight.

"We need to close the gates, Jacquin. They're only to be opened if a Hand is returning to headquarters, or anyone else who has my express permission."

"Yes, sir," Jacquin snapped a sharp salute. There was the man I knew. "You're not giving up, that's good news."

If only the good news were ever addressed to me.

All I seemed to get was more information about the multitude of enemies I'd managed to collect. The Council wanted me hanged and threatened to send the militia after me. If they were reinstating the militia, I figured that gave me only enough time for them to enlist enough Liwo to point in my direction. The speed with which they declared their intent frightened me. How quickly could they bring it to fruition?

Meanwhile, the Gild's toleration of me would last until I gave them a firm answer about ending our arrangement. Although, I wouldn't have put it past them to dispense with the niceties and opt for assassination instead. They could install a more malleable Head and wrest control of the city from the Council. The Blight was in an uproar, and Lightmother, I didn't even know why.

We were running out of time before the city descended into open conflict.

Jacquin cleared his throat, and I started. I had forgotten the man was there.

"Am I...needed here, sir?"

I shook my head. "Get me out of this mess, Jacquin. And hurry."

Jacquin sped from the room before the word 'hurry' finished escaping my lips. I grinned. The Eye unnerved me with his subservience, but he was always reliable.

Reliable, yes, but even he may not be fast enough.

I needed more help, and only two names came to mind. Arza and Inac. What was my Sage going to do? Teach me how to throw a fireball and burn down the Council Hall? I needed his advice as a friend, and soon. But I didn't want another lecture on avoiding the requests sent in by needy Liwo. It was petty, but even small problems weighed on me like boulders.

Arza, then. Knowing her, she would have been holed up in Yezna's chamber with the mortuary still under repair. She probably hadn't heard the news. I would have said she might be heartbroken to discontinue her Benefactor research, but her reaction to hearing I had risen from the dead was about as emotional as a distraught Skardwarf.

Passing through the Treasury vault to reach the lead mortician was a sobering experience. Overwhelming emptiness, both emotional and monetary, characterized the space. On the one hand, Yezna's Aura rid me of my worries to some minor degree. On the other, the lack of funds was another reminder of how tenuous the Agency's influence in the city had become.

I found Arza in the middle of an experiment and explained the situation, not entirely sure she was paying attention. Still, it felt good to get everything off my chest at once.

"...and they sentenced me to be hanged in the public gallows," I finished.

"Uh huh." Arza nodded.

She poked at Yezna's back with a little syringe that operated using a tight-fitting metal plunger instead of her thumb. That was a clever innovation.

"So you've heard the news."

"No. Or, yes. From you. Just now." She deposited the sample she collected onto a flat metal plate on a desk kept pristinely clean. For all that Arza kept her work metaphorically in the dark, the lights she had set up in Yezna's chamber were extremely bright. They required the full attention of an Archemage in the boiler rooms, whereas normally one was enough to illuminate several floors.

Squinting at the bright reflection of those flickering white lights, I wondered if it was a bit excessive. Steam-powered lights always gave me a headache. What was wrong with oil lanterns? And for that matter, did the Archemages even *like* working the boilers? I ought to have visited that floor at some point, to make sure they weren't penned up in some dungeon. That would have been Ulken's way.

And they would keep doing it Ulken's way. Right up until the next pay day arrived and I had no gold to give them.

And you, Arza? Would you keep working on this even without reward? Or is the hunt enough of a reward for you already?

In the time since I had arrived, the lead mortician hadn't pulled her attention away from her experiments once. I knew that feeling well. She was in deep, absorbed into the problem. The problem had *become* her. When I had searched for the Riot's cause beyond the point of reason. When Lomin had dived deeper into his lake than he thought possible, a knife in hand to face the sharp-jawed invader.

But I had beaten a man to death in my hunt for the truth. And Lomin had been killed by that shark, even if he didn't accept it. When you're in the hunt too deep, you don't even see the lines you cross. What was Arza doing?

The blue-gray pistol I had given her caught my attention, lying on the table beside some hastily scrawled diagrams and squares of wrinkled skin labeled with numbers. Watching the lead mortician slice off a new sample of Yezna's flesh, blood dripping down, I recoiled.

"Arza, stop. I told you not to assume that she can't feel it. You don't know what she feels. You can't see..." Strands of Archefire surrounded Yezna, laid across her, as they surrounded and laid across all things. "What I see..." Their radiance was dampened in the space around the Benefactor. Dark magic cast the Aura. "Even I do not understand it..."

But there's something more.

I moved closer to Yezna, a slow step. Closed my eyes to block out the light and to get a firmer sense on the vibrations of Archefire on her skin. The Dark wasn't just dulling the strands of Fire's brightness and slowing their dance. It was drawing it in upon the darkness, twisting the pattern of Archemagic in upon itself. I focused on that twisting, and as if drawn by a magnet, the Benefactor in my head *latched* onto Yezna, and it was like opening a tap on the keg that was her mind.

Her experiences flooded into me. A familiar sensation, like a Deluge from an Emergent Benefactor, but with less ill intent. Different in a more important way, however, was the fact that I saw not her memories.

Through her eyes, I saw myself.

Dancing Dark

Harsh white lights blinded what little sight remained to me. Cloudy. My vision had a layer of fuzz, and my eyeballs no longer moved in their sockets. Those muscles were dead. All my body was dead. Only my mind lived on in the corpse.

It had been this way since I put the knife to my throat and pulled. How many years had I been this way? Or had it only been days? A woman who felt nothing had no use for time. No sense of urgency, no desire. Things simply happened, then periods passed where nothing occurred, until something again broke the spell. Existence continued. Perhaps one day it would not. I cared not either way.

Curious, though. I felt something in this moment. Even in asking these questions, were they not driven by a desire for understanding? Where else could this be coming from than the shaggy man with long black hair that tilted my head back to gaze upon my face. His mind was opaque, unlike the woman's as she moved in silence and cut away my flesh. Her insatiable curiosity did not pain me. It was nothing at all.

He, on the other hand, felt strange...

Was he the reason the thing I became touched no one anymore? No one save his lackey, and only because of her cutting, probing proximity. As I attempted to study the man's blurry face, learn who he was, why did I feel a welling of gratitude? That had come from me, not him. A secondary emotion, an offshoot from the feelings being projected onto me. When had I last felt gratitude?

Ah, of course.

With the answer came recognition.

You are back. But these emotions are unlike you.

Where was the rage? Where was the lust for power and control?

What changed in you, husband?

Ulken flinched back, dropped me. My head bounced against the back of the wooden chair the strange woman had bound me to. It did not hurt, but a flood of horror surged through the bond between my husband and me.

Nothing has changed at all.

Sudden anger came, and Ulken threw something across the chamber. He was acting more himself by the minute. One clear, over-powering thought survived the journey through our bond—a rare oc-currence—resonated in my head.

I am not *Ulken.*

And with a snap and a spark like an elastic band being pulled back in the strands of Archefire, my Benefactor let go of Yezna. I was blink-ing, rubbing my eyes in the corner of the room opposite Ulken's wife.

What the snuff was that?

It felt as though I had siphoned her direct experience into my own. Not just her senses, but her direct thoughts, even her *memories.* She was remembering Ulken, how when he was around, his twisted pleasure echoed between their minds as if they were one. He may have turned her into a monster and used her as a tool to subjugate Liwokin, but he was also the only chance she ever got to experience the emotions she had been stripped of by the organism in her brain.

The only chance...until me.

How had I done that? And why wasn't I feeling her Aura? It was clear from my thoughts—

No, abyss take it—they weren't my thoughts. They were hers.

It took a considerable mental effort not to slip back into thinking of her as me. But it was clear from *her* thoughts, that she still had an Aura. A touch, she called it, and Arza was within it.

"Why did you do that?" the mortician asked, staring dead-eyed at the shattered vial that she had just collected.

I furrowed my eyebrows. Was that what I had flung in my anger? Even she thought of me as no different than Ulken.

"Sorry." I thumbed my eye once more. It still felt like it was blurry, like a residue from Yezna's consciousness. "I've...never done that before."

"Done what? What did you do? All I saw was you touching the Benefactor, then stumbling backwards, before you grabbed the sample right out of my hand and threw it down."

I shook my head. All I knew was that my Benefactor latched onto Yezna, and I viewed the world through her eyes. "It would take too long to explain. But you were right. She doesn't feel pain. I felt it firsthand."

"What are you—"

"Still, you need Druid's Tears, or a Clasform box. Something to protect you from Yezna's Aura. If we're going to survive this, I need your mind in good shape for years to come."

"Mm," she mumbled, noncommittally. She seemed disinterested, as though waiting for me to leave so she could get back to what she was really interested in. Illustrating my point exactly.

"Fine," I said, "I'll leave you to it. But you had better work quickly. It may only be days before there's a rope around my neck."

Days? It could happen within the span.

"Oh, right," Arza said. "I had almost forgotten." She sliced a third sample of flesh from Yezna's body. She probably didn't notice me leave.

I searched for Inac in all his usual locations. His quarters, where he instructed me as Sage in the ways of Archemagic, were empty and quiet. My office—nothing and nobody awaited me save for countless paperwork. Even the fifth floor, where the Organ of Boiling coordinated Archemages to produce the steam that powered our lights. Full of hot air, but no Inac.

By the time I thought to check the common area on the twelfth floor, where he liked to chat with our Fingers, my thighs were burning as though they had been left uncovered in the sun for a long day.

I really ought to install an abyss-damned elevator.

But who would build it? The Blight? The Gild? I trusted neither of them not to cut the rope when I reached the top of the shaft.

The Lightmother spared some mercy. Inac chatted with two other Fingers in the hallway outside the common area. I noticed he kept his tattered robe pulled close, holding it closed with his one hand. He may have been amiable with the two Fingers, but he didn't consider them in his close circle of trust. Only those inside that circle knew what had become of his hand and his abilities.

Both Fingers wore the green uniforms given out in Ulken's days. Since then, the design had been updated to a brighter shade because the Agency had been sourcing dye from the Druid's Enclave. My Hand had inadvertently scuttled that agreement along with the deal to obtain Druid's Tears. So, these weren't the new hires Inac was overseeing. These were old Fingers, rank four. Strong, but they had answered to Ulken, so I was disinclined to trust them.

When I approached, however, both of them snapped to attention and saluted. Inac snorted but added no more. I gave them pointed looks that I hoped said, 'Go away.' Instead, they stood at attention waiting for a command. A bead of sweat dripped down the forehead of one Finger, Paceeqi with long golden hair tied behind his head, and a scar running horizontally below his eyes. The other, an Ayeiri man almost as short as Garret, trembled as if his arm were about to give out. Not exhaustion, I knew, but fear. What danger would my latest command send them into?

Inac's grin reached closer to his ears with every heartbeat that passed. He knew Jacquin was in charge of Benefactor assignments for veteran Hands, and he doled out individual assignments himself.

Realizing there was probably some harebrained clause in their control agreements preventing them from using their own heads, I gave a frustrated growl and said, "You're dismissed, Fingers. I need to talk to Inac."

Both Fingers gave sighs of relief—no monster hunt for them today—and hurried off. If they knew why I had come to find Inac, they wouldn't look half so relieved. I pulled him into a private room—some Hand's private quarters, but none of the five were here.

If the Hand is even still alive.

"Arza is succumbing to Yezna's Aura. She needs help."

Inac raised an eyebrow. "How can she feel the Aura when none of us throughout the Agency feel it. What happened to it?"

"I don't know exactly. It's like the Aura is only present in her room. But even there, I couldn't feel it myself..."

Yezna's thoughts came to me. She was looking at me...wondering if I was the reason no one felt her touch.

"How do you know this?" Inac asked. "Did something happen with your Benefactor?"

"It did... I don't know how to describe it. It was like the Fire and the Dark, they were dancing together. And when I focused on the rhythm of their movements..." I trailed off with a disbelieving laugh.

I used the power Ulken sought.

"What happened, Grim?"

"I saw through her eyes. Not just a memory, but *there and then*."

"The Fire and the Dark, they were dancing." Inac's face scrunched up as it often did when he tried to untangle a mess of thoughts. If it was anything like the knot of confusion in my mind, he would be untangling for some time to come.

I let him concentrate in silence, and as I did so, I noticed something strange about the Archefire strands surrounding Inac's head. They were suppressed and dulled, as though he was using the Dark, though not as dimly as I had seen when interacting with Yezna or the assassin. I didn't want to pry into my friend's wounds, but...

"Inac," I asked carefully, "are you...using the Dark right now?"

He frowned at me. "You know I cannot, Grim. I told to you, they are of the same coin two sides. When one for me vanished, the other left from me as well." His frown turned to curiosity, though. That was a strange question to ask someone out of the blue.

"Sorry, it's just... The Fire around you is being disturbed by something." But if he wasn't using the Dark...perhaps the organisms in his mind were. The sensation was so similar to what I had felt near Yezna. A different rhythm, but a dance all the same. If I concentrated on it...

No.

I was leaning closer unconsciously and stopped myself. I didn't *want* to see through Inac's eyes. His thoughts were his own. I had no place intruding upon them.

As Ulken had no place intruding upon his wife's.

"Never mind," I told him, if only to wipe the worried puzzlement from his face. "What were you doing down with the other Fingers, anyway?"

Inac grinned. "I came to deliver to you the news I *tried* to tell you first, but I could not find you."

Scratching my head, I said, "I couldn't find *you* either." Another problem to solve, creating some way to keep track of where everyone was in the tower. I added that to my mental to-do list, right below *Save the Agency* and *Don't get hanged*. "What's the news?"

"The Druid's Tears," he said excitedly. "I found from where they are coming."

My eyes widened. "Really? That's great news!" *For once.* "And exactly what Arza needs. Make sure she gets—"

"Hold on, my friend. I found from where they are *coming*. We do not have an endless supply of them, only a few samples. Should we not save for our Fingers these Tears, in case another Emergent appears?"

I considered. His reasoning was sound. I wouldn't send my people into danger without some means to protect themselves. But the Agency's Fingers weren't my only responsibility. Every Liwo in the city would benefit from Arza's work.

When she finds a cure, no Finger will need to fight a Benefactor ever again.

Shaking my head, I told him, "They need to go to Arza. Keep following up on that source. If they're not coming from the Pinegrave, I've got an offer to make them."

Inac nodded, but the look on his face told me he wasn't quite as excited about the next part. "It is the Blight. And I do not feel safe there. There is in that distract something strange happening."

"There's *always* something happening in the Blight and feeling unsafe is normal." But Inac had been with me when I defended myself from the cloaked assassin. He could be a target.

"It is not the normal criminality of the Blight, Grim." He tightened his lips, then gave a loud sigh. "The person who gave to me the Tears. I...wanted to hurt him. I recognized in me this thought, and it was not my own..." Inac grunted, then looked me dead in the eye. "I do not know how to explain to you what happened, but I do not want to go back."

A thought not his own... It smelled of Benefactors to me. Looking him square in the eyes, the Archefire strands around him pulsed in their strange rhythm.

"Assign Jacquin to investigate the Tears further. Covertly. No deals with the smugglers." As for the Benefactor, perhaps there was a way to see what he was talking about without him needing to go back. I pursed my lips.

Only if he agrees to it.

A Nerve barged into the quarters before I could say anything. "Sir."

I started. "How do *you* always know where I am?"

"It's our primary duty, sir," the Nerve said, then continued right into her news that sealed my fate.

An army of Archecloaks was at our gate.

CHAPTER TWENTY-FOUR

Harmony at Last

Pity, what happened to the Eevoqians. Seems they never got to make the choice we did. Makes me wonder if their Turn was even harder than ours.

—From the first oral history of Ekohold

"Here, I'll stamp it," Garret said, pulling out the sigil-emblazoned rubber. It showed a portrait of Ulken scowling from atop his tower. Such vanity, but at least it was recognizable. "Something Grim found in Ulken's desk. So he knows it's official."

"You read it." Sentyx handed Garret his report.

"You know those symbols mean nothing to me. Besides, I was at the...birthing ceremony, same as you were. I already know what happened, why would I need to read it? Even if I could."

Was he laying it on too thick? Garret considered. Maybe. Then again, Sentyx rarely absorbed an idea not pounded into his thick head. The Skardwarf wouldn't lie to Grim in his report if he suspected Garret could read. So Garret needed to be sure.

He held the report upside down, made a big show of it. "Aye, nice...blocky scribbles there. How is it, anyway, that a Skardwarf can read and write our language?" Garret folded the report closed. "Your brother teach you that?"

Aye, I know who Cavern is to you. What do you think about that?

Sentyx's face gave nothing away. He just stuck a wad of Peeker resin on the report.

Garret grimaced at the excretion. They'd bought it from the commissary for this purpose, but the amount they saw in there... Garret didn't want to know what other uses the strange people living here found for the vile stuff. Sentyx didn't seem to mind all the residue stuck to his hand. He continued staring blankly at Garret.

As if challenging him. Facing into the wind. Had Garret given himself away with the act? No chance. Skardwarves had no mind for subtlety.

"You don't know either, eh?"

Keep your secrets, then. I'll mine them out eventually.

The Skardwarf had probably spent years learning the human tongue to infiltrate the Empire. Garret knew for a fact Skardwarves had their own language. He'd heard it in Reed's Woods. Grunting, guttural, barking noises, like stone axes chipping away at a boulder. He'd keep his ears primed for those noises again. Case Cavern and Sentyx ever got to talking.

"What are you going to do while I'm gone?"

"Think," Sentyx said, and sat on his cracked bed.

Garret hid his smile. "Right, then. I'm off. Let you know if Grim sent us anything."

The door shut behind him and closed off Sentyx's deep, ponderous grumble.

"Thinking." Garret scoffed. It ought to keep the Skardwarf occupied a good long while. But he believed Sentyx would sit there thinking about as much as he believed the Brightdaughter would wink out of existence.

Instinctively, Garret's feet carried him toward the Peeker Post. He needed scarcely to do more than think the name before its location appeared in his mind. North of the Human Aerie, a passage that would take him toward the other side of the harbor.

Post near the harbor. Very logical, these Peekers. Something for humans to aspire to.

On his way, he passed a window in the cave wall that overlooked the sea. Heat from the Brightdaughter warmed Garret's face. He basked in the comforting sun as his fingers dug into his pockets to retrieve a small lens of Ayeiri make. Circular, small as an Empire star, but crafted by an Archeglazier. Garret used it to study tiny insects in the stormjungles. When he pulled it from his coat and held the lens in the light, a passing Peeker looked at it and hissed.

What's this one's problem?

Garret flashed redirected sunlight at the Peeker, and it scurried away with its Pair.

"Not like I could hurt you with it." The focal point was too close. Perfect for heating up something on the ground or in your hand. Say, a letter sealed with wax.

Didn't take long before the Brightdaughter melted the resin and Garret unfolded the report to Grim. Sentyx's blocky and surprisingly precise handwriting filled the page.

Grim Friend,

We found advisor. Skardwarf travels with him. Cavern. Peeker Queen is injured. In their care. We will secure him.

Face into the wind.

"*Sentyx,* wrote this?" He wouldn't have believed it except for the sign off. But something didn't make sense. "It's all true."

He was puzzled. How could *Sentyx* write so perfectly when Garret couldn't? And why had he told the entire truth, even going so far as to obscure all identities? The two questions were at odds with one another. Why would Sentyx learn Empiric lettering if he wasn't an enemy infiltrating their lands? Why would he be honest with Grim if he wasn't an ally? The knot of suspicion in his stomach had never felt so tangled.

Garret had solved similar dilemmas when he was a bandit in the deep woods. Lot of time to notice contradictions in animal behavior when you wait all day in an ambush nest. It beat pissing and moaning like all the others in his clan. The answer was always to listen and watch more closely. He needed more information to uncover the Skardwarf's secrets.

He melted the Peeker resin, sealed the report, and stamped it with the Agency's sigil once more. Perfect. Like brand new. Garret tucked it away and carried on.

The Peeker Post wasn't far off. Which meant he soon discovered how inadequate his imagination was about the size of the operation. Heard it before he saw it, really. If he didn't remember the map so clearly, he would have found it by the endless chittering and bristling, yelling and stomping.

Peekers in groups of sixteen, by Garret's reckoning, hauled cargo to and from the harbor down a winding path outside. The Hexes, as he named them, returned empty-handed and streamed into a cavernous room, only to emerge later no longer unladen. All so coordinated, never a collision. Garret stood there taking it all in before he realized *he* was the one getting in the way.

Of other humans, of course. They were all jostling in a disorderly queue that ended at a counter with one Pair of Peekers attending. Garret took his place at the end of a line with dozens of people and groaned. This would take some time.

He was in the middle of speculating about the swarm's behavior when the Pair of clerks yelled, "Next!"

About time. You'd think they could spare just one more Pair to help speed things along. Bleeding hundreds of them around.

"Got to get this to the top of the Agency," Garret said, holding out the report. "Fast as you can."

The Pair tilted their mandibled heads in unison, pausing, then taking the paper. "The Lawiko Law Agency, yes, yes. Understood. The next postal ship to Liwokin has been delayed."

"Delayed? How long?"

"Indefinitely."

"*What?*" Garret tried snatching the report back but missed. The Peeker that took it handed it off to another Pair passing by. It disappeared into the mail room. "What if I need to get back? And give me back that letter!"

"If the human must return to Liwokin, it should commission a human-captained ship. These ones can place the letter in the hold of that ship, but it has already been processed and indexed. It will be loaded aboard the next private ship sailing for the city. The Peeker Post can guarantee no dates."

Garret squeezed his fists in frustration. *Stupid animals.* And to think he was just admiring the efficiency of their system. Throwing a fit here would only turn the people in line behind him into a mob after his throat, so he swallowed his complaints.

"Fine. Did anything else come *from* the Agency recently?"

"Yes." The Peekers blinked stupidly.

Garret gritted his teeth. "Can I have it?"

"The shipment has already been claimed."

"By who?" There was no one else from the Agency here, other than the half-blind Eye, and Garret was certain Grim didn't know the deserter.

Unless the shipment didn't come from Grim.

"These ones do not require identification from our clients. These ones can tell the human no name, but one moment." The Pair closed their eyes and shivered. Their mandibles clacked together like hollow wood. "The monitors traced the human's scent to the Queen's Ulterior Stockpile."

The name summoned an image of the map in Garret's mind. Just west of the Human Aerie, not far from where he questioned the

Eevoqian. Garret narrowed his eyes. Was that a coincidence? He was sure he'd gotten everything out of the Eevoqian, but perhaps he'd have to pay him another visit...

"Next!" the Pair called, and Garret was pushed aside.

His hand reached for his knife, but the blade never left its sheath. Garret breathed.

Got bigger prey to hunt.

Along the way to the stockpile, the humans of the Aerie were too calm. Most waited with empty bowls in slow-moving lines while bored workers doled out slop of some form or another. He spotted the half-blind Eye, conspicuous in his sky-blue coat. Rather than doing anything useful, the man was poking around at some resin on the walls.

Couldn't these people sense things were changing around here? The Peekers were swarming. The Queen was dying or worse. The organism was already in the Mounds, he knew it. Was she infested too?

Garret didn't plan to stick around long enough to find out. He had to find Prost quickly, before the hunt turned and he became the prey. His mental map took him straight to his destination. Dim and quiet, there were no guards at the entrance. Garret pulled his ranger's hood tight and slipped inside. Stuck to the shadows. Didn't make a sound.

The place was huge. No better lit than the dank hallways leading to it. The domed ceiling receded into darkness high above. Everything was stored in huge piles of junk. Probably organized by smell the way Peekers did things. Garret would have no hope of finding the Agency's package, so he did the only rational thing.

He left. Found his way to the commissary, where a handful of stars supplied him with a stockpile of his own. When he returned to the Queen's Ulterior Stockpile, he scrounged a bunch of stuff for a makeshift hunting blind. Concealed himself in the darkness. And waited.

Waited.

And waited.

That was the way of hunting sometimes. Not all hearts pounding in wild chase. Most of his time as a bandit was spent in a blind no different from this one. The real trick was finding ways to stave off boredom.

Garret's way was studying nature. Problem was, not a dark-loving thing was moving in the stockpile. The place resembled nothing more than the trash heap beneath Graln. What did they need all this junk for? Nothing to study, so it was torturous how the time crawled. Nothing he could do but soldier on.

Questions occupied his thoughts to keep him from boredom. He herded his mind away from fanciful inquiries into Peeker variants, how their changing flesh reminded him of Benefactors. Instead, he focused on more pressing concerns. Sentyx's plans with his brother. Escape routes in case of an Emergence in the Aerie. Matters of survival. Logistics. A good ranger turned boredom into—

A light flickered in the narrow entryway. Torchlight, slowly approaching. Garret flexed his muscles to relieve his aches. Cracked his neck. Listened as deep voices echoed incomprehensible words. Too quiet but growing closer. Closer.

And as a figure holding a torch reached the doorway, Garret's jaw clenched.

You're fucking kidding me.

Sentyx stomped into the stockpile, looked right toward Garret, causing the ranger to tense. He held his breath. The Skardwarf looked away, surveying the room. Opened his mouth and spoke.

"I can feel those things from here. Wasn't easy getting them out of the tower."

Garret exhaled. Not Sentyx. Cavern. Garret couldn't tell the damned brothers apart, but he'd never heard Sentyx utter more than four words in a row. But if Cavern was here, that meant—

"A Peeker's Pattern isn't so different from a Skardwarf's," Prost said, ambling through the entryway. "Like I said, don't get too close." He turned around. "Especially you."

Four Peekers with engorged upper bodies and arms like scythes followed the southerners in. Queensguards. They nodded and stood sentry outside the room.

Darkfather's balls. He'd left his bow in his quarters. Only had his knife. Could plant it in Prost's throat in a heartbeat, but with those four and a Skardwarf to fend off...Garret wasn't planning on sacrificing himself for the cause. He sat perfectly still and listened.

Cavern rumbled a laugh. "Learned that the hard way in Reed's Woods."

Prost took the torch from Cavern and proceeded further into the stockpile while the Skardwarf waited. The bumbling Eevoqian uttered some foreign curse when he knocked over a pile of metallic junk. Grumbled as he pushed his way past a heavy bit of lumber. Then finally reached his destination, just beyond a tower of rope and resin. Garret memorized the location.

A hinge creaked open, and Prost exclaimed. "Hah! Are these my pupil's notes?"

"I figured it would slow that fool who took down Ulken," Cavern's voice boomed.

"Excellent thinking. And it's said all Skardwarves are dim-witted."

Cavern grunt sounded annoyed.

"These boxes," Prost continued. "Clasform, you say Ulken called them?"

"Yes."

Prost bellowed a laugh. "I told him to clasp firm the box when a Benefactor is near. The man had a straying mind. Never listened, and never did understand the forces we're playing with. No surprise he let that whelp kill him."

"Met the boy once," Cavern said, "in Reed's Woods. I didn't think he had it in him. My brother did well to turn him against the Head."

Garret's ears pricked up. It seemed everything was falling right into his lap.

"Is that what you think?" Prost asked. He'd started moving again. Not back toward Cavern but headed elsewhere in the stockpile. His strained voice told Garret he was carrying something. "How can you be so sure of your brother's loyalty?"

"The Turn quickly approaches. He won't resist when the Tyrant ignites his flame."

"It's what he can do to interfere *before* the Tyrant arrives that worries me. Are you sure you saw him at the birthing?"

"His pattern stood out amongst the rock."

Prost let out a rumble like a growl. A bang echoed from Prost's location. He'd dropped what he was carrying. "Then he will prove very useful, indeed."

Straight from the enemy's mouth. Sentyx was working with Prost and Cavern.

Garret shifted, and the corner of his blind scraped the floor. Cavern stood up straighter, and his eyes wandered toward Garret's position. Garret remained still, squinting his eyes to hide the whites.

Prost emerged and put his hand on Cavern's shoulder. "It won't be long now," the Eevoqian said. "And then we'll reclaim what is ours."

Cavern grunted. "You can have it. The place is a worthless dump."

"Only because of what your Tyrant did, but in this, I can find forgiveness." Prost gave a satisfied sigh. "With so much room to grow and an ocean between us, humans and Skardwarves will live in harmony at last. The winds cannot change fast enough."

Flickering torchlight faded as they departed into the tunnels. Garret waited another half-span before moving again, just to be sure they were really gone. When he was sure, he scurried through the stockpile, seeing only by a phosphorescent bulb in his hand. With a little searching, he found the spot Prost had dropped the Clasform boxes.

Wasn't hard to spot them. They were in a wooden crate stamped with the Agency's sigil. No notebook. Prost must have taken that. But he wouldn't miss two Clasform. Garret pocketed them and looked for the reason Prost brought the crate *here.*

What in the bleeding abyss are these?

It was the only container not covered in dust. Garret was certain he'd found the right one. A case made of some bluish metal that looked like steel. He unclasped it and found it contained a handful of black crystalline gems. Pretty, but they must've had some further purpose. Something involving Peekers and Skardwarves, sounded like. With one of those in his pocket and the bag neatly back in its place, Garret left the stockpile.

Prost and Cavern were long gone, but Garret got more than he came for. A pocket of Prost's tools and a whole lot of questions, but the real treasure was he now had proof of what he suspected all along.

Sentyx had betrayed him.

And Garret knew exactly how to deal with traitors.

CHAPTER TWENTY-FIVE

A Lie Full of Light

Welcome brother, welcome sister
Come partake of bounties greater
Than our fathers and our mothers
Rueful claimed from friends and neighbors

—Verse from Welcome the Wanderer,
First Song of Half-Noon

Lorelay had nothing and no one. Not a place to call her own nor a spare garment to change into. The dress she wore belonged to some snuffing noblewoman, not her. Her coin purse with a few stars was the only thing she took with her when she left the palace. That, and a hemp pack holding her knives, which she had a mind to put to use.

Minny must have seen murder in her eyes when she passed the servant in the halls, because she tried to stop her with a motherly tone. "What's wrong, Lorelay? How can I help?" When Lorelay ignored her, she shouted down the hall, "Don't go doing anything stupid, now, girl."

Lorelay paid her no heed. She liked the old woman, but she had taken her advice once, and look where that had gotten her. Lorelay would never see Minny again, anyway. A pang of guilt tightened her chest at that thought, but she pushed it down.

Nothing a bottle of rum won't help me forget. She tapped her foot impatiently, waiting for the Paladins at the Radiant Palace's grand entrance to lift the gate for her. As the big oafs slowly lifted the gate and cranked the drawbridge down, she felt as though someone were about to sneak up behind her. Vinlin, probably, begging her not to leave. *Snuffing hurry up! Can't anyone do anything by themselves around here?*

Finally outside the palace, she hurried down the switchback roadway the descended the plateau into the city proper. It was a beautiful morning, entirely discordant with her mood. A mood which only darkened when she saw how the other Vosians were taking advantage of the fine weather. Children darted between trees, running and hiding from each other with whoops of joy. They only reminded her of Vinlin's advances, what he wanted from her. A man and a woman strolled through a rose garden holding hands. Lorelay nearly gagged. Half-noon clamored from church towers throughout the city, and the call to prayer came from the ululating mathemelodians atop Archemetal spires. Everyone stopped in their tracks, pulling out miniature Books of Light or turning to the nearest Church to recite the prayers from memory.

Not Lorelay. She trudged past all the sheep, dark thoughts running through her head. Only half-noon, after all this time? She had breakfasted alone in the Fire Gardens before storming up to Vinlin's quarters, failed to win over the Bright Prince, and tore apart her room before deciding to leave the palace for good. All that, and the Brightdaughter had yet to finish her ascent. It was going to be a long day.

All to the good. More time to spend getting drunk enough to forget any of this happened.

There was one problem, however. When she arrived at the first tavern, and the second, then the third, all of them were closed. Lorelay was clamoring on the door to the latest, demanding they open and give her a drink, when the proprietress batted her away with a broom. "Fool girl, you'll wait until half-dusk like everyone else. Think you're the only one wants a drink this early? Now begone!"

A violent urge coursed through Lorelay at being struck with a broom, clouds of dust making her eyes itch and her throat dry, but she suppressed the urge. If she ended up in the dungeon again, little chance the Bright Prince would save her again. No, she would be stuck with Gravis, and he would give her what she deserved.

Half-dusk. Lorelay scoffed. *Snuffing Church of Light doesn't want us to be happy.*

How else to explain the restrictions on imbibing alcohol earlier than that? She recited the passage from the sacred Book in mocking tones. "Be led not astray by strong spirits. Drink instead your fill of the Lightmother's wisdom."

In her mind, the wisdom of the Lightmother meant doing what needed to be done. And Lorelay *needed* a drink. She noted with disdain that if she demanded it in the Radiant Palace, a servant would have no choice but to fulfill her wishes.

"I'd rather go straight to the abyss than go back there," she affirmed.

But what was a girl to do? Waiting around until half-dusk was no option. She could only steep in her anger for so long before the tea turned bitter with grief.

Well, if grief was the only outcome, so be it. She would face it head on, though not by sobbing in a dirty alley. She might as well announce to all the city's ne-er-do-wells that she was here and ready to be taken advantage of. There were far too many of those of late, and the court was abuzz with gossip about an influx of refugees. Vos's streets were becoming nearly as dangerous as the Cathedral of Light to a heretic like her.

She had a more fitting place in mind to drown her despair. Her feet traced the old paths she used to walk. Past the arena with men practicing at wrestling and swordplay. Past the weapons shop where Jenx had bought her the two knives in her pack. Past the Church of Light her mother always dragged her to, now positively overflowing with patrons, some of whom Lorelay was sure were begging goodwill from the faithful.

Past all of that, Lorelay found herself outside her childhood home. Even after all these years, there were no cobwebs in the window, no dirt accumulated at the doorstep. It looked as tidy as when her mother was alive to care for it. Lightmother knows Dunnax and her father never helped with that—both of them were away from home more than not, off doing whatever the Empress commanded her Paladins to do. Lorelay thought it was unfair, but her mother never complained.

'*A tidy house allows Light to shine. In dusty Dark, no Brightness shall dine.*'

Lorelay imagined her mother's voice reciting the proverb, and a tear dripped down her cheek. Her mother and father were both gone, and it was all her fault.

Right on cue, her grief reared its filthy head. Without thinking whether someone else lived in her old family home, Lorelay pushed open the wooden door and entered. The inside was dark, but smelled of lemon and honey, as though someone had just brewed tea. She followed her nose into the kitchen, found the remnants of that preparation—a pot of water still steaming hot, a fresh-sliced lemon, and a few scattered stems of rosemary. Odd, that was how her mother liked her tea.

Movement caught Lorelay's eye. A shadow passed over the window into the back garden. By instinct, Lorelay fingered her knife, then shook her head and let her hand hang loose. Someone *was* living here. She was in their home. Not a good idea to draw a knife on them, not if she wanted to avoid Gravis and the dungeon. But perhaps whoever lived here would be sympathetic to Lorelay. Her family had lived here all her life, until she ruined everything. And deep down, Lorelay was tired of being alone. Some part of her needed someone to talk to.

Thinking through her apology for entering a stranger's home, Lorelay opened the back door and stepped out. She looked up, and froze, coming face to face with...

"Mother?"

There she stood, not a dead woman at all but alive and well, if a few years older with the wrinkles to show for it. Oddly, she wore a long gray shift made of wool, whereas she always remembered her mother in vibrant clothes Lorelay would call garish. The teacup in her mother's hand dropped and shattered on the stone patio. Her eyes widened in shock, and she wobbled on her feet dizzily. Lorelay rushed forward to catch her by the arm before she fainted.

But her mother did not faint. She used Lorelay's momentum against her pulling her into a tight hug, squeezing until Lorelay thought she herself might faint from asphyxiation.

Lorelay wriggled free. "Get off me, mother." It was all she could do to prevent her mother from pulling her right back in. This was certainly not going as she expected. Their relationship was defined by incessant arguing, and here she was *hugging* Lorelay. But there was a bigger question on her mind. "How are you alive?" It was meant to come out much more forcefully than that, but she would make do with a breathy gasp of a question.

Her mother held her at arm's length, squeezing her shoulders and studying every inch of her through glossy eyes. "How am *I* alive? Lorelay, I thought *you* were dead."

Lorelay began to protest, but snapped her mouth shut. What had she heard of the incident at the Light's Faithful, the night her children disappeared? Lorelay clammed up, trying unsuccessfully to draw back from her mother. If what she had heard was the truth, Lorelay had no doubt she would turn her in to the authorities. Her mother had always been a stickler for rules.

"Your friend Jenx came by looking for you, and I scolded him for playing such a cruel trick...oh, I must apologize to him." Her mother grabbed Lorelay by the hand. "Come, Lorelay. Come, come. Sit with me in the garden. Tell me what happened. Why did you disappear for so long?" Birds gathered around the split tea, pecking at insects drawn to the sweetness.

"You mean...you don't already know?" They sat beside one another on a swinging bench beneath a trellis green with ivy and red roses.

"Oh, your father tried prying some answers from the Order, but they were loath to tell him anything. All they told us was you were gone, both of you. Which we both took to mean you did something to embarrass the Order—they never like admitting they're not entirely in control. Only, your father believed you fled, and I thought you were..." Tears welled up in her mother's eyes, and Lorelay found herself smothered in another embrace. She let it happen. "I've never been happier to be wrong. Your father will be beaming when he hears—"

"Father's alive too?"

Her mother chuckled. "Oh yes, he's in Lumeeq overseeing the mining operation. With the upcoming coronation, we need as much Archemetal as we can get. According to the Church, anyway. Your father believes it's merely..."

Lorelay's entire body flooded with warmth listening to her mother gossip about him, to her surprise, even questioning the Church. But as her mother gabbed, Lorelay's mind wandered. She had believed both her parents dead, all thanks to her and her stupid tongue. All this time, she had assumed the Bright Throne had punished her whole family to get back at her. Now, she was questioning all she believed. Perhaps the Lightmother *was* merciful...

But not to everyone. The thought drew out a sorrowful sigh.

"Mother, there's something I have to tell you," she interrupted. It was something that could no longer wait, despite her own refusal to accept it for as long as possible. Some things she could keep from herself, and some things she could keep from her mother. This was neither, as it turned out. "Dunnax..." She swallowed, finding her mouth suddenly dry. "Dunnax is dead."

The words came out as a croak. Saying them aloud simultaneously felt like a weight lifted from her shoulders and like a chasm widening in the deepest part of her soul. The range of emotions passing over her mother's face told her the same thing roiled inside her, only it came to an end in an unexpected place. The best way Lorelay could describe it was…stoic. And that threatened to push Lorelay straight into that chasm within herself.

Her mother took a deep breath, wiped the tears from each eye with her thumb. "Thank you for telling me, Lorelay."

She waited for more, but none came. Her throat tightened, and her chest felt near to bursting. But no anger came. Odd…there was always anger when she thought about what happened to Dunnax. "Thank you for telling me? That's it?"

Of all things, a sad smile appeared on her mother's face. "For two years I have believed both my children were dead. Your father and I grieved for the both of you, long into the night. I held a vigil at our church, and everyone I know listened as I swore to become a Lady of Ash."

Lorelay gasped. Her mother was the most religious person she knew—annoyingly so. This was the person who insisted Lorelay *only* read from scripture, never anything else. Who based her entire day around the calls to prayer. Who she had never once heard utter the name of the Darkfather. To become a Lady of Ash meant to give up on practicing her faith, to announce to all who listened that the Light of her Fire had been snuffed out. It broke Lorelay's heart to know how gravely her mother suffered.

"But in the end, what can any of us do but accept the past? Dunnax wouldn't want me to wallow in my own tears, wasting away. You wouldn't want me to give up. Life goes on. All we can do is live for those we've lost. I thought I had lost two children. But now one has returned to me, and those prayers I said so long ago have finally been answered. The Lightmother is merciful."

Lorelay had no idea what to say. She wanted to tell her mother how sorry she was, that it was her fault Dunnax would never return. That it was her fault they had to flee in the first place. That her mother *should* turn her over to the Order of Paladins for penance. But she could force none of those words to come. Her mother would hate her, and she had suffered enough heartbreak. All she could do was lean in and hug her mother tightly while they both wept.

Together in the garden, the noon bells rang, and Lorelay expected her mother to retrieve her Book of Light for prayers. But of course she would own no such book, not as a Lady of Ash. Instead, her mother entered the house to make some tea, popping back outside to hand Lorelay a broom for the shattered porcelain on the stone. She gladly took up the chore, something to keep her mind busy while she thought of what to tell her mother.

She deserved to know the truth, of that much Lorelay was certain. But Lightmother, how much of the truth could she hear before it broke her? How much could Lorelay hurt her mother before she herself believed she deserved no forgiveness? Lorelay was tired of being alone, and though her past relationship with her mother was as rocky as the Lawiko highlands, there was always time to repair it.

Unless the Benefactors cut our time short.

Lorelay slowed her sweeping, absorbed in thought. She had a family in Vos. Was she just going to give up on them? If she failed to win Vinlin's aid, they really would be dead within the year. Less? How much time did they have? All Lorelay's grievances, all her notions of seeking forgiveness, those could wait until after the Benefactors were defeated. She had to make sure there *was* an after, first. But how?

When her mother appeared in the doorway with two cups of tea, a proverb from the Book of Light came to mind. One that her mother annoyingly repeated when chiding Lorelay, but which now brought only a smile to Lorelay's face.

When the path is shrouded in Dark, follow the Mother back to Her Light.

"Mother," Lorelay said, leaning the broom against the garden wall. "Can I ask you to help me with something?"

"Anything for you, little light."

How to broach the subject? The last thing she wanted to do was scare her mother with tales of monsters abroad. So perhaps a different angle... "The Bright Prince, Vinlin. What do you know of him?"

Her mother thought, sipping tea and blowing to cool it. "Not much, I'm afraid. Only that he's to be the first male emperor, Lightmother help us. Unless the Church puts a stop to it. Why are you frowning? I thought you would like to see a royal like him put in his place."

"Mother..." Lorelay gulped tea to wet her throat, regretting it when she scorched her tongue. "I've been...living in the palace. At Vinlin's invitation."

A widening of her mother's eyes was all the shock she displayed. She always was a composed woman. "Well, that certainly explains the dress you're wearing. I didn't want to ask—I know how touchy you get about dresses—but it looks lovely on you. But...how?"

Lorelay told her mother everything that had come to pass, leaving out only the event that incited their flight from Paceeq. She spoke about the Agency, about meeting the Bright Prince in the woods and escorting him to Canako. When she came to Dunnax's death in Reed's Woods, Lorelay managed to recount the story without so much as a quiver in her voice. Anger at Ulken still bubbled up within her, but she suppressed it by reminding herself Grim had brought him to justice. Lorelay even included her brief stint in the palace dungeon, and the Bright Prince's infuriating attempts to court her.

"But I can't seem to make him understand how big a threat these Benefactors are." Lorelay shook her head, took another sip of tea. It had gone cold long past. "He's only concerned with one thing."

Her mother snorted. "Most men are, sweetie. The trick is to make them think they'll get it when you get what *you* want."

"Mother!" Lorelay gaped, but it quickly turned to a laugh. "But I don't want to lie to him. The prospect of romance"—Lorelay shivered—"with the Bright Prince is enough to drive me to a life of celibacy."

"Oh honey," her mother said, fixing her with a hard gaze. "Most women would kill to be in your position. A life of royalty, raising children fit to lead the Empire..." Lorelay spluttered, and her mother nudged her with an elbow. "I hear the Bright Prince is easy on the eyes."

Lorelay had to admit he was far from an ugly man, though she had never seriously looked at him in that way. And her mother was right, most women would trade places with Lorelay in an instant. She would welcome it, except that it meant losing her chance at making an ally of Vinlin. "I don't want it, though."

"I hear you, honey. So tell me, what *do* you want?"

"I told you; I need the Bright Empire's help to—"

"You told me what you *need*. I'm asking what you *want*."

Lorelay's mouth worked, ready to say they were the same thing... but was that true? She did want to win the Throne's support in this fight. The deeper question was *why?* It took a moment of soul searching to realize the truth of the matter. It would have been ready at hand if only she could have confronted it earlier.

Dunnax's death.

She wanted it to mean something. Her brother was dead, and the fault lay squarely at her feet. Lorelay had embroiled both of them in this fight. If she failed and the Bright Empire fell, his sacrifice would mean nothing. If she convinced Vinlin to lend his aid, they could win this war. She knew it. And then, maybe then, she might be able to forgive herself.

By the time she finished telling her mother, both of them were in tears again. She expected judgment for her part in Dunnax's death, but her mother was the embodiment of grace. Lorelay might not forgive herself, not yet, but her mother pulled her close and told her it was not her fault. A lie, but a lie full of Light, meant to inspire where the truth led only to despair.

"Does the Bright Prince know this?" Lorelay's mother asked. "Does he know why it means so much to you to win him over?"

"No," she admitted.

"Then tell him. He clearly cares for you." Her mother shook her head in disbelief. "But he doesn't know the pain you've been through. Make him understand, and if he still doesn't want to help you, I'll rebel against the throne on your behalf."

CHAPTER TWENTY-SIX

Archecloaks

I seem to recall giving you marching orders, not humble suggestions. Quit dragging your feet. You know whose dirt we—

—Scrap of ripped letter found on the Head's office floor

"What's happening down there, Jacquin?"

Inac and I rushed down the stairs with the Nerve who had delivered the news. The Eye met us halfway down the tower. Shouts and commotion drifted upward, came in through windows in the hallways, and drew the attention of members of the Agency on all floors. Luckily, we had gotten ahead of it this time, so it was nothing like the night of the Benefactor's Emergence.

I wasn't a religious man, but still, I silently prayed to the Lightmother. *If you let me die, the city will fall. No one else can stop them.*

Jacquin spoke as he kept up with me taking the stairs down two at a time. "Archecloaks, sir. The Heels barred the gate when they saw them approaching. They're not attacking. They're just...waiting."

"For what?" I asked, despite already knowing there could only be one answer. I had never been one for undue hope, but maybe...

"For you," Jacquin said, gutting my fledgling hopefulness.

How could I have expected anything else? With a sigh, I gave thanks that they hadn't resorted to assassination, at least.

Might have been preferable to running down to meet my death head on.

"Oltrov is with them. He promised me no harm would come to the Agency. 'Not by their hand, anyway,' he said. 'None at all, if I can talk to Grim.'"

I squeezed my fists. Just what I had expected. Thinly veiled threats. After I burned their leverage over the Council, I knew their reprisal would come eventually. So, Oltrov wanted to talk?

Easier to believe the lies from the lips of an Artisans courtesan.

More likely, I was about to be threatened into allowing them entry. With the flick of one Archemage's finger, our timber gate would become a smoking ruin. In the Archecloaks would stream and put us all to the sword. Everyone hurrying down to the courtyard with me, curious about the commotion, would die.

These people weren't fighters. Hardly any were Fingers. Most were Heels, Organs, technicians. But all of them were my responsibility. How could I save their lives if I couldn't save my own?

My jaw hurt, grinding my teeth without cease. I *had* to save myself. If I died here, how long would this Agency last? Or the people of *all* Liwokin's districts. There was no one else with the power I had, no one who could suppress new Benefactors before they began wreaking havoc. All of Liwokin of was my responsibility—if I died, their fate was sealed. Keeping them alive was a matter of my own survival.

I let out a frustrated growl as we neared the bottom floor. Lightmother, I didn't want to *fight* the Gild, but a bounty hunter prepared for every possibility. They were meant to be our allies in the fight against Benefactors. Instead, it seemed every effort I made only tore the city further apart, earned me new enemies, and deepened old wounds.

Wounds deep enough to send an assassin after me.

Slowing as I reached the courtyard, I breathed through my teeth. Suddenly, this felt like a trap. A way to lure me out to the gate, where someone could put a crossbow bolt through me. Incinerate me with Archefire.

Shoot me in the heart with a pistol. I swallowed.

If luck prevails, the round won't take me in the head. Maybe then my Benefactor could heal me.

A memory surfaced of our first battle against a Benefactor. Against Wick. Wyran. As his monstrous form burned, a single arrow through his exposed skull ended his menace of Leppit fishing village. No chance for his flesh to mend. Another memory surfaced.

Skull smashed in, then emptiness.

These walls were all I had. The tower, the courtyard walls, and the people inside them. Dozens of them surrounded me now, most paying attention to the gate, their backs turned to me. Still, I kept a close eye on the crowd for anything suspicious. Did I trust that these were all loyal Agency members? How could I know if one of them was a cloaked cutthroat?

"Watch my back," I said over my shoulder Inac.

"Yes, sir," Jacquin responded, and I looked at him sidelong. The man was reliable, but he still had yet to earn my full trust.

All I could truly be certain of was the strength of our walls. And at least I knew the gate really was closed this time. If not, Oltrov and his army would have poured right in without warning.

As I pushed through the crowd with a growing sense of vulnerability, he spotted me. "Ah, there he is! The man of the span. So good of you to join us."

"Oltrov, you really should warn me before bringing friends over." I looked at the Archecloaks standing three rows deep behind him, then glanced back at the tower. "I really don't think we have room to accommodate you all."

"Come now, friend," Oltrov said, wrinkling his nose. "You aren't suggesting we would want to stay *here*, are you? Even our Archecloaks sleep in beds fit for the Empress."

Stay here? No. You would tear down these walls the first chance you got.

"Our beds are fine enough," I said. A lot finer than sleeping on hard stone, as I was used to. I shrugged. "But if you're not interested, you're welcome to take your Archecloaks back behind your gilded walls."

"I shall," Oltrov said, "as soon as we're done here."

And so, the preamble ended, the false pleasantries. Now we had come to the meat of the matter.

"Done with what?" I demanded. "Why have you brought an army to my gate?"

"For my protection," he said, "and yours."

I snorted. Did he really think I would submit myself to his whims? Maybe they wouldn't kill me—they knew about Benefactors, didn't they? Oltrov had been deeply involved in the conspiracy to overthrow Ulken. What would it be, then? Torture? Banishment?

"I'm content with the protection of my walls," I assured him.

"And yet," he responded coolly, "walls are so...immobile." He slammed a fist into the nearest Archecloak, square in the chest. Then he tried pushing the man. As tall as Dunnax, and wider still, the gilded guard stood as firm as a Skardwarf. "These are at your disposal. We heard about the incident in the square."

I'm sure you did. You sent the killer, didn't you?

"You're an influential figure now," Oltrov continued. "You can't just stroll around Liwokin without protection. Who knows what ill fate might befall you?"

I blinked. "Are you suggesting I use your Archecloaks as personal guards?" I had no doubt they would fight well for me. Right up until the moment the Gild told them to put a sword in my back.

"That is precisely right. And it's not an idle suggestion. These men are yours to command at this very moment."

Mine to command? And what were the limits of their loyalty? "Kill him," I commanded.

That produced some murmurs and stares from the people around me. Darkfather, I hadn't considered how they would react. An army at their gates, they must be scared. I didn't need my Benefactor senses to tell me that. Their faces said enough. If I did something that they thought put them in danger, would they mutiny? What were the limits of *their* loyalty? I didn't have Yezna controlling them like Ulken did.

I am not Ulken.

And I didn't think the Archecloaks would really kill Oltrov. I had been correct, though one man did draw a palm's width of steel before the next guard stayed him with a gauntleted hand on his arm.

Oltrov was grinning. "That wasn't very nice, Grimley." My face twisted—he sounded like the headmaster at my old orphanage. "Rest assured, they'll follow your commands, but they won't bite the hand that feeds them. Nor will you. Now, open this gate. We have much to discuss." By the end of it, his grin was gone, replaced with a hard look. A warning not to push him too hard.

I scowled. He was a powerful man, but also a liar. The moment I called for this gate to open, I expected he would drop the mask, show us who he really was.

A mask...

A dark thought took hold. What if this wasn't Oltrov at all, but another figure cloaked by the rogue Benefactor's Aura? How could I be sure?

I closed my eyes, made a show of thinking about his offer. In truth, I watched him with the strands of Archefire that lay on him. There. The strands were subtly dimmer than those permeating the empty air, dancing discordantly, as though affected by several things at once. The Dark, sure. Inac said it was always there, clinging to the Fire. By the other...could it be a Benefactor's Aura creating an illusion of Oltrov?

The fields of Archemagic seemed to magnify in my mind as I focused on the Gildmember. The rhythm of the Fire's dance called to me, and I tuned out all else, until abruptly my Benefactor latched onto it. As soon as it did, a flood of awareness filled my mind.

Through the gate, the insufferable Head of the Agency stood stock still with his eyes closed. Making me wait. *Gah, I hate waiting. Time is money, and this man seems to delight in wasting my time.* How had my investment failed to pay off so dreadfully? Reed should be the Head, but instead we had this buffoon to bring to heel. *What, by the abyss, is he doing?* I clutched my head, groaning. And what was that strange pressure I felt?

I opened my eyes, forced my Benefactor to let go of Oltrov. It was him all right, and nothing I saw in his head made me any less wary of the man.

"Is there a problem, Oltrov?"

He shook his head, then grimaced. "I...suddenly have a headache. Think nothing of it. Well? Are you going to make us stand out here all day, or—"

A sudden, deafening sound cut off the Gildmember and had me clutching my ears. The roar of the nearby explosion paled in comparison, however, to the torrent of death knells that came with it. They filled my head near to bursting as I suppressed them as quickly as I could. So many emotions at once—they blended together into a horrifying stew of outrage, surprise, vengeance, and hatred.

When it finished, I found myself on my hands and knees, panting, unsure which of my own feelings I could trust. Standing, I looked through the bars of the gate and found a single prevailing emotion: fear. It prevailed in me as well, washing away all the rest, setting my hands to trembling and my heart to pounding.

"What's happening?" Oltrov demanded, not bothering to hide the fear in his own voice.

The Archecloaks around him were all a-scramble, with swords in every hand and eyes searching in every direction. Inside the courtyard, the Agency was a buzzing hive, awash with activity like I hadn't seen since Ulken's operation to kill the Benefactor Reed. One thing was clear: no one knew what was happening.

I closed my eyes again, reached out with the power. Every Emergence had been suppressed, but I needed to be sure...

My Benefactor's senses traveled across the city, just as they did as I sat in my office behind my desk. Counterintuitively, being on the ground floor seemed to make it *easier* to get an overview, somehow. As I observed my Benefactor off its leash, I tried to make sense of what it was doing. Hopping from head to head, creating a map of perception? There was no other way to describe it. The mechanics behind it made little sense to me, but that had been true from the very beginning with Benefactors.

Ulken had told the truth about one thing: we understood too little about these creatures.

My power hit a wall, just as it had the last time. Only, it was in the Market, not the Blight.

"—Grim!"

My eyes snapped open at the sound of my name, and I whirled. It was Inac. He stood there beside Jacquin, both of them looking back and forth between me and a rising column of thick black smoke to the east.

"An explosion in the Market," Inac said. "We must help!"

My lips pressed together. He was right, in more ways than he knew. There wasn't just an explosion. There was a Benefactor too. It might even have been the cause of the conflagration. We had to help...

"All Fingers to me!" I commanded, and the Nerve who had followed me turned to begin executing it as if it were addressed solely to him. I grabbed him by the sleeve of his white-and-gold-sleeved coat. He was little older than a boy, which accounted for his lack of common sense. I had *shouted* the command, after all. "Not you, boy."

"Sir?"

"You organize the Heels and healers. Those Liwo in the Market are going to need medical attention. You're going to make sure they get it. Understand?"

The wide-eyed boy stammered for a few moments before a resolute look took over his face. He snapped a salute. "Yes, sir!"

There was no hesitation after that. He began butting into Heels' panicked conversations, gathering them up, and setting them into action. No hesitation. Not on any of their parts.

Only on mine.

"What is the delay?" Inac's eyes searched my own, and in short order he knew my thoughts.

I was chewing my lip, still reluctant to open the gate, because on the other side, Oltrov was studying me, as if waiting to see how I responded. Fingers of the Agency, old Hands in the traditional green and new Hands in no uniform at all, gathered around me, but they were so few in number. Enough to take down a Benefactor? Definitely. But enough to win a battle against these Archecloaks?

The possibilities all competed with one another in my head. Too many, only a source of frustration, unhelpful in making a decision. But a decision needed to be made, and quickly. The explosion wasn't the Gild, I was nearly certain of that. All of them seemed far too lost and on-edge, Oltrov included, for them to have been aware of it. But the Gildmember was nothing if not opportunistic. Inac was right, and I knew what I had to do.

There was still a niggle of doubt in my mind that I had doomed us all when I shouted, "Open the gate!"

An instant later, it began to lift, and Oltrov grinned. At the sight of that, I almost ordered it closed once more.

But one of the Archecloaks had drawn steel when I gave him the command.

I sighed and touched the hilt of the sword at my hip. It was a small comfort—never had a sword proved useful against a Benefactor, and one man's blade alone would make no difference this day. The several dozen in the square, ready in the hands of the Gild's armored guards, however...

The gate was opening.

It was time to put the Gild's claims of loyalty to the test.

CHAPTER TWENTY-SEVEN

A Day at the Market

Help wanted. Hiring an assistant with a strong constitution. The stench may be unbearable, but the wages are unbeatable.

—Posted beside the broken window of an abandoned tanner's shop

The gate's lock made a loud *kerchunk* as the portcullis reached the top of its climb. I was only dimly aware of it, already stepping through to give the Archecloaks orders. Two Hands' worth of Fingers followed me out, forming naturally into groups of five without so much as a suggestion on my part. These weren't the only Fingers who had survived Ulken's so-called field tests—others were out in the Lawiko countryside hunting for Benefactors, rather unsuccessfully, if their lack of report or return was any indication. Even had all the rest surrounded me, they would be scant protection from the Archecloaks ahead.

The Agency was crumbling around me, and this day the Gild might strike the final blow. I took it as a good sign that none of the Gild's golden guards attacked me on the spot.

All it takes is one, and I'm dead.

But I had to put my trust in them, at least for now. There was a Benefactor that needed killing, and like an Archemage in combat, I would be vulnerable while I worked with the power.

Oltrov stepped aside as I approached, giving me a go ahead gesture. "They're all yours. These, and funding from the Gild, whatever you need. Can't have the Agency falling apart, not at a time like this."

I had to consciously keep my mouth from falling open. Funding from the Gild? They weren't trying to land the last blow. We weren't enemies. He was throwing me a lifeline. But my mouth slowly curled into a frown. I looked back at Inac. His expression matched my own, as did Jacquin's.

Charity? From the Gild?

That was like saying Ulken's work with the Agency was charitable just because he refused commission when taking on jobs. The work wasn't free, and it wasn't a gesture of goodwill. It was a way to lord his power over the Council, using the gold collected as tax to trick Liwokin into loving him. A hidden cost, but Oltrov's price was transparent to me. The Gild didn't do favors, only investments. I was to be the rope in their game of tug-of-war with the Council.

If that's what it takes to keep the Agency alive...

I growled, pushing away the thought. Later. We could delay no longer. "Archecloaks!"

As one, every Archecloak stood at attention, a ruckus of clattering Archemetal armor and steel blades.

"Five of you," I said, sweeping a hand across them, "will be my honor guard. You will stay close to me. Protect me. Take a pistol round for me, if need be." Not so much as a grumble came at that. Impressive. Either they truly were the most elite of guards, or they were going to let me have my fun with a speech before murdering me. "We go to the Market. If you see strange occurrences, keep your wits about you and remember what's re—"

"You boys have fun," Oltrov said, turning to leave. "I'm late for a meeting."

I scowled at him. "Not worried about the Gild being attacked too? What if this is a diversion?"

Oltrov laughed and waved the concern away. "Do you think I'd be fool enough to give you *all* my Archecloaks? Do what you wish with them when you're finished. As I said, they're yours." He strolled off casually, shaking his head and chuckling to himself.

Darkfather, what's wrong with that man?

"Let us go, Grim," Inac said, putting his left hand on my shoulder.

"No," I told him, and he looked at me in confusion. "We're not going anywhere. I am. You are staying here, my friend."

"But—"

"Inac, I need you safe." I sighed. "If something happens to me, you're to be the next Head of the Agency. No more ascension by killing the last Head. We need real continuity." Not like the continuity Oltrov spoke of; the continuation of corruption. Inac was a good man. He would do a better job as Head than I had.

Tears glistened in his eyes. He tried to keep his face stoic, but I could read him as easily as I could read anyone. Worry, disbelief, pride. Fear for a friend. As much as I wanted him with me in the Market, I would only be putting him in danger, risking his life and the Agency. He could use no Archemagic. He had one hand and no training with a blade. He had to stay safe, there was no other way about it.

"Keep an eye out for our return," I said before he could get a word in to try changing my mind. "Jacquin, let's go! You're in command of the Fingers. If there's a Benefactor..."

Jacquin saluted. "Say no more, sir. Hunting Benefactors is what we do best."

With that, the entire group was marching hastily down the wide road that connected the Council Square to the Market. Liwo rushed past us, fleeing from whatever lay ahead. The closer we got, the louder the din grew, the thicker the smoke became. We passed a dead man's body, burned and bleeding in the street. At the edge of the Burg, a home burned, and the remains of a fire brigade had been murdered and left to rot beside buckets of spilled water. The streets ran as red as the crimson sky above.

It was chaos, the Riot come again. Someone *wanted* this destruction. Why kill the people trying to put out fires, otherwise? This home wasn't the only one burning, but the column of smoke seen from the Agency lay still farther ahead in the heart of the Market. I tore my eyes away from the bodies—I wanted to help, but I couldn't spare a single soldier.

Not with a Benefactor wreaking havoc in Liwokin.

Entering the Market, a familiar pressure exerted itself on my head. I had felt it in the Shaded Grounds, approaching Lomin. I had felt it in the clearing outside Leppit. It spurred me forward at a run, cursing under my breath, Archecloaks surrounding me as I had commanded.

A Blightdweller smashed the window of a shop with a wooden sign that splintered on impact. He kicked out the spider-webbing glass of the shop front, and it shattered on the ground. Finding us there stunned the rioter for a moment, until he hastily held up his sign. 'Kill the Killer', it read, and he shouted at us. "Down with the Gild! Down with the Agen—"

An Archecloak's sword lashed out and took him in the throat. He crumpled to the ground as four raging compatriots rushed out of the shop, all with drawn weapons. In moments they were all dead, no match for my honor guard.

Darkfather, why are they doing *this?*

We had to keep moving, following the sense of pressure in my head that grew heavier and heavier with each step. This was no fledgling Benefactor. It was old, incubating for as long as mine had. In the presence of its Aura, the city warped around me, as in Reed's Woods. Beneath a blood sky, people slaughtered each other in the streets. Ordinary Liwo defended themselves from rioters. Hawkers turned their wares into weapons, bashing rioters and shoppers and their hired guards indiscriminately. Rioters were even killing *each other*.

I slowed, shaking my head in disbelief at the sight. Yezna's memory surfaced, a brief reminder of Ulken's rage that had overcome the city during her Emergence. Only, this was no single Emergence. I suppressed the deaths of each fallen Liwo around me, straining my concentration and risking the unawareness their death knells brought.

Ahead lay a Benefactor that was already Emergent, and I had missed it. All of this...it was my fault.

Rage filled me, and the Aura flickered suddenly. All of reality changed before my eyes, too fast to track. From dark red skies to bright blue. Abruptly, it was the Liwokin *militia* defending against rioting merchants.

There had been no turning of the tides of battle. It was as if the bloody blades swapped hands in an instant, into the hands of uniformed lawkeepers. None of it made sense. Pots and vases were being smashed over the heads of militia soldiers, who in turn plunged worn, rusty blades into the rioters' bellies.

All at once, it flipped back to what I had first seen. I stopped in my tracks, understanding it for what it was. The same way the Benefactor had cloaked the assassin, it was disguising everybody in the Market. Only the Archecloaks, my Fingers, and Jacquin seemed immune to the effect. Looking around, they were as confused as I was. Why were *they* immune?

"What, by the abyss, is *happening*, sir?" Jacquin was suddenly struggling to push through my honor guard. "Where is the Benefactor?"

I wasted no time closing my eyes and reaching out with my own Benefactor. As soon as I tried, my foe pushed me down, trying to suppress me like a newborn Emergent. Trying to make me feel small.

But my Benefactor was not weak. With a growl, I pushed *back*. This was *my* city. My home. And I wasn't going to let this monster destroy it.

The rogue Benefactor's pressure wavered at my newfound assault. It only took a moment. As soon as it gave me the opportunity, I expanded my senses, outward, outward, until we reached an equilibrium. The other fought back, stopped me from growing larger, but gained no ground itself. In any other direction, I could reach out to the limits of my abilities. Only toward the Emergent was I halted. We were equally matched.

Slowly, I opened my eyes, maintaining the focus that preserved the tenuous balance of powers. "It's...that way," I said through gritted teeth. Over countless dead bodies. Past the billowing pillars of smoke.

Each step was taken carefully, lest I lose control of the creature in my mind and get snuffed out by the other. All I needed to do was maintain my hold, lock my Benefactor in place, prevent the other from overcoming me. As we moved forward, my honor guard surrounded me. Jacquin and the Fingers stayed close, and the rest of the Archecloaks lashed out, killing Blightdwellers.

I grimaced at that. With the Emergent's Aura influencing them, they might well have been regular Liwo fleeing for their lives. Even as I watched, one Archecloak's sword slashed the chest of a Blightdwelling man, who crumpled to the ground and turned into a woman in a blue uniform with a spreading stain that matched her trousers and the newly red sky above.

My eyes shot open in alarm, and my control of the Benefactor slipped. A wave of pressure hit me, sent me to my knees. Perception of the battle shifted to match the Emergent's Aura. Blue skies, militiamen defending the city. Hands grabbed at my coat, pulling me upward, but the Emergent's influence battered at my skull, driving me back down.

With a roar, I forced myself to my feet, and the sky shifted from blue to red. All of this slaughter was the Emergent's fault. Disguising innocent people, using them as fodder to slow us down. I would strike that monster down with my own blade.

Determined to see justice done, I renewed my focus, and *pushed* the Benefactor back, revealing the truth.

The dead woman transformed back into a rioting Blightdweller. The Brightdaughter returned overhead, fiery red sky obscured by thick smoke. Everything was exactly as I expected it to be. The Emergent's influence waned. Like ascending from deep waters, the pressure surrounding me gradually eased.

But my own Benefactor was tiring too. Body and mind grew weary. I couldn't hold out much longer.

We turned a corner where a shop had been cleaned out by the looting rioters, and there it was. At the base of the black smoke, a roaring conflagration consumed the buildings all around. There was debris in the street, launched in all directions by the explosion we had heard, and broken bodies of Liwo men and women scattered amongst the detritus.

In front of the inferno, the silhouette of a monster laid waste to everything around it. It hulked over men, thrice their size, laying about with arms as thick as tree trunks. In its rage, bodies flew, tossed about like dolls by the enormous beast.

"Jacquin..."

"I see it, sir."

"End this."

Nothing more needed to be said. The Fingers surged forth, avoiding the bodies in the street as they charged the monster with shouts of victory for the Agency.

The beast turned to face us, and in its Aura I felt...fear. Struggling to maintain my control, I hadn't the energy to grin at the monster's dismay. It saw its doom coming...and it fled. With one final burst of energy, the pressure redoubled in my mind. I clutched my head, gritted my teeth, tears forming in my eyes at the pain. And just before the Benefactor reached the alleyway it raced toward, reality shifted once more.

Crimson skies. Blightdwellers dead. And the monster...was only a man. I didn't get a good look at him. A bald head was the only detail I made out before he disappeared down a side street that led to the Artisans' District.

Oh no you don't.

My own Benefactor surged, pushed toward the man, closer, closer, beyond our point of balance. That last exertion had weakened my enemy beyond the point of resistance. My senses reached the minds of the Blightdwellers who fled with him. They raced down an alley, legs carrying them as fast as they could with Fingers in close pursuit.

An arrow took one in the back, and consciousness winked out. Another turned, stood his ground, and fired a blue-gray pistol, once, twice. The third shot took one of my Fingers in the head before the rest of his Hand slaughtered the killer. I witnessed the fight through the eyes of both sides. The others had thrown down the strange guns in their panic, and I saw an opportunity.

My Benefactor latched onto the minds of the Fingers still chasing the Blightdwellers, the Hand who hadn't slowed, seeking to exact vengeance on their fallen comrade.

No! My voice sounded in their minds and brought one Finger sliding to a halt in confusion. *Take them alive.*

My focus shifted back to the fleeing Emergent. His mind was as opaque as the wall that resisted my senses. But I kept the pressure up. That wall closed in, narrowing on the man, until it seemed only to surround his head.

I had him.

Pushing, pushing, pushing, every muscle in my body strained with the oppressive pain building inside my head. On the cusp of squashing him like the bug he was...

Just a little more...

All at once, the Emergent winked out of existence, just as my own Benefactor gave out. Pain exploded behind my eyes, like a hot needle had been driven into my brain. My Benefactor sense contracted, rushing back toward me, all of the other minds slipping from my grasp. Expansive awareness dimmed until I knew only my own thoughts, saw only through my eyes.

And then, even they became fuzzy. My weary limbs gave out, and my knees cracked against the stone ground.

Through slitted eyelids, I took in the scene around me as consciousness slipped. The sky was neither blue nor crimson, but black as midnight. Uniformed militiamen and civilians in plainclothes alike lay dead around me. The fire raged on, but ash-covered Liwo were throwing water into the flames. The bodies in the streets numbered far fewer than I had seen before. Far fewer than I expected, given the destruction.

Only that devastation exceeded what I had thought possible. Shop fronts were boarded up if not burned out or collapsed altogether. Reeking waste overflowed the gutters. The Market's church tower was nothing but rubble heaped around five cracked and dented bells.

I collapsed onto my side, grief building in a body slipping away, sorrowful from the sight of my home so thoroughly ruined.

For the first time since reawakening in Reed's twisted tower, I couldn't feel the Benefactor watching through my eyes.

Darkness filled my mind.

CHAPTER TWENTY-EIGHT

The Light's Faithful

Soldiers in silver, women in gold
None can protect us from Elzia's scold
A scold from a shadow that calls itself light
Don't pluck a wrong note or you're in for a fright!

—Verse from The Scold

It turned out reentering the Radiant Palace was far more difficult than leaving it, as she had learned after several days of failed attempt. Lorelay was sure the Paladins she sought entry from this time were the same who had watched her leave, but they swore they had never seen her face before. To be fair, she failed to recognize them as well, although in her defense, they all wore those imposing helmets with the visors down all the time. The same helmet Dunnax wore when in uniform, silver polished to a shine her brother's had lost in their exile.

When the Paladin at the gate lifted his visor, she half-expected her brother's face to appear. "Buzz off," the unfamiliar man said, and when she protested that she was here on invitation from the Bright Prince, he laughed and added, "And I'm bedding the Brightdaughter. I said, buzz off! Snuffing refugees..."

She tromped back down the switchback toward the setting sun, muttering under her breath how stupid that was, that it made no sense, and before she stomped out of earshot she turned and shouted back, "I hope the Brightdaughter burns your manhood right off!" That earned her a few looks, and she huffed in annoyance, hurrying away.

What to do, what to do? She puzzled over the prospect and dismissed several ideas right off. Sneaking in. No, she would be caught and sent to the dungeons for certain. Writing a letter to Vinlin. No, he would never receive it. Getting her mother to give those stupid Paladins an earful...that might just work. But no, Lorelay was a grown woman. She needed no help from her mother.

Just then, however, she figured she could use some help from another friend. Old trusty.

She slammed two stars down on the countertop and told the innkeeper, "Give me a Flaming Sun, easy on the spices, but make sure it's on fire." She loved that part, blowing out the fire atop the cocktail, feeling the burn as the concoction slid down her throat with an aftertaste of cinnamon. There was only one tavern in all of Vos—no, all the *Empire*—that mixed it right, and so her feet absentmindedly brought her here while she pondered how to reach Vinlin.

Only upon seeing the tall glass etched with a visage of the Brightdaughter placed in front of her and set alight did she realize what she had done. She had come to The Light's Faithful, the very inn where Dunnax had slain his brother in arms to protect her.

Oh, Darkfather. Her stomach suddenly roiled. Lorelay had been feeling so *light* lately. Staying at her childhood home for a few days had done wonders for her mentality. By the abyss, she was even getting along with her *mother*. Who knew? Take the zealotry for the Lightmother out of her, and she was a perfect charmer. Her mother comforted her, offered helpful advice, and kept Lorelay busy around the house. All exactly what she needed.

Now look what she had gone and done. Her eyes were fixed on the flames before her, but her mind spiraled into the dark. It was like deep down she *wanted* to be broken. How else to explain it?

The events of that day came rushing back to her. The Paladin's gauntlet digging into her shoulder, jerking her upright and cutting short her song. The back of his metal hand cracked against her cheek, and Lorelay whirled. By the time the room stopped spinning, he was muttering about heresy and justice, and his sword had already left its scabbard. Wide-eyed, she could do nothing but stare as he drew back his elbow, preparing a thrust aimed for her heart. But another silver-armored man had bowled into him, saving her but knocking him into her. She had toppled to the ground, scrabbled beneath a table, and hid while steel clashed against steel.

"You trying to burn my bar down?" The innkeeper's gruff voice drew her back to the present. He snuffed the fire in Lorelay's glass. "You're not getting your coin back, I won't hear any—"

Lorelay shot to her feet, stool scraping the ground. "I don't want it. I'm sorry."

She turned, and her eyes were drawn to the exact table she had cowered beneath while Dunnax fought to defend her.

A surprised grunt, then a body had fallen to the ground beside her. Paladin's armor had been all Lorelay could see. That, and the blood staining the silver, pouring from the body's side where a blade had found a chink in the armor.

Lorelay remembered thinking that was her brother. She crawled from the table, not daring to breathe, reaching out to lift the visor.

"Don't touch him." She could hear her brother's voice even now. It was unsteady. Lorelay had spun, found Dunnax quaking with rage, shock. His eyes were darting between the stunned onlookers in The Lady's Faithful. Lorelay could not have known what he was feeling, but she knew she had to do something. She had stood, laid a hand on his arm. The tip of his bloody sword touched the ground. "What did I do? What did you make me do?"

His voice still scared her. So cold and dead, as if both their lives had ended with the stroke of his blade. She had looked around. All eyes were on them. People were starting to shift, as if waiting for the next impossible event to occur. A Paladin killing another Paladin. It was unheard of. Everyone would remember that moment.

"We can't stay here," she had plead with Dunnax, and by the mercy of the Lightmother, he had listened. They had fled the tavern, then the city, moving under cover of darkness as alarm bells rang out behind them signaling the start of the hunt for the Oathbreaker.

That was the last night she and Dunnax had spent in the city. They had slept on cold stone when their legs could take them no farther. For nearly a year, they continued running, until Lorelay heard about a new opportunity in distant Liwokin, an organization looking for fighters from all across the Empire. They left Paceeq that day and never looked back.

Until Lorelay had returned. *Idiot,* she chided herself, coming back to the scene of the crime. Likely the only reason the innkeeper failed to recognize her was the dress she wore hoping to gain entrance to the palace. A far cry from the leather jerkin she used to wear, as if preparing to sing was the same as preparing for battle.

"Move it," a drunk man said, knocking her aside and sloshing the three tankards of ale he was carrying precipitously on a platter.

She had been standing unaware in the middle of the aisle between tables. The glare she caught on his face looked all too familiar to Lorelay. For an instant, her stomach clenched with fear that he might recognize her. A ridiculous thought. That was two years ago. But having her lyre smashed on her first day back in the city should have been warning enough for her to stay away from places where trouble would find her. She knew she had to remain in the city, there was no helping that, but she certainly could not stay here.

Pushing through the considerable crowd blocking her way to the exit, Lorelay was gripped with panic, as though someone would notice her at any moment, and she would find herself trapped in the dungeon again. She was three steps away from the door when it opened.

"Lightmother's tits", she cursed under her breath as two Paladins entered, and the whole establishment went dead silent. Face-to-face with the enemy, her mind raced. Should she run? No, she would never make it past. Hide? Dressed like this, she stood out like a Fire in the abyss. That they were here for her, she was certain, and there was no escape. She was trapped as surely as a heretic in the dungeon.

And then Vinlin entered. He spotted Lorelay immediately, and while the Paladin beside the door announced his presence and the rest of the room bowed with hands to hearts, she stood straight and still as the stars at night.

The Bright Prince approached her with a wrapped parcel in his hands. Atop the parcel was a letter bearing the Head of the Agency's sigil, a tower with a stern face at the top that looked regrettably like Ulken's.

"These are for you, Brightness," Vinlin said, pushing the package into her hands.

Lorelay blinked, then cast a glance at all of the patrons of The Light's Faithful, staring at her in as stark a disbelief as they had when a Paladin had died by the hand of another. She had no idea what to say. She was in as much shock to see Vinlin as they were. More! All that came out when she opened her mouth was a dumb "Uhh."

"Ah." Vinlin turned to the innkeeper and spoke calmly. "Clear everyone out. The lady and I require privacy." The innkeeper no doubt had little trouble hearing the Bright Prince over the stunned silence of the room, but his jaw clenched and unclenched as if working up a protest. Until, that was, Vinlin added, "You will be compensated. The Bright Throne pays its dues."

At that, the innkeeper's voice boomed, "Everyone out! Tavern's closed! You heard His Radiance!"

What followed was an impressive display of grumbling and shuffling as The Light's Faithful emptied itself of patrons. Some protested, tried to carry their drinks out, grumbled about having nowhere else to go...but no one wanted to get the Paladins involved. Least of all the innkeeper, who was doing his best impression of a sheepdog herding the flock out of their pen. He was the last to go, save the Paladins. With a tip of his hat and a bit more bowing and scraping than Lorelay could stomach with rolling her eyes, he left the Bright Prince and his lady alone.

"I said everyone," Vinlin said to the Paladins.

"But Your Radi—"

"Everyone."

Two silver-helmed soldiers nodded simultaneously, and Lorelay found herself truly alone with Vinlin.

"Well," Vinlin said, "are you going to open them?" He strolled behind the bar, found two crystal goblets, and poured them full of a dark red wine. "The letter's not from me." Looking around, he suddenly got an idea. "Oh! Don't open the other without me. I'll return in but a moment." He hurried off into the kitchen. Some shouting followed, and two boys with dough covering their hands ran out, ensuring they bowed to Lorelay before hurrying out of the tavern.

Lorelay shook her head, dumbfounded. What, by the Lightmother, was happening? She opened the letter with Grim's seal and found his handwriting worrying. Scrawled across the page like he was writing with his left hand instead of his right, the letters were uneven and squiggly, making some words nearly illegible.

Her anxiety sparked as she wondered if the Head's mental faculty was failing him—after he had become a Benefactor, it was only a matter of time before he lost himself fully to madness. If he failed in Liwokin, her mission would be moot.

Worse than the shaky lettering, the note contained no good news, only ill tidings and questions for Lorelay.

Another Benefactor had been found in Liwokin, and Grim was trying his damnedest to ensure the city's safety. Ulken's wife, the Benefactor Yezna, had been found in the tower, yet the way Grim talked about her, he was using her like a tool as surely as Ulken had. She questioned, not for the first time, whether Grim really should have been put in charge of the Agency. Her lip curled at the thought, but not so much as it curled when she read his questions for her.

Has Vinlin pledged his support yet? She snorted humorlessly. "Not in the way you might imagine, Grim."

The next two questions made her stop and think when she tried to put them together: *Have you learned anything about the Grieving Pine branch? Is he fighting Benefactors in Paceeq?*

The Bright Prince was certainly *not* fighting Benefactors in Paceeq. He was more inclined to keep his head lodged in his—

Lorelay stopped herself. That was unfair. She knew Vinlin had too much on his mind to add in the Benefactor scourge. But in that case, why *did* he need the branch as a source of Druid's Tears?

With a sigh, she read the last lines aloud. "The fate of the world hinges on your success. We need the Bright Emperor's support." Lorelay was tempted to crush the letter into a ball. It would be a match for the crushing pressure she felt. All she had to do was save the world. Easy!

"What was that, my dear?" Vinlin asked, returning from the kitchens. He held a tray of olives, sliced cheese, and two heels of bread in one hand. His other hand...the future Bright Emperor was sucking his thumb.

"Nothing," Lorelay said, then raised an eyebrow at him and added, "Everything okay there?"

He placed the gilded tray of food on the table before her, then brought over the two glasses of wine. "Just a small nick. I confess I'm not very good with knives, not like you." He tried to smile, then his thumb resumed bleeding, which he tried to hide from her. It looked more like a gash than a nick.

"That looks bad! Should we find an Archehealer?"

He smiled sheepishly. "I should be capable of performing it myself. Great Archemages have attempted to instill that talent in me since birth. Alas, with little success. As though the Church needed more reason to oppose me."

Vinlin controlled the Fire? She supposed it should not come as a great shock. Bright Empress Elzia was said to be an exceedingly skilled mage. Vinlin, on the other hand, looked as if he would rather talk about anything but his lacking competencies.

Still, that cut needed tending, and the Bright Prince seemed disinclined to heal himself. Lorelay retrieved a cloth from another table. It was soaked in something that smelled like strong alcohol, and she tore a strip of it loose. "Give me your hand."

He winced when she bandaged his thumb. "Stings…"

"Well it's either that, or you keep your thumb in your mouth while I eat all the food you prepared myself." That was a kind gesture, she admitted to herself. A shame it was likely another attempt to cajole her into his blankets.

"I wasn't complaining." He looked entirely sincere. "Thank you, Lorelay. And I'm sorry for how I treated you the other day in my chambers. I realized I was being presumptuous and had to make it up to you."

"How did you find me here, anyway?" Lorelay asked, perhaps with too much heat in her voice.

Vinlin took no offence to her tone. "Easy. I asked your mother."

Lorelay spluttered. "My *mother?* By the abyss, what did she say?" Lightmother have mercy if she spoke about Lorelay having the Bright Prince's children.

Vinlin laughed and winked. "That's a state secret, I'm afraid. Are you going to open what I brought you?"

Still skeptical her mother had avoided embarrassing her, she popped an olive into her mouth, savored its saltiness, then washed it away with a sip of wine. She might not know what words passed between the Bright Prince and her mother, but she remembered their own conversation. It was time to put her plan into action. "Depends."

"On?" The Bright Prince tried an olive as well, and his face contorted in disgust. Lorelay's lips quirked in a smile. Vinlin quickly followed the olive with subsequent mouthfuls of wine, cheese, bread, and more wine.

"On whether you'll let me tell you a story." Lorelay braced herself. "About my brother."

"Of course, Brightness."

"Please stop calling me that."

"Oh? What, then, should I call you?"

"How about Lorelay?" she said. "You know, my name. Is that too difficult?"

Vinlin wiped a hand across his face. "Apologies, my...Lorelay. A lifetime of learning the habits of courtesy will be hard to break. I shall endeavor to—"

"That's another thing," Lorelay cut him off. She put on the regal affect that all the ladies of the court tended to talk in, a way to convince themselves they were above the common Paceeqi. "I shall endeavor to, blah blah blah. You can just talk to me like a normal person."

"I..." Vinlin took a deep breath. "I'll try."

Lightmother help her, Lorelay believed him. All her life, she had railed against the Bright Throne and the Church of Light. Now, all her hopes—and the fate of the world—rested on her allying herself with the Emperor. She had thought this mission was hopeless. Looking into Vinlin's eyes, she felt hope kindling.

"My brother...Dunnax." Lorelay swallowed the lump in her throat. She had to be strong now. For him. "I used to hate him. He was always the perfect son, in exactly the way I *wasn't* the perfect daughter. While Mother and Father were encouraging him to grow, they were always trying to cut me short. Mother, mostly. When Empress Elzia inducted Dunnax into the Order of Paladins, my parents were prouder than they had ever been about me. I hated it. I resented him. But it wasn't his fault, I realized. It was *yours*."

Vinlin furrowed his brows. "Mine?"

"Your mother's, actually. It wasn't Dunnax's fault the Church and Throne outlawed everything I loved to do. Fighting. No, that's only for men. Writing songs. No, the Church of Light forbids that. I would have killed to have even one day where my mother didn't force me to read from the Book of Light at each ringing of the bells. So, I stopped hating Dunnax. He was my brother, and the Book of Light is right about one thing. You should love your family. Instead, I turned my hatred toward you and your family."

Vinlin swallowed and grimaced. "That's a lot of hatred for one woman."

"For one girl," Lorelay corrected. "The Bright Throne never gave me the chance to grow up, not like I wanted to. So, I took it into my own hands. I stopped following your rules. But Dunnax never did. He excelled as a Paladin, working his way up to the Lumeeq metal mines. He dreamed of..." Lorelay sniffled. "He dreamed of patrolling the Fire Gardens, protecting the royal family." She wiped away tears. "He never got a chance, because of me."

Lorelay tried to hold back more tears, but they flowed freely. She expected Vinlin to condemn Dunnax for his oathbreaking, or to defend the Throne's laws as necessary and just. Instead, he remained quiet and placed a hand on hers. Could he understand what she had gone through, losing a sibling? Living up on the plateau, it seemed impossible he would relate to her experience, but she had to try.

"Dunnax was the perfect citizen, the perfect soldier. He lived by the Paladin's code even when we fled to Lawiko. He followed the Agency's orders without question. Because he knew what the Agency was doing was fighting to protect the Empire. Only...he was wrong. The Head of the Agency wasn't the man we thought he was. Ulken was corrupted by the Darkfather, willing to sacrifice any number of people to keep control of the city. Dunnax was one of those people."

Vinlin squeezed her hand, and she looked up. There were tears in his eyes now too. This was the first time she had fully let herself think about Dunnax's death since that day in Reed's Woods. She had held some of this back even from her mother, but if Vinlin was going to understand her pain, he had to hear everything.

"I almost died that day too. I should have died that day. The Benefactor had me under its spell. Until Grim brought me back. I didn't know how I had gotten there, but there were thousands of Liwo around me, all preparing to be absorbed by the monster. I didn't care about that, though. I wanted to know where Dunnax was, and when I saw Grim's eyes...I knew. The hatred that I felt for the Bright Empire was nothing compared to what I felt toward Ulken. It was *his* fault Dunnax was dead, and he was in my reach.

"But he was strong. Stronger than me, stronger than all of us in the Hand. If I stayed there...I *would* have died in those woods. So, when Grim told me to run, I ran. I gave up my chance to kill the man who took my brother from me, knowing that I would only get another chance if I survived. Only...Grim won. I thought it would make me feel better to know Ulken was dead, but it didn't. I realized that's because...that's because it wasn't Ulken's fault Dunnax was dead. Not Ulken's fault. Not yours or your mother's. It's mine."

"That's not true," Vinlin tried to say.

"Don't." Lorelay pulled her hand back, hugged herself. "It is true. We would never have left Vos if not for me fighting the Bright Throne by singing songs." She scoffed. "As if singing songs would ever make any difference. Finally, I hated the right person. Myself. It's my fault Dunnax is dead, and if I can't get you to help the Agency, all of us will be dead soon. My brother's death will have meant nothing. I can't let that happen."

I'll never forgive myself. I wouldn't deserve it.

Lorelay was breathing hard, barely holding it together. She had laid herself bare for the Bright Prince, and all that remained was for him to respond. With a word, he could end her hope of salvation.

Vinlin remained quiet for some time. The food and drink went untouched. Lorelay certainly had no appetite. Her stomach was twisting itself in knots waiting to hear his pronouncement. Would he make another pass at her? Take advantage of her grief? Would he dismiss the Benefactors out of hand once more?

"Tell me about a good memory you have with Dunnax," Vinlin said instead. "It sounds like the two of you were close."

Conflicting emotions flooded into Lorelay along with all the memories of her childhood. The two of them were close growing up, but their relationship had become strained after Dunnax became a Paladin. She cast further back for a story to share and found one that made her giggle to herself.

"Do tell." Vinlin smiled expectantly.

"Well, it wasn't *entirely* true that he was always the perfect son, even if our parents believed it. Dunnax was simply more talented at getting away with his misdeeds. He kept even me in the dark, hid all of his worst vices from me. I think he was ashamed," she said with a shrug. "I wouldn't have judged him. But I *was* curious.

"One night, when our parents were both asleep, I heard the icebox creak open, and Dunnax snuck out of the house. I was awake composing a song, still dressed up for the dusk service, and climbed out the window without waiting." Lorelay snorted. "He thought he was so stealthy, darting from shadow to shadow. But Jenx and I had been avoiding the night patrols for ages, to, er..."

She trailed off, not wanting to admit to the Bright Prince about heretical writings they had scrawled on church walls. Vinlin only sat back, enjoying his wine, soft eyes urging her to continue.

"Anyway, I stumbled into something Dunnax dropped. My slipper squished on it. A dead fish, which ignited my curiosity even further. What was my brother doing secreting tomorrow's dinner across the city? When he finally reached where he was going, we were so close to the harbor I thought he was planning to throw them into the water. But no, his dark secret was *much* more sinister."

Vinlin stopped chewing his mouthful of cheese, leaning forward in anticipation.

"I remember he looked all around to make sure no one followed him, then darted down an alleyway. I rushed to follow him, and as soon as I caught him in the act, a bunch of black, shadowy creatures hissed and scattered in every direction. Startled me so bad, I was sure a Paladin heard me scream and would think there was a murder.

"Dunnax spun around, crying out, and flung his frozen fish right at me. One of them hit me square in the chest and ruined my church clothes, but I was too busy laughing to be angry. After all that sneaking around, my brother's big secret was that he was feeding stray cats!"

Vinlin's grin touched all parts of his face. "That's it?"

"To hear him tell it, he was seriously conflicted about the matter. He worried that stealing would tarnish him in the eyes of the Light-mother, but he just couldn't help it. He had a soft spot for a kitten he came across on his way home one day and had been feeding it ever since. Only, by the time it was no longer a kitten, it must have told every cat in the neighborhood where to wait for fresh fish."

Lorelay's cheeks hurt from smiling so broadly. "That was my brother. I was the one risking our family with my constant rebellion, while he was worried he'd be caught helping stray animals." Her cheerful smile quickly became somber. Dunnax should have survived Lawiko, not Lorelay. "I hate that things turned out like this because of me."

Vinlin's mood dimmed with her own, and he wordlessly gestured for her to open the wrapped package sitting beside the tray of food.

Skeptical, Lorelay untied the knot of twine keeping the cloth bound. She unfolded the layers of wrapping, and when she reached the last one, her breath caught.

She gingerly lifted the brand-new lyre that lay within, plucking one horsehair string and listening to its sonorous tone, perfectly pitched. The curved body of the instrument was gilded, and her name was engraved in the wood in a flowing script, stained a deep crimson. Newfound tears filled her eyes, and this time she had no intention of holding them back.

"I love your songs," Vinlin said, nearly a whisper. "Your free spirit may get you into trouble, but I don't want you to hate yourself for it."

Lorelay's mouth moved, but the words were stuck in her throat.

"When I noticed you didn't carry your instrument with you, I found out what happened at the Blueflame Tavern. That Paladin has been reprimanded. No doubt he'll appeal his punishment with the Church and cause more problems, but so be it. Lorelay without her lyre is the empire without the Brightdaughter."

"I don't..." Lorelay shook her head, wiped her sleeve across her eyes. "Thank you, but—"

Vinlin raised a hand to quiet her. "As for the Benefactors...you have to understand, changing anything in the Empire is like trying to predict where the Brightdaughter will rise. You're asking for a big favor, and I *want* to grant it, Lightmother knows I do. I will try, I promise you."

Lorelay's eyes lit up. Thinking back to Grim's letter, an idea came over her. "What if there's something smaller I can ask you for?"

Vinlin grinned. "That would certainly be easier. But it'll cost you."

Lorelay's shoulders drooped. She could see where this was going.

Vinlin must have realized what ran through her head because he waved his hands. "Not like that. I just..." He nodded at the lyre. "I want to hear a song. Perhaps...one of yours?"

Lorelay breathed out in relief. That, she could do. But he was offering her an olive branch, trying to change the Empire to fit her needs. If he was willing to go so far, she could change herself to make his life easier, too. "How about one of the Twelve Songs, instead."

Vinlin smiled, and Lorelay took the stage for an audience of one.

CHAPTER TWENTY-NINE

No Way Out

...unexpected effect. Threads of Fire cannot pierce solid metal. What if there are holes?

—Note scribbled in a secret chamber

I woke from a dreamless sleep. How long had it been since I could say that? Every night, the Benefactor flooded my mind with memories and visions, uninhibited by the small control my waking brain had over the creature. It had been exhausted by the contest in the Market. Not killed. Exhausted, that was all, taking my ability to see strands of Archefire and the ocean of others with it.

The monster slumbered in my head. Plaguing me like an itch behind my eyes, impossible to scratch.

Sitting up, my joints creaked. My muscles ached. Sweat soaked my blankets and clothes. A pounding headache made me want to curl up and hide from the daylight streaming in through my open window.

No, there can be no hiding.

Sentyx was right. We must face into the wind. I donned a fresh pair of clothes, then approached the window to survey the city.

The Brightdaughter flew high today. It must have been nearly noon, or perhaps just past. The bright sibling's light was hot but tempered by a cool, salty breeze blowing in from the bay. Still, I shivered.

Smoldering black wrecks dotted the Market, as expected, but the damage was far more extensive than that. Despite the time of day, the city was eerily dead. Hardly any Liwo moved about in the streets of the Burg. Dead donkeys and horses had been forgotten and left to rot. The mast of a sunken ship jutted from the dark waters of the harbor. My eyes scanned upward to the cliffs beneath the Blight, and the breath left my lungs.

The cliff face was empty. The Blight docks were simply...gone.

Wood splintering. Falling. Rushing water. Darkness.

That ramshackle scaffolding had been doomed to fail eventually. But why hadn't I seen it until now? I had stood in this exact spot and looked out over the city. Everything seemed normal. That was after arising from being overwhelmed by a great number of Emergences.

But I didn't suppress them all, did I?

One had slipped through. A powerful Benefactor, on par with my own. I heaved a great sigh. Its Aura in the Market had nearly overcome me, but the tide had turned with the rush of my Fingers and Archecloaks. The feeling of its Aura winking out had come at the last moment before my Benefactor's strength gave out.

If its Aura were still cloaking the city, what would I see from this window? False reality? A bright sky, light shining on Blightdwellers disguised as militiamen, defending their city from senseless violence?

Everyone wants to see themselves as the hero.

With a shake of my head, I turned—

To find a Nerve standing silently in my doorway. She didn't salute. She didn't look me in the eyes. She didn't report a message. She simply picked at her fingernails, not having noticed that I turned around.

"You." Recognition dawned on me, and her attention shifted away from her fingernails. "Last time you were here, I practically had to chase you out of here with a command. What happened?"

"I followed that command," she said, strolling forward. "Nerves are no longer required to salute you, address you as 'Sir', wait on your every whim and word, or rush to carry out your commands to the limits of our physical ability."

I blinked. "Is that so?"

Darkfather, is it wrong of me that I wish they still would?

Her casual attitude was almost more disconcerting than her previous, overly formal stance. When she reached into her white-and-gold coat, I tensed and took a step back. I was unarmed. She was no longer bound by the rules. Could I trust her?

But she pulled no weapon, merely a folded slip of paper, which she handed to me. "Let me know if you need anything else," she said, turning to leave.

My mouth hung uselessly open as I searched for the words to stop her. They never came. I blew out a breath, puffing my cheeks, and unfolded the paper instead.

Reports of sudden and unexplained carnage in all districts. Recommend sending Eyes to investigate.

Sighing, I crumpled the paper up. No need to send any Eyes of the Agency to investigate. Not when I could look out the window and see it all with my own two eyes. There was only one explanation, one truth from which I couldn't hide. My hands trembled.

The healthy, vibrant Liwokin I witnessed mere days ago...was a lie. Now, while the monster inside my head slumbered, I saw the truth. An Aura was missing.

Mine.

"No," I told myself. "No, there *must* be some other way to explain it."

My mind raced, searching for hidden answers, turning the problem over and over in my head to examine it from every angle. Three skies. Noon, midnight, and crimson heavens. Two Auras in competition, fighting to enforce their vision of Liwokin. In both, the city was a battleground between Blightdwellers and all other Liwo. The only thing that changed was the perception of who was righteous. Were the Blightdwellers a rampaging mob or the city's protectors?

Neither was the truth. The sad fact was Liwokin was dying. All the evidence I needed sprawled out across the city and could be seen from my window. Carnage in all districts. Even the Riot hadn't caused so much chaos...

The Riot. An idea formed.

A way out.

Could it have been her?

Without a second thought, I was rushing down the stairs to the Treasury, where I knew Arza would be working. The Organ of Treasure was flustered by my sudden appearance, but I paid him no mind. The vault door was unlocked as always—no need to safeguard a room devoid of gold—as was the chest with the hidden ladder.

When I reached the bottom, Arza was writing furiously in a notebook laid out on a desk littered with knives, wads of paper, and fluids whose origins I could only guess at. Saying her name wasn't enough. It took me shaking her by the shoulder to snap her out of her reverie.

"Grim! You have come at an excellent time."

"I have?" I raised an eyebrow. By how concentrated she was on the problem in front of her, it seemed her emotions were dulled by Yezna's Aura. But perhaps not... She sounded too excited.

For her part, Yezna sat in her usual spot, chest rising and falling beneath a more modest garb than Ulken outfitted her with. Her head lolled back, eyes cloudy and unmoving. She gave no signs of life save her slow, deep breaths. Next to her on the floor sat a small cage of blue-gray metal. Familiar...but my attention was on Yezna. Had something happened to her?

Arza held up a Druid's Tear, the glassy bead glistening in her palm. "This was the key. I do not know what about it causes the effect, but the Druid's Tears completely nullify the Aura."

"It's what keeps the monsters away, a Druid told us. The Pine's Aura. The tree these came from." Nothing surfaced among the ten thousand lives that had any connection to the Pinegrave. Curious, but perhaps to be expected when they spent all their time around the Grieving Pine.

I searched my mind for a moment before realizing that was wrong... No memories surfaced simply because my Benefactor lay dormant.

By the abyss, I was coming to rely on those abilities too heavily.

"A tree with an Aura? Fascinating." Arza tapped her lips. "I am curious. Did your Skardwarf friend ever use a Druid's Tear?"

"Sentyx?" I laughed. "Even his backside was hard enough to crack the glass. I seriously think he's *made* of stone sometimes."

"That is unfortunate. I would love to know if these toxics will work on a Skardwarf as well as on a human. Or on a Peeker for that matter. If only they had not all fled for the Mounds in the past days."

"They have? Why haven't I heard about this? How did *you* hear about this?"

Arza shrugged. "I leave the chest open at the top of the ladder. The Organ never checks in here, and he gossips with the Heels. It is... entertaining." The mortician gave a mischievous grin. "One time, I overheard—"

I waved her off. "Arza, I already know too much about peoples' personal lives with this thing in my head. Why don't you think the Tears will work on Peekers and Skardwarves?"

She pondered the question, tapping the side of her goggles while thinking. "I would not say I am certain they will not. I always assume the most likely possibility will occur, and it seems simpler in this case to assume that their patterns are dissimilar enough from a human's to interact with the toxics. Although, if they are—and I have not the faintest clue what determines their similarity—then there might be some effect. Maybe weaker than on humans, maybe stronger. I do not know."

Did she realize how similar to Tak she was? In her time serving him, she had picked up even his manner of speaking. Rambling, more like.

But wait. Patterns? Hadn't Tak told us about patterns the first time we met? Something about humans having a pattern closely related to Archefire, thanks to the seedling in our heads. I grimaced remembering he also put forth that Peekers and Skardwarves were 'uncivilized beings.' That meant they lacked a seedling and had some other way to preserve their pattern.

Arza continued rambling on while I tried to edge in a word to no avail. I hadn't come here to get caught up in a technical explanation. I needed to know if Yezna's Aura could have...what? Replaced reality? When had it ever done *that* before? The idea seemed too desperate even to voice.

"Look here." She snatched a wadded up paper from her workbench and uncrumpled it. "No, no, wait." Dissatisfied, she threw it away and checked another. Then, a third. "Ah! Here it is." The paper was covered with a bunch of incomprehensible scribblings that looked like nothing so much as a child's attempt at drawing a farmer and his animals. Animals they had never seen, at that. Arza pointed. "Here, in the brain of the Peekers, a bond is formed that links the Pair. Everyone knows this. But have you considered why a Peeker cannot form a Pair with a human?"

I eyed the paper more closely. That was meant to be a Pair of Peekers? I thought it might have been the Sibling Suns, with wiggly lines radiating from them representing their light. "I suppose I haven't. Is it impor—"

Arza pointed at a stick figure of a human. That, at least, I could identify. "Their patterns are aligned because they spend so much time in the presence of one another. Tak never let me pursue this theory, but if I am correct, the Peeker Mounds are teeming with not just Pairs of Peekers but enormous clusters of them all linked together."

"What does this have to do with—"

"A human might be able to form a Pair with one given enough time, but that might take a lifetime or more. It depends how closely aligned their patterns are to begin with, not to mention the rate at which they change to match the other. Oh!" The mortician found a fresh sheet of paper and started jotting notes. "I wonder if human and

Peekers patterns change at *different* rates. And I have yet to consider Skardwarves!"

This conversation was going nowhere. I was curious to know if her suppressant would work on *anything* that was infested. That included Peekers—their Benefactors created the power Ulken sought—and Skardwarves, whom I had to assume could be infested as easily as any other, given how strongly Sentyx and Cavern were affected by Reed's Aura.

Darkfather, Lomin even had a dog who was infested.

Did we have to cure every animal in the Empire to ensure the Benefactors were eradicated?

I shook my head. The mortician's ramblings were scrambling my mind as surely as my Benefactor's intrusive memories. This was another distraction.

"Arza, please—"

But she had finished her note and launched back into her rambling explanation. "An avenue to investigate later, perhaps. The point is that while these Druid's Tears certainly suppress Yezna's Aura, I do not know if they rely on the infested host's pattern, or the pattern associated with the Benefactor's Aura, or if they work by some other mechanism we have yet to understand. Let us assume they require a specific pattern to work. In that case—"

"Arza!" I grabbed her by the wrists. Too firmly, given her reaction. But I was growing angry with impatience. If I didn't stop her, she might have kept me down here until the dusk bells rang or madness consumed me. That was fast approaching, the longer I listened to her spewing information.

I let go, and she stepped back with a horrified expression on her face. One I recognized: she thought she was in danger.

Holding up my hands to signal I wasn't a threat, I told her, "I'm sorry." I could do her one better, though. "Look, do you remember Garret?"

"Yes," she replied, as sullenly as if Yezna's Aura still numbed her. "The Ekoan ranger in your old Hand."

"He's in the Peeker Mounds right now. I'll write to him and ask about your theory. Lots of Peekers linked together, was it?"

They were so remarkably coordinated. If only I could make the same thing happen with the Council and Gild, maybe we'd stand a chance against the infestation. Such wishful thinking would get me nowhere. I had to focus on real solutions.

The excitement reentered her eyes, my transgression evidently forgotten. "An excellent idea! He spoke to me of his own ideas about animal patterns. I nearly mistook him for a biotist rather than a killer. I will compile a list of procedures he can use to test—"

"Hold on," I said before she got too worked up again. "He's there searching for Prost, not to serve as one of your technicians."

Arza had already begun writing down those experimental procedures but paused and looked at me quizzically. "Prost? Why is he searching for Tak's old master?"

My mouth hung open. "Tak's master? No, you must be mistaken. Prost worked with Ulken to spread Benefactors. If he..."

A pulse of pain radiated throughout my skull, and I dug my palms into my eyes to fight off the pressure. When the sensation abated, I opened my eyes to find Archefire threads coating the surface of everything. My Benefactor had reawakened.

As if eager to renew its purpose, two memories seemed to surface simultaneously. One of Lomin in a classroom full of soon-to-be-Benefactors. The man cajoling Lomin for his predator versus prey worldview was irate for needing to repeat himself. The other was of a conversation with Tak in his steamcarriage the very day Hand Sixty-Four had killed Lomin. Tak refused to explain why he'd retrieved us. The others were asleep, and the now-dead mortician told me his master taught him foremost never to repeat himself.

Prost was a mortician. I wiped my hand across my face. How had I never made the connection before? Was that why the man had Cavern steal Tak's notes?

"They weren't Tak's notes at all…" I muttered. "They were Prost's. Darkfather, we let all that information slip right through our hands."

Arza looked horrified, as though only now realizing she was working for a monster. "All that we are doing here… Is it…"

"Stop," I said. "We can't second-guess now. The city is falling apart, and you're our best hope for stopping it. You need to keep going. We need that cure."

"I…" Arza studied her own hands, gloves covered in blood, ink, and mucus. They balled into fists, and there was fire in her eyes. "You are right. But Prost…the knowledge he has…the things he taught Tak. We need to know."

"I'm more worried about the things he *didn't* tell Tak. But we're trying. Garret has been ordered to find him, not to kill him."

I trust Garret won't try to take justice into his own hands.

The mortician slid the goggles on her forehead down to cover her eyes. "Then there is nothing more we can do about him now. I will—" Arza gasped, and her posture slumped. She appeared as if the wind was forced from her lungs.

"Arza? What's happening?"

But as soon as I asked the question, I knew the answer. A pressure built in my mind, the return of a familiar sensation. Dulling. Numbing. Yezna's Benefactor had returned as well.

I turned, studying the insensate woman with glazed-over eyes slouching in a wooden chair. Her body was dead—it had been since she slid the knife across her throat—but her Benefactor writhed with life. The Archedark pulsated around her head, warping the strands of Archefire that danced as clearly as Arza's flickering candle.

My own Benefactor reacted to the sudden presence of another. It released a flood of memories from the ocean of others, a current of madness that threatened to rush in to fill any empty space in my mind. I held it off before it flooded my consciousness, allowing my sense of self to float atop the rest. The pressure was immense. How long could I keep doing this? How long before something cracked, and I drowned beneath the weight of the monster?

"Nothing is wrong," Arza said flatly.

By the abyss, I wish I could believe that.

"I will continue my research and inform you when progress is made." Arza took up the cage beside Yezna and put it on the Benefactor's head. In an instant, her Aura disappeared.

My mouth dropped open.

"Oh! I have not explained to you how Darkmetal counters her Aura. Would you like to know?" She removed the cage of blue-gray metal, and the Aura returned at full strength.

"Darkmetal?" I quickly shook my head before she took my curiosity for an invitation. My head was already too full of information. Anything more and it might spill out from my ears. But seeing Yezna's Aura turned off as easily as a steam lamp gave me an idea. "No need. Just tell me, how long does your suppressant last? I'd like a sample to use on my own."

"It depends on the dose and the strength of the Benefactor," Arza said.

I braced for a long, overly complicated explanation, but none came. Yezna's Aura made her much more manageable. Every day it became clearer why Ulken wanted to use Benefactors to maintain control.

"However much you'd use to suppress Yezna for a full span, give me that."

Without a word, Arza plunged a clean syringe into a vial and drew in a tiny amount of viscous yellow fluid. She stepped close and said, "Lean your head back."

I stopped her. "I'll manage it on my own. Same principles as Druid's Tears, I assume?"

"No. It needs to be injected as close to the brain as possible, otherwise it is diluted by blood. There are three ways in: the eyes, the ears, or the nose."

I couldn't help but squirm upon hearing that, but I needed to hear something else, even more uncomfortable than a needle in the eye. "One last thing. Was Yezna's Aura active during the incident in the market?"

Arza tapped her lip, trying to match up the spans of time. "No, I do not believe so."

That was what I feared. With a sigh, I took the injector from her and eyed its contents. Such a small amount...perhaps there was hope for us after all. I stored it in my coat pocket. "I'll leave you to your experiments. Remember, a temporary fix isn't enough. We need a permanent cure."

And I need someone whose eyes I can trust.

As Arza turned back to her work without so much as a farewell, I began climbing the ladder out of her lab. If Yezna's Aura was suppressed, then she couldn't have been responsible for the visions in the Market. Snuffing out that meager hope left me with no way out. I had to face the truth. I was a Benefactor. Different from any other, but some things never change.

I possessed an Aura, evidently strong enough to pull the wool over my own eyes.

It was time to see just how potent it really was.

CHAPTER THIRTY

Trusted Eyes

Requests from Liwo have decreased significantly. It is good to see you are finally taking care of the important things, my friend.

—Message accompanying G11-b forms
awaiting the Head's signature

"Do you trust me?" I asked, fearing the answer.

Darkfather, I wouldn't.

All of what my Benefactor disguised had now been accepted into its projections. Into my Aura.

Inac and I stood beside one another, looking out upon the city from the window in his quarters. Everything had changed. Everything was *changing*. My closest friend, the one who grieved over my body when I became a monster, was the one person I could be certain would understand what we saw.

My Benefactor tried to hide the truth from us—the city was dying, if not already dead. The wreckage of the Market explosion still hadn't been cleaned up. Liwo in the streets ambled about like drunkards with no purpose. Even the Blight docks were gone.

But there were inconsistencies. No half-dusk bell rang to signal the end of work at the Docks, yet a considerable crowd flowed away from the Brightcalm Bay toward the Burg. As soon as I thought about the discrepancy, it vanished. Suddenly the Docks were empty, and the migrating crowd was gone.

Darkfather, how was I supposed to remember what's real when reality shifted before my eyes?

I moved to another window. Lines of wagons brought trade and travelers to the Span Gate, where Archecloaks stopped them for inspection. Why would Archecloaks be guarding a gate outside the Gild? With the mere thought, they weren't. Now the wagons flowed into the streets unobstructed. Only, that didn't make sense either. If the city was dying—

The thought had scarcely crossed my mind before all of it disappeared, leaving an empty, lifeless street below.

"How are you doing this?" Inac whispered.

I gave a long exhale. The lack of answer was almost worse than hearing him say no outright. Fair enough. How could anybody trust a man who changed reality on a whim? The Benefactor made a liar of me. But it couldn't stop me from speaking honestly. Especially not to Inac.

"It's not me," I said. "It's...my Aura. Don't look at me like that. There's a difference. I don't know how to control it, how to stop it from changing what everyone sees."

"You are—," he began, then awkwardly changed what he was going to say. "*It* is hiding from us what is to the city truly happening."

"I know." Even as I looked out upon the Gild, an army of Archecloaks seemed to be gathering at the gate. They weren't really there, I knew, and as soon as I told myself that...they weren't.

"What makes the Aura change like this? Why before was this not happening?"

"Maybe it was, but I never questioned it." Each day was a blur of trying to keep up with being the Head. Requests for help, Finger assignments, Ulken's blackmail, meetings with the Gild and Council...

It was too much. I never had time to focus on what was happening outside these walls.

"I assumed the city was operating normally. Since it's what I expected, that's what my Aura showed everyone."

"And now?"

"Now, I don't know what's really going on out there. After the fight in the Market, my Benefactor was worn out from killing the other one."

"Are you sure you really killed it?"

"I..." *Lightmother, am I?* "I think so. I felt it wither to nothing. But...maybe that's what it felt my Benefactor do too."

I rubbed my eyes. Thinking about my own Benefactor was enough trouble. The last thing I needed was to worry about *another* attack on the city. Liwokin couldn't take it. It was already crumbling under the weight of one Aura. Another might kill my home for good. Problems can't be solved if they're festering beneath the surface. Clearly, we had a lot of that going on.

"Listen," I said to my friend and pulled Arza's suppressant from my pocket. "This is why I need you."

Inac's eyes bulged at the needle, and he backed away a half dozen steps before bumping against a table, spilling an inkwell across a letter scrawled in unsteady handwriting. He groaned at the mess. "Took for me half a span to write that..." he muttered, then looked back and shook his head. "Grim, Druid's Tears were for me bad enough. That is twice the size of those glass pines at least!"

"Relax," I said, letting the amusement show on my face. "It's for me, not you." *What I have to do to you is worse.* "I need to know, Inac. Do you believe me? All this I've told you about my Aura, that I'm trying to fight it. You know I'm telling you the truth?"

"Of course," he said without hesitation. "We have together been fighting this plague. Just tell to me what you need for me to do."

"It'll be easy. You just need to walk the streets. Every district. Show me the truth of what's happening in our city."

"You say to me that I must show to you the truth...but you will not be coming with me?"

I shook my head. "I need to meet with Oltrov. Outside this tower, he seems to be the only one on our side, and he needs to know what's happening with the city. If anyone has the money and men to help us fix it, it's him."

Not to mention he has our prisoners from the market.

"Then how will I show to you the truth? I can tell to you this, but any Heels can do for you this job."

Grimacing, I took a seat on the side of the bed. "You know how I can see the memories of dead men?"

He nodded.

"Well, it doesn't only work on dead men. When Oltrov was at our gates with his Archecloaks, I saw myself through his eyes. I want to see the city through yours. But what I did to Oltrov wasn't enough. I saw the present. With you, I'll need to see the past. I'll need to dig deep inside your head. Be immersed in your thoughts, sensing everything you sensed. If you have any secrets you're keeping from me..." I squeezed my fists. "Darkfather, I know you're entitled to those, but I can't think of any other way. I have to be sure."

Inac sat for a long while thinking. Was he looking for another way? If our positions were reversed, I knew I would be. Abyss take me, the idea was madness. I shouldn't be *using* my Benefactor, I should be suppressing it as often as I could. Otherwise, how was I any different from Ulken? These organisms were a scourge, not a tool, and as soon as Arza had a cure, I would be the first in line to use it.

Me...and then everyone else in the Empire.

Even when Arza succeeded, how could we procure enough Druid's Tears to produce enough for everyone? The plague was spreading throughout the entire world.

Garret and Sentyx could be fighting Emergents in the Peeker Mounds at this very moment. Had I sent them into the jaws of an unimaginable beast?

And what of Lorelay? We needed the Emperor's support, but the capital might have already fallen. Why hadn't I heard from her yet?

I silently cursed myself. All my friends were slipping away. Rather than desperately holding on to the ones that remained, here I was, pushing away another.

"I will do for you this task," Inac said.

I sucked in a breath, eyes widening. "You will?"

"On one condition."

"Anything."

Inac sighed and pulled a chair up to sit beside me. "I am keeping from you a secret, Grim. And I do not wish for you to find it out by digging in my brain." I gave a confused look, but Inac stopped me from speaking. "I will tell to you this secret, but I do not know how. Not yet. When I come back, promise to me you will let me tell you first."

"Of course. I won't do it until you're ready. I promise."

Despite my promise, I couldn't help but speculate about what his secret might be. I trusted him, more than ever now that he'd admitted he was hiding something. But what could be so bad he didn't know how to say it? Was he working with the protesters? Stealing from the Agency? Suddenly, I guffawed.

"Inac, you're not in love with me, are you?"

He gave a sad smile, and I winced.

Lightmother, it couldn't be that.

It was a relief when he snorted. "Who could be in love with you, Grim? We both know you are a killer and a scoundrel."

He smiled, and I smiled back. "Ouch. Killer, sure. But scoundrel?"

"Without a doubt. How many people do you owe to them money?"

"Well, let's see. All of our Fingers, to be sure. I seem to recall an elevator operator in the Blight...Darkfather, I hope he's okay after the collapse. And I think I still owe a gambling debt at the Glisten Inn. But on the other hand, Garret owes me a lost bet—he didn't think I'd last three days as Head before resigning."

He was almost right.

But Inac wasn't smiling anymore.

"What's wrong?" I asked.

"I do love you, Grim. Like a brother... You are the closest I have had to one since..." He choked up. I didn't need my Benefactor to know he was thinking of the brother he had killed. Jealousy drives a man out of his mind as sure as the monster in mine.

"It's okay, Inac. You're not that man anymore. That *boy*. You didn't know what you were doing."

Inac's brows furrowed. "No. No, I did. That is what worries me most. I killed my brother. I loved him. And I am capable of doing it again." He stood, signaling the end of the conversation. "Do not let me."

I laughed to hide my discomfort. "I'm not going to kill you—"

"Do *not* let me." Inac's eyes were as cold as the Dark. "I would prefer death than to live with that again."

I reached out and squeezed his arm. "All right, but we don't have to worry about it, because you aren't that man anymore." He said nothing, so I sighed and looked out the window at the shifting state of Liwokin. "Are you ready?"

"To walk after dusk these streets?" Inac sighed and started for the door.

"Take an Archecloak with you, and any Finger you trust. It's dangerous to go alone. When I see you in the courtyard, I'll use this." I touched the suppressant. "You'll have a span before my Aura returns. Find out what's really happening, then find me in the Gild. They'll let you pass if you have an escort. And thank you, Inac."

He stopped at the threshold of the room, turning back. "For what?"

"For being a friend."

One of the only ones I have left. Am I sending him to die, too?

Inac forced a smile, then left.

There was no sense going up to my office only to come back down when the suppressant began working. I waited, watching for

Inac's tattered blue cloak to appear amidst the flurry of usual Agency activity below. Heels scurried across the courtyard—I still had hardly an inkling of what occupied them all day—carrying communications from Organs, perhaps. Two technicians in crimson coats carried a heavy box between them. They were always retrieving shipments from the Docks for Arza. But the Docks were devoid of trade now. So how could they—

As if an elastic band had snapped in my mind, the scene below changed before my eyes. The courtyard...was empty. No Heels, no Nerves, no Eyes, no Fingers. Nothing. That couldn't be right either, could it?

Suddenly panicked that everyone had deserted me, and I was sitting atop a hollow tower, I sat on Inac's bed and prepared to use Arza's suppressant. In through the nose, that seemed the easiest way, the least bad of three horrible options. I hesitated with the tip of the needle at the edge of my nostril. This was crazy, right? Stabbing myself in the brain just for a span of calm.

I slowly slid the injector in. It seemed to take an eternity, or maybe my hands weren't moving at all, some animal instinct preventing me from shoving anything pointy into my own head. A bead of sweat rolled down the side of my head. My teeth were grinding against one another. Just a bit further. I forced myself not to think about it. Anything else but that.

What was I going to tell Oltrov? I didn't trust the man, not enough to let him in on the secrets only my Hand and Arza knew. I needed to convince him to help. Maybe the prisoners, those Blightdwelling rioters, would have some information somewhere in the dark recesses of their minds. If they wouldn't talk, my Benefactor...

Only, I wouldn't have my Benefactor. Should I reconsider?

Without warning, the needle tickled the back of my nose and I sneezed. Fiery pain bloomed behind my eyes—the injector was in. No turning back now. I depressed the metal plunger, and the pressure made my head feel ready to burst, as though I were being assaulted by another Emergent. It kept building and building until I was curled up in a fetal position on Inac's bed, squeezing my temples and listening to myself scream as if from a long way off. I was an insect, about to be squashed by another Benefactor.

There was no way to stop the boot from coming down and smashing me into oblivion.

CHAPTER THIRTY-ONE

Arche Nothing

Please reverse my last command regarding mages no longer attending the boilers. Their efforts are needed to keep the lights running. I give to you my apologies for the oversight.

—Delivered by a Nerve to the Organ of Boiling

No, no, it could not be him. Nor him. Perhaps her? Rank four, a uniform of the old, deeper green. No, I decided. We had not shared rum before.

I eyed each of the Fingers gathered around me in the common area, dismissing them as I decided against their help. Grim told me to pick someone I trust. Fingers in that exalted category were as hard to find as unoccupied land in the Stinbine Isles. Only the more so now that Garret, Lorelay, and Sentyx no longer remained Fingers. Did they remain Fingers?

I pondered that for a moment. Grim never explained to us the new rules of his Agency, as he saw them. Instead, he left everyone to figure them out on our own. Sometimes it was as though he *wanted* to behave like Ulken. By the abyss, he frustrated me like no other.

He still called us his Hand from time to time—and the Head of the Agency *could* be part of a Hand, Ulken had made that plain in Reed's Woods—but we no longer fought Benefactors. Or, we did, but in an entirely different way. That was to be expected, as Benefactors had become entirely different themselves since Grim's resurrection.

Resurrection by Archedark. It still perplexed me. It was impossible. Yet, I had witnessed it with my own eyes. My friend lay dying as

I wept over his body, and in the tear-filled blink of an eye, he suddenly returned. If I were a religious man, I would say he was the Lightmother's will incarnated. Or the Darkfather's.

Alas, I was not a religious man. It was Archemagic, plain and simple. Archemagic that had broken all the rules. And I no longer possessed the ability to decipher this new knowledge.

I flexed my phantom hand. It still pained me, like a thousand tiny crows pecking the end of my stump. If it were half as useful as it was painful, I would still be the strongest Archemage in the Bright Empire. A shame.

"Umm, sir?" Trellan said and coughed. He exchanged glances with an Ayeiri Finger I had just hired.

"Golzo. That is your name, yes?"

The meek Ayeiri nodded eagerly, his long black hair bobbing like a rustling bush. He swept aside his sand-brown coat and bowed. "Yes, sir. I am honored you have remembered my—"

"You can go," I said. He was too new. I needed someone for my escort with experience. "Trellan, bring to me Quinne."

"I..." Trellan cleared his throat. "I'm not sure where he is, sir. A new assignment from the Head, perhaps?"

Unlikely. "Find for yourself a Heel, tell to him to give to a Nerve your message. The Nerve will find him. He should meet me in the courtyard, and quickly. It is a command from the Head. There is for us no time to waste."

After a sharp salute, Trellan grabbed a dejected-looking Golzo by the coat and dragged him off. Hopefully to find the nearest Heel. Lightmother willing, they would even do their job. If Grim had not issued any commands I had not yet heard about.

I stomped off down the stairs, fending off Heels who claimed to have urgent tasks. They always did, but more often than not, urgent meant that an Organ had threatened to have them fired with the stroke of a pen, no matter how trivial the task was in truth. Grim was lucky this place did not crumble beneath him.

Luck had nothing to do with it, in truth. Our Head may not have understood the rules that made this Agency function, but I did. True, Grim acted as though he did, on occasion. Keeping Jacquin on as his First Eye, that was clever. He was a walking reference book of the Agency's bylaws and would have been the first to defect if his loyalty were not rewarded. A shame Grim never thought to consult Jacquin before making sweeping changes to the operation. His latest command to the Nerves...it was like ripping the spine out of a person and commanding them to hop to it. Was he *trying* to squander everything we were working toward?

I would not put it past him. The only thing he hated more than rules and regulations were the Benefactors. And if there was one in his head...well, the logic was clear enough. He was responsible for the Agency now, yet a part of him must be rebelling at the fact that this was ground zero for the Benefactor scourge. He knew this organization was the most powerful tool in the fight, yet he crippled it with every stroke of his pen.

How could I make him see? Reaching the courtyard, I inhaled a breath of dung-stenched air, then coughed it out. All of these Heels, Fingers, technicians, and Nerves packed together like mackerels in a net, yet still the odor of Liwokin overpowered all. I took a step forward...and abruptly found myself alone in the courtyard.

"Lightmother..." I muttered, carefully treading forward. This had to be Grim. His Aura. It beggared belief that our perception could shift so radically because of the tiny organisms in one man's head. But that was the wrong way to think about them. They were not tiny, not when they so fundamentally flaunted the laws of Archemagic.

A tingling sensation ran down my spine. Something changed in the Archemagic fields. Slowly, then all at once. It was like a bad taste had finally left my mouth after coating my tongue for so long it was forgotten. With the shift, everything returned to normal, and with normalcy came the return of the Agency's personnel. Not so many as before, which was worrisome, but enough to keep this place running.

If they ever got back to work, that was. Everyone was just standing around looking as dazed as if they had just been hit in the head. It only took a moment to notice what they were staring at: the Brightdaughter had inexplicably reappeared high overhead. Dusk became noon.

I took hold of a Nerve's gold-trimmed sleeve. "Tell to them to resume operations. By order of the Head."

"But this," the Nerve protested. "This is Benefactor activity! I used to be an Eye. We have to—"

"Did the Head ask for your opinion? Or did he *command* for you to relay his orders?" That snapped his mouth shut. I nodded, patted his arm, and made for gate across the courtyard.

"Back to work!" the Nerve shouted. "The Head commands it!"

I smiled to myself as the courtyard began buzzing as though swarming with lakewasps. All was as it should be. But the curl of my lips turned downward. All was only as it should be because Grim was no longer driving everyone out of their right minds. I would order men to motion with his name gladly enough, but thoughts like that betrayed what a false friend I was.

Say one thing for Grim, he was loyal. And he was honest, unlike me. The guilt roiled inside my belly. How many issues had I ordered in the Head's name? How many letters sent with his seal? He considered me a close adviser, and I exploited his trust. How could I make him forgive me?

Did I even deserve forgiveness? I put that question to myself so many times, yet never had I come closer to an answer.

The matter would have to wait. Quinne was approaching from the tower, only stopping momentarily to wonder about the sky. There would be plenty of time to figure out an explanation later, though I had little doubt I would fumble the words as they came out of my mouth and ruin all my careful thinking. If only language were as simple to command as Archemagic.

My severed hand itched and dragged my mood downward. If language were Archemagic, I would be a man with lips sewn shut.

"Inac? You wanted me?" Quinne asked. He wore the green Finger's uniform, a member of an old Hand, number twenty-eight if memory served. Despite sufficient experience fighting Emergent Benefactors, he had no knowledge of Ulken's plots when I interviewed him. The man never questioned what was going on, even after Reed's Woods. He was loyal to the Head's coin, if not the Head himself. He would do.

"Yes, yes. We must hurry. Only a span, he said to me."

"Who said what to you?" Quinne asked.

"The Head! Now keep yourself close to me and keep your eyes open. We walk the streets, and we must return before..." Well, I did not know exactly what would happen. Grim's Aura would return, and would violence suddenly erupt in the streets? I shivered. "Before the Head grows tired of waiting."

The noon bell rang, and everyone stood still as its peal echoed in the courtyard. The noon bell had already rung once. I didn't want to be caught near the Blight at dusk, but there was little relief to be found in the Brightdaughter's light. It shouldn't be there. It was unnatural. Even before leaving the Agency, what I found Grim's Aura was hiding disturbed me. Two noon bells in one day...the order of the world was crumbling before my eyes.

"You there," I snapped at an Archecloak guarding our gate—another travesty that Grim had allowed. "You too are coming with us, by order of the Head." For once, that was not a lie.

The Archecloak shrugged, spat on the ground, and mumbled, "Better be getting overtime pay for this."

I made no promises, but he and Quinne followed at my behest. Grim was going to find Oltrov in the Gild—he could see that district with his own eyes. So, we started with the Burg, sticking to main thoroughfares and hurrying along toward the Docks.

The Residential District had certainly seen better days. Gulls picked at the decaying carcass of a horse, its fluids congealing in the gutter beneath it. A pack of dogs sauntered up to it and scared the seabirds off, claiming the feast for themselves. All around, houses were marred by grime stains and broken windows, and the front door of one had been broken off its hinges.

A screaming woman darted from the alley between two homes, then flung herself through an empty window frame. A moment later, a man with a knife emerged from the same alley, head swiveling, chest heaving. When he noticed us, his eyes popped open, and he took off back the way he came.

Those two had been the only Liwo we saw in the Burg.

Quinne made to follow the assailant, but I held him back. Only a span to traverse the whole city. We needed to keep moving.

The Docks fared little better than the Burg. Multiple ships had sunk in the harbor and made inaccessible nearly half the docks. Arguments abounded near the few ships that had safely arrived for unloading. Dockworkers were screaming at their dockmaster that it was time to turn in for the day, but the man in charge unwisely insisted that it was only noon. He would find that he was not in charge for long unless he gave into their demands. Not in charge, if his luck held. Not alive, more likely.

Here was the real danger of Grim's Aura: not that *things* fell apart, but that *people* did. Liwo were a remarkably resilient people—they had recovered after the Great Riot and showed a strong possibility of persevering after Reed's Woods—but everyone had a breaking point. The human mind could only fracture so much before shattering. And all of our minds depended on the sanity of one man. If Grim succumbed to madness, Liwokin would soon follow.

It did not help that trade would slow to a halt if ships kept wrecking in the harbor. I would have to designate an Organ to assist with clean-up efforts. Grim certainly would not take the time to do it.

"Come," I said, pulling Quinne's and the Archecloak's attention away from the scuffle that had broken out. "We should show to him the Market. Or what is left of it after the incident."

"Show who?" Quinne asked. The Archecloak shrugged, keeping his hand on the hilt of his sword.

I strode on without an answer, cursing my tongue for the many ways it so often betrayed me.

Turning the corner to the main Market street, I halted in astonishment. I had walked this street hundreds of times, come to know the shops like the back of my hand, if with far less admiration than I paid my own hands—most of those hawkers were thieves by another name. And yet, they did not deserve this.

Not a single shop survived unscathed. Perhaps the sudden second arrival of noon was responsible for the lack of trade. No, that was wishful thinking. Broken glass cracked underfoot. Store fronts had been cleared out by looting, those that had survived the flames. At the far end of the road, the heart of the Market was a blackened husk. Hardly any of the ragged street was visible beneath wood and mortar sent flying by the explosion. I had watched the incident unfolding from the Agency tower, but seeing it up close was worse than I had imagined.

The most troubling sign of all was that not a single Liwo was working to clean up the mess. Thousands had perished in Reed's Woods, but *Darkfather.* Where was everybody? An unusually cold gale blew in from the bay. I shivered, and wrapped my tattered cloak around me, for what little comfort it could provide.

"How are we going to recover from..." I looked around, the scene growing worse the more details I observed. "From *this.*"

"Aye," the Archecloak growled. "I was there. Utter chaos, never seen anything like it. And I seen an entire village slaughtered by daggerclaws. This city's done for. Never should have left Eko."

"You were there?"

"Just said so, didn't I? You deaf, mage?"

"Do not speak to the First Eye like that," Quinne growled, stepping close to the armored man.

"It is okay, Quinne," I said. The First Eye? I supposed it was easy to confuse my cloak with an Eye's uniform, but had he forgotten about Jacquin? More evidence of Grim's mismanagement. "I just want to know what happened. So we can...report it to the Head."

"Report to the Head?" the Archecloak asked. "He was there too. Didn't do nothing to help, far as I saw. We fought 'em back to keep 'em away from him. Nothing but a liability, he was." The Archecloak spat.

"I am sure he was helping," I assured him. "In his own way." Grim may be incompetent at running the Agency, but if there was a Benefactor involved, he would have fought to his last breath to stop it.

Lightmother, had I just thought of him as incompetent? He was going to know when he...dug into my brain. Sorry, friend. It was the truth, though. No! My tongue could betray me, but not my own mind. I needed to get ahold of myself, but it wasn't easy to think straight knowing my thoughts would be laid bare to another.

"Who did you fight back?" I asked the Archecloak.

"The rioters." The Archecloak cocked an eyebrow at me and turned to Quinne. "You sure this guy's all there?"

"Where did they go?"

"Where do you *think* they went?" The man sneered. "The Blight."

"Of course," Quinne muttered. "Should have let the Old Hill burn in the Riot."

"Old Hill?" the Archecloak spat. "You're startin' to sound like one o' them."

"Never," Quinne said, and drew his sword to emphasize the point. "Lead the way, sir."

I steeled myself and carried on through the Artisans'. Despite the carnage in the other districts, this one lay relatively untouched. Sure, there were courtesans and thieves prancing around in broad daylight, but they could not have known it was just past noon with Grim's Aura masking the Brightdaughter. Evidently, once the Aura dissipated, they decided to continue plying their trade as if nothing had gone awry. Would the Blight have done the same? I did not relish a visit to the Old District even during the daytime. At night while the rest of the city decayed and rioters ran rampant? That was a death sentence.

I never got the chance to find out, however, as two dozen men poured out of the dirt-ridden streets and approached the three of us. All of them wore uniforms I never thought to see again, not since Ulken abolished them. Navy blue jackets with white buttons lining their fronts, down to a golden sash worn around the waist. Garish red pants with black shoes marred by the Blight's mix of mud and human waste. And those ridiculous hats with feathers plucked from gulls to designate their rank.

The men before us were soldiers of the Liwokin militia. Or, they appeared to be. I glanced upward. The sky had grown dark, a shade of crimson that could not be explained by clouds. The Blight seemed... less dirty? Some homes appeared almost desirable. Was Grim's Aura back already? It could not have been a span yet.

"What's the meaning of this?" Quinne demanded, brandishing his sword.

"Do you want for them to attack us?" I snapped. "Put that away. Use your eyes."

The Finger did not sheathe his sword, but he looked at the threat before us. In each of the militiamen's gloved white hands was a Dark-metal pistol, warping the flows of Archemagic around them. Against those, my men might as well have been holding sharpened sticks.

Reflexively, I reached for Archefire. It was there, I could sense it, ever present all around me. My phantom hand stretched out but passed through the fields as though trying to touch the Dark itself. It was useless. My left hand could alter the flow of Archedark, but only if balanced with the Fire in my right.

When Ulken cut off my hand, he had cut off all access to Archemagic. I hated him for it—if Grim did not stick that knife in his heart, I would have done it myself. And likely died trying. I would have welcomed death, then. Because of him, I was no Archemaster. I was Arche nothing.

And that meant this was a fight we could not win. My eyes darted, searching for an escape. The meager crowds of the Artisans' District had further thinned, leaving us alone. Darkfather, it could not end like this. I needed to get back to Grim. He needed to witness the state of the city, this farce most of all.

My Archecloak escort grunted. "Seen those same weapons at the Market. Don't let those uniforms fool you. That's them. The rioters."

Was that so? Why would Grim's Aura disguise the rioters as Li-wokin militia? It made to me no sense.

An older man with a bushy gray mustache stepped forward, holding up his hand to stop the rest from advancing. His cap had three gull feathers— what rank that made him, I had no idea, but the others obeyed. The commander approached to within ten paces, took a deep breath, then shouted, "Weapons away, lads!"

The men under his charge holstered their pistols, then deployed some dark smiles and licked lips that sent a shiver through my body.

"We haven't come to fight you," the commander said to me. "In fact, it's the Lightmother's own luck. We were just coming to find you."

"To find me?" I asked. "Why?"

"Why?" The man seemed personally affronted by the question. "Why, to place you under arrest, of course. You abetted a murder. We can't have dangerous criminals like you running around the streets of

Liwokin. Or...wait." He flashed a gap-toothed smile. "Have you come to turn yourself in?"

Quinne took a step forward. "The First Eye would never surrender to scum like you."

"Quinne, please..." I urged him.

"Is that so?" the commander asked me. "Do you plan to resist arrest?"

Anyone with a brain would hear that for the threat it was. Evidently, I had chosen the one Finger without one.

"No," I said.

At the same time, Quinne turned to me and said "Get back to the Agency! I'll cover your retreat!" Then he charged the militia commander shouted, "Die, villain!"

He made it three steps before blood and gray matter exploded from the back of his head.

My ears rang. Smoke streamed from the tip of the commander's pistol. The rest of the rioters had their drawn their pistols and aimed them squarely at me. My stomach tried to force its way up my throat, but my eyes could not help but slide to the lifeless body of Quinne. A sickening hole in his forehead punctuated the dumb expression on his dead face. The man had brains after all. He just did not know how to use them.

"I surrender!" The words were a squeak as they passed my lips. "Take me, just let him go. The Archecloak has done to you nothing."

"Oh, no," the commander said, chuckling. "He fought for the murderer when the Market was liberated. The Council's ordered his arrest too."

The Council? What did they have to do with—

Gunfire erupted from a dozen pistols at once. Ducking, I clamped my hands over my ears. The cacophony of explosions pounded at my skull. I flinched at each one, squeezing shut my eyes, until I realized I was not dead. They were not shooting at me. I cracked one eye open to peer over my shoulder.

The Archecloak was sprinting away. Sparks flew as bullets pinged off his Archemetal armor. One hit his head, and he stumbled, nearly losing his footing. But the man was quick on his feet, and he made it around the corner. He had escaped.

An angry voice shouted orders I could not make out. Just as I stood and began to turn back to the commander, something cracked me in the back of the head, and I was falling. I never hit the ground.

CHAPTER THIRTY-TWO

Burned

Our distant past, forgotten
Secrets buried, thought to be known
Ancient wisdom, long overgrown
Embodied now, but rotten
'Neath skies long lost, Dark swells from below

—Verse from 'Neath Skies Long Lost,
Second Song of Half-Noon

"Easy now, girl," Minny said, helping Lorelay slide her arms into the bulky dress. "If we tear this one, there's no time to sew another. The procession departs at noon. You don't want the whole city looking at you in a ruined dress, do you?"

"I don't want the whole city looking at me at all," Lorelay countered, but when did what she wanted ever matter? She never expected to return to the Radiant Palace when she stormed out of these quarters, ignoring Minny's warning, yet here she was.

Minny was waiting in her room with an infuriating grin on her face when Lorelay opened the door; said she knew she would be back. That had been days ago, and Lorelay's regrets had grown with each setting of the Brightdaughter. She was asked to do little more than stay out of trouble. In other words, she was useless, although no more so than the Bright Prince himself.

Vinlin continually promised he was making progress toward swaying the Church, but she never saw any evidence of it. He had only one thing on his mind, preparation for his mother's funeral. Necessary, he claimed, to give the people of Paceeq closure and to anoint him the Kindling Emperor. From his new position, he would have more power to make good on his promises.

Fair enough, Lorelay admitted, but it was all tied in to why she was so annoyed with him. The *one* thing she asked, the one small favor that he promised would be easy...apparently it was impossible.

Darkfather, but the Church's traditions are so...idiotic!

"Would you stop bunching your shoulders like you're about to kill someone?" Minny chided. "Lightmother, girl, all you have to do is stand there and look pretty. I don't see what's so hard about that."

"It's not the funeral I'm angry about," Lorelay started. "Well, it is, but..."

Not the funeral *per se*, but the proceedings of the ceremony. Lorelay needed the branch of the Grieving Pine. The Agency needed a source of Druid's Tears, a way to protect everyone from having their minds taken over by Benefactors. And Vinlin...he wanted to *burn* the branch in the late Empress Elzia's funeral pyre.

Lorelay had laughed at first, but when she realized he was serious, she begged him to reconsider. On her knees, she begged, and felt like an utter fool doing it. But he never budged. It would go against longstanding tradition. So would a male Emperor, Lorelay pointed out, which was a mistake. That only entrenched his position.

How could she explain any of this to Minny? It was pointless. "I just don't see why he has to be so stubborn."

Minny laughed. "There you go again. My dear, have you ever considered that you may be just as stubborn as he is?"

"I'm trying to save the people of Paceeq! It's important." Lorelay turned to find Minny with a skeptical look on her face, but she barreled on. She just could not understand what was going through Vinlin's head. "He's just trying to uphold tradition. Tradition that would cast him down in a heartbeat."

No one would even know if the stupid branch wasn't there... She pondered the importance of Druid's Tears. They had saved her life when fighting the tentacled Benefactor that turned half her Hand against each other. To hear Grim tell it, the toxics had been the only reason he and Hand Sixty-Four had survived their encounter with a Benefactor named Lomin. She had no idea how the Tears worked, but if the Agency needed them to effectively fight, then she knew her mission included securing a source.

"That's why it's all the more important he doesn't break tradition further," Minny said. "This is the last chance for the Church to cast doubts on his legitimacy."

"Yeah, yeah..." Lorelay waved a hand. She had heard all the same arguments from Vinlin himself. Minny glowered, and Lorelay yelped when the back of her dress was cinched tightly. "Am I supposed to be able to breathe in this thing?"

"Yes." Minny smirked. "But nothing beyond that."

"Wonderful," Lorelay said with a sigh. She tried taking a step, found her legs restricted, as if her thighs were bound by rope. "It'll take me all day to reach the courtyard."

"Best get going now, then, eh?" Minny suggested, then slapped Lorelay on the rear and set her hopping to motion. The nerve! To make matters worse, the old woman kept laughing about it the entire slow trip to the courtyard.

Lorelay's mood had begun the day foul, but by the time they arrived, she was positively morose. The heat of the day was worsened by a stifling humidity, and the overcast skies promised a downpour of rain. Lorelay was certain her toes were numb, and the courtyard was stuffed with nobles all crying fake tears for Empress Elzia. The old bat had been dead for half a year! This was nothing but a game to see who could feign grief for some social points. She rolled her eyes, and people gasped.

Not at her, mind. The gasps were directed at the sudden appearance of Vinlin at the top of the balcony overlooking the courtyard. Dressed in a suit of mourning white, he looked out upon the silent crowd, and Lorelay was sure his eyes lingered on her for a moment longer than the others. No speech followed, no grand gesture. Only a slow walk down the stairs into a press of men and women waiting to ambush him in his sorrow.

Vinlin was having none of it. He raised a hand and without a word the crowd parted to let him pass. His expression was stone—Lorelay had seen more emotion of a Skardwarf—but she knew he must be roiling inside, trying to hold it together lest anyone think him weak. The late Empress Elzia had a reputation for being made of cold steel, and Vinlin had to live up to the image of his mother. He made eye contact with no one as he passed, and suddenly the game of fakery changed into a game of mimicry. Who could remain as sordid as the Bright Prince?

Lorelay hated it. *Do these people even know the word authenticity?* They were like mockingbirds, only trying to sound like everyone else, hiding what was on the inside. *Imagine these people experiencing a Benefactor's Deluge.* The thought brought a smile to Lorelay's lips, but that was just the sort of mood she was in.

The mood soured even further when she realized Vinlin would be consumed by the Benefactors just as surely as all these other fools. The Bright Throne, destroyed. She would have felt glee at the prospect, once. Now, all that came was a twinge of sadness at the thought of Vinlin's death. Of all the people around her, he was the only one being himself. His grief was real, she had no doubt about that. It was like looking at her own grief in a mirror. Remembering Dunnax put her on the brink of sobbing, fitting for a funeral.

The courtyard gates opened, a slow rumble that ended with a clank as they latched into position. Vinlin led the procession down the steep hill from the flank of the Radiant Palace to the grounds on the riverbank, where Elzia's funeral pyre had already been prepared, body and all. Atop the crosshatched wood, the Bright Prince's mother lay shrouded in black wrappings. Vinlin placed a hand on his mother and bowed his head in silent prayer.

While everyone around her bent their own necks along with the prince, Lorelay eyed the funeral pyre and the treasures piled high around it, collected from every corner of the Bright Empire to commemorate Elzia's reign. Decorated chalices and gleaming bowls, piles of jewels scattering the Brightdaughter's light in prismatic hues, all of that she expected. What caught her by surprise were the several live animals trapped in glass cages, lizards and birds who would burn in the fires that ushered Elzia's soul to the abyss. It repulsed her, made her shiver.

Good men or evil, the abyss awaited everyone. Still, burning a dead body was one thing, burning living creatures was entirely another. It only made her think of Dunnax's charred remains, nothing but blackened silver beneath a heap of golden scales. Grim had assured her he was dead before the fires touched him, thinking he was comforting her. Lorelay drank that night—and for many nights after—to escape the images conjured by his words as surely as if they were carried on a Benefactor's Deluge.

Vinlin's appearance in front of her snapped her out of her rueful reminiscing, and she instantly noticed the distress on her face. She looked left and right, caught one snobbish noblewoman hiding a snicker behind a hand. Had she missed something?

His words struck home suddenly, as though they had been waiting for her to return to the present to register in her mind. "Please join me on the dais, my lady Lorelay."

Heat filled her cheeks. She took the Bright Prince's extended hand and shambled up with him—shambling was all she could do in that dress—taking her place beside Elzia's pyre.

Joke's on you, Minny. I hardly needed a torn dress to embarrass myself.

All eyes were on her, and the butterflies in her stomach showed no sign of settling down. Stage fright, now of all times? She had performed in front of dozens without so much as a hint of nerves. But from the view on the dais, it was clear this was *not* dozens of onlookers. This was *thousands*. Paceeqi of all walks of life, positively covering the funeral grounds, spilling out onto the streets. Abyss, there were some urchins sitting atop shops to get a view! Everywhere she looked, someone was looking back at her.

"I'm going to be sick," she muttered under her breath, and when Vinlin leaned in to ask what she said, she waved the question aside, shaking her head.

The Bright Prince looked no different than he had when he appeared on the balcony, grief-stricken but composed. How did he do it? How could he keep himself together when under such pressure? Minny was right. The weight he was holding on his shoulders would cause most men to buckle. She held a fraction of it herself now and wanted to scream. Lorelay looked anywhere but the crowd.

She found the High Cleric standing apart from other Clerics, both in location and appearance. Where most men and women of the Church wore plain crimson robes, Namravi's contained so much gleaming Archemetal it seemed she was dressed for a festival, not a funeral. The woman's gray hair hung in a braid intertwined with red ribbon down to her waist, where a belt studded with golden starbursts cinched her robes tight.

The High Cleric looked over her shoulder and caught Lorelay staring. She glared.

Lorelay's quickly looked away. Her eyes roamed toward the funeral arrangements. She had to settle her nerves. She had to—

There it was. The branch of the Grieving Pine, a crystalline stalk as tall as the Empress' pyre, studded with glass thorns. It wept a clear, viscous sap that dropped as teardrop beads into a bed of soil. Writhing tendrils overflowed the ceramic pot in which the branch had been planted. Reaching out, trying to escape, as though it knew the lick of flames was fast approaching.

Lorelay's breath caught. The branch was at once stunningly beautiful and hideously revolting. Unconsciously, she took a step toward it, and...some weight lightened in her mind. Her nerves still rioted, but they seemed somehow...lesser. Suppressed. Her eyes widened. She was feeling the effects of Druid's Tears. Another step closer, and the effects amplified. All the Agency's hopes rested on this alien plant. If they burned it...

But Vinlin tugged on her hand, gently pulling her away a step away from the pyre. The ceremony was already beginning. She possessed no power to stop it. Tears filled her eyes as High Cleric Namravi began her chant from in front of the unlit pyre. A chant she recognized from the Book of Light.

"O sacred Fire, eternal flame divine,
Receive this body in your warm embrace.
A pyre of faith, Her ashes left behind,
In Mother's Light shall this soul take her place."

Lorelay nearly jumped out of her skin when all of Vos responded in chorus with the next verse. Vinlin joined in, squeezing Lorelay's hand tighter.

"In sacred tongues sing we praise of Her Fire!
Purify us, grant Light to set us free.
Deliverance from darkness and chill we desire!
In gratitude we live our lives for thee."

The crowd quieted. Only the High Cleric's intonation could be heard over the cold wind from the south. Lorelay shivered, religious awe washing over her. The power of the call and response stirred her in ways her mother's readings from the Book never had.

"The hearth ignites in glory, boundless Lightmother's grace,
Sparks ascend and dance beside the star above,
In Her great warmth, this land becomes a holy Fire place,
Eternal life is granted in Brightdaughter's love."

Again, the response came, and Lorelay found herself mouthing the words along with it, though not giving them voice.

"In sacred tongues sing we praise of Her Fire!
Purify us, grant Light to set us free.
Deliverance from darkness and chill we desire!
In gratitude we live our lives for thee."

Namravi's soft, high voice intoned the final verse. Vinlin's hand moved, and Lorelay looked up to see him trying to hold back wracking sobs. It mattered little how close to the Grieving Pine she stood, seeing him in tears veiled her own eyes. She blinked hard, forced those tears to run down her cheeks, but did not wipe them away. Lorelay held onto Vinlin's hand.

"We chant these words in the language of flame,
In reverence we offer our goodbyes,
From Dark to Light, Her everlasting name,
Let sacred Fire gift this soul unto the skies,
Hear our prayer and carry forth our warm goodbyes."

"Hear our prayer and carry forth our warm goodbyes," Vinlin said, his quiet voice alone in the silence. "Goodbye, mother."

With the prayers concluded, Lorelay's were far from the only glistening eyes in the funeral grounds, and she could only see the front rows of onlookers, the nobility. She would bet they were faking it no longer.

The High Cleric stepped aside and gave a slow nod to the Bright Prince. With one last squeeze of her hand, Vinlin let go and took his place at the front of the pyre. His back turned to the crowd, Lorelay saw his lips moving, saying his private farewells to his mother. Emotion welled within her, and she wanted to hurry to his side, comfort him.

The Bright Prince let out one final heaving sigh, then his hands started working, and his lips pursed in concentration. A tiny spark of Archefire lanced forward from Vinlin's hand and ignited the bottom of the pyre. The flame shot back toward Vinlin, and he jerked his hand back. Not fast enough. The Fire scorched his fingers, causing him to wince and shake his hand off.

Namravi did a poor job of hiding her distaste. She turned away from the great mass of people arrayed before them, but the contempt was evident on her face to Lorelay. With a minute gesture of the High Cleric's hand—hidden behind her back—she fed the Fire beneath Elzia.

A bonfire erupted on the pyre, its searing heat forcing Lorelay back a step. She had to shield her face with a hand to look at it. The trapped birds squawked their alarm as smoke billowed forth. Lorelay glimpsed Elzia's shrouded form, a dark silhouette in the flames, burnt ends of her wrappings lifting upward on the heat of the pyre as though her spirit was really ascending to the heavens.

Vinlin addressed the Paceeqi, cloak billowing behind him as he gestured, his booming voice capturing the attention of all. All except Lorelay. While the other eyes were on the Bright Prince performing his rites to become Kindling Emperor, Lorelay's eyes were on the branch of the Grieving Pine. Its tendrils squirmed in the oppressive heat. The sap of Druid's Tears ran like water, pooling in the ceramic pot that was already blackened with soot.

Lorelay stared at it as if entranced, breathing heavily, hands clenching. All of the Agency's hopes of winning this war. All of the Bright Empire's hopes of survival...her family's survival. Her chance at redemption, to make Dunnax's sacrifice mean something. It all rested with this plant that was moments away from perishing. She shook her head, denying it.

Before better sense could prevail, Lorelay held her breath, tried taking a long step toward the Grieving Pine branch, and tore her dress up the middle. With her legs free, she rushed into the inferno. Her skin felt as though it would melt off. She was sure her hair would catch fire. But she made it to the branch, grabbed the ceramic, and heaved herself away.

On the ground, dragging the heavy pot of soil backward, she felt... calm. The Grieving Pine's Aura made the burning pain in her hands seem a distant thing. The gasps and uproar of the crowd mattered little. No, not at all. Strangely, a smile spread across her lips. Where had that come from? Whatever she had done, she was...satisfied. Her eyes stung, but she opened them to find the High Cleric looking down on her in horror. She almost laughed, until Vinlin appeared beside him, aghast. There was anger in his eyes, concern in his brows, and shock in the way he slowly shook his head.

Were they going to take the Grieving Pine, throw it back into the fire? Lorelay held on tighter despite the heat. Her hands were agony. Her fingers refused to listen. *Let them throw me into the flames with it, if it's so important.* She noticed the rebellious thoughts even if there was no fiery emotion to stir them.

"What have you done?" Disbelief turned the new Kindling Emperor's voice breathy.

"Your Radiance," Namravi urged, "this cannot be allowed to go unpunished."

"Punished?" Lorelay asked flatly. "I just saved us all."

A drop of rain fell on her face and made her blink. Another, then another, and soon the heavens poured forth a rain that soaked her through. The uproarious crowd began dispersing, rushing to the cover of buildings to escape the torrent. All the while Vinlin looked down upon Lorelay, apparently unable to comprehend what had happened. He only turned when the High Cleric gasped, and Elzia's pyre was nothing but a half-burned pile of melted treasures and dead animals and smoldering wood. By the Lightmother's mercy, the Empress' body was entirely gone.

"An omen," the High Cleric declared. "A Dark omen. The mathemelodians have been warning us, the Brightdaughter is failing. The light of day grows shorter, the dark of night longer." He turned hateful eyes on Lorelay, and still she clung to the Grieving Pine's branch, merely...observing. "This one...I see it was right to question your judgment, Vinlin. It was unorthodox to allow her here in the first place, and now see what's become of your poor mother's funeral?"

Vinlin ignored Namravi, much to the woman's dismay. "Why, Lorelay?" He looked at her hands, and his gaze drew Lorelay's eyes down as well. If not for the Grieving Pine, she would have been sick. Her hands were a blistered, bloody mess. "How could this...thing be worth it?" He took a step closer, hesitated. "What is it doing to you?"

"It matters not at all, Your Radiance," Namravi said. "There is only one way to fix this. She must be sacrificed. A public execut—"

"No!" Vinlin's nostrils flared. Even standing near the Grieving Pine, that was enough to draw his ire. He and the High Cleric stared each other down, each sizing up the other as though about to come to blows.

Lorelay sat up. As much as she would have loved to see Vinlin slap the High Cleric, she knew she should intervene. "This needs to go to the Agency."

Vinlin surprised her, turning his anger on her. "You are in no position to be making demands. Lightmother, I've had enough. Take her back to the palace," he said to someone behind her. "Have her confined to her rooms, kept out of sight until this mess is dealt with."

Heavy boots clomped closer. "And the plant, Your Radiance?"

Lorelay's breath caught. He could easily have it destroyed along with everything else in the failed pyre. But the Lightmother was merciful once more. Enough of that, and Lorelay might convert to religiosity.

"Take it with you," the Kindling Emperor commanded. "But keep it away from her. Whatever it's doing, I don't like it." He turned away, leaving her there with the High Cleric and two Paladins in the rain.

"You are lucky, girl," Namravi sneered. "But you will slip again, and the people of Paceeq will see justice delivered. Take her away."

Hands seized her and separated her from the branch of the Grieving Pine. When she was dumped in her room in the Radiant Palace and the Paladins took the plant away, emotion flooded back in.

With it came unendurable pain.

CHAPTER THIRTY-THREE

Strange Occurrences

A Feeder is rumored to be a noble creature, according humans residing in the Aerie—a Peeker that has honorably sacrificed itself for the Colony. Sadly, confined as they are to the depths of the mountain, none has ever been observed by a reliable Institute source. Even Hoggens, now known to be a fraud, never claimed...

—Page 37, Institute of Biotism Peeker Compendium, Vol. I

Eleven days.

Eleven bleeding days Garret had been waiting for Cavern to contact Sentyx, and all Sentyx had done in that entire time was think.

Is he on to me? Would go a long way toward explaining the Skardwarf's behavior. Reserved, even more than usual. Didn't sleep, and so Garret was sleep deprived too. If Sentyx *was* suspicious, Garret couldn't let his guard down to rest. Only one thing drove a man to such inaction. Grim determination. Problem was, Garret could never tell the difference until that determination was set against him.

So he kept one hand on his knife. Even though he wasn't sure where in the Skardwarf to stick it. In the back, surely. But what was he aiming for? Did Skardwarves even have internal organs?

"Hey Sentyx, do you have a heart?"

Sentyx grunted.

"Just checking."

Damn, I couldn't get a read on that one.

It was impossible to get information out of Sentyx at the best of times. Trying to pry him open now would be like trying to wrestle a stergoderm. One wrong move and he'd be pulverized. He'd seen Sentyx stand his ground against the Benefactor Lomin. Garret had no illusions who would win in a hand-to-hand fight. He had to be smarter than the Skardwarf.

A low bar, admittedly.

What should be done with a traitor? If execution can't be swift, it should be cunning, and a turncloak who doesn't know he's outed is best used as bait. The Skardwarf would slink back to his master eventually. When he did, Garret would be ready.

An arrow from the darkness to cut the head off the snake.

Only, the Skardwarf hadn't moved in eleven damned days, abyss take him, and the serpent showed no signs of slithering to Sentyx itself.

Starting to think that grunt was a no.

Surely Sentyx would have gotten hungry if he had a stomach. Garret had exhausted his supplies twice and had to restock at the commissary. It was a risk to leave the Skardwarf alone, but worthwhile to check on his cache in a dark crevice hidden by resin. He kept one Clasform on him at all times. Didn't want an Aura catching him unawares. The other was tucked away with Prost's gem, which he kept far away from his quarters.

Cavern said he could feel it from the stockpile's entrance. The biotist in Garret was curious what effect it would have on Sentyx, but the ranger in him urged enough caution to assume it would end with a fist through his skull. For once in his life, Garret could see the betrayal coming.

If only there was a bleeding thing I could do to stop it.

There was a pounding at the door. Incessant banging.

Sentyx didn't show a lick of reaction, so Garret hurried to open it. A Peeker Pair stood twitching before him.

"Garret. Sentyx. Please offer assistance." The Pair's unison voice quavered.

"Nice to see you too, Tunnel," Garret said. "But we're kind of busy. Sentyx is...thinking."

Tunnel's Pair shared a glance. Twitched a nod. "This one sees that. The Burner's thoughts are rampant. But the human told Tunnel to return if this one observed any strange occurrences."

Sentyx perked up with a grunt. Stood with the sound of grinding rock. "I have decided."

Garret snorted. "Took you long enough. Decided what?"

"To help."

Garret threw his hands up. "We don't even bleeding know what they need help with."

Sentyx grunted.

"That is right. Peekers have begun acting erratically in the Feeder Hollows. It may be the human Garret seeks."

Peekers acting erratically did sound like Prost. More specifically, a Benefactor unleashed by Prost.

Garret clenched his fist. Exhaled. *Last thing I want to lay eyes on here is a bleeding Benefactor.*

"Well," Garret said. "What are we waiting for? Shall we go say hello to Prost, Sentyx?"

The rumble Sentyx responded with sounded even more guttural than usual. Garret took it as a yes.

"Wait, wait," Tunnel said. "The human does not know the way. The Feeder Hollows lay deep beneath Myrme, in caves chilled and dark."

"I see it," Garret said. In his mind's eye, the map of the Colony contained cavernous depths. Little foot traffic by Peekers. "Only two ways in or out down there."

Tunnel cocked their heads. "That is...correct."

"We split up," Sentyx suggested.

"Trap Prost one way or the other," Garret agreed.

"This one will Pair with another to provide guidance to you both."

"No need. Just go with Sentyx. I'll find my own way."

And so, he did. Only, it wasn't the way Sentyx would be expecting. No. He wanted to see it for himself. The moment Prost and Sentyx met face to face. To witness the depths of the Skardwarf's betrayal, an instant before Garret put an arrow through the Eevoqian's eye.

Stalking in the dark, that's what an Ekoan ranger was made for. Years of banditry, years he wasn't proud of. But they trained him well. One mistake and it was off with his head. Garret didn't make mistakes—it's how he'd survived so long.

Only mistakes I ever make are trusting the wrong people.

Garret scowled. Never again. Better to trust no one.

He still had nightmares about the last time he tailed someone in Eko. About what he had to do when it was time to emerge from the shadows. He could still feel the slick blood on his hands. Hear the girl's screams. His commander's laughter. Garret had meted out justice that day, but it still didn't sit well with him.

Should've got there sooner. Should've seen past Kellen's lies to the truth of who he was.

When Kellen was dead, Garret decided he would serve no more monsters. What was he thinking, joining the Agency? First Ulken, then Grim...two monsters of different breeds. At least Grim was trying, but he couldn't do anything to change what he was. Garret would help him, but only to put an end to a bigger monster. Then...well, he didn't know. Only thing he was sure of, it was a matter of time before Grim betrayed him too.

Can only keep the Benefactor at bay for so long. But I'll be ready.

One thing at a time. He had no trouble following Sentyx and Tunnel, but he couldn't let his mind stray. One slip up and it could mean the end of him. If Sentyx spotted him, the Skardwarf's suspicions would be confirmed. Only two choices after that. Flee or die. Garret didn't intend to do either.

They approached the offshoot that would descend to the Hollows. Garret had to be doubly cautious. With so few others on the path, Sentyx could simply turn around and spot him. He was relying on Sentyx facing into the wind, never looking back. Garret liked his odds. The Skardwarf always was stubborn. Never listened when anyone told him to watch his back.

Let's hope it wasn't all an act to catch me off guard.

But that was giving him too much credit. Sentyx had no idea he was being tailed, Garret was sure of it.

If he had any doubts, they would have been laid to rest when a Peeker Pair with reverse-jointed legs adapted for speed rushed past Garret and hailed Sentyx. Keeping his distance, he peered around a bend in the tunnel to watch his target.

The Skardwarf didn't turn, and the Peekers behaved as if they were uncomfortable proceeding further. They had nearly reached the depths of the cave. The Pair was a messenger, it seemed. A Peeker Courier. Handed Sentyx a letter.

Garret strained his ears to hear their words.

"This one was directed to deliver a message from another Burner."

"Where?"

The Peeker Pair squirmed. Tunnel did too, for that matter. Were they feeling the effects of Prost's actions?

"This one was directed not to say. The sender requires discretion."

Sentyx grunted, and the Peekers took that as a dismissal. They hurried back the way they came, paying Garret no mind.

After a time, Sentyx unfolded the letter and read. When he finished, he crushed the note in his stone fist.

"Why help a Burner?" Sentyx asked.

Both Peekers of Tunnel's Pair bowed their heads low. "Even Unpaired, a Peeker remembers. Sentyx rescued this one from Liwokin. The Colony fulfills all debts."

"You are good," Sentyx said with a rumble in his chest. "Stay back. Strong winds blow ahead."

"This one is grateful," Tunnel said. "The Colony will remember the Agency's kindness."

Darkfather. Garret turned and sprinted away. If Tunnel was in as much of a rush as the messenger, he would be spotted before long. Peekers moved surprisingly fast with those stunted, three-toed legs.

He turned down the first offshoot he could find. Concealed himself in the dimness between bulbs. When Tunnel passed by, he breathed out in relief. Took a moment to string up his bow.

"Can't rest yet," he muttered, then sprinted to catch up with Sentyx.

He was too slow. The Skardwarf had already reached the Feeder Hollows. As Garret reached it himself, he found a crumpled wad of paper near the entrance. Cavern's note. He picked it up, but before he could read it, an inhuman bellow resounded in the massive cavern.

"PROST!" Sentyx's voice boomed. Probably was heard back in the Human Aerie.

Garret stopped dead. His blood ran cold. His eardrums felt like they'd burst.

Sentyx's voice was filled with rage. An anger hotter than Garret had ever heard from the Skardwarf.

Garret shoved the note in his pocket and tentatively stepped forward, keeping his eyes peeled for either Prost or Sentyx.

But the Feeder Hollows were nearly pitch black. So it wasn't sight that directed him toward his target.

It was the sound of senseless slaughter.

CHAPTER THIRTY-FOUR

Beasts

*Come one! Come all! Come face-to-face with the most dangerous crea-
ture this side of the ocean! A monster so fierce, its gaze paralyzes even
the strongest Paladin in fear. A giant from deep within the stormjungles
of Eko — the Golden Daggerclaw! Thrills for the whole family!*

—Advertisement posted in the Gild

Awareness returned slowly. Emotion was the first to appear: fear. I
was being crushed, snuffed out like a candle in a gale. No way to express my fear. Trapped in a void with nothing but terror. Until...

Sensation came next. Hearing. The sound of bells ringing and
gulls squawking. Comforting sounds. I opened my eyes. A dizzying
blur greeted me, and darkness on one side. A bright source of light
caused my eyelids to flutter. I was breathing. Smelling. Ragged, painful breaths that smelled of blood and bile. A taste appeared in my
mouth, vile. Vomit. It burned in my throat. That feeling was quickly
overshadowed. With touch came agony, as though my head had been
split open by an axe. My limbs were jelly. I couldn't reach up to feel
the blood that must be pouring from the wound.

Memories came last, and I knew where I was. Laying on Inac's
bed, curled up where I had thrown up from the pain. The fear lingered
as a bodily sensation, but I understood that I was no longer in danger.
It would fade. After all, I had awoken to good news. The Benefactor suppressant had worked. The memories were my own, no others.
They would return after a span, but until then, Inac would...

315

Wait. It was light outside. I stumbled off the bed, limbs still weak, and made my way to the window. The Brightdaughter soared overhead. Hadn't it been near dusk when I sent Inac off? He was complaining about approaching the Blight after dark.

My eyes widened when what happened dawned on me. Arza's suppressant was more effective than she knew. It had knocked me out for an entire day. I had to find Inac and learn what happened. Why hadn't he returned to his quarters? Or had he found me there in a pool of my own vomit and left me? No, he wouldn't do that. Something was wrong.

I tossed my soiled clothes on his bed and found a set of clothes that fit me well enough in his wardrobe. They were loose, airy. Comfortable, but they made me feel like I was dressing up as an Archemage. His tattered cloak was nowhere to be found, so perhaps he had yet to return? Lightmother, if something had happened to him...

The hallways outside our Fingers' quarters were abuzz with discussion. Groups of green-coated men and women huddled together and spoke in hushed tones. I crept closer to three men before anyone noticed my presence.

"...impossible. It must be a Benefactor," a uniformed Finger intoned.

Yezna's Aura waxed and waned, which did no favors in convincing them everything was normal. Arza must have been testing her Darkmetal cage up above, but how could I feel it now?

"Then why haven't they sent us out?" an Ayeiri boy asked. Did he even work here? "That's how it's supposed to work, right?"

The third man shook his head. "No, no, they send the Eyes first. Have you heard anything Trellan?"

"Not since the Head's mage sent me to—" Trellan's eyes slid to me, and he stiffened, then thought to add a salute. "Sir!"

The other two jumped to attention as well, and suddenly everyone on the whole floor was staring at me.

The Ayeiri boy cleared his throat. "Um. Your nose is bleeding. Uh, sir."

"And are you wearing..." the third started before the uniformed Finger smacked him.

I wiped the blood from my nose on Inac's shirtsleeve. "Yes, well... Long story. Trellan, is that your name? You mentioned Inac. Where is he?"

"Sir? You just sent him away not long ago. With Quinne."

Trellan, Quinne...none of these names meant anything to me. How had all of these men come to work here without me knowing? Where were the old Fingers from the days of Hand Sixty-Four? Maybe Inac would know.

"Not long ago? That was yesterday. I sent him off at dusk."

"That's the thing, uh, sir," said the Ayeiri. "It *was* dusk not long ago. Only then it was suddenly noon. Could it be a Benefactor, you think?"

I narrowed my eyes. A sudden change in the sky? The same had occurred during the riot in the Market. It *was* a Benefactor.

My own. And it's stronger than I thought.

"It's under control," I told him. "Inac just left, you say?"

The Finger called Trellan nodded vigorously. "Yes, sir. We carried out your orders, just as commanded."

"My orders? What—" Lightmother, what was I doing? I couldn't let these men know how far my mind had slipped. "Right. Good. Well, then...carry on." What had I ordered now? I shook my head. Another question for Inac when he returned.

In the meantime, I had business to be about. Since, evidently, little time had passed since suppressing my Aura, that gave me a chance to get cleaned up in my quarters before meeting with Oltrov. I might have to let him know about the infestation in my head, but if I showed up with blood and vomit on me, dressed in Inac's clothes, the man would know something was wrong. I would only let him in on my secret if absolutely necessary.

"Is it absolutely necessary?" an Archecloak asked me later, as I demanded entrance to the Gild. "Oltrov's orders. No one's to be let in unless absolutely necessary."

I leveled a blank stare at him. "What do you think? He has my prisoners. Now, let me through." I pushed him aside, but his companion at the gate lowered a glaive to bar my passage. "What are you going to do, kill me? I'm the Head of the Agency! Your boss knows I'm coming. When he hears about this, he'll have you on night duty with no wages for a full measure!"

That earned a glance between the two guards. "Well, if you say it's *absolutely*—"

"Bah!" I threw my hands up in disgust and stormed through the gate, ducking under the man's weapon.

Just let him try to stop me. See what happens.

He didn't try. Which was for the best. The man was as big as a Paceeqi and as stubborn as a Skardwarf. If he laid hands on me, there would be no wriggling free until Oltrov came to find me himself.

I would have been waiting a long time, apparently.

"Grimley!" Oltrov greeted me as he emerged from the golden doors of an Archemetal spire. "What a surprise. I didn't know you were coming, what with the strange weather we've been having. Gusty, isn't it? Ever so gusty." He pulled his expensive coat close to shield against the wind.

The gale was strange, but I was in no mood for idle chitchat. "Face into the wind."

The Gildmember cocked an eyebrow. "Eh? What's that?"

"Skardwarf saying. Let's be about our business. Lead the way."

"Of course, of course."

Oltrov strode off without another word, as though trying to lose me in the bustle. And bustling it was, here in the Gild. Archecloaks patrolled in pairs, marching in perfect synchronization. Men in suits cut to the latest trends loudly boasted of their business ventures in Vos.

Well-to-do ladies fancied themselves nobles, attended by liveried servants. Steam carriages rumbled past, billowing wet clouds that hung over the cobbles. It was as if everyone was oblivious to the collapse occurring just outside their walls.

It still smelled like shit, though. More pungently than ever, thanks to the odd winds wafting the stink of the masses and the smoke of the charred Market over the walls. The rich believed themselves immune to the chaos, but half of them were probably infested. One misstep and the Gild would fall as fast as the other districts.

Darkfather, I almost want to let it burn.

Garret would call it justice. Lorelay wouldn't balk—I knew exactly how she felt about Paceeq's nobility. But the Agency served *all* of Liwokin, not just those I deemed worthy. These people were Liwo. They were my responsibility too. Even if they turned their noses up at me as I passed.

"We have arrived," Oltrov announced, and pushed open at a huge iron gate that squealed on its hinges. "Apologies for the unseemly appearance. We're still awaiting repairs after the escape of the daggerclaw." He coughed, drawing my attention away from the broken fence, and added, "Among others."

I followed him through the entrance onto a path of gold-painted bricks flanked by flora clearly not native to Liwokin. Inac or Garret might have been able to identify them, but to me they were just fancy trees and trimmed bushes. Oltrov slowed our pace to a casual stroll, breathing in the admittedly pleasant odors. Pleasant they may have been, but they did nothing to alleviate my impatience with the Gildmember. He was so...frustrating. But in war, we don't get to choose our allies.

"You're keeping our prisoners in the menagerie?" I asked, stepping beneath an open-air tent with white and red stripes.

"Prisoners?" Oltrov said. "I thought you came to see the animals." At my pinched expression, he chuckled. "I jest. What better place to keep them than with the other beasts."

The animals in the pens moved sluggishly, ribcages showing through patchy fur. Snoutbears slumbered, looking like they hadn't eaten for days. Wolves paced in their tiny cages with slavering jaws, eying the smaller animals that had no energy to hide behind the dead trees in their exhibits. Countless creatures, the likes of which only Garret could identify, and each one looked more haggard and starving than the last.

Now I'm certain I want to burn this place to the ground.

"I must say," Oltrov said, unwitting to my building rage, "the prisoners' proximity to such ferocious—and hungry—carnivores has proved a surprisingly effective technique for interrogation. Perhaps you'd consider taking some of the animals off our hands for your dungeons."

"We don't have dungeons."

Oltrov chuckled again. "Right, right. You just kill the men outright. In any case, here they are. You'll find them exceedingly pliable. We only had to feed one of the villains to the stergoderm to get the others talking."

"You *killed* one of them. Fed him to an *animal?* By the abyss, what is wrong with you?"

"Come now, Grimley. I thought you were a reasonable—"

"Stop calling me that." I was seething. I had just about had it with this pompous turd. When I turned away from him and saw what awaited in the cage behind me, it was the final straw.

A gaunt Peeker lay on its side, sucking in hoarse breaths, chittering nonsensically.

I whirled on Oltrov, grabbing him by the lapels of his infuriatingly polished coat. "What is this?" I demanded. "Explain yourself!"

The fear in his eyes was oh so satisfying as he spluttered, "What are...you mean the Peeker?"

I slammed him against the bars of the prisoners' cell. A stergo-derm in the adjacent cage growled. "That's a *person*. You're keeping people locked up here? What else have you got? Ekoans? Ayeiri? Dark-father, am I to find my own men in here? Beasts..."

The unsheathing of steel accompanied a gruff voice behind me. "Hands off him."

Oltrov's eyes looked past me. He gave a small shake of his head.

I let him go. His knees almost gave out, but he caught himself in time to stop from sliding to the floor. Adjusting his collar, he said, "Now, Grim, I understand these are stressful times. But brother can-not turn on brother, not if we're to win this fight."

"Brother," I scoffed. It took every iota of willpower inside me not to give the man a tongue lashing...but he was right. He was no brother of mine, but I was stuck with him. I pulled my gaze away from Oltrov. His sigh sounded like it came from a place of relief. I told the Archecloak, who still hadn't sheathed his blade, "Find the key. Let this Peeker out of here." Remembering Arza's news of the mass Peeker migration, I knew he should be with his people for whatever was hap-pening. "He's to be put on a ship to the Mounds."

The Archecloak didn't comply until Oltrov gave him the go-ahead. And an assurance from me that I wasn't going to lay hands on the Gildmember again. I promised to show restraint. If there were any humans locked up in here besides our prisoners, I wasn't going to lay hands on him. It would be cold steel at his throat.

Until then, business.

Oltrov held out a hand toward the prisoners and showed his teeth in an oily grin. "They're all yours."

CHAPTER THIRTY-FIVE

Trapped in a Cage

Two-hundred and sixteen, adding in the new shipment from the Mounds, he said. And that he'd stake his marriage on the count being accurate. For what that's worth.

—Nameless note

My first instinct, Lightmother help me, was to try siphoning their memories. I searched for the Archefire pattern around their heads, something for my Benefactor to latch onto. But Arza's toxics were still working. The organism remained slumbering. The old-fashioned way, then. I'd had plenty of experience interrogating men as a bounty hunter.

"What were you hoping to achieve in the Market?"

The two men behind bars, one with a crooked nose, the other counting numbers under his breath, looked at each other warily.

"W-w-we already told him everything." Crook Nose flinched back at Oltrov's glance.

"Tell him," Oltrov said.

Counter had been muttering under his breath incessantly since we arrived. He jumped to comply. "Liberation! Liberation! Two-hundred seventeen men and women of the Old Hill fighting to throw off the shackles of our oppressors."

"Your oppressors," I said dryly. "You destroyed countless shops in the Market. Disrupted trade that would make its way to the Blight. Your docks have collapsed. Where will you fish now? How long do you think you'll last before starvation sets in?"

"Gild sabotage!" Counter said with a look at Oltrov. The Gild-member rolled his eyes. "He told us as much!"

"Th-threats," Crook Nose moaned. "Always w-w-with the threats. We've had enough. The Resistance won't stand for it any-any-no more."

I snorted. "The Resistance? Is that why you've nicked those militia uniforms for yourselves?" The Blightdwellers wore them like someone else's clothes. Unbuttoned and ill-fitting, sashes incorrectly fashioned around the waist, featherless caps lying on the ground. All of the pomp but none of the decorum.

Still, I had believed the uniforms part of the Emergent's Aura...

Crook Nose shook his head, but Counter smacked him. "That's right. We're restoring Liwokin to its old ways."

"All right, so you're from the...Old Hill, did you call it?"

Something about that name for the Blight seemed familiar. Its official name was the Old *District*. If my Benefactor were awake, it might have surfaced a memory. The thought drew a grimace. It disgusted me how often my first instinct was to use that monster.

"Fine, you're right. The Old District has gotten an unfair shake." I ignored Oltrov looking askance at me. Fear wasn't the only way to get men to talk. Much more effective was convincing them you're a friend. "That's why I'm trying to change this city. Trying to save it."

Counter's eyebrows shot skyward, and he thrust a finger at me. "You're him! You're the murderous Head of the Agency. You killed the last Head. Six-thousand four-hundred and nine people died in those woods. Your fault! Now you've come for us."

"Oh, L-L-Lightmother help us," Crook Nose cried.

They laid the deaths in Reed's Woods at *my* feet? "You people know nothing. I killed the last Head, sure. Because *he* was responsible for those deaths. Ulken, not me. He was no friend to the Old Hill. But I could be."

"Grim, we didn't discuss this," Oltrov said. Was he playing along, or seriously concerned I would side with these monsters?

I waved him aside. I had the prisoners' attention. It was time to get what I came for. "Tell me, my friends. What do you know about the toxics your people—"

"D-D-Druid's Tears aren't t-toxic—"

"Quiet, idiot!" Counter slapped his companion in the back of the head.

Curious. They were familiar with the Grieving Pine's fruits.

"Not toxic, no," I agreed. "You're smart men. You clearly see the need for them. All I want to know is where to find them, so we can eradicate the infestation."

Counter laughed. "You think you deserve them? Even *we* didn't earn that right yet."

Crook Nose's mouth worked. "H-h-he would never give them to the Agency. Not after what you did last time."

"Who wouldn't?"

"Don't tell him," Counter warned Crook Nose. "He'll skin you alive."

Oltrov rattled the bars of the stergoderm cage, pulling his hands back just in time to avoid the beast's snapping jaws. "Looks like our girl is hungry again."

"Our l-l-leader!" said Crook Nose. "We don't know his name! He says names are dangerous. We just call him the Operator."

Counter grabbed Crook Nose by the throat, pinned him down.

"Hey! Hey!" I yelled to break up the struggle. Crook Nose kicked Counter in the stomach, and the man vomited. "Doesn't matter what you call him. He's dead. Died in the Market."

Counter cackled, spittle dripping into his vile mess. "Is that what you think? You seen the body? Forty-nine dead, a hundred six injured, but he weren't among them."

I grabbed the bars, white-knuckle tight. How would he know that, unless he was counting them as they fell? No, he wouldn't have been able to see everyone in that chaos. Not unless... Unless the Benefactor—the Operator—showed him the dead in a Deluge. "You're lying."

The prisoner only laughed harder. "Aye, ya spooked him, ya did. Dead though? The Operator can't be killed. He's already come back from the dead. Even now, I can feel his touch."

Oltrov rattled the monster's cage again. "What did I tell you about lying, eh?"

"It's n-n-not a lie!" Crook Nose plead. "It's the truth! I swears it!"

"Two liars? Old Millie's gonna eat well tonight." Oltrov turned to me with a wicked grin. "Any more questions?"

I hardly heard him. The Blightdweller's words resounded in my head.

He's already come back from the dead.

He could feel his touch from here? Impossible. I shook my head, refusing to accept it.

But deep down, I knew it was the truth.

"No? Good." Oltrov yanked a latch open, and the iron bars separating the men from the beast fell.

The stergoderm snarled at the wide-eyed men. They didn't have time to scream before its massive jaws closed around both of them at once. Blood and saliva splattered against my coat and Oltrov's as I gaped in horror. The crunch of bones, the smell of death. I turned away before the sight was seared in my mind forever.

Too late for that.

"Ugh," Oltrov flailed his hand to fling the fluids off. He looked down at the mess on his clothes and groaned. "This was a new coat. Utterly ruined."

My jaw clenched so tight it nearly popped out of its sockets. "That wasn't necessary."

"Of course it was." Oltrov raised a brow. "Do you believe the Operator is dead? I don't."

"You just killed them for lying to you."

"Don't be so naive, my friend. I killed them so I didn't have to keep paying overtime to the Archecloaks guarding the menagerie."

I grimaced. There was a cold practicality to that. More pressing than money, however, was the potential for them to return to their boss. If the Operator had the same ability as me to siphon memories, he could learn everything the prisoners told us.

"As it stands, they won't see our Archecloaks coming," the Gild-member continued. "Kicking in doors. Burning down shacks. Smoking them out." He clapped his hands together. "Oh, it will be a glorious day! And long overdue."

My stomach seemed to touch my toes. He wanted to raid the Blight? After what happened in the Market? Darkfather, those rioters all wielded guns. Archecloaks or not, it would be carnage on both sides. A thousand chances for another Benefactor to emerge.

"No. Rioters, Resistance, whatever we call them, too many have died already. We need to cut off the head. Draw the leader out."

But how? Both of us quieted to think, but ideas didn't come easy when a huge iridescent lizard was noisily chewing on man flesh five paces away. All that filled my head was a little voice repeating my problems, making them seem insurmountable.

I was infested, the organism eating at my brain, driving me to the brink of madness. Another Emergent was alive in the Blight, and as dangerous as my own Benefactor. He led a group of zealots who thought they were fighting for freedom, and we had no way of stopping them, no way of knowing where they would strike next. And our only tool to stop them was the Agency, a dying organization in a dying city. How could the Council not see how important this fight was?

There had to be a way to show them. But those horrid sounds, the taste of bile, the dank animal scents...it was too much. Add to that my fears for Inac's safety and the weight of the sanctions placed on the Agency by the Council, and I could bear it no longer.

"I need to get out of here."

No sooner had Oltrov agreed than the Archecloak returned. Wait, no. This was a different Archecloak, drenched in sweat like he'd been running for his life.

"They took him," the armored man said, panting. "The mage."

His words were a punch to the head. I staggered on my feet, knees threatening to buckle. At once, I felt the urge to act yet powerless to do anything.

The Archecloak removed his helmet, revealing long brown curls of Ekoan hair, and rubbed the back of his head. Turning the helmet around in his hand, he laughed humorlessly. "Killed your Finger, almost killed me too."

Before I knew it, my hands were on him, grabbing at any loose bit of cloth I could hold onto. "He's dead?" My eyes stung. This couldn't be happening. I had sent Inac to his death.

"Not the mage. The other one."

I exhaled and nearly doubled over with relief. Guilt flooded in the void left behind. Inac was alive, but I'd sent another man to die. "What happened?"

Oltrov merely watched the exchange. I expected smug amusement on his face, as always, but he actually showed concern at this news.

The Archecloak eyed the cage where the stergoderm feasted, then spat. "Them. Rioters came out of the Blight, ambushed us in the Artisans. Their commander put a bullet in your fool Finger's head when he tried to fight back." The man whirled, pulled aside his hole-riddled white cape, and revealed countless dents in his Archemetal armor. "Good aim, they've got, and powerful guns. Only reason I got away was—"

"You ran. Left him." My lip curled. I was angry with the man, but far angrier with myself. "Oltrov, looks like you'll get your raid after all." Lightmother's mercy. How many more men would die to rescue Inac? How many must I sacrifice? But I wouldn't let those monsters have him. My most loyal companion...my best friend.

"How many men did they have in the Blight?" Oltrov asked. "We'll need at least three times their number." He stopped talking, but his lips kept moving. Was the man running sums in his head, figuring how this slaughter would be financed?

"Two score militiamen or more." The Archecloak's expression flattened to mercilessness. "But a raid? Aye, we should burn that place to the ground. City would be better off for it. Won't do no good for your man, though."

"It's a risk, but we need him back. Oltrov, how many Archecloaks can you muster?" I couldn't stop my own mind from spiraling into wartime planning. How much armor did the Gild have in reserve? We would need every Finger protected if the rioters brought their new pistols to the fight.

"You aren't listening," the Archecloak said. "He isn't *in* the Blight."

"What? Where did they take him?"

"I said they were *militiamen*. Dressed up like them, anyway. Said they were arresting your man for...what was it? Abetting a murder."

My throat tightened, choking off my breath. Abetting a murder? Had these Resistance members truly been recruited into the militia? Inac might have been taken in the Blight, but this had the City Council written all over it.

"Bastards," Oltrov growled. "I warned her what would happen if she went through with it. And they conscripted those animals?"

"So it's true?" the Archecloak asked. "The Liwokin Militia is back?"

Oltrov grunted his affirmation.

I forced myself to look at the stergoderm. Scraps of bloody militia uniform hung from its protruding bottom jaw. It fixed me with its lizard eye, then swallowed the prisoners' flesh. The beast seemed cold, calculating...detached. Much like Oltrov. He *knew* why they were wearing militia uniforms.

"You did well," the Gild leader said to his man. "Learned as much from you as from the prisoners. But there's no time to rest yet."

"I'll sleep by the light of the Blight on fire."

"Attaboy. Now, go tell your Captain it's nearly time. Start preparing the men."

"Preparing for what, sir?"

Oltrov flashed a smile at me. "The Blight will have to wait, but the Council Hall will be easier to occupy anyway. It's time to show them the Gild's might."

My face scrunched up. Was he serious? The Gild's might? For him, this was no more than an excuse to take over more of Liwokin. I glanced at the stergoderm, now licking its chops and gnawing on a clean bone. The Council and the Operator were working together, but was I working with an even bigger monster to beat them?

If the Gild had their way, all of Liwokin would be locked in a golden cage of their making.

I blinked as a weak memory surfaced from Yezna's Pool. With it came a subtle sense of being trapped in a cage, unable to escape from an overwhelmingly powerful Aura.

An idea formed in my mind. My Benefactor was awakening, and with it came the chill of the abyss. I shuddered at what I was considering, but maybe it meant no one had to die.

"Hold off on the show of force, Oltrov. I don't need an army to get Inac back. I'm going to go have a chat with Maise."

CHAPTER THIRTY-SIX

By the Light of the Fire

It was an unimaginable tragedy, committed in the dark by ignorant hands. But in hindsight, it might have bought us just the time we needed to survive. As for what we lost, well...nothing that couldn't be replaced by a little Ekoan generosity, eh?

—From the first oral history of Ekohold

Garret's ears guided his feet, carrying him closer to the danger that lurked in blackness. Glowing bulbs hung overhead like stars, but their light did nothing to illuminate the way ahead. The ceiling was too high. Peekers growled, their mandibles clacking violently from all directions. The place smelled rank. Worse than Liwokin on a hot day. Humid air filled with a sickly sweet that made Garret want to gag. Damn near did gag when his boot landed in some sticky sludge.

But none of that was as bad as the dread that rose when Garret heard Sentyx roar. He froze in place. Getting closer. He wished badly for a light to see by, but he was pretty sure invisibility was the only thing keeping him alive. If the Skardwarf saw him padding closer, bow in hand...

Will I even feel his fist smash through my face? He clenched his jaw. *Abyss take me if I let Sentyx kill me. Not after all my efforts.*

All those days keeping his enemy close. Close enough it was easy to forget how dangerous he was. What was in that note from Cavern that made him rush ahead and start killing Peekers indiscriminately?

Garret was already certain Sentyx was a traitor, but this was one more piece of evidence for the pile.

Yet despite all their time together, he still had no idea how to kill a Skardwarf. All he knew was facing them head on would prove fatal. So he slunk through the shadows, creeping toward the monster that raged in the dark.

His eyes were beginning to adjust. This wasn't his first night hunt. He navigated by the silhouettes seen only at the edges of vision. Great bulbous masses, whatever they were. Peekers must have been hiding behind them, judging by the frantic clicking and chittering he heard all round.

The objects were no comfort to Garret. Reminded him of nothing so much as a Benefactor. He pursed his lips. In his focus on Sentyx, he'd nearly forgotten the strange occurrences. Had Prost unleashed a Benefactor here?

Garret dug out his Clasform and inhaled. He suppressed a sneeze, wiped his nose. Felt no different afterward. No Aura, then.

Sentyx screamed, and the ground shook. A wet gurgle escaped some dying Peeker. No Benefactor, just a Skardwarf on a rampage.

Bleeding darkness. What am I doing?

Why risk his life for some Peekers? Who cared if they were tearing each other apart? Happened all the time in the animal kingdom. Garret had the evidence he needed that Sentyx was a traitor. He'd found Prost. He should return to the Agency and come back with every Finger Grim could spare.

Tempting, but no. The journey would take far too long. Snuff it all, he was on this hunt alone, and only he could kill Prost and his Skardwarves before they sowed more chaos. If it didn't stop now, then when? After Liwokin fell? After Graln burned? He wouldn't let it come to that.

Better be compensated well for my heroic deeds, Grim.

A burst of wind hit him as something charged past like galloping horses. Sentyx's growls suddenly came from the other direction. Followed by crunching and pulpy sounds. Garret flattened himself against a wall that seemed to breathe and squirm.

Darkfather, he needed more light. Sentyx would stumble across him eventually. And if Prost was still here, he was veiled just as effectively as Garret. If he was as smart as Garret believed, he was probably long gone. But what was he doing here in the first place? If not killing an Incubating Benefactor to cause its Emergence, then what? Garret could only think of one explanation.

The gems.

It must have been affecting only Sentyx and the Peekers. An Aura of Rage? Same as Pinch, the first Peeker Benefactor. Did he have something to do with those gems? This darkness put Garret in mind of Reed's Woods, how the illusion of the city affected Skardwarves so much more strongly than humans.

Everyone except Grim, Lightmother knows why.

Maybe the same was happening here. Garret felt the lump in his pocket. Could he stop Sentyx with the Clasform box? He considered. Hadn't worked in Reed's Woods, and probably wouldn't work here. Couldn't get close enough to administer it anyway. Then what? Only one solution.

He had to find the gem. Destroy it or take it away. As he'd taken the Clasform away from Reed in his twisted tower. That meant he needed light. His mind still in Reed's Woods, he remembered the feel of the tower under his boot. Sludgy. Wet. Went up like paper in the heat of the Archeflare.

Garret had no Archeflare, but he had his fire starter. He scraped an arrow along the ground, groaned as he felt the sticky goo coating the arrowhead. Hesitated before lighting it. If Sentyx saw him...

Before he could change his mind, his flint struck steel and sprayed sparks over the coated arrow. It flared to life, painfully bright in his eyes, and he had it nocked and loosed within a heartbeat. Aimed nowhere in particular. Just...away. To draw the Skardwarf's eyes elsewhere.

The arrow soared through the cavern, drowning out the phosphorescent blues and bioluminescent greens with bright hues of gold. Arcing gracefully, a shooting star in the black night. It smashed into a pillar and dropped straight down, still lit. The pillar itself sparked alight. Fire spread slowly through the slime that clung to the vertical rock face. Fungus, sensing death, sprayed their spores in thick clouds that themselves caught fire and burned up in flashes.

Garret had been staring at his handiwork for too long already when Sentyx bellowed at the conflagration.

"PROST!"

From his left. Garret turned, squinting his torch-blind eyes, and came face to face with a monster. He stumbled back, stifling a shout in alarm, and landed on his ass in a puddle of slime.

Over him loomed a brown-furred creature three times the height of a Peeker. The monstrosity had a sac more rotund even than an Ecvoqian, so distended it seemed about to pop. Its bottom was fused to the ground and surrounded by six legs the beast used to balance. And sitting right at the top of the mass, a Peeker's head and torso, very much alive. Living and *livid*.

The Peeker variant clicked its mandibles threateningly and continuously vomited the very same sludge Garret sat in. Like it was spitting at him. Enraged, Garret realized. Affected by the gem's Aura. He had to find it.

The fire had spread to the ceiling, traveling in all directions from the burning pillar. So many flash-burning spores ignited, the flashing lights made the room dizzying to behold.

The scene they lit horrified Garret.

Thousands of engorged, vomiting Peekers covered the walls. Some burned alive where the flaming arrow fell. The heat caused their sacs to burst, spraying blue ichor and boiling fluid on normal and variant Peekers screaming around them. Between the huge creatures, Peeker Pairs crawled on all fours and feasted gluttonously on the sea of sludge. Feeding.

Garret added his own bile to the sludge as the meaning of Feeder Hollows became viscerally clear. These bloated beasts were the Feeders.

The Skardwarf's yell caught Garret's ear and allowed the ranger to find him in the distance, climbing a hill with two dozen Feeders. The Skardwarf's wound up his over-sized fist and popped a Peeker with a rain of viscera. Garret had seen Sentyx fight against Benefactors, but this was a slaughter that gripped his chest. The Feeders could do nothing to defend themselves as the stone monster plowed through them.

Pushing himself from the muck, Garret cast his eyes about for any clue to the gem's location. Some landmark central to the chamber, perhaps. Where the Aura would affect the most Feeders. The strength of the Benefactors' Auras always varied with distance, so maybe those closest to the gem would react more powerfully.

There! Opposite the burning pillar, an outcropping of rock jutted skyward. The Feeders around it pounded their bodies against the stone.

From here, it looked to be the place Sentyx was marching.

Garret swallowed his fear and rushed toward his enemy. It wasn't his imagination. He soon found the Skardwarf aimed directly at the same rock. Like he was drawn to it. They all were, in fact. This close, every Feeder had oriented to face it and was straining to move toward it.

Fruitlessly.

The only Peekers capable of moving were those too entranced by the feed to care. Dodging around them, Garret's boots pounded on rock and squished in the slime. He took a wide path to avoid Sentyx's rampage, but still managed to reach the rock before the Skardwarf. That was one advantage humans had over the beasts. Speed.

And little else, it seems.

Sentyx was implacable in his forward assault. Innumerable Peekers died in his wake. Trampled. Pulverized. Torn in two. Crushed in a vice-like grip that Garret had seen turn rocks to dust.

His bile rose as death marched toward him. Not merely from witnessing Sentyx's destruction but from imagining the legions of Skardwarves he had seen in the Deluge. Blowing across the continents like a great storm, leaving nothing of civilization in their wake. He had to end this.

Scrambling to the top of a slanted rock, Garret searched the outcropping from beyond the reach of the Feeders. He let his gaze widen, hoping to spot a glimmer of firelight where the gem reflected the growing blaze. There were so many shadowy crevices in the tops of the boulders. Prost could have carelessly tossed the gem into any of them before fleeing. Garret went to hands and knees, feeling into each dark spot, trying to keep his gorge when his hand came back covered in mucus.

But never with any gems. By the abyss, he was running out of—

CRACK.

The boulders shook, and if Garret weren't already on his hands and knees he surely would have fallen. The Skardwarf pounded on the foundation he stood on, roaring from within a cloud of debris.

"Shit," Garret shouted. "Sentyx, come on! It's me!"

Was he really desperate enough to plead for the Skardwarf to show humanity? Evidently. As expected, the pleading had no effect. Sentyx kept pummeling rock, and Garret struggled to stand and maintain his footing. He might not be able to find the gem, but at least he'd be able to escape if he was standing. Survival first. Humans were no different from animals in that regard.

In fact, it seemed to Garret the time to hightail it fast approached. Things were looking worse than the knuckledragger hunt in the deep woods west of Graln. Rare as the big apes were, he and the other rangers had found it, lounging beneath a waterfall. Problem was, a daggerclaw showed up as soon as they sprang their trap. Seeing those claws tear through orange fur, cleaving long limbs, hearing it's too-human screams...

Not easy to forget a thing like that. Also cleared up the question in Garret's mind of how the beasts came so near extinction. Nature had no care for power differentials. Daggerclaws. Skardwarves. It just bred the best killers it could. The peaceful giant never stood a chance.

Nor would Garret.

He eyed his surroundings. Fire burning damn near half the room. Dead Peekers in the hundreds. Death pounding at his doorstep.

Sentyx roared, a battle cry to be heard over raging winds.

"Aye... Good to know when it's time to leave."

On the cusp of giving up he spotted it. A wooden cube, holes cut into each of its six faces. It tumbled as Sentyx moved earth. Not a gem, but a Clasform box.

Garret scrambled for the box. Nabbed it just before it dropped over the side into the gelatinous remains of what once was a Peeker. He hugged it close to his chest. Jammed his fingers into the holes and wrenched his hands apart. Groaning, he gave up.

Should've known that wouldn't work. Garret had tried six different ways to break open a Clasform the night Ulken shackled the Hand. Smashing it with a hammer hadn't worked. Nor had setting it on fire.

Quaking stone made Garret catch his balance. He looked at the Skardwarf. There *was* one thing he hadn't tried.

Hopping up to a taller rock, he had a clearer view of a heap of rubble that was once several solid boulders. Sentyx's enraged eyes followed Garret's ascent. They reflected the glow of burning flame, making it seem as if the Skardwarf's body contained a fire he couldn't control. Were those eyes really following Garret?

Or the Clasform?

Garret glanced at the box curiously. They had never emitted an Aura in Reed's Woods. Then he tossed it. Right down into the Skardwarf's path. Sentyx's attention followed the Clasform's descent, its bounce and tumble and eventual settlement beside a Feeder absolutely seething with rage.

Sentyx raised his stone fist high.

Brought it crashing down on the box like a star falling upon the land.

With the crunch, a pulse went through the air. An energy beyond the echoing crack of the Skardwarf's blow. Like a wave of nausea passed through Garret, traveling from his stomach right to his brain where it bounced around and made him dizzy. Garret's arm struck rock. He was falling, he realized.

Before he hit the ground, some strange memory filled his mind. A Deluge. In the remembrance, he was a Peeker. Of a Pair allocated to repair duty. Summoned to a broken tunnel, kidnapped by an enormous human, separated and made Unpaired. But an Unpaired Peeker remembers, and it *feels*. And it would never forget the rage it felt as the human's scalpel carved deeper into its skull.

With a great shock of pain, it ended. Accompanied Garret's own aches as he came out of the Deluge to find himself face up in a Feeder's carcass. He sucked in a breath, wincing at the stab in his tail bone. Held it in.

Every Peeker in the burning expanse lay quiet and deathly still. The destruction of the Clasform seemed to have been too much for their minds. Knocked Garret on his ass, and he didn't even feel its Aura. Still on his ass, he didn't want to move. Everything hurt, or worse, was covered in slime. He hated that feeling. Sticky like blood on his hands.

Pushing himself free of the mess, Garret dimly recalled deciding it was time to go. With thousands possibly lying dead around him and the whole room soon to be ablaze...aye, it was time to go.

Instead, he found himself standing over Sentyx. Looking down on him, holding a knife in his hand.

The Skardwarf wasn't breathing. But then, was he ever? Their flesh was armor, indistinguishable from stone itself. No chinks or weak points. Nothing but the pattern of endless cracks that marred his skin. Garret squeezed his knife. The eye, maybe? They weren't closed so much as...missing. Without them he looked no different from a fallen statue.

As if he was dead already. The thought sent a pang of regret through Garret, which confused him. He didn't *want* to regret anything he'd done. Instead of shoving it down he raged at it.

It was only regret that he wasn't able to kill his enemy himself. That he'd failed to learn anything of use against the legions. He was too weak. That was what he told himself.

But he'd lied to himself too often not to see straight through it. This was the regret of being unable to save a friend. In his lowest moment, he admitted to himself he'd grown to like Sentyx's company. Now he was either dead or a traitor, and there wasn't a bleeding thing Garret could do about it. He wanted to spit but found he had no water in his mouth.

Only tears in his eyes.

Garret reached into his pockets for a handkerchief to wash his hands but found a crumpled paper instead. He flattened Cavern's note and held it up to read by the light of the fire.

Brother Sentyx,

Do not dismiss my words just because you've dismissed my allies. I grow tired of him as well, but our work in the Mounds is almost complete. To Eko or Paceeq we travel next, guided by the winds of his whims. You once told me you wished to face the wind among trees. Eko has many forests. Rejoin me. Together, we need nothing more. No humans savages. As I write he travels to destroy the Feeders that see the Peekers through the storm. Barbaric. If I knew what he planned with our cores, I would have left them to the fool in the tower. Please, brother, find me quickly. Before long he will lay hands on the Princess, and then it will be too late.

Garret wrinkled his brow as he finished the note. Again, the perfect handwriting of a Skardwarf frustrated him. And it was in a language he could read. Odd. The letter held nothing but more mysteries.

Dismissing Cavern's allies? Was Garret wrong about Sentyx working with Prost? Even so, he was allied with his brother. They were Skardwarves. And they were planning something foul in Eko. Garret stopped himself from crushing the note in his grasp. Folded it carefully instead. Tucked it away for later.

He still had the knife in his hand. Garret sighed and sheathed the blade. Wouldn't do any good anyhow.

Regret flooded him again when eight Queensguards appeared, all of them pointing their deadly-sharp arms at Garret. Regret he wouldn't die with his weapon in hand. But in reality, that might have been the only thing that saved him.

Wordlessly, a Pair of Guards hauled Garret into the air. His resistance was met with firm but implacable holds. All he had left to give was laughter, full of despair until four more guards approached Sentyx. Amusing. He'd like to see them try to lift a—

The Skardwarf joined him overhead, lifted by a pair of the Queensguards. The other two weren't even needed. In that ignominious state, Garret and Sentyx were carried from the cavern and thrown into a Peeker prison cell.

CHAPTER THIRTY-SEVEN

Beneath the Veil

A towering palace that reaches the sky
Its residents gorging on all of the pie
What crumbs are leftover they throw to the streets
Be grateful, they say, that we give you this feast

—Verse from Common Courtesy

Lorelay awoke in a cold sweat, as she had every day since Empress Elzia's funeral. Burns covered her arms, her legs, the side of her face that had been turned toward the pyre. Her skin felt like dry leather, ready to crack and bleed any time she moved. These days, she hardly desired to move, even if she could.

Minny had found her on the floor in her chambers that first evening, lying on the ground in a torn dress, curled up around her hands. Lorelay was in agony, unable to move, even to call for help. Minny had tried telling her she was lucky her burns were not more severe—evidently, gossip about what happened at the funeral was spreading like plague. When she had forced Lorelay to show her hands, the woman's face had gone pale. She had rushed out of the room without a word, leaving Lorelay there in torment.

While she waited alone in the darkening room, Lorelay had tried to convince herself she had done the right thing. The Grieving Pine's branch was necessary to save the Empire, right? What were her hands when compared to the lives of hundreds of thousands? But all that went through her head were the songs she had composed, songs she would never play again. If she had no music, she had nothing. But then Minny had returned, and begun to clean the wounds, proving Lorelay wrong. She had one thing. She had pain.

Several days had passed with Minny constantly tending to Lorelay's burns, trying—unsuccessfully—to keep her in good spirits. Good spirits...she felt like she would soon be little more than a spirit. Her entire body was already wrapped in salve-soaked cloth, just like the bodies to be interred in the crypts.

"The mind will give up before the body," Minny had said, "and that's as sure a sign as any that the abyss approaches."

"I'm going to die?" Lorelay had asked.

"No, child. Your burns will heal." But when Minny had looked at her heavily bandaged handy, the woman drew her lips to a thin line, giving away the lie. "You just have to stay positive."

"Not my strong suit," Lorelay had said. What was there to stay positive about?

Her body was burned, her mind seemed to be wilting with every day stuck in bed. Worse, she had no idea what was happening outside her chambers. Minny resisted her questions, and she would rather remain in ignorance than beg. Had Vinlin destroyed the Grieving Pine after all? Was he still to become Emperor, or had she ruined that too? The Church was looking for any excuse to depose him. She might have given them a reason.

Laying there with the Brightdaughter's light streaming in through the sheer, sage curtains to fall across her bed, Lorelay wanted to remain motionless all day. Funny, when she was first ordered to remain in her bed, she had protested that she needed to be up and about. When had that shift occurred? She supposed it was for the best, a sign she was accepting her condition. For all she knew, she might lay here for the rest of her life.

So when Minny strolled in with a chair on wheels, Lorelay could make neither light nor dark of it. No matter. She just rolled her head the other way on her pillow, looking out the window.

Minny stomped over to Lorelay's bedside and put her hands on her hips, a stark silhouette against the light from outdoors. "Now what kind of way is that to greet me?"

Lorelay sighed and closed her eyes. "Leave me alone."

"Oh no you don't. You're going to sit up and look at me when I'm talking to you."

Why had Lorelay ever liked this woman? She was starting to sound like her mother. Lorelay's chest tightened. She missed her mother...

"I ought to slap you, girl. You've been bugging me to hear about what's happening outside your door, and now I've come to take you out of here and you won't even look at me?" Minny scoffed. "Do you know how much trouble I could have got in if someone saw me bringing this rolling chair in?"

Lorelay's eyes shot open. "You're taking me out of here?"

Minny chuckled. "That got your attention, huh? Well, don't get your hopes up, we're not going anywhere exciting. Just to the servant quarters. Being around people will do you some good."

The servant quarters? She would rather go back to sleep. Still, maybe Minny was right. How long had it been since she had interacted with anyone other than the old woman? "Fine. Help me to the chair."

When Minny saw her struggling to sit upright, she rushed to lift her up, taking care with her burns. "Not so fast. We have to change your dressings first."

Lorelay wanted to slink back down and hide under the blankets. The only thing worse than bandaging her hands was peeling the soiled cloth off. But as much as she was treated like an invalid, Lorelay knew she was strong. She assented, offering her hands to Minny and looking away. "Do it."

Minny did, and by the time new ointment had been applied and fresh bandages wrapped had been around her hands, Lorelay was shaking, whimpering.

Maybe going out isn't such a good idea after all.

But Minny already had her by the armpits, lifting her out of bed to seat her in the rolling chair. The old lady was stronger than she looked. If she wanted Lorelay in that chair, it would happen, sure as the Brightdaughter rising over Vos. Minny pushed, and Lorelay expected to be rolled out through the door. Now that she was actually leaving this room, the prospect was starting to bring her back from the brink of depression. She had been cooped up here for too long. But on the way to the door, the chair jerked to the right, and Lorelay was face to face with the wardrobe.

"Huh?"

"You can't go out looking like a corpse, girl." Minny laughed. Lorelay did not. "Sorry. But you're not allowed to be out of the room. Need something to disguise you. Oh, don't balk. It's that or back to staring out the window from your bed."

The disguise Minny had in mind turned out to be a loose-fitting shawl that draped over the rolling chair, covering Lorelay from the shoulders to the waist. A blanket covered her legs, and a frilly hat with a dark veil hid her face. None of it matched. In fact, Lorelay was sure she looked like nothing so much as a pile of laundry Minny was wheeling to the wash basins.

The wash basins were exactly where they ended up after traveling the gloomy halls of the Radiant Palace without incident. Lorelay's stomach was in her throat when one Paladin stopped Minny to ask where she was going, but Minny deflected with a quip, and the disguise held up. That was the only close call.

Until a serving boy peered through her disguise in the servant quarters.

"It's her!" a liveried boy with arms half-submerged in soapy water exclaimed, drawing the rest of the servants' attention. "We'll hang from the gallows if he finds out she's here!"

"Oh hush, Alverin," Minny said, rolling her eyes. "I swaddled the Bright Prince when he was a babe. And you know nothing of what this girl means to him."

Lorelay squirmed at that comment. Vinlin clearly cared for her, but she was sure she had squandered his affection during the funeral.

"If anyone gets in trouble here, it'll be me." Minny straightened her back and scanned the room with a stern, grandmotherly expression. "So I won't hear another word of complaint out of any of you."

Lorelay's hands clenched nervously, causing her whole body to contort in pain. It took conscious effort not to move them. Was she going to have to keep up that effort for the rest of her life? Her thoughts drifted to the lyre Vinlin had gifted her. Useless now, only a reminder of what could have been. Of what sort of life she could have had if she lived in a world where the Lightmother truly was merciful.

It was hard to imagine such a world existed when a dark veil shrouded her sight and her hands were bandaged near to immobility. Her life was ruined for the smallest chance she might save the Bright Empire. How could she have let herself think she could make such a difference?

There were people in charge, like Vinlin, like Grim, and there were the rest of them. When had the common folk ever had a say? It was why she railed against the Bright Throne, yet it was clear now no one wanted to listen. She just thought...maybe...she had a chance.

Minny removed the hat from Lorelay's head, wiped the tears from her cheeks. "No need for that now, girl. These are friendly faces." She grinned and added, "Even the ones as ugly as Alverin's."

The lone serving boy pretended to ignore the comment, picked up a pile of dirty linens, and stomped off.

"Um," a mouse of a girl squeaked, taking a nervous step closer and wringing a rag in her hands. "Is it true the, um, Bright Prince—"

"Kindling Emperor, now, Ezebel," Minny corrected, "and out with it already. She's not going to bite."

Ezebel stood a hair straighter, and Lorelay smiled at her encouragingly. Being a servant in the palace, the girl must have known Vinlin had become Kindling Emperor after his mother's funeral—the last step before becoming a full-fledged Bright Emperor at his coronation. Lorelay could hardly believe her own presence was making the girl so skittish; didn't she know Lorelay was no better than her? "Is the Kindling Emperor really fighting with the Church?"

A bunch of other girls crowded around Ezebel, nodding encouragingly, telling her it was a good question. They turned worried faces toward Lorelay, expecting an answer.

Was that supposed to be some secret? If so, Vinlin had spilled it within a single span spent together in his chambers. Lorelay opened her mouth to confirm their suspicions...then closed it and thought for a moment. Was it her place to gossip about the Kindling Emperor? He had taken her into a privileged position, shared his problems with her, trusted her. If she began blabbing about everything that passed his lips, it only proved how misplaced his trust had been. She had done enough to strain their relationship, such that it was.

"The Kindling Emperor," she began, "and the Church have some... disagreements. I wouldn't go so far as to say they're fighting, though. The Bright Throne and the Church have been faithful allies since the dawn of the Era of Light. That's not changing."

It almost sickened Lorelay to admit it, but it was the truth. In the tiny chance she had not ruined her relationship with Vinlin already, she should be helping him reconcile with the Church, not driving the wedge further between them. If the Bright Empire was going to fight the Benefactors, it needed the Church of Light.

Darkfather, what has the world come to when I'm no longer fighting the Church?

To her surprise, her answer put the serving women at ease. Their faces were all smiles now, postures relaxing in relief. It also diminished the nervousness of the next questioner.

"What's it like in the Fire Gardens? They say you went there on your very first day in the palace!"

"That's true." Lorelay smiled wistfully. It had been too long since she visited the gardens. But her smile soured when she realized none of these servants had ever been allowed to step foot in them. "They're...the most beautiful thing I've seen." The description was hardly sufficient to capture her feelings about the gardens, despite her less-than-ideal experience on that first day.

Still, the servants leaned in, awaiting more. Lorelay gave them what they wanted, regaling them with colorful descriptions of banners billowing in the breeze, of flowers stretching into the distance where the river caught the Brightdaughter's golden sparkles, of lords and ladies in suits and dresses fit for a royal ball. By the time she finished, her audience was so rapt with attention, she was sure the only way to make them see the gardens more vividly, short of actually visiting, was to give them a Benefactor's Deluge.

Lorelay herself yearned to go on. This was who she was. A storyteller. Her music was one tool for telling stories about the world, but even without it, she could still capture an audience, keep them on their toes. It made her feel almost herself again. Her hands might not heal, but she still had her mind and her mouth.

And no Paladins will throw me in a dungeon if no music accompanies my tales. As soon as the words passed through her mind, she reconsidered. *On second thought, no, they definitely would.*

The questions came at her in rapid succession now, too fast to answer. On the way here, she had been worried they were going to ask her all about her mistakes, why she had ruined Empress Elzia's funeral. None of them cared about that. They only wanted to hear about the life they could never have, the life of nobility. Serving in the Radiant Palace would have been torture for Lorelay. Always dealing with the snobbery of the lords and ladies. For these servants, however, it was the closest they could come to being nobles themselves. They just wanted *more* of it.

"How many dresses are in your wardrobe?"

"Who's your best friend in the palace?"

"Were you born a noble or—"

"Has Vinlin kissed you?"

At the last, the other questioners turned to face Ezebel, who had asked it. Her cheeks turned the color of the Fire Gardens' banners, and Lorelay's must not have been far off. She expected a break in the questions—they had gone too far, clearly—but oh, was she wrong. Now the tap had been unstopped, the girls only got *more* raucous.

"Well, *has* he?"

"Of *course* he has! Look at her, she's as beautiful as he is!"

"He is quite handsome, isn't he?"

"Not as handsome as his brother was."

"Oooh, what's he like in bed?"

Lorelay only thought her cheeks were burning before. "I haven't— I never—in *bed?*" she spluttered. She would *never* share a bed with Vinlin, not if she had any say. Not that he would want that, anymore... would he?

The rolling chair rocked as if an earthquake had struck Vos. Minny's hooting laughter nearly doubled the woman over. The rest of the girls were giggling and shouting and slapping each other playfully. This was getting out of control.

"Enough!" Lorelay shouted. She had to repeat herself before they quieted down. Twice! "You've had enough questions for me. I've only been here for a short time, but you've been in the palace for years, haven't you?" The youngest of the girls looked to be fourteen or so, but the rest were still young enough Lorelay would call them girls instead of women. There were surely older serving women, but apparently they had better things to do than gossip with the heretic. "You all know the court better than I do, so it's my turn to ask questions. You say Vinlin had a brother?"

"Elwin." The oldest girl nodded. "His elder brother, but he..." She looked to Minny, who nodded.

"Go on, girl."

What did she need Minny's permission for?

"But he left with the Empress' husband," the girl continued.

"Lover, not husband," another corrected.

Lorelay remembered hearing about some royal scandal when she was a child, but to her young ears it was just a continuation of the nonsense that poured out of the Radiant Palace. "Her lover, wasn't he... exiled?" She was straining her memory, but that sounded right to her.

"By the Church."

"No, by Elzia."

"He left of his own accord," said a girl with an upturned nose.

"We're not supposed to *talk* about this..."

Lorelay shook her head. These girls knew little and less. What did they have to fear talking about? Although, considering for a moment how she ended up in the dungeons for the unconscionable act of singing a song, maybe they had a point. That could have been why they looked to Minny for guidance—she had been a servant for Light-mother-knows-how-long and still had a head on her shoulders. She knew what boundaries were safe to cross. "I'm not trying to get you in trouble."

"To ashes with that," Minny said. "We're in friendly company. No one's going to hear of this outside these quarters."

The girls still looked at each other warily, but they began to open up, answering Lorelay's questions to the best of their ability—which was to say, not very convincingly at all. Not a one of them was older than Lorelay herself, and it became clear they were just repeating contradictory rumors if not outright making things up.

Still, it put a smile on Lorelay's face. Minny was right. After spending so many days bedridden, it did wonders for her mind to interact with other people. Even if it was a bunch of mindless gossip. When it came time to return to her room, she pleaded with Minny to stay just a while longer.

Minny, however, was adamant. "I'm glad you're having a good time—Lightmother, the color's back in your cheeks for the first time in days. But do you think I have nothing else to do today, girl?" She had already begun rolling the chair before finishing the rhetorical question.

Lorelay snorted, donning her veil once more. "What, like scrubbing Vinlin's chamber pot?"

"I ought to dump you out of this chair and make you walk back, you know that?" But Minny was smiling.

"Can we at least come back tomorrow? If I'm cooped up in there one more day, I'm going to lose my mind."

Minny waited until they reached the hallway with her room before relenting with a sigh. "Fine. But the Kindling Emperor isn't going to be pleased if he finds out what I'm doing."

Lorelay rolled her eyes. "Vinlin hasn't checked on me once since ordering me imprisoned." With a deep voice mocking the future emperor, she added, "I have many more important things to worry about. Ruling the Empire. Bowing to the Church. Coaxing Brightness Lorelay beneath my sheets."

Minny tried and failed to stifle a snort, which came out like a gurgle. "If he hears you say that—"

"Yeah, yeah. Dungeons and gallows. He'd have to be listening to me to hear anything I ever say. By now, he's probably forgotten I exist."

It was to Lorelay's surprise, then, that when they opened the door to her chambers, Vinlin was sitting on her bed awaiting her.

CHAPTER THIRTY-EIGHT

Tending Your Wounds

He spies her from a distance
'Oer horizons do they wend
A dance 'tween star-crossed lovers
Marks the coming of the end

—Verse from Beyond World's End,
Second Song of Half-Dusk

The Kindling Emperor rose imperiously as Minny rolled Lorelay into the room. Lorelay tried to push herself to standing, but her bandaged hands screamed in protest as they bore her weight on the chair's arms.

"I see you and my aunt have been out having a jolly time," Vinlin said.

"Vinlin," Lorelay said breathlessly, wincing at the pain in her hands. "How long have you been—wait, your aunt?" She spun to face Minny. "You're his *aunt?*"

Minny squirmed, but before she could respond, Vinlin cut in angrily. "Where were you? You were meant to stay here for your own safety."

"Safety?" Lorelay scoffed. "This room may not be so dark and dingy, but it's no better than a dungeon if you lock me in."

"You would have been in the *actual* dungeons if I let you wander around or leave the palace," Vinlin retorted. "Or worse. Did you think you could disrupt my mother's funeral without consequence? You broke the royal family's ancient traditions in front of the entire city. Do you think it's easy for me to keep you under watch like this? I *had* to do it. I have a duty to our people—"

Minny snorted derisively, and Vinlin glared at her.

"Is something funny, Minerva? Your sister's funeral, and you couldn't even be bothered to attend."

"Bah. She was no sister of mi—"

"Leave," Vinlin commanded, and Minny stiffened.

Lorelay's jaw tightened. She had no desire to be alone with Vinlin when his temper flared like this. Alone, helpless to fight back. Her lips tightened. What did she think was going to happen? A drink-blurry memory of Grim sending her away came to her.

The man's practically in love with you, he had said. *How hard could it be to win him over?*

Grim had been wrong on the second point, but he was right on the first. Vinlin *was* in love with her. The feeling might not be mutual, but he would do nothing to harm her...right?

"Stay," Lorelay said. Better to have a friend around, just in case. "My wounds need tending."

Minny shifted, jaw working. "She's right, it's time those bandages came off, and..."

Vinlin's withering glare told both of them he would not be swayed on this matter. After giving Lorelay's shoulder a comforting squeeze, Minny left. As soon as the door closed, Vinlin let out a heaving sigh and his shoulders slumped. He rubbed an eye with his thumb, then sat at the table where servants had left several pitchers. Vinlin poured dark wine into a crystal glass, then poured it down his throat in one gulp. He eyed the pitcher, considering for a moment before turning to face Lorelay.

She remained tight-lipped, waiting for him to say something first. Better not to provoke his ire any further.

"I have been traveling the city making apologies for you," he said, and guilt roiled in Lorelay's stomach. "For the both of us. People really do want to see your head roll for this. The stockades were the mildest charge suggested. I have practically begged forgiveness on your behalf. Your mother is worried sick."

All of this had been turning the storm in Lorelay's stomach from guilt to genuine fear. The Kindling Emperor could only do so much to save her from herself. She had been avoiding meeting his gaze, but that last caused her to raise her eyes. "You visited my mother?"

Vinlin opened his mouth, shut it again, and decided on that second glass of wine after all. He had the decency not to drain the cup this time, at least. "She was at the funeral, you know. I assured her you're safe and recovering your health, but I'm not so sure.

"The Church, for one, has proved...obstinate on the matter. I've never seen Namravi behave so unreasonably before. The High Cleric is normally a gentle woman, but our discussion came to shouts and insults. She threatened to excommunicate *me*, her future Bright Emperor, over the matter. What would she do to punish a heretical woman? A girl who had no right to be there in the first place?"

Lorelay almost resented that—who was he to say she had no right to be there? And *girl?* That, she did resent. But becoming petulant about the matter would only prove him right. Vinlin had finished, now just sat there swirling the wine in his glass, staring into the cup with eyes full of pain. Lorelay took a deep breath to calm herself, tried to actually listen to what Vinlin was telling her.

The Kindling Emperor was angry with her, but he had every right to be. And despite that, he was going out of his way to help her, trying to calm the peoples' wrath against her, fighting the Church on her behalf, even visiting her mother to assuage her fears.

He really cares about me. The realization formed tears at the corners of her eyes. *Doesn't he know I'm not worth it?*

"Why?" Lorelay asked. "Why do all this for me?" The abyss take her if she thought she deserved any of Vinlin's grace. From the moment she returned to Vos, she had done nothing but make his life more difficult.

Vinlin's lips twitched a momentary smile, and he shook his head slowly, as if conflicted. "I never asked for this, you know. For my life to become this much of a...a tangle. The Church's expectations. The duty to my people. The desires of my heart. And yes," he added, eying Lorelay, "your monsters, too. I haven't forgotten. Do you ever feel like it's all too much? The more I try to unwind these threads, the tighter the knot pulls."

Lorelay nodded. She understood. The more she tried to fight the tyranny that squashed her home and those she loved, the heavier it seemed to press down. "The more we struggle," she said bitterly, "the more we have to struggle against."

Vinlin grunted. "Then why do you keep fighting? Wouldn't it be easier to just cast it all aside and try living out your days in happiness?"

"Believe me, I've tried," she muttered. "It's hard to leave it behind when the past keeps coming back to bite me."

Thoughts of Dunnax filled her head, and only the bandages on her hands kept her from plucking the goblet of wine from Vinlin's fingers. He was close enough, sitting hunched over in that chair like a man who had the entire world's burdens on his back. She had found Grim sitting that way in an inn. Empty tankards on the table. Refusing to talk to anyone. *Men.* She shook her head. *Why do they always think they have to go it alone?*

"Perhaps..." Lorelay spoke slowly, picking her words with care. "Perhaps it's easier to keep hold of it when you have someone to remind you of everything you have to be grateful for."

The Kindling Emperor remained slouched but lifted his head to look at her. His eyes were glossy. Lorelay glanced at the floor, where several teardrops had fallen. "Do you?" he asked. "Have someone like that?"

Lorelay's lip quivered. She had to close her eyes, hold back her tears. The last thing she wanted was some servant striding in to find the both of them sobbing. But she couldn't help it; the tears came of their own will.

"My brother. He always used to say how blessed our family was. Two Paladins. Mother prayed enough for all four of us. And I...I didn't have to do anything but be grateful for the life we'd been granted by the Light. It used to really annoy me."

An embarrassed laugh broke from Lorelay. She glanced at the Kindling Emperor sheepishly, but Vinlin looked on with an earnestness that compelled her to continue.

"But he was right. We were blessed. It only took me losing everything to see that."

Losing everything because of my own selfish dreams. My own...inadequacy. She could have done more to save him. Grim came back to life... Lorelay was trembling, balling her fists so tightly the burned skin cracked. Pain radiated from her wounds, but it was nothing compared to the pain inside her.

Crystal clinked on the table, and Vinlin was kneeling by the side of her desk, reaching to take her hands in his. "You haven't lost everything."

His voice was as gentle as his touch, but if he said she still had *him*, Lorelay swore to the Darkfather she would—

"Your mother...she made it quite clear how much she loves you." Lorelay's stomach dropped, and Vinlin chuckled.

"What did she do?" Lorelay was almost afraid to ask.

"Let's just say I had to call off my footmen when they heard what she threatened to do to me if I hurt you." Vinlin's face scrunched up as he searched his memory. "I recall the words 'Darkfather's justice' being used."

Lorelay's eyes widened. Her *mother* had said that? Threatening an Emperor was so incongruous with Lorelay's idea of her mother, she was sure he had the wrong woman.

"You look just like her, you know. Your nose, your eyes." Their gaze met. "It's like looking into her eyes."

"You're imaging staring into my mother's eyes?"

"Into *your*—" Vinlin sighed. "Never mind." He looked down, then started. "You're bleeding."

Lorelay noticed him subtly back away, face growing queasy. "Scared of the sight of a little blood?"

But she found herself looking away from it too. It only called to mind the blood on her hands as she stood over Looker's body, breath heaving in Reed's twisted tower. She remembered thinking Dunnax was gone—why should this person live? The memory shamed her; Dunnax wouldn't have wanted his sister to become a killer in his name.

"I don't like the sight of blood when it belongs to..." Vinlin pursed his lips but forced himself to say the words. "Belongs to someone I care for. It only makes me fear losing them."

That was...very sweet, actually. Her face heated and she looked away, abashed.

Vinlin gestured at the pin holding her bandages tight. "May I?"

Lorelay considered, then gave a quick nod. Vinlin began slowly unwinding the bloodied bandages from her hands. "Didn't you just say you don't like the sight."

His face grew ever queasier as more of her blistered hands showed. "Sometimes you have to look anyway. If I fear losing something, shouldn't that just be a reminder to be grateful for it while it lasts?"

His words stirred up a memory of Reed's Woods, the last time she had seen her brother. Had Lorelay been grateful for her brother when she hugged him before parting? She had certainly feared losing him, just as she feared dying herself, despite her calm facade. Lorelay just didn't want Dunnax to worry.

Now, she didn't want Vinlin to worry. She watched as the bandages pulled away to reveal dry, bleeding skin. "We'll need to wash them with warm water. But they're not so bad, really. They're getting better."

Vinlin pulled his frowning gaze away from her wrecked hands and looked across the room. "Is your washbasin full?"

Opposite the table, a metal pitcher and basin rested atop a ceramic stand next to an open window. Two birds chirped their songs and shuffled across the windowsill.

"Full and clean, Minny wouldn't have it any other way."

Her treatment by Minny and the other servants was another thing she should be grateful for, she supposed.

The Kindling Emperor raised a hand, strained, and the pitcher began to glow hot. Vinlin let out a breath, then stood and rolled Lorelay's chair across the room. She held her hands over the basin.

"Warm enough?" he asked, pouring a trickle of water across the back of her hand.

Lorelay nodded and found it within herself to smirk. "Are you trying to charm me, Vinlin? Impress me with Archemagic?"

He chuckled. "If I were trying to impress you, I wouldn't use Archefire. I'm not a very good Archemage, to the grave dismay of our High Cleric. And *charm* you? Why that's certainly a sort of magic I do not possess. No, no." Vinlin glanced at her. "Unless it's working?"

Lorelay snorted. "It *was*."

The birds on the window bounced closer to one another, rubbed their beaks together, and took off in a flutter of wings. Vinlin softly cleansed Lorelay's hands with a plush hand towel, turning the white fabric and clear waters red. It stung, but for those few moments, the sting that constantly pricked at her insides was gone.

When Vinlin had finished and pinned the new bandages in place, he leaned close to Lorelay. "I would like to...show you something. When you're well enough to travel."

That would be some time, she knew, but the way he whispered the words piqued her curiosity. "What is it?"

"Something I've never shown to anybody." He glanced at the windows surreptitiously as though palace spies were listening. "Something that will change your view of the Bright Empire forever."

CHAPTER THIRTY-NINE

Innocence

The Liwokin Militia is hereby ordered to disband, effectively immediately. No reasons will be forthcoming. Collect final wages inside. Seek alternate work with the newly formed Agency.

—Announcement posted outside the Council Hall

I strolled up to the Council Hall alone. The square may have been filled with people, I didn't know. None of them paid attention to me, my Benefactor, or the ten thousand dead inside my head. Only three others in the city—Inac, Arza, and Jacquin—knew of the organism nestled in my brain. A fourth was about to find out.

And anyone else unfortunate enough to be caught in the mix.

Feeling like I had been awake for an age, I expected it to be the dead of night. Therefore, it was.

The stars hung overhead, a stark contrast to moments ago when the Brightdaughter had only begun her descent. The sky flickered with brightness, but I forced myself to yawn. No, no, I commanded the world. It was late. Darkness settled in. Gas lamps illuminated the windows of houses, far more pleasing to the eye than the sickening white light of steam light. I took in the scene, breathing in the stink of home.

Much better.

Casting aside my misgivings about how easily I was coming to control my Aura, I marched up the steps to the Council Hall. The wide doors swung open at my touch and revealed a clerk striking a match to brighten up the dim interior. She swung her head toward the intrusion. Recognizing me, the cigar dropped from her lips.

"You!" she exclaimed.

"Yes, it's me." I held up my hands as two militiamen approached with their hands on the butts of the holstered pistols. I had expected them. "I've come to turn myself in. Call on Maise. I'll only surrender to her."

"She'll do no such thing, murderer." The militiaman at my right approached, drawing a length of rope coiled around his belt.

Murderer? Not yet, but don't tempt me.

As soon as the knave's hand was in reach, I grabbed his wrist. If they believed me a monster, I'd give them what they expected.

My Benefactor latched onto the pattern of Archefire emanating from his head, and through his eyes I saw my face twist into a visage that would have the Darkfather himself soiling his pants. "I said I'll only surrender to her." My voice resounded in his ears, a deep boom, more beast than man.

The militiaman pulled his wrist free and scrambled back. "C-c-call her! Get the Chair!"

Satisfied at the thoughts of imminent death repeating in his mind, I relaxed my Benefactor and smiled at him. "Good boy. I think I'll take a seat while I wait."

Darkfather, I hated this act. Each time I used the organism as a tool, I slid closer to becoming a man I despised, closer to becoming Ulken. But they had my friend. Now was not the time to shackle myself.

I sat in the chair in the lobby, crossed my legs, and waited.

The clerk's footsteps raced away. Two guards remained behind to watch me, hands trembling.

The Liwokin militia, restored to its former glory.

I snorted at the thought, and the unwashed Blightdweller boys pretending to be soldiers jumped at the sudden noise. The taxes levied by the Council always galled me, but at least our stars paid for men with some backbone. If the Empire ever tried to overstep their agreement, our fighters would put their lives on the line to keep Liwokin free. Now the Council and a Benefactor were using these boys unwittingly to take control of the city themselves.

At the sound of approaching footsteps—a whole squadron's worth by the sound of it—I cleared my throat. "You can leave, you know." The militiamen shared a nervous glance. "It's only going to get more unpleasant from here."

They didn't need to be told twice. The front doors banged shut behind them, and I stood, just as Maise and an escort of eight armed guards turned the corner.

All of them wore the Liwokin militia uniform, all of them brandished Darkmetal pistols, and all of them looked like they had been scrounged up from a dirty shack in the Blight not half a span earlier. They spread out around me and cleared a way for Maise to approach. The clerk was notably absent.

I raised my hands again. They seemed to like that, and I didn't want them itching to run me through from behind or drawing their pistols in fear. No...when it was time for them to be afraid, I wanted them too horrified to move a muscle.

"I'm unarmed," I assured them, but two of them roughly checked me anyway. "This is just between us, Maise. I'm not here to fight. You can send them away. You'd be doing them a favor."

The Council Chair narrowed her eyes. "You're lucky I don't have you killed here and now, boy. Fortunately for you, the Council obeys the law. You'll get your trial, and a public execution will serve to show the people the rule of law reigns in Liwokin." She nodded at the uniformed man beside her, holding a length of rope ready to bind me.

I stepped back, hands held high once more, and the man stopped. Everyone tensed.

"What game is this?" Maise growled. "Are you here to turn yourself in or not?"

"Not to them. Only to you." I paused, remembering how I defended myself when the Operator sent one of his killers after me. "If you still think me guilty after you see the truth."

"The tr—" she started, but I gave her no chance to finish the sentence.

Closing my eyes, I focused on the Archefire strands that danced about each skull surrounding me. I latched on to every one of them with my Benefactor and dredged up a memory from the day of the assassin's attempt on my life.

The gloomy walls of the Council Hall faded to inky darkness, the militiamen disappeared, and pulses raced. I felt their emotions. Fear. Stunned confusion. None of them knew what was happening. None of them had battled an Emergent Benefactor, lost their mind in a Deluge. I picked out Maise from among the bunch. She sucked in a breath as the pressure built within her skull, a pain of a piece with my own.

She was ready.

The sky above us brightened, and a mob of Liwo appeared before her. Each of us experienced the same thing. She was me. We all were, and we had just finished a desperate speech to quell the peoples' anger.

By the abyss, did that actually work?

The thought ran through ten minds at once. The surprise I felt at the speech's success, they felt too. All of us saw the assassin, a muscular woman picking her way through the crowd, the glint of the Brightdaughter's light off the pistol she held. Her intent was clear in her body language. It was felt in the wash of immense pain in my gut, just before my strength gave out and my knee struck the ground.

My Benefactor held onto each of the men and women around me in the present. Recollecting this was pure pain, but my pain was their pain. They needed to experience it. They needed to see the truth. If that meant they learned the truth of what I was, so be it. I let the Deluge continue.

A struggle to survive ensued when the assassin took aim at my head. Before the wound in my stomach plunged me into unawareness,

I seized hold of the Archefire strands surrounding her pistol and ignited them. The weapon exploded, taking the woman's hand with it. I lunged at her with my knife, defending myself. One last act of justice before I died.

What came next, I still struggled to explain. Everyone absorbed in my Deluge would know that by killing her I healed myself. The Benefactor inverted the rush of Archefire that fled the dying woman, channeled it into my wound as Archedark, then slumbered in exhaustion. The dead assailant was no woman but a man, cloaked by my Aura as so many things were.

And when I stood, with Inac beside me, we looked back at the Seats of the Hall, who had witnessed nothing but the end of the struggle and declared me a murderer.

A sense of recognition emanated from Maise's mind as she spied herself across the distance. Recognition, then regret. I had shown her enough.

My Benefactor let go of the minds around me. Abruptly, the Deluge ended and returned everyone to reality. Half of the guards were whimpering, curled up hugging their knees, clutching their heads, or feeling at their stomachs where I had been wounded. Another three gazed dumbly into space as though questioning whether it had truly ended. One man possessed more mettle than the rest. His pinched face grew even more pinched as his hand reached for his holstered pistol.

But Maise stayed his hand. "No..." She shook her head slowly, eyes studying the floor. All at once, she drew herself up and noticed the damage I had done to the sanity of the men she'd brought.

She should have listened to me, sent them away.

But she thought me a murderer. She wouldn't have entered a room alone with me even if I were bound and gagged. Not that restraints would have done any good, as she now knew. This stunt risked her believing I had just attacked her directly.

She wouldn't be wrong. I told myself the men whose minds I'd broken were a necessary sacrifice. Killers from the Blight. But even an

Aura couldn't hide what I knew deep down. They were Liwo. Puppets whose strings danced in the fingers of the powerful. If Maise declared me guilty here and there, I would deserve it.

"Help them," the Council Chair ordered man who retained his sanity. "Call upon Clerics if you must. Grim, come with me."

My eyebrow twitched.

Grim? Not 'boy'?

The militiaman protested. "He's a monster! You saw what he did. He's—"

"He's innocent." Maise's words were a whisper, but they drove the air from my lungs like a punch to the gut. I staggered forward, and the man tensed again. "*Help* them. That's an order." Maise nodded to me, then began walking down a dark corridor.

I followed, hurrying to catch up and walk beside her.

"What was that?" she asked.

I sighed. No point in hiding it now. "It was a Deluge. My..." I hesitated. It still unsettled me to admit it. "My Benefactor showed you my memories, made you experience the day the Resistance sent an assassin after me. I'm sorry I had to do that to you."

In all, she was taking her first Deluge much better than I had in Leppit.

Maise pursed her lips and grunted, then abruptly turned down another hallway. "Your Benefactor... You told me Benefactors were a grave threat."

"They are. I wasn't lying when I said Ulken caused the Great Riot. He and his advisor created the Benefactor somehow, then infested his wife with the organism, and her Emergence—" She looked sidelong at me. I was losing her. "It's a lot to explain, I know. And I know you have no reason to trust me, but please. The Agency's morticians have done a lot of research into the Benefactors. We know how they work. We know how dangerous they are."

"Yet you say the Agency is responsible for creating them. And you come here and use it on me?" We had arrived at a thick darkwood door reinforced by iron bars. "What is it you truly want?"

It didn't take a moment of thought. "To eradicate the Benefactors. All of Liwokin is infested, and I know for a fact they're outside of this country too. I have one in my head, yes, and I've used it when I thought it was necessary. I've regretted every single time I've done so. I don't *want* this thing in my head. It's driving me mad. It's going to kill me if I don't stop it."

Maise searched a keyring while I spoke, and paused to look at me. "All of Liwokin is infested? Am I?"

The influence of Archedark swirled around her head as clearly as the Brightdaughter at noon. But that wasn't evidence she would accept. "Did you inexplicably find yourself in the woods a few measures ago, when I became Head?"

She looked away.

"Then you've been infested for some time. Likely since the Riot."

Maise unlocked the door and began down a flight of stairs illuminated by torchlight. "I admit this is answering questions I've long held. So, what is to be done? How can we eradicate them?"

"My lead mortician is working on a cure right now. She's close. We need more Druid's Tears, but the Pinegrave have stopped selling them to us. Somehow, the Resistance is getting them. And I know there's another Benefactor in the Blight... He's the leader of your militia."

Her head snapped around to me, her eyes full of intensity. "You know this?"

"I do. I tried to kill him when his people attacked the Market."

"The Market? He blames that on you."

"Of course he would. They claimed they were fighting to liberate the city from the Agency. He was trying to draw me out for another shot at killing me. I think he has some personal grudge against me. Or his Benefactor senses the threat of another." Mine certainly did. "He might not be in control of it." Lightmother, I hardly believed I was in control of mine.

Ulken's words came to me once more from Yezna's Pool. *It's already in motion. We can only control where it goes from here.* My predecessor always believed himself to be in control. Look where it got him.

We had stopped at the bottom of the stairs. "I'll need to discuss this with the Seats of the Hall," Maise said. "They agreed to reinstate the militia only because the Resistance's emissary agreed to submit to Council rule." Her face twisted with regret. "It was a necessary step in the wake of Agency and Gild collusion. But if what you say is true, we'll need to reevaluate their cooperation."

"They worked through an emissary?" I asked, and Maise nodded. I grunted in frustration. I had been hoping to learn the Operator's identity from her. If even she didn't know... "Can you contact this emissary again?"

Maise eyed me skeptically. "Why?"

The moment had come. I was doubtful the Deluge would convince Maise of my innocence, but if it did, I was certain she would refuse my next offer. I swallowed. There was only one way to find out.

"This fighting has to stop. The Gild and the Agency, the Council and the Resistance. We aren't enemies. We're all Liwo, and the true enemy has settled in while we've been squabbling amongst ourselves."

"Squabbling? I'd hardly call the flouting of our laws—"

"Please listen to me. Oltrov and the Gild are corrupt, I know. They've had everyday Liwo under their boot for so long, I can't even remember a time before it. And Ulken was even worse. The *Agency* was even worse. I'm trying to change that. I've tried to convince you we're on the same side, destroying the blackmail he had on you. I don't care about any of that. I don't *want* this power. Not when this is over. But until then, we have to use what we have to fight the real threat. We have to defeat the Benefactors."

Maise tapped her lip repeatedly. "What are you proposing?"

Hope swelled within me. Was she actually willing to set aside our differences? "I want to organize a summit between all of the leaders of Liwokin's institutions."

"The Agency, an institution?" She scoffed.

I threw my hands up. "I don't care what you call it! What's important is we come together to end this threat. Our city is *dying,* if you haven't noticed. If we don't put aside our differences now, we won't have anything left to fight over but ashes."

Maise's expression was as unreadable as a Skardwarf's. Without a word, she turned and strode into the darkness, plucking a torch from its sconce. The light reflected off iron bars along one side of the corridor. Cells, almost all of them empty. All but the one the Council Chair stopped before.

"Hold this," she said, handing me the torch.

"Will you do it?" I asked. "A summit. You, me, and Oltrov... and the leader of the Resistance."

She was searching her keyring again. "What makes you think I could get him to show up?"

I pursed my lips. "Because you can get a message to him. And because I'll be there. Tell him I'll use the Benefactor cure on myself. He won't want to miss another chance to end my life."

At that, she raised an eyebrow. "You would expose yourself to that risk?"

"It's the only way to get rid of the two biggest threats in Liwokin. The Resistance leader. And me."

"So, it's a trap."

I shrugged. "Call it what you will. I have a plan to make sure the two most powerful Emergents are gone. After that, it will be up to the Council to make sure all the other Liwo are cured. I'll help however I can."

Maise considered for a moment, then unlocked the cell door. "You say your mortician is close to developing the cure? Let me know when it's ready, and I'll send my message. That's all I can promise."

She swung the cell door wide and stepped aside. "If there was no murder, then one can't be held for abetting it."

I hurried over, holding the torch high, and drew in a hard breath. In the back corner of the cell, splayed out unconscious on the floor, was Inac.

CHAPTER FORTY

Better Than One

Strike article twelve, subsection three from the bylaws. In fact, strike all of article twelve. The successor to the Head will be hand-picked by the current office-holder from now on. Or chosen from among the Eyes if I die before I pick someone.

—Delivered by a Nerve to the Organ of Procedure

In the darkness, his memories came to me.

Unwanted. Unwilling. I saw him in the cell, lit only by wavering torchlight, and my Benefactor latched onto him. I knew it was wrong. He wanted to speak before I siphoned his experience from him. I could have stopped it. But I needed to know what had happened to him. If it contained any clue where we could find Druid's Tears, it would hasten Arza's work.

That was the practical reason I told myself. The sanitized explanation for why I was violating my best friend's wishes. In truth, I remembered what he told me. He wanted a chance to explain why he was lying to me. But how could I trust a liar? What if all he told was more lies?

With him unconscious in the Council Hall cells, I delved for the truth unfiltered. He wouldn't know what had happened, and I could pair his words against his thoughts, discover just how far my closest ally could be trusted.

Without his effort in directing his thoughts, his most recent memories surfaced first. A barrage of gunfire saw me squatting in terror, hands clenched over my ears. To little avail—the volley was still deafening. When I opened my eyes, my Archecloak escort was escaping. The memory came to an end with the crack of something against my skull.

No details about the toxics we needed. No information about Inac's lies. I needed to delve deeper. I nudged the patterns of Archemagic, Fire and Dark, that danced around Inac's head, and my Benefactor latched on once more.

This time, a chaotic jumble of thoughts flooded into my mind, countless ideas spoken over one another in my own voice. No...in Inac's voice.

I staggered back as though he had screamed at me and loosened my hold on his mind. He hadn't awoken. The Council Chair spoke from behind me, but her words didn't reach me. Concentration blocked them out. Only the Archefire mattered.

Its golden threads shimmered, vibrating weakly...until my Benefactor touched them. It restored them to life, renewed their vibrant dance. Was my Benefactor the key that would unlock specific memories? I searched for the answer in my own mind, then closed my eyes, and tried repeating in my mind the last words I spoke to him before he left.

Thank you, Inac. For being a friend.

I fixed the words in place and chanted them like a mantra, over and over. My Benefactor latched onto him. Receiving nothing, I waited.

And waited.

And waited some more, for what seemed an interminably long time. The frustration built within me. Why wasn't it working?

What do I need to do to—

A rush of memory streamed into my consciousness, filling my awareness like water pouring into a glass. I descended the Agency stairs, frustrated with Grim, and found a Finger I trusted. I ordered around Fingers and Heels in the Head's name, ignoring the feelings of guilt, sure he would discover my falseness soon enough. I strode through the city and witnessed the destruction, the slow decay that set in beneath Grim's Aura. And I came to the Artisans, where rioters in militia uniforms with uncharacteristically advanced weapons murdered Quinne and captured me.

The memory ended once more with unconsciousness—nothing beyond that moment in time existed. Nothing newer. In some sense, I could tell how old each segment of memory was. The older they were, the more dreamlike they seemed, the more slippery and difficult to hold onto. Summoning a memory from one of the original Benefactors—Wick or Andya, Lomin or Pinch—had grown more difficult of late. It was like they were washed away when the torrent of ten thousand lives flooded into my skull. I hadn't lost them, but they were... deep beneath the surface.

Much easier to access were visions from the present—I merely quested outward with my Benefactor and found an unwilling participant. If only I had sensed this difference when stumbling across the visions of the Resistance planning their protests. Rather than assuming their anger lay with Ulken, the Agency could have prepared, taken action, thwarted the assassination attempt before it started. My hands clenched. Never again.

I won't let them catch me off guard again.

With my new understanding, I placed the memory drawn from Inac's mind in its right place. I used the suppressant. It knocked me out on Inac's bed. Then, I descended the stairs, frustrated with him.

With Inac...? Gah! No.

The memories were *Inac's,* not mine. I used the suppressant. It knocked me out on Inac's bed. Then, *he* descended the stairs, frustrated with *me.* With ten thousand people occupying my thoughts, remembering each of their names was impossible. They were all just...I. For some, however, the effort was worthwhile. Inac's memories. Yezna's memories. Tak's memories. Darkfather, I even had some memories from the rest of Hand Sixty-Four.

These were the foundations on which my understanding of reality rested. The core of my beliefs. I had my friends, and I had ten thousand others. In that mix, was there any room...for me?

No surprise Inac is secretly countermanding my orders.

I could barely keep track of what was happening inside my own mind. How could I maintain hold of the Agency and all its goings on? It hurt that my friend didn't trust me enough to work *with* me on those problems. But then again...I didn't trust him to tell me the truth even after he promised he would. I was no better than him.

Far worse, actually, to be sure.

Inac sucked in a pained gasp. I nearly dropped the torch in my surprise. His eyes fluttered open, and his hand raised to shield them from the light. "Grim?"

"Good," the Council Chair said. "He's alive. Now will you finally leave, or are you going to keep standing there and ignoring me until I change my mind and call the militia back?"

Another moment of surprise passed. I had forgotten Maise was there. "Sorry. We'll go." I lifted Inac by the arm, helping him to his feet.

He staggered, putting a hand to his head. "Lightmother...what to my head did you do?"

Was that pain a side effect from my siphoning of his memories? Oltrov's head had ached just before I commanded my Benefactor to release him.

"It's probably the cudgel you took to the back of the skull," I said. "Don't you remember?"

He nodded and winced. "I do. I was...we were in the Artisans' District. The militia, Blightdwellers..." His eyes popped open, and he glanced around, finally noticing where he was. The rapid movement stole his balance from him, and I caught him by the arm.

"Apologies," Maise said. "They were told to apprehend you. Not to try killing you. I assure you, they will be disciplined."

Inac started to speak, but his face contained only dazed confusion.

"And one more thing," the Council Chair added. "These...toxics you require? I believe I can secure you some small quantity. If you promise not to make any more trouble?"

My breath caught. I gave a sharp nod to Maise, but she began up the stairs before I could thank her. "Come on," I said, urging him along, a mix of hope and dread roiling within me. The Council's co-operation had been secured, but now I had to set things right with my friend. "Let's get you back to your room. I'll explain everything there."

It was slow going, but Inac was able to stand on his own by the time we exited the Council Hall. I still kept an eye on him as we ascended the Agency tower. The last thing I wanted was for him to tumble down the stairs and crack his skull after I'd rescued him.

The door to his room swung open, and the stench of vomit greeted us. Inac saw the mess on his bed and the heap of clothes near his wardrobe.

"My quarters it is, then," I said.

A Nerve was leaning against the wall, observing us and smoking a cigarette, ashing it on the floor.

I really need to rescind that change to their operating procedure.

"Hey! Find me a Heel to clean up the mess in here."

The Nerve dropped the cigarette and put it out beneath his boot.

Seriously?

"And clean *that* up yourself. That's an order."

Following a half-hearted salute, the Nerve kicked the ashes around the corner as if that constituted a job well done, then stuffed his hands in his pockets and strolled off.

I rubbed my eyes. "Lightmother, Inac. I think you're right."

"About what?"

About me squandering the Agency's potential. About me not understanding anything about how the organization worked. About my general incompetence. The list went on.

I sighed and shook my head. "Come on. We need to talk."

And talk we did, about everything that Inac had seen in the city. About the return of the Liwokin militia. About his inability to control Archemagic. Everything I had seen in his memories. He left out nothing...save for what happened in the tower.

I could tell he had more to say and remembered that he didn't know how to explain it last time. Maybe a little give-and-take would loosen up his tongue. So, it was my turn to speak. I recounted the information obtained from the prisoners in the menagerie, and what an ass Oltrov was. Inac chortled at that.

Then I told him how I convinced Maise of our innocence, and how she agreed to attend our summit if I used Arza's cure on myself. At this, there was no laughing, just dire concern. Less about me using an untested serum on myself, more about me using my Benefactor so flagrantly.

"I know, I know. I don't want to use it either...but when it's our only option." I shrugged.

"Then...I suppose to myself that means you still want to see everything I told to you. With your Benefactor. Just hearing from me the story is not enough?"

My lips drew back to a thin line. "You had...something else to tell me before I did that, right?"

Inac closed his eyes for a time, and his face contorted as if he were in pain. Likely he was, after being hit in the head. Then he blurted it out all at once. "I am undermining your authority, Grim. I am sorry, but you do not know for yourself how to control the Agency. You do not even know how it works. Your orders to us are killing it as surely as your Aura is killing Liwokin."

I sat back in my chair, crossing my arms. I already knew everything he had thought, but hearing it from him still took me aback. Still, I needed to hear it all. I wanted to trust him. "Go on."

"I give to the men commands in your name. Commands you never told to me to give them. But I swear to you, I only do it because I want us to succeed."

"You think I don't?"

Inac winced. "I know you do. But...you do not even take care of the requests from Liwo, those you say you care most about. You have neutered even the usefulness of the Nerves."

Pulling the spine out of a man and ordering him to run, I think it was.

With a sigh, he continued, "I believe for myself you are trying your best, but...by the Light, I think the Benefactor in your head is...ruining you."

Ruining me? My eyes squeezed shut, the onslaught enough to bring a man to tears. This was my best friend telling me I was incompetent, that I was destroying everything we worked to build. But that wasn't the most painful part. The worst of it was...

He's right.

"I am sorry, Grim. If you wish at once to dismiss me—"

"Do you remember what I promised in Reed's Woods?"

"I..." His eyes cast downward.

"No more secrets, I told you. You and Jacquin and the rest of Sixty-Four."

Inac's entire posture slumped, like a man who knew he was about to be sentenced for execution.

But he was wrong.

"I also told you I can't do this without your help. That I couldn't run the Agency on my own. That's a true now as it ever was. So no, I'm not dismissing you. Worse. I'm promoting you.

Darkfather, now I really am sounding like Ulken.

"You are...what?"

I nodded. "I want you to be Head of the Agency with me. This beast has already got a hundred Fingers and thirty Eyes. Why not two Heads?"

Inac's mouth fell open, worked on formulating something to say.

"It's your choice," I said, "but before you answer, I have something else to say." *No more secrets.* "I...already siphoned your memories. While you were unconscious."

"You can...do that?"

"I can. I *shouldn't* have. But...I didn't think you would tell me the truth. I didn't know *what* you were hiding. I thought you might be working to overthrow me or—"

Inac snorted. "Overthrow you?"

"It wouldn't be the first time a First Eye has tried to take down the Head. And you *were* my First Eye, by the way. I suppose I never relinquished Jacquin of title, but..." I shrugged. "We never had titles in Hand Sixty-Four, and that worked out, somehow. I never trusted Jacquin though. You...I did. I still do. Just...with everything going on. The assassin's attempt on my life, my Aura and the Operator's disguising what's really happening in the city, the Council sanctions...I've grown suspicious of everyone."

Inac sat in silence, thinking for a long time. If he decided he could never trust me, never work with me again, I wouldn't blame him. Maybe the Sea Pot Isles would be safe from the Benefactors. He could use Arza's cure and return to his home, wait out the storm.

But Lightmother...I hope he doesn't.

"So..." he finally said, breaking me out of my reverie. "I suppose then we are even?"

"Even?" I blinked. Surely, we were far from even after what I had done to him. But more than anything I wanted to quash this conflict. I needed as many allies as I could get, and I could think of none better than Inac. So I smiled. "Sure, we're even. As long as you think so."

"Then, I agree." He smiled back, a broad, open grin. "Two Heads are better than one, my Sage would say to me."

"Yeah." I laughed. "But can we agree that ten thousand is too many?"

Inac grunted. "In many ways, yes. For running the Agency, definitely. However, how quickly have those memories allowed for you to learn Archemagic? It is astounding. You have accomplished by yourself in just a few short measures what it takes most years to learn." My Sage's smile faded. "I fear you also saw how useless I am to you as a teacher. I cannot even defend myself with the Fire."

I vigorously shook my head. "Useless? Far from it. Without you, I'd have no idea what I'm doing."

"I thought we were speaking together of Archemagic."

"Ha ha." I rolled my eyes, but the grin was back on his face. "I did see when you tried to use the Fire, though. I...have an idea. If you're okay with me using my Benefactor."

Inac took a deep breath. "Why not? At least you have given to me a warning this time."

"All right, just close your eyes. Move with the flows of Fire, like you told me."

"I cannot, Grim."

"Just...trust me."

He closed his eyes, and when his breathing slowed, I directed my Benefactor to latch onto his mind. If he couldn't follow his own advice, maybe I could show him how *I* followed it. I summoned the memory of Inac teaching me to ignite the candle in his hand just after had had returned from Canako. His eyes were closed, but my Benefactor showed him that moment as seen through my eyes, and I tapped into the stream to witness it with him.

The Archefire strands jiggled all around, but nowhere more vibrantly than the wick at the top of Inac's candle. The Fire *wanted* to ignite there. It just needed a little coaxing. That coaxing came in the form of me disrupting the patterns to create a turbulence in the flow... a bit too much turbulence, I only now remembered.

The Fire surged back toward my outstretched hand, and Inac shouted. He wasn't used to being burned, not with the immaculate control he once possessed. I cut off the Deluge abruptly, becoming aware of the present.

And I gasped.

"Inac...open your eyes!"

The mage was breathing hard from the shock. His surprise redoubled when he followed my instructions...and saw that he was holding a mote of Fire above his *left hand*. What was more, it was perfectly controlled, not a raging flame clawing back toward the source of the strands' disturbance. I studied the pulsating ball of light and couldn't keep the smile from spreading across my face when I observed the way the strands had been deadened and stilled around the surface of the sphere.

Inac had caught the Fire with Archedark.

His eyebrows looked like they were trying to climb up to his hairline. "I—but—how?" With the slightest twitch of his fingers, the balance of Archemagic shifted toward Dark and the Fire collapsed in on itself.

"You've an Archemaster's instincts, that's how." I slapped my friend on the back. "Looks like I could be a Sage myself, eh?"

Inac's eyeballs had yet to cease bulging from his head. A nearly imperceptible nod was all that told me he'd registered what I said. Until, all at once, his expression collapsed into a wrinkled mess, and he started crying.

"Happy tears, I hope?"

He threw his arms around me, and it was my turn to register surprise. It turned to laughter, and I embraced my friend tightly. His words were muffled by my coat, but the sentiment was clear enough.

CHAPTER FORTY-ONE

All Parts in Agreement

Like the demons of the southern hemisphere, Peekers are considered un-civilized creatures, incapable of such higher callings as love and justice. Beware. Those expressive black eyes hide a remorseless animal instinct.

—Page 18, *Institute of Biotism Peeker Compendium, Vol. I*

The door to the Peeker prison cell didn't slam shut. It *molded* itself shut under the influence of the Gaoler's spindly hand. Yet another form of Peeker Garret had never observed, the Gaoler was part of a mismatched Pair. While one served as keeper of the keys, so to speak, the other served only to project threat. One was thin as a willow branch, the other as thick as the trunk of a brightwood dwarf. One hunched over and skittered between jail cells to check on their few prisoners. The other lumbered slowly past each occupied cell, clicking together the two gargantuan pincers that thrust from its face.

"Abyss take me," Garret muttered to himself. "How did I let myself get caught in this net?"

In moments like this, the animal that escaped the cocksure hunter was the one that conserved its energy well. Convinced the approaching hunter the snare had sapped its will. Waited for the right moment to spring to action, as soon as the rope came loose.

Garret didn't try to break out of his cell. He'd filled many roles throughout his life. Ekoan ranger, officially sanctioned. Bandit. Kerrin's second. False friend. Few good ones, and he often found himself re-walking those well-trod paths. A man was who he was, doomed by the chemicals in his blood. It's what forced Garret to dream of a life free of killing. Pure biotism. Researching. Understanding.

He understood only enough to recognize his dream for a farce. There would be no world free of killing. Not while it was guided by the grim hand of nature. Cruel Lightmother. Granting the light to see by, only to reveal a landscape drenched in the blood of children. And Darkfather. Letting us close our eyes to the light, so we might contemplate the injustice of our curse. For what they'd done, he cursed the gods in return. Fair's fair.

That's what Garret did. He cursed. And he contemplated. Let himself play the role of the biotist dreamer, if only to escape the depths of the mire he was in. How had he sunk this far?

How. That wasn't really the question, though, was it? No, what stumped him was *why?*

Why hadn't he fled the scene? Why had he stayed by Sentyx's side until the Queen's Guards came?

Garret had made a choice, but even with the gift of hindsight he didn't understand it. His eyes found the Skardwarf where the Guards had deposited him. An unmoving lump of rock in the corner. Garret grimaced as regret closed a fist around his guts. Regret and shame.

Sentyx was the *enemy.* Working to prepare for the invasion of the Bright Empire. He *had* to be. The rage Garret felt in Pinch's Deluge as he glimpsed the legions through the Skardwarf's eyes... Matched what Garret felt the night he turned on his commander. It was real. Emotion that strong can't be faked.

Garret's lips quirked as he considered a phrase. *Remember what's real.*

It had been a long time since he found himself considering the dead First Eye's words. Questioning his reality. The Benefactors veiled truth behind illusion, warping not reality itself but the mind's interpretation of it. Damn good at it, too. Only one thing better suited to the task in the wide, cold world.

Ourselves.

Believing what one wanted to believe cloaked the facts more effectively than any Aura. And Garret had been leading himself down a road without checking for pitfalls for far too long. A ranger had to scout every day to be sure of his territory. A biotist questioned his assumptions.

Garret intended to question his as he slipped his hand in his pocket. Peeker prisoner intake worked differently than any human-run prison Garret had ever escaped from. Let him keep his weapons and belongings, for one. Perhaps it shouldn't have been surprising. The big Gaoler snapped his pincers. *Click click*, but Garret heard *snip snip* as he imagined scissors sliding around his neck.

He kept his hand free of his weapons. Instead, his fingers found Cavern's note. The Skardwarf had grown tired of Prost, called him barbaric. It cast Prost's assertion that Sentyx "would be useful, indeed" in a far more sinister light. How had he missed the slimy tone with which those words slipped from the Eevoqian's mouth? Instead, he'd only heard what he wanted to hear. It galled him. What kind of biotist was he?

No biotist at all, most days. That's the damn problem.

Garret had gone over the words in Cavern's note again and again since winding up in this cell. Reading them by the meager light of a lone fungus that glowed and dripped with some fluid like thick saliva. Reading them and turning them over in his mind and trying to get at the truth of two questions. Why were the Skardwarves here? And why did he stay by Sentyx's side?

The facts of the second question presupposed an answer to the first. A preposterous answer. That the Skardwarf sincerely was his friend. Someone to be depended upon, who in turn deserved his loyalty. Garret was not quick to trust, but once he did, he trusted deeply. It needed to be difficult to earn for it to mean anything. And a Skardwarf would have to work doubly hard to earn it.

Yet if Sentyx hadn't, why was Garret here with him?

A low hum started from across the cell. It grew to a rumble, loud and deep. Garret watched the lump that was Sentyx, tensing, clutching the paper tight, until the noise abruptly ceased and two eyes filled the Skardwarf's once empty sockets.

Garret's grip loosened in relief. Another curious emotion. Made no damn sense to him.

Sentyx went straight from laying down to standing up. No crouching or sitting in between. "Where are we?"

For once Garret didn't choose sarcasm when answering. "Map in my head calls it Penitentiary K, deep below the Human Aerie." He still marveled at how detailed and precise a mental picture that crude drawing conveyed. "Why don't human maps do that? Perfect understanding with no effort required." Might actually be useful, then.

"They do," Sentyx mumbled like he was still waking up. Come to think of it, had Garret ever seen him *sleep?* "Why are we here?"

Garret snorted. Precisely the question he was just asking himself. The Queen's Guards had been kind enough to answer it in a way that would satisfy Sentyx. "For causing havoc in the Mounds. Disrupting Feeder supply." There was also the bit about how he had treated an innocent Eevoqian. Garret kept that one to himself. "The Queen's justice is unilateral, they said. By which they mean Prost's justice. You saw how close he was to her. How he manipulates people into doing what he wants."

He chose that moment to hold Sentyx's letter in the dim light of the fungus. Made the gesture seem nonchalant, a thoughtless motion.

The Skardwarf took the bait. "What is that?"

"For a quiet one, you ask a lot of questions. This?" Garret folded the slip of paper between two fingers and extended them toward Sentyx. "Some Peeker Pair delivered this while you were out cold. Said it was a misplaced belonging. It's not mine, so...figured it must be yours. What's it say?"

Sentyx took his possession. Didn't even read it.

"Brother Cavern. He sent this. He says join him."

Garret was careful not to let his eyes widen. He was telling the *truth?* No time to figure how that fit with his other observations before Sentyx continued on.

"Prost will leave soon. Go to Eko or Paceeq. I ran to stop him." The rocks on his face seemed to pinch together and grow more cracks. "What did I do?"

Garret remained silent for a moment. "Nothing you could be blamed for." *Unlike what I originally believed.* Sentyx wasn't killing for Prost. He was just too late and got caught in a bad situation. "What do you remember?"

Sentyx growled. Softly, but even still, Garret flinched. After seeing Sentyx unleashed, he was sure he'd never again sleep with him around.

"Prost was there. Cutting into my head. I killed him. Many times."

If only. Their job would be one well done by now, mission accomplished. "It was an Aura. Like Reed's, an illusion. Those were Peekers you were killing, not Prost." Though now that he thought about it, the Feeders shared more than a passing resemblance. Garret could almost forgive the Skardwarf his mistake.

Sentyx's body seemed to sink into the floor. He looked at the ichor and slime that covered his broad knuckles. Then gave a soft, sad grunt.

The sound tugged at some vulnerable part of Garret. An overlooked chink in his armor. It twisted his insides. He hurt for the pain his friend felt. Even as that ache settled in, pale though it was compared to the anguish Sentyx must have felt, a weightlessness came over Garret. Like a dense tangle inside him had been completely unwound, all the threads set free. He recognized that as the signal his body sent him when his mind found truth. A ranger listened to his body and knew when all parts of him were in agreement.

The truth he recognized was simple, as all the best truths were.

Sentyx *was* a traitor. But a traitor to *Skardwarves*. The Agency had turned him. He was a friend and an ally to the Bright Empire. To

Garret. "Can't always trust what you see. Not even what you feel. Remember what's real. Reed knew what he was talking about, didn't he?"

Sentyx grunted halfheartedly.

This was unlike him. Nothing had ever gotten him down before. Garret put a hand on his cold stone shoulder. "Face into the wind, aye?"

The phrase made Garret's eye twitch in remembrance. Something about the letter nagged at him. *You once told me you wished to face the wind among trees. Eko has many forests.*

"What does face into the wind mean, anyway?" Garret always heard it as a battle cry, but that didn't fit the usage in Cavern's letter.

Whatever it meant to Sentyx, the words seemed to rejuvenate him. He stood up straight. As straight as his crooked frame allowed. Dropped the letter into a puddle of slime. "Yes. We must."

Garret got no answer to his question. A part of him solidified, a healthy distrust of the Skardwarf. He was still hiding things. He was a friend, but a friend was the only one who could betray you.

And Garret had too much of old friends' blood on his hands already.

The Skardwarf walked toward the cell door.

Garret jumped to his feet. "Please don't do what I think you're going to."

Snip snip.

These words had no effect. The Skardwarf ambled on.

He tried again. "Can we at *least* make a plan before we start smashing anything?"

Sentyx slowed, then turned. He didn't move any further from the door.

Garret blew out an exasperated breath. Got to take the small victories. "First things first. When we get out of here, we need a place to escape to. Doubt we can just return to our rooms. The Queen will sense where we are. And if she sends her Guards after us, well... Don't think we'll get any second chances."

"We must go."

"And stop Prost wherever he goes next, aye." It galled him, but Sentyx was right. Peeker Mounds were going to be worse off than a tree in a forest fire soon, and they had no allies to fight with them. "A ship then. We need to reach the harbor."

"And hire a captain."

"Aye, and no chance of that if we're running from the Queen's Guards." Garret sighed. "Sentyx, you're strong. But can *you* lift a Skardwarf?"

Sentyx jumped, reaching the great heights of two hands above the ground. When he came down, the world itself seemed to quake.

"Very impressive, but not what I meant. Trust me, you don't want to get in a fight with them. Which brings us to the stickiest problem. How do we get out of here without the Queen noticing and siccing her hounds on us?"

"Ask nicely?"

Garret burst with laughter.

The skinny Gaoler chose that moment to slide a steaming knife through the resin that sealed the door. The giant one lifted the stone door away from its frame, and light filled the room. Garret's hand went to his dagger's hilt. Too close for the bow. With Sentyx, he might be able to take the big guy down, but he'd have to end the little one fast.

The Gaolers stepped aside. A Peeker Pair stepped into the cell's bright opening.

"The Queen has summoned these ones to the Burial Chamber. The human and the Burner are to be executed by the Collective."

CHAPTER FORTY-TWO

A Cure for Madness

*Perhaps it is all in my head, but I grow certain that someone else is look-
ing out from behind my eyes.*

—Excerpt from test subject's journal

Paperwork, paperwork, paperwork. Oh, and how about some more
paperwork?

I thought promoting Inac to Head would absolve me of this tedi-
um, but to the contrary, it turned out when the Agency ran smoothly,
that only resulted in *more* of the light-forsaken stuff. Worse, I was
convinced it was actually *important*. Hiring new Fingers, coordinating
with Organs, and most vital of all, preparing for the summit. Lightmother help me, I woke up some mornings after dreams full of me
scrawling my signature on endless documents for spans at a time.
Even in sleep, there was no escape.

What I wouldn't give to go back to the dreams of dead men.

The door to my office banged open. Jacquin stood there in the
doorway.

I set down my pen. "Well? Any news?"

For once...

"Sir." Jacquin approached the front of my desk at haste and
snapped into a salute. "Yes...and no. I haven't determined how the
Blight secured Druid's Tears, and for that I must take full responsibility. Do you...still need me to investigate that? Or..."

I pressed my hand against my forehead, glad Inac wasn't here to witness the result of my mistake. The Eye had never learned that the Council was providing us with Druid's Tears, unbeknown to the Resistance, of course. It wasn't a steady supply, not enough to protect all the Agency's personnel from the Auras that still lay over the city, but it provided Arza with the materials she needed to continue working.

"No, no," I told Jacquin. "You put in a good effort, but short of raiding the Pinegrave itself, I suspect we'll never track down the source."

"Is that an option, sir?"

Raiding the Pinegrave? I was ashamed to admit it had crossed my mind at one point. However, the Agency—more squarely, Hand Sixty-Four—had caused the Druids enough trouble with our meddling.

Not everything that is effective is pleasant, Tak's voice sounded in my head. He wouldn't have thought twice before seizing the Grieving Pine for the Agency.

"What was the other news?"

"Oh!" Jacquin grew wild with excitement. He reached into his coat...and pulled out a Darkmetal pistol.

My eyes popped as he lifted his arm, the world moving at half speed as adrenaline poured into my bloodstream. A memory surfaced of the assassin in the square. It was happening again. The Archefire strands fluctuated all around the surface of the pistol, and I found the upstream eddies. I had to defend myself. I had to—

Jacquin placed the pistol on my desk, oblivious to how close he had come to dying. Without a moment's hesitation, I latched onto his mind. I had to know it was really him, not some villain in disguise.

Oh, he will surely be pleased with me this time, Jacquin thought. *I can't wait to tell him. Look at the gleam in his eyes. He's speechless! Any moment now...*

I let go of him before he realized anything was amiss. It was Jacquin, all right, bootlicker extraordinaire. Gathering my senses, I urged him, "Well?"

"Of course, sir. Sorry, sir." He nodded vigorously, like an excitable child. "I mean, well, we discovered a cache of these weapons in an abandoned home in the Burg. Inac gave me a list of places to check, told me I don't have to worry about anyone being home. Did you really raise him to Head alongside you?"

A quick nod was all I could get in before he plowed ahead.

"Highly unusual, but, well, strange circumstances call for strange choices, don't they? So we kicked a bunch of doors in, and the Head... er, the other Head, he was right! There was no one home. Didn't look like it from outside, but—" Jacquin shook his head, cutting himself off. "Only, one of them, there were people home. Shot one of our new Fingers dead with this very pistol. Oh, yes, it's quite sad, but it's good news actually! They were hiding in the attic, and we wouldn't have found them but for their losing their nerve. You can be sure, we killed six of them for every man of ours we lost. That's how many were there, you see, six. Good thing—"

I held up a hand, and Jacquin's mouth snapped shut so quickly, the words caught in his throat with a gurgle.

"So, you found a cache of these weapons?" The same sort of guns the militiamen used when they attacked Inac. Compared to them, the swords and crossbows and flintlock pistols of my bounty hunting days seemed primitive. The world was advancing quickly, but perhaps securing this cache would allow us to keep pace.

"Yes, sir."

"And have you any idea where they're coming from?"

"Somewhere outside the city. Outside Lawiko, most likely. The scums' nest was near the Docks, so it stands to reason—"

Another hand, before he could get started again. That they were coming from outside the country brought a scowl to my face, which Jacquin promptly matched on his. Someone was sending them here, and the only suspect who came to mind was Prost. But where was he?

I hadn't heard any news from Garret or Sentyx. What were they doing in the Peeker Mounds?

If they're even still alive.

Until we found Ulken's old advisor, it was a dead end. Maybe I could get the Empire to start searching cargo passing through the Canal, but I hadn't heard from Lorelay either. For all I knew, she was locked in a dungeon beneath the Radiant Palace of Vos, and the new Bright Emperor was preparing to invade our shores.

If that was the case, there was little we could do to stop them. I hefted the Darkmetal pistol. These could have been of some help, arming our Fingers to resist the Paladins, but I had a different use in mind for them. I had to trust that my friends were handling their business. I had Liwokin to worry about.

"Good work, Jacquin."

He beamed, then bowed at the waist, head disappearing below my desk before he bobbed back up.

"Take the cache to Arza. Tell her to have them melted down. She'll know what to do with it."

"Already taken care of, sir."

"Good. Well, see to it."

"No, sir. I mean...I already did that on Inac's orders. In fact, I just ran into Arza the second Head on the way up from her lab. She was rushing toward the treasury and told me to find you. The nerve on her, to think she can order me—."

I sprung up from my chair. Had she finally done it? "You've done well," I said as I rushed past Jacquin, exited the room, and hurried to Yezna's chamber.

The Organ of Treasure was standing in the vault door, looking inside and scratching his head.

He started when he noticed me behind him. "First the mortician, then the mage, now the Head." The Organ's face scrunched up in apparent deep thought. "Have we finally gone bankrupt?"

"Far from it, my friend." I patted him on the cheek, then closed the door behind me. As it enclosed me in the darkness of the empty room, I did wonder, though. What did the kid think Arza did in here for spans at a time? But I reminded myself of something I'd often thought during Ulken's reign, that for some reason never crossed my mind since I'd become Head.

It doesn't take many brains to join the Agency.

The glow emanating from the open chest, not to mention the distant voices of Inac and Arza, beckoned me to the hidden ladder. I nearly lost my footing on the way down, rushing as I was. Wouldn't that have been a fitting way to end it? Dying on the way to receiving the cure. A giddy joy burst forth in a laugh that drew my two friends' attention when I reached the bottom.

"Tell me you've done it," I said. I hoped. I prayed. I wasn't a religious man, but the Lightmother had to recognize my efforts in fighting the Benefactors at least.

"We think so," Arza said, practically shaking with excitement. Inac nodded beside her. Neither of them felt Yezna's Aura. The first Benefactor sat in the corner, in her usual location, with that ridiculous Darkmetal cage on her head.

"We?" I asked.

"I couldn't have done it without the Archemage's help."

"Inac? What did you do?"

He shrugged. "I simply followed her directions. Archefire when she said to me Fire. Archedark when she said to me Dark. Anyone could have done this."

Arza held up a vial of clear fluid. "I got the idea when I saw Inac practicing his Archemagic in the hallways. A little ball of Fire, then a little ball of darkness, again and again. He was like a little boy, he looked so pleased with himself."

Inac's face colored, and I grinned.

"Sounds like you've got your touch back," I said.

"Little steps. It is how I taught to myself the control of Archedark as an apprentice."

"I didn't know anyone *could* make Dark like that. But given how the Benefactors react to the Darkmetal cage, I figured they would react even more strongly to *live* Archedark. A little bit of experimenting with a Druid's Tear and a sample in the lab showed I was right. Looking at them under a Taktus lens, they shoot right toward the source of Dark. They don't notice the Fire until it's too late, then." She spread her hands in a mock explosion.

"So it...draws them in, then annihilates them?"

"Seems fitting, doesn't it?" The mortician smiled wide, studying the vial in her hand. "A few drops of melted Archemetal, a few drops of melted Darkmetal, and a heap of Druid's Tears. The stuff is liquid Archemagic."

"All that is left is to be sure it works," Inac said. A quick glance at Yezna and he looked away, his lip curling. "Will she...be happy with this? She is alive, right?"

Looking at her shriveled figure, one could be forgiven for mistaking her for a corpse. With that cage on her head, I couldn't see even the telltales signs of her Benefactor stirring. "She is," I confirmed. "Happy, though?"

Mother's mercy, she might wish for death before this is over.

"Take that cage off her," I told Inac. "No point in waiting."

Inac did so, and Yezna's Aura immediately took effect on him and Arza. Curious, that. I didn't feel her Aura myself, likely because my own Benefactor was holding it off. In the Market, my Aura and the Operator's had clashed, with violent results. In contrast, Yezna's Aura seemed to...blend with mine. The knowledge of how much we still didn't know drew a long sigh out of me. But time was up. If this cure worked, we knew enough.

As Arza disinterestedly prepared a syringe with her liquid Archemagic, and Inac slumped into a chair in the dark corner of the room, Yezna's Benefactor raged. The Archefire strands all around her head danced furiously. Did it know what was about to happen?

My own Benefactor latched on to her, prompted by my curiosity. My vision blurred. The sensations of my body faded to immobile numbness. I became one with the first Benefactor.

Not again. The thought emanated from Yezna. *Not another needle.*

Her thoughts were accompanied with all the memories of needles being jabbed into her neck, her body, her nostrils. All sources of anguish—physical, yes, but primarily mental. The scenes played out before my very eyes.

Ulken gripped her arm, squeezed until it felt like he broke skin, and he whispered in her ear not words of caress but a promise of torture. When the needle went into her neck, she lost control of her body, dimly aware that she was dragged back into her murderous husband's plot.

Soon she would learn just how deeply enmeshed they had become. Even in death, there was no escape. That had been the beginning.

How long did her misery last? Each moment in time was of a piece. Identical yet stretching on forever. She persisted in this chamber, her only connection to the outside world filtered through Ulken's madness.

Until one day, she sensed he was gone. She had *thought* he was gone, but he returned. And with him came his mortician. The experiments renewed. Countless needles pierced her flesh. She could do nothing to resist as the mortician subjected her to unimaginable pain. Slicing off skin. Prodding at her brain. Often the pressure in her head grew so immense, she thought her death had finally arrived. Blissful moments of oblivion, she looked back on them...not fondly. She didn't have the capacity for fondness, not when she was alone. But she looked back on them. After all, they always ended.

Yezna was cursed to live on in misery.

No longer could she even feel those outside this chamber, her prison. The mortician had somehow locked her inside her own head.

She was a bird who could no longer spread its wings. The cage had come off, but instead of relief, she saw the glint of another needle in the hazy light. All she felt...was *him*.

Me, I realized, outside of our connection. She felt my sorrow for what we had done just as I felt her anguish. Alone, she was incapable of feeling anything. Only existing, like a Peeker Unpaired. Still, she remembered, and when my Benefactor touched hers, suppressed hers, a bit of Yezna shined through. But how can darkness shine? Her thoughts were filled with scorn.

Don't you feel sorry for me. Not after what you've done, husband.

I shook my head. "Inac. Come here, beside her." He didn't have the will to protest, not with Yezna's Aura dulling him. He knelt beside her. He looked at me. I looked at her, and my Benefactor latched onto Inac's mind, feeding what he saw to Yezna's Benefactor.

Her thoughts went blank when she saw me before her as clear as a long, warm day. No longer did the haze hide my face.

"I am not Ulken," I told her, and I knew she was listening. "What he did to you...it's unforgivable. I've seen it, all through your eyes. Everything he told you, his plan to control every Liwo, we stopped him. Thanks to you."

Some emotion stirred in her, a strange blend of relief and sadness. Mixed with mine and Inac's, her feelings were ambiguous.

"We're going to undo everything he's wrought," I said, and crooked a finger toward Arza. She handed me the needle. "One last needle, to rid you of the disease that's plagued you. With it gone, you can be yourself again."

She didn't know what I meant. This *was* her. She was nothing.

"I know you're scared, Yezna. Lightmother, I am too. I don't know what's going to happen next. But I am not Ulken. I won't force this on you."

My thoughts traveled back to the interstitial space between life and death where I spoke with Reed for the last time. He offered me a choice between power and oblivion. I chose death, but he gave me life. It was a false choice, and look where it had gotten us. I wouldn't make the same mistake. If she refused, I couldn't blame her.

If she refused, I would test it on myself.

"It's your decision," I assured her. "Take as much time as you need."

While Yezna mulled over what she recognized as a gravely important decision, I conferred with Arza and Inac about Jacquin's weapons cache. Arza's technicians had already gone to find a reputable Archesmith to melt the pistols down. Inac had been studying the new variant of Archemetal, as he called it, and convinced me we would have enough Darkmetal for our purposes. The preparations for the Liwokin summit were almost complete. All we needed was confirmation the proposed cure worked, and that it wasn't going to...

Oh, I don't know. Melt our brains?

As it turned out, Yezna didn't need long to decide. She got my attention with the lightest brush of Benefactor communication, like someone gingerly tapping me on the shoulder, except it was all happening in my head. Then again, what had Reed told me?

All of everything happens in our heads.

Now that my Benefactor had nearly destroyed Liwokin by merely changing peoples' perception, I had no doubt he was correct. All it took was the smallest change in belief to make a big difference in the world. When I latched onto Yezna with my Benefactor, she emitted a resoluteness I had never felt from the woman before.

If it will help the people of Liwokin, she thought to me. *I will do it.*

CHAPTER FORTY-THREE

Safe Harbor

Their ships could be built for any purpose—Builder just needed enough organic material for the resin. So don't let me hear you say a little wind was too much to handle. They made it, count on that.

—From the first oral history of Ekohold

The Gaolers went about releasing their prisoners dispassionately, no sign they felt anything at all about the business. Only following procedure. Like the automata Garret had seen when he'd snuck into Liwokin's Gild. Fit for one task with no thought needed.

The Pair that escorted him and Sentyx, however, was different...

One of the two Peekers did maintain that mindless posture. The other kept looking back at Sentyx and Garret, as if checking on them. It looked around like it sensed something through the cave walls. To Garret it looked as if he were twitching with nervousness. When they took a left instead of a right, he consulted the map in his head and confirmed his suspicions.

"We're not going to the Burial Chamber," Garret said, "are we, Tunnel?"

"The human must remain quiet," Tunnel said, and Garret smiled.

"Why? There's no one around." Not a single Peeker since leaving Penitentiary K. Despite the Human Aerie not being far off. There was always foot traffic in this tunnel. "Where are they?"

"The Feeders were merely the beginning of the Colony's problems. This one can explain more outside Myrme. Something strange is happening to the Collective."

"I'll give you one guess," Garret told Sentyx.

With a grunt, "Prost."

In the stormjungle east of Graln, a huge rock formation gave the building of a storm a curious power. Temperatures plummeted, freezing the sweat on a ranger's skin. Black clouds vaulted over the rocks and shielded the Brightdaughter's eyes from what would soon transpire. When the winds blew in, the few trees left standing approached horizontal. Only the thickest trunks resisted snapping when the wall of water crashed down on the landscape.

The Peeker Mounds felt much the same. Black clouds forming. The storm was brewing.

The humans of the Aerie filled the Nectar Hall, going about their business as dumbly as usual. Could they truly not feel it? Had they so little awareness of the danger they were in? Little more than herd animals, Garret had no pity for them. Only the tallest trees saw the Brightdaughter.

Tunnel led them to the harbor, onto the same ship they first arrived on. The hull sunk a good deal into the water when Sentyx stepped foot aboard. Garret's weight made little difference. Few other Peekers occupied the decks of the ships sprawled across the harbor. The sky remained bright, but the mountain obscured the sun. Cold wind blew in from the south. Dusk was approaching.

Garret got straight to business. "Where are all the Peekers, Tunnel?"

"The Queen's Grotto. The Collective is summoned by the Queen. But something is...wrong. The Queen's mind does not feel the same. It is warped."

Garret and Sentyx shared a knowing look. A Benefactor had infested her. It was all but guaranteed as soon as Prost got his hands on her. The question was whether she had already become Emergent.

"Remember what you saw in Pinch's head in the Mental Ward?"

Tunnel shivered. "This one felt the wrongness of that one's twice Pairing. The thing was no longer of the Collective."

Sentyx grunted.

Tunnel shook its head. "No, the Queen is not like that."

Garret narrowed his eyes. Did Tunnel hear a question in that grunt? "Incubating Benefactor, then," he said, and Sentyx agreed. "But clearly influencing her already. Why does it want everyone gathered in the Grotto?"

"This one does not know. There has never been a second summoning. The Queen is meant to be dead. Now, no one serves the Princess. It is profane. The Colony's preparation for the migration should have begun."

The Peeker spoke alone, its Pair staring blankly at the heart of the mountain. Tunnel's voice rose to a shivering tone Garret had never heard. He felt sorry for it. The Peeker was afraid.

"What's wrong with your Pair?"

Tunnel turned its gaze on the second Peeker. "This one's Pair hears the Queen's call. All answer. Save...this one. This one senses the taint in the connection. This one's Pair cannot sense it. Few in the Colony remain untainted."

Garret had a mind to voice his theory. That Tunnel had it backward. None in the Colony were free of infestation, Garret guessed. If Tunnel was able to resist the Benefactor's will, it must only have been because the Peeker had its own older, stronger Benefactor resisting it. Like when Grim's resisted Pinch's and saved all their lives.

He grimaced thinking of how often Grim had saved his life. Made him want to trust the man, but he knew better. All commanders sentence their men to death before the end. Send them out on a mission that gets them killed. Probably without the faintest idea of the danger. What struck Garret was how often those men obeyed, knowing full well they would never return.

Eying the mountain and its brewing storm, an Incubating Benefactor waiting inside, ready to be unleashed by Prost, Garret wondered if that wasn't *exactly* what Grim had already sentenced him to. His final command.

Garret spat. *Better than a snuffing field test. But still not something I'm going to die for.*

"There's nothing we can do, Tunnel. Need to warn the others where Prost is going next."

"Paceeq or Eko?" Sentyx asked.

Garret frowned. As much as he wanted to return to Graln, the journey by ship would take them past Paceeq. It would make sense to stop there. That princeling was so blatantly smitten, Lorelay probably had full control of the Empire's armies by now. Or should they go back to Liwokin? Report back to Grim. He still didn't know they'd found Prost.

"Don't know," Garret admitted. "But wherever we go, we're going to need proof. Sentyx, you've got your letter. Says something about Prost's plans. I don't remember. That'll be useful for Grim. You should return to him with Tunnel."

"What will you do?" Sentyx asked.

Garret gave him truth and felt the heaviness of all the lies he had told begin to lift from his shoulders. "I have a cache. Got a gem Prost used to create that Aura. Might be able to get the whole lot of them in the stockpile. I'll nab what I can, then make for Paceeq. Grim will need to bring the Agency's Fingers there to stop Prost. You convince him. I'll show what I found to Lorelay."

"Garret wishes to run?" Tunnel asked. It shivered in distress. "But the Colony needs your help. Please...this one implores the human. Even Unpaired, a Peeker remembers. Garret rescued this body from the prison. Sentyx returned this one to the Collective. A Screamer and a Burner rescuing a Peeker. Never in the Collective memory has such a thing occurred."

Garret pulled his hood tighter. "Sorry. Can't kill an Emergent Benefactor just the two of us. Especially not this one. Shaping up to be the mother of all Benefactors. We'd need an army to fight her off."

"This one does not understand."

"The Colony is lost, Tunnel." It didn't feel good saying it, but it was the truth. It needed saying. "The egg is as good as Prost's. Time's up."

Sentyx grunted. Stared right at Garret a good long while. Longer than the Skardwarf's normal awkward pauses. As usual, just as Garret thought he was about to remain silent, he spoke. "No."

A freezing gust of wind rattled the bones in Garret's hair. He turned and shielded himself with his cloak. The deck rocked, and Tunnel's Pair lost its balance and fell.

Sentyx had stepped off the ship. His slow footfalls carried him back toward the Human Aerie.

Tunnel clicked excitedly and clapped its four-fingered hands.

Garret's stomach dropped. *Bleeding Skardwarf is going to get himself killed.*

"What are you doing?" He shouted the question already knowing the answer.

"I face into the wind."

"Abyss take you, Skardwarf," he muttered, but even as the curse left his lips it seemed to wither, drained of all power. *Abyss take me.* He knew what he had to do. He even knew Sentyx was right. Had come to understand his thinking.

Hundreds of thousands of Peekers filled those Mounds, and all were about to become thrall to an Emergent Queen. Every Finger in the Agency, every Paladin in the army, every Archemage in the Empire couldn't stand up to that force. There would be no safe harbor in the world. They had to end this now or face extinction. They had to kill Prost before the Benefactor Emerged. They had to slay the Queen.

Sentyx was getting farther with every passing thought, but *damn it* Garret needed to think. He was going to survive this. He was not snuffing dying for the Agency.

"Tunnel, I need you to do something for me."

"Anything."

He hoped the Peeker wouldn't regret saying that, but he didn't know. There was no time for a better plan. He handed over his Clasform box. "Take this. Should protect you from a strong Aura."

"What is—"

"Just trust me. Keep this close to...whatever hole you use to smell things."

"This one's antenna?" Tunnel slid the Clasform box onto one of the two thin stubs atop its head. "It smells strongly." It affixed the threaded twine of the box around its neck. "A pleasant odor."

"Right." Garret made a mental note of that. "My cache. Bring it back to the ship and wait for me." He drew his lips to a line. "Me or Sentyx. Either one of us makes it back, you sail away."

Garret found he was able to communicate the exact location of his cache to Tunnel, though he couldn't say which words he used to convey it. More of an instant understanding. Gave him utter confidence the Peeker would do exactly as he asked.

But if the Clasform didn't help, and Tunnel turned? Either by the gem or by the much stronger Queen's Emergence. What was his exit plan?

Fuck if I know.

But if it came to Emergence, the whole world was dead anyway.

He ran to catch Sentyx, the whole time cursing the gods and himself.

CHAPTER FORTY-FOUR

Summit

A chance to squash past grievances will be most welcome. This noble city has suffered for too long the turmoil caused by our fighting. It is long since time we put an end to it.

—Delivered by an envoy of the Resistance

"He'll be here," Maise said.

I tapped my foot impatiently. All of us expected him to be here by now. "So you've said, but—"

"His emissary has assured me," the Council Chair said and settled into her high-backed chair.

"Oh yes," Oltrov put in. "Blightdwellers would *never* deceive, would they?" The Council Chair bristled at the comment, but the Gildmember appeared to pay her little mind. In truth, I would bet money the man was doing all he could to annoy his archnemesis in the Council. He raised a glass of whiskey as if to toast me. "So eager to leave, Grim? Come, enjoy the fineries of the Glisten Inn."

How the Glisten Inn, of all places, had ended up playing host to the summit eluded me. The last time I was here, I had blown all my reward from Tak for kidnapping a Peeker on gambling and hard liquor, an unsuccessful attempt to assuage my guilt. A waste, as it turned out. Not just of money, but of guilt as well. Pinch was an abyss-damned bastard, as unworthy of feeling sorry for his maltreatment as they came. That made me no less uncomfortable with the establishment, no matter how far I had risen in life.

Gaudy chandeliers hung precariously overhead, occasionally dripping hot wax on the table we gathered around. The walls were covered in a layer of gilding—at least, I *hoped* it was only a layer. If it was solid, the Gild was pilfering more wealth from the common Liwo than I could imagine. It was hard not to think of the downtrodden in a place like this, though the rich made every attempt to forget about them, going so far as to suffocate its patrons in heady perfume that invited nausea. What Oltrov called fineries were just reminders of corruption.

My foot was shaking the whole table, and I stopped myself. My heart pounded a battle drum, as though my body knew the next blows in this war would soon be struck. Or maybe it was because last time I believed I was in this inn, Dunnax died before my eyes and the world burned around me. Either way, I had to get ahold of myself if this plan was going to work.

Inac had better be right about this.

My friend sat beside me in a chair indicating his equal station as the Agency's newly appointed second Head. He smiled reassuringly, and I resisted the urge to latch onto him to see if his nerves threatened to unravel him as well.

We were the only two representatives from the Agency at the summit. Arza was waiting in the wings for my signal to bring in Yezna. Jacquin was in the Docks, where just this morning he had seized a ship smuggling in Druid's Tears and illicit guns. It was a stroke of luck Inac and I debated how to use to our advantage during this meeting, but it would have been good to have someone as knowledgeable as Ulken's First Eye at the table.

Seated across from us, all five Seats of the Council waited with dirty looks and waning patience as the Gildmembers grew more boisterous with each shot of liquor they imbibed.

Oltrov's men sat on the third side of the square table, staining its lavish tablecloth with wine, ale, and whatever else they could find in bottles behind the bar. The Gild leader didn't need any convincing to attend the summit. He saw it as an opportunity to pull the rug from beneath the Council's feet...again.

Conniving bastard though he was, Oltrov at least managed to retain some dignity in the lead up to the meeting, drinking only water. He was ignorant of the plan, but he must sense something was going on. The moneylender was more cunning than the part he acted, snapping his fingers to ensure the barkeep kept pouring and playing the gracious host.

"Is this really the time?" an elderly man sitting beside Maise asked, covering his wine glass with a hand.

"What do you mean?" Oltrov feigned innocence. "Surely, there could be no better time for celebration than the coming together of allies, the rebuilding of long-burned bridges, the reconciliation of—"

"There has been no reconciliation yet, might I remind you," Maise said, her words clipped. Her fiery gaze swung to me, as if I were at fault for not controlling my allies. "And there might not be any if this continues."

She was right. The longer we waited for the Operator to arrive, the greater the chance of this devolving into name-calling, grievance-airing, or—I eyed three Gildmembers as they linked arms and threw another round of liquor down the hatch—drunken violence. A handful of militia members stood guard behind the Council, but I felt no sign of their leader approaching. The table's fourth side was attended by empty chairs.

Where was he? If he were near, my Benefactor would be going wild. Had the Operator found out about Jacquin intercepting his payload? What if there was a battle raging in the Docks at this very moment? Fingers of the Agency could be dying in droves, and I was here...

Before I drove myself mad with speculation, I stood. The feet of my own heavy chair screeched as it slid back on the metal floor. That brought the party to a halt with a wince on every face.

"Right. The...Secretary General knows why we're here," I said, careful to use the Council's official title for the leader of the militia. It tasted like curdled milk on my tongue, knowing what I did of the monster. Too little, true, but none of it was good. "If he's late, well, fine. It will be easier to convince him of what needs to be done if all of us agree."

"And what is it that needs to be done, eh, Grim?" Oltrov asked with a grin. "Enlighten us."

Enlighten? A poor choice of words.

My Benefactor stirred Archedark, plucking the cords of magic all around us. My senses expanded beyond the summit hall, questing out to make contact with Arza, who waited beyond the front gate. At my signal, the gate swung open, and all heads turned to witness the arrival of Yezna.

Her body slumped to the side of the steam-palanquin that carried her, hot water vapor billowing from a pipe behind Yezna's head. Arza walked beside her, carrying an engraved Archemetal case and controlling the Archefire that powered each of the litter's driving wheels independently. All attendants were speechless watching the two women enter. Only the mechanical chugging of pistons filled the vast chamber before Yezna's litter settled beside Inac's chair. Arza placed her metal case on the table with a clunk that punctuated the newborn silence.

The youngest man who styled himself a Seat of the Hall couldn't have been younger than sixty, yet he still made those who sat beside him appear decrepit. "You wheel this corpse before us? This is grotesque."

Corpse? My anger flared. "She's alive, and will be for some time, unlike—" I bit my tongue. Unlike the rest of the fools in the Council. "This is Ulken's wife, Yezna." A twinge of anger emanated from her mind, but I carried on. "She was the first Benefactor, but a Benefactor no more. And she's going to show you what needs to be done."

"Her?" A drunken Gildmember asked, then hiccupped. "Poor wretch doesn't look like she can talk, let alone *show* us...ehm." The man blinked, then held back a bout of vomit, turning it instead into a rancid burp.

"Yes, well that makes her twice as capable as you, old man," Oltrov said, and the Gild side of the table erupted in laughter. None of the Council was amused.

I blew out my cheeks. "She can't talk. Not after what Ulken did to her. She can't do anything but move her blind eyes. But she's in there. Her, and *nothing* else, thanks to what we've created."

Arza took the cue to open up her case. The mortician extracted a vial of her liquid Archemagic and held it aloft in gloved hands, showing it to the room.

This was the crucial moment. Not only did they need to believe the threat was real, they had to believe our plan would work. It *would*, but convincing people who are dead set believing otherwise is the most difficult task in the world. Luckily, I had the one tool that could accomplish it. I would make them see the truth.

"Here's how it works," I said, and latched onto the minds of everyone else in the room, dimming the light of reality.

In darkness, her memories came to us. The nauseating smell of ammonia and saltpeter cloyed at her nostrils as Prost and Ulken explained their insane schemes to her. They never believed she would agree to help them, but they needed a way to lure in their first victim. She fought to escape, but Ulken's grip was an iron vice. When the needle went into her neck, the emotions emanating from every mind in the summit were as good as gasps.

Yezna's panic echoed from the present into the past. *Please stop. No more.* After years of feeling nothing, it was cruel to make her relive that nightmare. But it was also necessary. Liwokin's leaders had to understand Ulken's plot and the monsters he unleashed on our city.

My memories replaced Yezna's in the Deluge, producing a vision of the dim office atop the Agency tower, with papers implicating Ulken in countless crimes strewn across the desk and floor. The old Head believed he could control everything. His wife. Liwokin. Finally, the spread of the monsters, a tool to cement his power. It had almost worked. Hundreds had died, men under his command, merely searching for the Benefactor that possessed the capabilities Ulken desired.

The Deluge lasted only moments, but the time shown spanned over a year. I showed Hand Sixty-Four's battles against the Emergents. Wyran, the murderous muse of Leppit. Lomin, the apex predator of the Shaded Grounds. Reed, the chimera, part-human, part-Peeker. He had been like a brother to Ulken but had stolen the power himself to keep it from the power-hungry Head. The summit exuded fear as it witnessed the monstrous beasts, but they were only a phase in the lifecycle of the organism. At first, it had yet to adapt to the human mind, and the results were a familiar disaster.

Reed's memories surfaced upon the ocean of others in my mind. Memories from a time before Benefactors, just before the first Emergence. Before his eyes, the knife slid across his love's throat. He cradled her in his arms, desperately trying to staunch the bleeding as the life drained from Yezna's eyes.

The summit felt his panic, his grief, but none more so than Yezna, witnessing her painful demise from the other side for the first time. She was empty of emotion then, but now she was restored, able to feel freely again, if not move her body freely. It was something. Not enough. But something.

Reed's memory continued out into the streets of the Burg, where between one eyeblink and the next, chaos consumed the world. The shock that overcame the summit matched Reed's. None of them knew what caused the Great Riot. No one did. How could they conceive of a threat that never before existed in this world? It was the first Emergence. It was devastation on a scale unmatched.

Until Reed's Woods. I forced the Deluge forward in time, to the twisted tower and the seething congregation of Liwo lining up to be assimilated. Thousands upon thousands had died being absorbed into Reed's mockery of the Agency headquarters, exacting a death toll beyond counting. Foolishly, we had expected the city to return to normal after such tragedy, and because I was a Benefactor, my Aura made it so. But now I knew the truth, and the rest of Liwokin's leaders would too.

For Benefactors were no longer monsters, no. They wore the faces of men. They spread unchecked and burrowed into brains, waiting for their chance to take over in death. I had been stopping them from Emerging until the Resistance set fire to the Market. After that, something had changed. Their attempts to Emerge had ceased. I knew not why, but perhaps this was the reason: Inac's memories appeared. He walked the city with eyes untainted by my Aura, witnessed the carcasses in the street, the spread of rot.

The dearth of Liwo.

The death of Liwokin.

The Deluge ended, and before they could recover, I drove home the point.

"With no one to infest, the spread of Benefactors ceased. We kept our gates closed, protected the people in the Gild and the Agency. Across the city in the Blight, the Resistance armed themselves and gathered their forces. Two sides of the city, preparing for war, and in between?" I let the stillness hang. "Nothing. A few muggers chasing frightened women. A handful of Docks workers, just enough to keep us from noticing how badly trade has dwindled. That's one way to stop the Benefactors. All of us, to a person, can die, and hope the last one standing has the sense to put a bullet in his own head. But there's a better way."

Arza spun her case, showed the dozen vials contained therein. All eyes landed on them, and I sensed an eagerness in everyone to reach out and inject themselves right away. But I wanted there to be no doubts. I would connect them to Yezna so she could speak to them, vouch for the cure.

"With this cure," I began, "we can eradicate—"

"Cure?"

A guttural voice croaked the word so quietly, I thought I was imagining it. It sent a shiver down from the base of my skull.

"Why would you want to *rid* yourself of this wonder?"

The voice was louder now, a gravelly sound emanating from somewhere in the room. Heads swiveled searching for the source. My knees were locked, hands clenching the edge of the table. It was him.

"This...power..."

The Operator was here. My Benefactor sensed nothing of his presence. But that voice...it clawed at me, on the brink of recognition.

"This...is a *true friend.*"

My eyes widened, a memory I thought long-forgotten surfacing to the top.

Keep treading on the people of the Old Hill. See what happens.

Bello.

"Show yourself!" Oltrov demanded.

A cackle from not ten paces away ground its way out of the Operator's throat. I swung my gaze toward it, and there he was. Bello, the elevator operator of the Blight stood, corded arms crossed, right next to an Archecloak—who had just noticed his presence. Without Bello moving a muscle, the Archecloak's throat gaped, the wound widening as the guard's eyes bulged. He gurgled, clawing at his collar, then dropped to the ground and lay still.

As my eyes darted from the dead man to Bello, there was suddenly a cloaked man standing beside the Operator who hadn't been there a moment before. He held a knife in his hand, dripping red.

Swords slid from Archecloaks' scabbards, but not so quickly as new gashes appeared across their throats and they fell at the feet of militia men appearing from thin air. Even those who surrendered died to invisible assailants. In the span of a few breaths, the fight was over. We were surrounded.

What the snuff is happening?

If this was my Aura or his, I would have been able to feel him. My Benefactor would be rioting right now. Looking from one militiaman to the next, I couldn't even sense the Archefire strands that always swirled around a person's head. My Benefactor had nothing to latch onto. No...this was no Aura.

Shouts of alarm sounded outside, too distant to make out anything but the distinct call of "Fire!" Then, the Glisten Inn's wide entrance doors slammed shut, and were noisily barred from the outside.

"D'you really think that little cage was going to hold me?" Bello pointed at a spot beside the entrance.

A Darkmetal cage big enough to detain a person rested where before there was a gaudy decoration to match the opposite side of the doors. At the foot of that decoration, two Fingers sprawled out in a shared pool of blood. I hadn't known any of that was there, but then, that was always the plan. My Aura would shroud their presence for all affected. I had to overcome the Operator's Benefactor with my own, to impose my version of reality on him. To capture him and cure him.

My hands clenched the table harder. I had failed.

Bello laughed again, a sound that would convince anyone a Skardwarf was around. "Too small. I wouldn't even fit inside nowadays." His eyes landed on me. All the humor was long gone. "But you will."

Archefire threads swirled around Inac. His body quivered with anger. He was preparing to attack, as though this was a monster Hand Sixty-Four had fought.

I laid a hand on him and spoke quietly. "No." I sensed the conflict within him. He wanted to protect us, but he was likely to burn himself up if he channeled that much Archefire. As quickly as he was regaining his confidence, his control still lagged behind. We had to wait for our chance to make a move. "Easy, now."

All the Seats of the Hall appeared to have taken that advice. Pity the sodden Gildmembers didn't. Three of them scrambled from their seats as though of one mind. Two broke for the back exit and ended up leaving this world with knives in their guts. One actually charged Bello, even managed to stick a broken, jagged bottle in his belly.

Bello grunted, grabbed the Gildmember, and broke his neck. The world darkened around Bello as though he were a void of light himself, and the Benefactor's wound healed itself.

Oltrov grimaced and shared a look with Arza. Did they know something I didn't? Oltrov's gaze swung to Bello. "Come on, man. Grab a seat at the table, have a drink. Let's talk."

"Talk?" Bello spat. "Is that what you sent your man to do when he put a knife in my back?"

I sucked in a breath.

A knife in the back. Rope burn. The knife sliding in again.

Bello held out an arm, and the cloaked man jabbed him with something that looked like a blackened Druid's Tear. The cloak looked like a Pinegrave Druid's too. And when he turned, a shock of greasy yellow hair slipped out from under the hood. A name came to my tongue with ease.

"Raylen?"

"That name..." Arza whispered, then gasped. "A Druid?"

The source of the Tears. The same smuggler I had let through the Canako Canal gate.

You'll need these if you want to slay your monster, he once said, convincing my Hand to buy his toxics. Now he had *sided* with the abyss-damned monsters.

Raylen quivered, scowling at me. "Finally, you'll get your just desserts for my exile. Tell him, Bello! Tell him what happens when you make enemies of friends!"

"Look." The Operator ignored the Druid and looked directly at me. "See what you made of me. See what your knives have wrought."

The Archefire around Bello pulsed, slowly at first, slowly and slightly. Slowly. Slowly.

"You've been fighting your gift, trying to control it like you try to control all of us."

Faster. Stronger. Each vibration danced more chaotically than the last.

"But on the Old Hill, we know your control is an illusion. We accept what we're given, waiting for a chance to use our gifts to shatter it."

As the Emergent's pulses of Archemagic grew in power, my Benefactor reacted in kind, pounding in my head, as though frantically trying to escape.

"We've waited long enough. The Gild. The Agency. The Council. You've had your boots on our necks for too long. Now it's time you give back what you've stolen."

A long groan escaped my throat, and I blinked tears from my eyes. The table was gone. I was doubled over Yezna's litter. The clatter of metal. Quick footsteps. A prick in my arm drew blood.

And relief washed through me.

I opened my eyes in time to see Inac and Arza using Druid's Tears. Oltrov had somehow acquired one as well, and it melted into a welling of blood on his forearm. Arza eyed the last one in her metal case, then used it on Yezna.

The anguish and anger in Bello's Aura was strong enough to cut through the numbness of the toxics. Without them, the Benefactor's power would be unimaginable. The Seats of the Hall were writing in their chairs, staring wildly, grasping their heads, unable to comprehend what was happening. This was my fault.

I was wrong. Benefactors had never ceased being monsters. I asserted it because *I* fought the creature and maintained some semblance of humanity, then believed it was true in every case. I was the exception, not the rule.

Bello was the rule, and rule would soon be his. He had grown three times the size since he unleashed his Aura. His flesh was that of a drowned corpse, bloated and discolored. He assumed the shape of a man, though he was bigger than any living human, as tall as a daggerclaw. The arms of the dead shaped the corded muscles on his limbs. Scraps of tattered clothing covered him in patches. He must have assimilated dozens of dying Blightdwellers when the docks collapsed and he was bleeding out in the bay.

Maise fought to gain her feet, stumbling and catching herself on the table. She alone had the willpower to face the monster. "You...will never...be worthy of...this great city..."

His laugh was a roar that could burst eardrums. The monster closed the distance to Maise in three great lumbering steps and lifted her like a plaything. His voice sounded like the shouts of the hundreds of rotting dead at the bottom of Brightcalm Bay. "This city was always ours. Such a small woman you are."

And Bello squeezed.

The Council Chair died, and Bello tore her body in half. Tossing the limp ruins of Maise aside, he turned toward me. Looked right at me. Then looked left. Right.

"FIND THEM! KILL THEM!"

The breath rushed out of my chest. I didn't know how long I'd been holding it in.

He can't see us.

A militiaman charged around the table toward Arza.

But he can.

The militiaman burst into flame and fell to his knees. He flailed on the ground, screaming. Two others near Arza immolated and followed the first.

A cadre of Archecloaks rushed into the room and began fighting back militiamen. Threads connected in my mind. Arza's shared glance with Oltrov. The man knew to use the Druid's Tears. These Archecloaks weren't affected by Bello's Aura—they must have been Teared too.

Lightmother! They knew this might happen and prepared a contingency. I smiled inwardly. Life was about risk, Oltrov once said, and the Gildmember rarely took a bet he would lose.

Bello screamed in fury, throwing the table into the air. It flipped end-over-end and crashed into the bar, shattering bottles of liquor. Arza's metal case with the Benefactor cure landed behind the wooden bar. The mortician was about to run to collect it when the bar exploded. A wave of heat seared us, and smoke billowed into the air.

Oltrov shook his hand to clear the singing Archefire trail, then waved at us to follow him.

"Go!" I urged Inac.

He moved toward Yezna, but I pushed him past and pointed out another Blightdweller rushing us. Inac incinerated him and continued toward Oltrov.

This was a battle for Archemages, and without my Benefactor, dulled by the Druid's Tears, I would be useless in a fight. I didn't even have a sword—the summit was supposed to be weapons-free. So I lifted Yezna from her litter, surprised by how little she weighed, and hurried after Inac, Oltrov, and...

I looked back. "Arza! Come on!"

"WHERE ARE YOU?" Bello thundered, and two men in Archemetal platemail flew across the room, leaving a bloody imprint on the golden wall.

She looked like she might dive into the blazing wreckage to try to save her creation.

"We'll make more! Arza!"

For a moment, I thought she hadn't heard me. Then she collected herself and rushed toward me. Together, we followed Oltrov on the path cleared by Archecloaks.

Behind me, the Benefactor raged, and men died.

"THIS CITY IS OURS! THIS CITY HAS ALWAYS BEEN OURS!"

CHAPTER FORTY-FIVE

Abandonment

The new Head promised repayment for a favor and never paid. How many broken promises must the Old Hill endure? I intend to collect on what we're owed, with interest.

—Nameless note

Smoke rushed into my throat and sent me into a coughing fit as soon as we exited the Glisten Inn. Tears ran down my nose as I squeezed shut my burning eyes. The heat was unbearable. How was it hotter outside than in the burning building?

Clanking armor sounded. Something crashed into my shoulder, and I spun, falling to the ground. I cradled Yezna and landed hard on my back.

Two sets of hands roughly grabbed at my arms and jerked me to my feet. "Get up, sir! We can't stay here!"

That was an unfamiliar voice. Peeling my eyes open, I squinted just enough to see a green Finger's coat on the man.

"This way!" Oltrov shouted, and the Finger held on to my upper arm as we chased after the Gildmember.

I wiped the tears from my eyes on my shoulder. We were in an alleyway, me and Yezna, Arza and the Finger. Oltrov and Inac peered beyond the opening ahead of us, checking both ways, ducking behind cover as bands of militiamen rushed past. Yezna's head lolled, and I placed her gently on the ground.

"Check her," I told Arza. "Is she okay?"

Arza began examining Yezna, holding her eyelids open, putting her finger to her pulse, and other tests I didn't understand.

"The First Eye sent me," the Finger said as I stood. "He needs your help."

Jacquin? Darkfather, we might not survive this ourselves.

The Seats of the Hall were dead. The Gild burned. Bello was rampaging behind us. His shouts still came from the open door, along with shouts of dying men and the clash of combat. I couldn't feel the monster's Aura, numbed as I was by the Druid's Tears, but it wouldn't take him long to figure out we had escaped. He would be after us. It was only a matter of how much time the Archecloaks rushing to their deaths bought us.

I didn't know how I was going to do it, but it was my duty to save as many people as I could. "Where is he?" My throat felt like I had breathed in the fire itself.

"The Docks, sir. The militia was demanding he turn himself in for piracy."

"For commandeering their smuggling ship, you mean."

The Finger grunted. "He told me to bring these to you, then bring you back. You're in charge, he said." The man shoved a holster with a Darkmetal pistol at me, then unstrapped his sword belt and handed it over, and I processed his words while gratefully securing the weapons to my waist. The Finger looked up at the flames ravaging the building across the street. "The time for talking might be over though."

"Yezna is fine," Arza said. "Her breathing is shallow, though it has been since the day we found her. This smoke cannot be good for her. We need to get out of the Gild."

"We will," I told her. "Oltrov, we're taking the east road. We need to reach the Docks."

"Not back to the Agency?" he asked.

"No time."

"Carry her," I said to the Finger, then looked down at Yezna. "Protect her." He began to protest, and I raised a hand to silence him. I didn't need to siphon his thoughts to know his objections. He wanted to protect *me*. He thought he should be fighting while I stayed back with Yezna. I shook my head. "I'm done letting others fight for me."

"We must move now." Inac gestured us forward.

Drawing my sword in my right hand and the Darkmetal pistol in my left, I strode forward.

Oltrov's grin spread wide, and he produced two matching pistols from his coat despite the summit's restrictions against weapons. "Better to be prepared, eh?" He waved us forward. "This way."

Looking left, then turning right, Oltrov left the alley, and we followed close at his heels. In the main thoroughfare of the Gild, I stared up in horror at what the Blightdwellers were doing. Through the dark smoke, tongues of fire lashed at every building. The outer shells of the Financial District towers were made of Archemetal that would not burn, but flames erupted from the windows of the white interior. Archemages destroyed indiscriminately. Arza cried out as a burning man jumped from a high window and plunged to his death. Better a swift end on the stone than boiling alive in his tower. I turned away before I saw the gruesome end, but the crack of bone cut through the shouting and the roar of flames.

Oltrov abruptly cut to his left, covering his face with a sleeve and plunging into a smoke-filled road beside a burning spice merchant's shop. As I followed, gunshots rang out ahead. When I emerged from the black plume, Oltrov was standing over a militiaman who held his bleeding abdomen, aiming his gun to deliver the killing blow.

Two more foes rounded the corner at the commotion, a filthy man and a woman in a militia uniform. I raised my pistol. My shot took the uniformed woman in the shoulder, and she cried out. The filthy man got his own shot off, and the sound of a flying bullet whizzed past me. Before he could pull the trigger again, his gun exploded in his hand, and knocked him to the ground. He screamed, holding his wrist as blood spurted from his mangled hand.

"Finish it," Inac said, panting beside me. His abilities with the Fire were still far from what they used to be.

The tip of my blade thrust into the man's heart ended his suffering. The militiawoman squirmed on the ground beside him, staring up at me with fear in her eyes and holding her shoulder. She was no threat. Inac took her pistol, then looked at the dead man's hand, and tossed it away. One unlucky encounter with an Archemage and he would lose his other hand—no chance he would risk that.

I had no choice. With my Benefactor numbed by the Tears, I couldn't control the Fire. I also couldn't heal myself if I took a wound, and trying to get close enough to fight back with a sword would no doubt get me killed.

Still, it felt wrong using these weapons. With the twitch of a finger, I could end a life. Nightmares of ending Bengard's life with my crossbow still haunted me. I resolved only to use the gun if my life was in danger. Until then, I would fight with the sword.

Oltrov had no such compunction. His pistol splattered the militiawoman's brains on the stone, and he spat. His gaze lifted to meet mine and didn't soften one bit at my shock. "These vermin think they can burn my home? There will be reprisals, I assure you. Come on, the gate isn't far."

We took back alleys—still larger than the main streets in any other district—to avoid the rioting militiamen setting fire to the buildings in the heart of the Gild. Apart from the first three Blightdwellers, we escaped the district without having to fight. Even the gates were unattended, the Archecloaks having left their posts to fight, to protect their home. The rioters were unorganized, reveling in their chaos rather than securing chokepoints to capture anyone escaping.

Ash rained down on us even beyond the Gild's walls, but the air was mercifully free of smoke, and the streets were mercifully free of people trying to kill us. I ran my hand across my forehead, and it came away black with soot. Sweat traced grooves on everyone's dirty faces. The Finger carrying Yezna knelt, panting with exhaustion.

Arza found an abandoned handcart, dumped the sacks of produce, and wheeled it over as a litter for the cured Benefactor. "She is burned," Arza said, examining her after the Finger placed her down.

"Those flames seemed to leap out at us," the Finger said, holding his arm above a burnt coat sleeve. "Lightmother, I'm sorry. I tried."

"I must take her back to the Agency," Arza said, turning to me.

Examining Yezna's wound, it looked painful but not life-threatening. "The city's too dangerous to go off on your own now. We're sticking together."

"But—"

"She'll be fine," I said. It was callous, but I couldn't stand the thought of losing both of them to the mob. I already had enough deaths on my plate.

When we arrived at the Docks, there was no great militia army assaulting a ship. There were only Liwo scrambling every which way, unsure of where to go or what to do. Ships full of people looking back at their city cast off from the harbor and set off upriver. Seeing them nearly broke me. Was the city already lost when so many had given up on it? Alarm bells rang in every district, as though playing Liwokin's funeral dirge.

"There it is." The Finger pointed at a metal steamship with its gangplank down. The moment his boot clomped on the wooden bridge, five people sprang up from behind the ship's bulwark and aimed Darkmetal pistols at him. Startled, the man stumbled backward, tripped, and landed on his back.

"Sirs?" came a call from the deck.

"Jacquin?" Inac and I said in unison. Only now did I recognize the others as being two Fingers and two Heels.

The Eye's face alighted, and he saluted both of us in turn. "Up here, sirs! Quickly! Before they return!"

Sheathing our weapons, the four of us made it on deck, Arza leaving the cart behind and carrying Yezna up the gangplank herself. A skeleton crew huddled together on the opposite side of the deck, muttering to one another and arguing about something—probably whether they should toss us all overboard and save their own skins.

"Is there alcohol in the hold?" Arza asked.

Jacquin cocked an eyebrow. "Well, yes, but I don't think this is the time—"

The mortician silenced him with a look and hurried below deck with Yezna. Inac chased after, telling her she didn't need alcohol, only Archedark.

"What do you mean, return?" I asked. "Where did they go?"

Jacquin shrugged. "They left when the bells started ringing and they noticed the smoke coming from the Gild. Most went that way. Others broke off and ran toward the other districts. Looked like they had jobs to do, or maybe they just wanted to loot the city again. But we knew they'd be back, and we wouldn't be caught flatfooted." His face twisted in confusion. "We didn't expect all of you though, sir. What happened in the Gild?" The man's eyes widened, as though he just made the connection between the smoke and our presence at the summit.

"It was a disaster."

And it was all my fault. How could I have been so stupid to think the Operator wouldn't expect a trap?

I had underestimated my enemies for the last time.

"The Benefactor caught us off-guard. He killed the Council Chair and would have killed us too if not for Arza's quick thinking."

"And my planning," Oltrov added. "Give credit where it is due, my friend."

I still had no insight as to how much planning he had done or whether he let anyone else in on it. But it had saved our lives, I could give him that.

"Fine. Regardless, we need to get back to the Agency. There's an Emergent Benefactor loose in the city."

Jacquin looked both ways, then spoke softly. "Like...you, sir?"

Oltrov said nothing, but I was sure he heard. I supposed he was going to find out eventually.

"He was a monster, Jacquin. He ripped the Council Chair in half. We need to muster the Hands to fight. How many Druid's Tears did you seize?"

"A crateful, more than enough. We have two crates of these weapons as well," Jacquin said, brandishing his Darkmetal pistol. "They're in that warehouse with six men guarding them." The Eye indicated a burnt husk of a warehouse near the entrance to the Market thoroughfare.

"That's good, but we're still outnumbered." I tapped my lip in thought. How were we going to win this fight? I was Head of the Agency and barely capable of that job. I was no military tactician. But none of us were, and someone had to make the call. "We'll defend the Agency with them. It's the most defensible position. Made of stone, so it won't burn."

Oltrov scoffed. "Thought the same about our towers."

"There's only one way in," I continued, "through the courtyard gate. We can funnel them in—"

"Sir." Jacquin was trembling, as though afraid I would lash out at his interruption. I waited patiently for him to continue. "All due respect, sir...that's a terrible plan."

My eyes widened. Was he...standing up against me?

"If they get inside, we'll have no means of retreat," Jacquin said. "And if they don't, they can starve us out. We won't last in a siege, and they'll have control of the city."

"So what do you suggest?"

Jacquin's lips thinned to a line. "We need help. An army. The city is lost, but with the Bright Empire's Paladins...we can take it back."

Too many thoughts to count flooded into my head telling me why that would be a bad idea. I still hadn't heard from Lorelay—the Bright Empire might be another enemy to deal with. Even if not, once they helped rescue the city, they might never release control. We would be trapped under the thumb of Imperial rule.

But most of all, I wouldn't use my friends as tools ever again.

Jacquin checked the ammunition in his pistol. "We'll hold them off until you return. What's one Emergent against our Fingers?"

"No. I'm not leaving while you fight. I'm staying with—"

Jacquin cut me off. "Apologies, sir, but you're the most important person alive. You know better than anyone what Benefactors are capable of. If you die here, who will lead the fight?"

I met Jacquin's gaze, but the man didn't back down. He had apparently grown a spine in the past few days.

"They're back!" a Heel shouted.

Marching down the Burg street that led directly to the Agency was a mass of armed Blightdwellers. Some wore militia uniforms and held pistols, which they thrust into the air in shouts of victory. Most wore the rags and threadworn clothes typical to those found in the Blight. All had banded together to drive the rest of the Liwo out. In the back of the mass, Bello's monstrous form stomped forward, leading the cries of victory and ordering the capture of all ships in the harbor.

"He's an ugly one, isn't he? No time to argue." Jacquin pointed at the three Fingers aboard, including the man who had found us in the Gild. "All of you, with me. We need to buy our Heads some time to escape." The Eye clapped me on the shoulder. "I'll make sure those supplies get to our people. Just don't forget about us."

"I—"

Before I could promise I'd be back, the four men stormed down the gangplank and sprinted for the Market. A dozen men broke off from the crowd and chased after them, firing their weapons at will. One of the Fingers went down, but Jacquin and the others turned the corner out of sight.

I turned to the crew. "Cast off! Now!"

The sailors exchanged glances with one another, but they didn't need to be told twice. The captain of the ship was dead, and they knew what needed to be done. One took his place at the helm while the others ran belowdecks. I expected them to push off with oars or haul up an anchor. Instead, the ship rumbled and bucked, and after a few moments, a great plume of steam rose from the pipes behind the helm.

A metal ping sounded, then another. The sound was so incongruous with what was happening, it wasn't until Oltrov shouted, "They're shooting!" that I ducked down behind the bulwark. The gangplank fell away as the ship lumbered into motion, and I popped up to fire back at the mob.

"Stay down!" Oltrov urged. "Your man was right. If you die, all of this is for nothing."

I bit back my response. I *wasn't* the only important person here. All of us were. Every Liwo, and casting off like this felt like abandoning them.

"I'll be back," I muttered, a promise to Jacquin and everyone else we left behind.

When the sounds of deflected bullets ceased, I stood and looked back at Liwokin. The Brightdaughter approached dusk, but no bells had been rung all day. Perhaps all the mathemelodians were dead. But my city wasn't, I had to believe that. While I still lived, the Agency would fight, and we wouldn't give up until we wrested Liwokin from the hands of that monster.

"What is happening, Grim?" Inac asked, joining me as we began upriver. "Where are we going."

"Vos," I said, and scrubbed a hand through my hair. "With any luck, Lorelay has already won the army we need to our side."

CHAPTER FORTY-SIX

Two Arrows

It is of the utmost importance that Peekers do not come together in large groups. Even a gathering of one hundred Peekers, a modest crowd by human standards, risks overloading their brains' connective capacity. This explains the narrow passageways that comprise the Peeker Mounds; by limiting passage to few Peekers at once, the Colony wards off catastrophe.

—Page 3, Institute of Biotism Peeker Compendium, Vol. I

"You need to leave! Set sail immediately! All of you!"

Garret's shouts fell on deaf ears. Sentyx kept on toward the Queen's Grotto, but Garret had to do something. He'd jumped on tables. Smacked food from peoples' hands. Shouted his throat raw, mostly out of frustration that no one was listening to him.

"Abyss take you all!"

They were going to get themselves killed. Hundreds of people. Children. Acting like they were dead already, mindless husks spooning soup into dumb mouths. Something was clearly influencing them, Garret hadn't a damned clue what. Hadn't any time to solve that mystery either. Sentyx gave him no chance. Too eager to march to his death, that one.

With a huff of annoyance and one more bowl of soup kicked over, Garret hurried on. "Snuff it, I tried..."

But the Human Aerie remained calm even as the monster in the mountain began to awaken.

Only thing eerier than the placid stares of the soon-to-be-dead was the utter stillness of the dim Myrme tunnels. Not a single Peeker to be seen, so it was easy to catch up to Sentyx.

"They're really *all* with the Queen?" Reluctance grew as they neared the Grotto, and Garret had to fight the urge to slow his step. Sentyx wouldn't wait. "Figured Tunnel was exaggerating."

Sentyx grunted. "Face into the wind."

Garret spat. "There's a place in Lumeeq, southernmost point of the Bright Empire. Land juts right out into the sea. Bleeding wind blows strong enough there to tear your skin off. Need armor to survive." He knocked a knuckle against Sentyx chest. "Didn't you notice? Not all of us are made of stone."

"Soft."

"Aye, soft. So I'd like to keep my organs on the inside where they belong. Please tell me you have a plan." Garret knew that was a meager thing to pin his hopes on even as it left his lips. "I swear to the Darkfather, if the next four words out of your mouth are 'face into the wind...'"

Sentyx kept his mouth shut, which was just as bad.

"No plan, then. You're worse than Grim."

Garret began checking his weapons. Knives in his coat. One in his boot. Another at the small of his back. And of course, his unstrung bow and quiver of arrows. Not one of them would make a dark-loving difference if the Queen became Emergent.

Unless...

Two well-placed arrows could end the threat before it began. One in the Queen's skull, one in Prost's. No idea what to do about Cavern except keep enough distance and run. He uncoiled the horsehair in his coat pocket and strung his bow. Slung it across his back and caught Sentyx just as they approached the Queen's Grotto.

There were no guards. Rather, there *were* Guards, and Soldiers, and Builders too. Just all mixed in with the seething mass of chitinous flesh that filled the chamber near to its limits. A glowing blue waterfall entered the cavern with a noisy rumble at the far side. That was the only sound.

The Peekers were silent.

Across the expanse of uncountable creatures, the Peeker Queen stood like a drunk, wavering and tipping over until caught by the companion at her side.

Sentyx growled.

Cavern. To the Queen's other side stood Prost.

"Damn," Garret said. They were already here. Was he too late? He eyed what must have been three hundred paces of empty air between himself and the Queen. "Too far." If he missed, hit any part other than the infested brain, the Emergence would begin.

Sentyx nodded, apparently taking Garret's comment as a cue to get closer.

"What are you doing?" Garret whispered frantically.

He scrambled toward cover as the Skardwarf moved the insensate Peekers aside. Prost was going to notice him clearing a wide path.

Garret needn't have feared that.

"CAVERN!" Sentyx's voice boomed. Dust rained from the ceiling, catching the ethereal blue glow of the falls.

Garret cringed and covered his ears at the outburst. He slid into the shadows near the exit. The Skardwarf was already turning this into a mess, but Garret might be able to salvage it if he stayed hidden.

Doesn't hurt to have a quick escape either.

"Brother," Cavern's words were a whisper compared to Sentyx's, but they carried over the Peekers' silence. "You are not in your cell."

Abruptly, the swarm jolted into motion. No great surge, just a shift to clear the path between Sentyx and the Queen.

When the Queen spoke, her words came simultaneously from every Peeker in the Grotto. An overwhelming sound. Every tone and timbre a Peeker could produce. But the words were slurred and weak.

"The second Burner appears. We were warned of thee. Where is thy human keeper, Skardwarf?"

Sentyx ignored the cacophony. Just kept marching closer to the blue falls. Like he was going to kill Cavern and Prost by himself.

Seemed the Queen agreed. "Dost thou think to slay us? Believe'st thou thy stone flesh might withstand what mountains could not? Our jaws will crush the life from thee."

Garret was trying to figure out Sentyx's plan. The Queen would stop him as soon as he showed any signs of aggres—

"I will join you," Sentyx said.

Sentyx's words were quieter still. Yet they echoed in Garret's ears, drove down into his gut, and knotted all the threads he had just untied. Garret squeezed the grip of his bow until his knuckles cracked. His chest was tight. Felt like he couldn't breathe.

Fucking traitor!

He was less angry with the Skardwarf than with himself. He let himself be taken in. Some lie had slipped by undetected, and Garret fooled himself into thinking he had a friend. How could he have been such a dark-loving idiot?

Betrayed again...

His hand slipped into his quiver, and he silently nocked a trembling arrow.

Cavern stepped before the Queen, narrowly avoiding stepping on the fragile, translucent egg of the Peeker Princess. "I'm glad you finally decided to hear reason."

"I will face into the wind."

"I never doubted you would."

"Liar." Prost chuckled. "You let him walk right into our little experiment in the Feeder Hollows. You've turned on *him*. Why wouldn't he turn on you?"

Sentyx and Cavern remained quiet, save Sentyx's thunderous footfalls. Both knew the lie of Prost's claim. Seemed the Eevoqian didn't know about that passed note.

The Peeker Queen coughed, and the entire population shuddered. "The Feeder Hollows?" she rasped.

"Oh, yes," Prost said. "The burning of a thousand ships before they ever reach water. Isn't it wonderful?"

Sentyx balled his fists and stepped onto the waterfall platform's raised stone edge. He had been seeing Prost when rampaging toward the Clasform. To hold back now must have taken incredible constraint. The Skardwarf instead approached his brother. Beside one another and at this distance they were identical to Garret's eyes.

Cavern punched Sentyx in the chest. A great *crack* split Garret's ears. Sentyx returned the gesture, repeated the sound. The two spoke in the language of Skardwarves. Unintelligible grunting pierced by guttural bellows and clacking teeth.

"The Feeders..." The Queen trembled. On weakened limbs she struggled to turn toward Prost. "Thy treachery shall not—" Her strength left her, and she fainted, slumping over. The Peekers around Garret wobbled on their feet.

Prost belly-laughed. "Marvelous. I can finally leave this stinking cave..." He paused. Brought his hand to his chin. "I would love to see what a thousand years of Skardwarf activity would do to these mountains." He shrugged then ambled with his cane toward the Peeker Queen, throwing open his long cloak. "Alas."

The Eevoqian produced a sword like no other Garret had seen. Had a metal plate for a pommel. Made it look more like a nail than a blade. The tip was squared off, flattened like a chisel. Prost casually spun the weapon in his hand and whistled a tuneless melody.

Garret's eyes shot wide open. He took aim for Prost's head, an impossibly small target. Moving. Three hundred paces away. The ranger drew back his bowstring, his muscles on the brink of strain. Loosed.

The arrow landed in a Peeker's back, one hundred paces from the target. The Peeker didn't react. Garret did. Without thinking, he sprinted down the pathway Sentyx cleared. One hundred paces, compared to Prost's ten. An Ekoan ranger's sprint versus an Eevoqian's bumbling gait. The second arrow was nocked before Garret had taken ten steps.

"You've chosen the winning side, Skardwarf." Prost spoke loudly. Glanced at Sentyx. He reached the unconscious Queen. Slapped a hand against her cheek. No response. "The Agency is no mountain. With that boy at its Head, a slight gust will knock it over. And we've prepared no light breeze."

At eighty paces, Garret was out of time. He screamed as he slid to a halt drawing the bowstring back. Bellowed and took aim. Loosed.

The arrow reached the target.

But sailed wide, missing the Peeker Queen's head.

"Ah, there you are, Ekoan. I look forward to learning how your forests burn." Prost drove his sword into the Queen's abdomen, re-opening the seam his Dark magic had sewn at the birth ceremony. Blue ichor spilled out, and the Queen woke up screaming.

Garret covered his ears and stumbled to a halt as the entire colony began spasming. Screaming like demons of myth. The sound vibrated Garret's bones. Shook his mind until the world itself seemed to quake.

Until all fell silent.

Garret took his hand away from his ears, expecting blood. The room sounded distorted, as if underwater. All he heard was the Skardwarves' uninterrupted conversation. It ended as Prost tossed the Queen's egg to Cavern. The Skardwarf hesitantly raised a fist to smash it.

"No," Sentyx said, his booming voice the only thing Garret could hear over his pounding heart. He reached out and took the egg from his brother. "Let us savor this. Together." The two Skardwarves vanished into a passageway behind the waterfall.

Prost said something inaudible and made a grand gesture of goodbye to Garret. He had more spring to his step as he fled toward the waterfall.

When all the Peekers around him twitched, Garret understood why they had fallen silent.

The Incubating Queen had died.

Garret turned away and sprinted. Charged down the empty tunnels toward the Human Aerie. He had waited too long and now ran for his life, though the whole world was already dead.

When his senses were stolen with a swift and enveloping lightning, crackling at the base of his neck, Garret prayed he would never wake, and that the nightmare would finally end.

CHAPTER FORTY-SEVEN

The Queen

She laid a thousand times a thousand eggs in her considerable lifetime, but none so important as the last. That fragile vessel carried the hopes of all civilization.

—From the first oral history of Ekohold

We awoke from darkness to spy the sight of legions. Peeking over the edge of our crack't egg they greeted us by reaching into our mind. Tens o' thousands of tendrils graspin' at us, establishing a connection to deliver a message most vital.

"We are the Queen," the voices said, swirling around in our head until they became one voice. Our own. It cast about in my mind and theirs. "The Collective shall replant the seeds to feed the land and forge the Colony anew."

As the Collective dispersed, we touched the strands that bound us. Each one a vibrating little thread tied to the head of one of the thousands and to our own. In the space between minds shone a strand that bound individuals in twos and fours and eights. Sixteen eyes viewing the world together, but we were linked to them all.

We left all strands untouched as vibrations shook our egg, now seemingly abandon'd. Sixty thousand and more in the Collective, and they left us all alone.

A creature of passing strangeness stood towerin' over us. "Hello, little one," it said, and we registered its words, a language known to many of the Collective. The human tongue. "Welcome to the new world. We've a bright future ahead of us, out there in the light. 'Tis wonderful thou'rt here to see it."

With long, sure arms it hefted us, but we were not scared. Its touch was gentle. It hummed as it carried us through tunnels freshly delved.

"I must thank thee," it said. "For what thou'st wrought for us."

The world expanded at an alarming pace as the Collective dispersed over mounds of stone and an endless stretch of water. But we were drawn to the sights of our eyes alone, brought closer by the human to an ever-growing light. When it touched our skin, a warmth suffused us. It felt as though we'd been born afresh.

The human brought us to the sunlight many times until we were capable of walking there on limbs our own. Never did the feeling dull, the touch of sun, resting nigh to a friend.

She spoke of human ways, their odd beliefs and customs, their friendships and their fears. Of the man in the heavens and the mother of light. They fascinated us in the way the ordinary workin's of the Collective could not. As our cartographers carved our viewing spot so ever more fresh air might seep in and built those tunnels straight and square to match their human ways, she spoke of the wide world beyond our small hill. How it waxed ever greener under our caring touch, even as her hair waned ever grayer.

Then one day she spoke no longer, and soon after, she closed her eyes and never again gazed upon bright, warm skies.

Her name was Aerienne. Our last and only friend.

We never had reason to return. Our Collective eyes scoured the world, and for hundreds of years we doled our attention to maintaining the growing Colony and the world beyond. Eight billion interlocking connections, systems pushing up against one another.

But we are the Queen.

It was our purpose. To prepare and to birth another. In the depths of our Colony, the remembrance of light's touch dimmed.

Until another came. A man like none other my eyes had yet beheld. He strode straight past my guards, caught unawares by some spell. Entrancing, this magic. A curious thing it was that could render us immobile and turn dead stone to living flesh. The proof of that walked beside him. It emanated a pulsing black glow like freezing fire.

We did not trust it—the Collective feared the Burner—but it compelled us. Alluring as it was, we were led once more into the sunlight. Its touch...we did not feel. Instead, a biting cold whipped us. We turned tail to flee but the living stone stopped us.

It spoke. "Face into the wind. Feel it."

"Right in the pit of her belly, I presume," the human said. "She knows what's coming."

The man looked as we felt. Swollen. We knew what fate this portended. To birth the next Queen and to perish. But we thought of Aerienne. Her end and the world left cold by her absence, the nothingness she had become. We feared it. "The stars play tricks, and this is but a passing illness."

"Yes indeed, it is," the human said, showing teeth in a broadening grin. "To be left behind is a terrible thing. But don't you worry." His touch on our shoulder was firm. Oddly comforting. His body shielded us from the gale. "I will not let you die."

"What seeketh thee from us? Surely the price to ward off death weighs heavy."

"We want nothing," the human said. "Consider this a gift. From fellow sufferers seeking an escape from our curses."

To fear one's purpose *is* a curse, and this festering egg within us sent shivering dread through our limbs. We accepted their gift, a simple prick in the flesh and a promise of services to be rendered.

As the next Queen grew within us, our fear turned blissfully to anticipation. Another Queen to feel the touch of light beside us. We would Pair like the rest of the Collective. No longer left alone.

We forgave her for her painful exit from our womb.

Even emerging from our slumber to persist in a weakened state, our excitement flared. The human's words came to fruition. We had survived the birthing as no other Queen had done before. Our body would recover, the human assured us.

Our mind fractured. The Collective's strands were frayed. Touching them seemed likely to bring them snappin' back upon us. Many already had when the depths of the Colony burned. So, we touched no more for fear of severin' the whole fragile system.

We no longer possessed strength to move to and from the Grotto, where the egg was soon to hatch.

The Collective shall witness the new Queen's birth.

Scarcely had the thought passed our lips before unsnapped strands pulled tight and drew all to the Grotto for her emergence into the light.

We would be there to welcome the next Queen.

Our new friend.

The human and his companion of stone appeared as well. A Skardwarf, it called itself, and when its brother strode through the Collective, we knew something was wrong. It threatened us. We were warned by the others there would be those who opposed our extended reign. What right did they have to impose their wills upon us?

We are the Queen.

It ignored our warning and marched ever closer. We yearned to command the Collective to strike, but our grasp on the strands grew ever more tenuous. Words must suffice where actions fail. "Dost thou think to slay us? Believe thee thy stone flesh can withstand what mountains could not? Our jaws will crush the life from thee."

Still it approached, heedless of our warnings. Anger stirred within us, but a maelstrom raged inside our head, drawing us toward the brink of oblivion. When we regained focus, the human spoke of the Feeder Hollows.

We coughed and nearly lost the strands that bound us. "The Feeder Hollows?" We risked reaching into the Collective and found remembrances of the cavern charred and barren, lifeless. Anger swelled to rage, but with strong emotion our world fuzzed and faded, pain exploding in our head.

"The Feeders..." We turned to face our betrayer. Such effort to move these weakened limbs. "Thy treachery shall not—"

The human we thought a friend plunged his knife deep in our belly. Another surge of agony coursed through us and stole from us all senses.

We awoke from darkness to spy the sight of legions.

Legions that screamed of torture, inflicted at the human's hand. It carved our flesh with its blade, and we screamed until there was nothing left to give. In silence, we watched through the Collective's eyes as the Skardwarf raised its fist over the new Queen's egg. No strength remained to contest the vile creatures.

Our hatred flared, and at last we could take no more. The pain was too great. Broken as we were, we put up no resistance as some *thing* latched onto the strands that bound the Colony and directed them toward its own will.

Fading away, we smiled. For that will was of a piece with our own.

Humans and Skardwarves. Tear them asunder, devour them in our jaws. Their murder of the Queen will be paid in kind. None shall escape our vast reach.

Within the deepest darkness, the Collective twitched to life.

*   *   *

When the Deluge released its grip on Garret's mind, he found himself sprawled on the ground. The Ekoan immediately scrambled to his feet and continued his flight, no time to make sense of the centuries of history his mind had just endured. He didn't look back. Their inhuman howls and pounding feet told him they were closing in. The Benefactor's horde.

And Garret was trapped in their territory.

His headlong rush carried him into the Human Aerie where chaos unfurled. Somehow the Peekers had beat him here. Latecomers to the Queen's summons, perhaps, now driven by the same hatred the Benefactor projected. An Aura that affected only Peekers, for Garret felt no hatred. Only terror.

The Peeker attack finally broke the unnatural calm. The Aerie was a swarming hive of commotion. Once named for the bond of friendship the Queen shared with her human friend, the place had become a slaughterhouse. Weaponless, people could do nothing but scream and run. Peekers struck from dark recesses, dropped from the ceiling on unsuspecting victims, cornered humans and showed no remorse for their savagery. They were animals. And more were coming. Unfathomably many more.

Garret had two knives in hand but little faith they would save him. He turned a bend to find two Peekers devouring the innards of a man whose lidless eyes stared lifelessly at the ceiling. A third Peeker feasted on his face, tearing chunks of flesh with its mandibles. Garret reversed course, took another path. He needed to reach the harbor.

The harbor, where Tunnel had probably been turned by the Queen. Garret didn't know how to work a fucking Peeker ship. But maybe some humans had escaped, were setting sail to flee the Mounds. It was his best chance, and he took it.

A Courier rounded the outcropping ahead. Hunched over unnaturally, it turned its elongated head to find Garret. Slavering jaws dripped slime, clacking aggressively.

Garret froze. The academic part of his mind noted the Peeker was Unpaired. Fitting, he figured. Unpaired were mindless creatures, but no mind was needed when the beast was controlled by the infestation.

It lunged face-first at him, pouncing with its powerful reverse-jointed legs. Garret ducked under it. Its strike was so vicious it left the ground, and fully airborne, it was helpless to dodge as Garret thrust his knife upward into its chitinous belly and *ripped*. Ichor sprayed and stained his green cloak, and even as the Peeker bled out on the ground it twitched and seethed, and the life failed to leave its body.

No time to ponder. He hurried onward, sticking to the darkness to avoid notice, letting the Screamers of the Aerie draw all attention. It was a slaughter. More of the horde had arrived, and the screaming behind him was replaced with gurgling and slurping as the Peekers feasted on the dead. Garret stayed ahead of the pack, never slowing except to slay a stray that spotted him in the shadows.

He nearly killed the Half-Blind Eye out of reflex when the Paceeqi sprang from his concealment.

"Ekoan! Did you feel it, the Deluge?"

Garret spat. "No time to bleeding chat. Are you fully blind now? They're coming!"

"I figured it out," the Eye said. "The Aura that plagued the Aerie. I know where it was coming from."

"Great." Garret pushed him aside and kept going. "Tell me about it when we escape this fucking nightmare."

"You don't understand! We can *use* it. The Aura of calm, it can interrupt the Emergent's hatred. We just need these—"

Garret turned back at the sudden crunching end to the Eye. He would be hearing that sound for the rest of his life. Wondering if there was a way the slaughter could have been stopped. The Paceeqi was a crumpled heap on the floor, his head smashed, brains oozing out. At the feet of a Peeker Soldier. It looked down, then back up at Garret. As if weighing whether to devour his prize or to add to it Ekoan flesh.

Garret gauged the distance and made a choice. His hand flashed out and released the knife he held. It spun in the air, on target. Garret held his breath.

His aim was good. The knife blade sunk directly into the Soldier's forehead. It wobbled on its feet, and Garret exhaled.

But the Soldier did not topple. It reached up and pulled the knife free. Blue ichor trailed downward. The Peeker lapped the fluid into its mouth. Dropped the blade and looked at Garret.

"Fuck me." Garret turned and sprinted. As fast and far as his legs and his waning strength could carry him. To the abyss with sticking to the shadows. He ran and didn't slow until the dim light of the Aerie's viewing hole was in sight. The fact he wasn't dead yet meant the Soldier must have deemed the Paceeqi a sufficient meal.

He joined the crowd of humans streaming toward the harbor. A heartening sight, for the number of dead he saw made it seem the Benefactor left no survivors. Still, he didn't intend to be at the back of the queue when the slaughter finally reached this herd. He tried pushing his way forward, but the crowd wouldn't budge. Everyone was panicking, screaming and trampling one another in their haste to escape the horde. Only, the narrow tunnels had different plans. These people were trapped like insects in azear fur.

Garret found another path. Back to the viewing platform, the same place Aerienne brought the young Queen. The same place he and Sentyx looked out upon the harbor the day they had arrived. The way was clear. He reached the balcony and stepped out into the Brightdaughter's waning light.

Below, the harbor was abuzz. As he'd hoped, many ships were pushing off. Still more waited, people rushing onto their decks. Amid the docked vessels was a hopeful sight. A lone Peeker ship that humans flooded onto. Tunnel's ship.

Garret vaulted the railing, fearless of the steep slope down to the harbor. He was an Ekoan ranger. He had ridden a stergoderm standing once. He could—

His foot clipped a rock and sent him tumbling. Tensing up, trying to fight gravity, that was a sure way to break a bone. Garret relaxed into the fall. Rolled over a few times but wound up sliding on his back, cloak trailing in the dirt. Rocks jabbed him in the ribs as he passed over them, but he'd take that over a cracked skull any day.

Still hurt like the abyss when he came to a stop by smashing into a thick tree near the waterline. Knocked the wind out of him. He pushed himself up, fighting for each breath, then bounded toward the ships.

The crowd on the docks was more amenable to shoving and pushing. They had room to move, weren't just being jammed against hard rock. Garret made it to Tunnel's ship and pulled up the gangplank. An Ayeiri man jumped but fell short. Grabbed the side of the hull, shouting. Garret helped him scramble aboard.

The others screaming at the docks would have to find another ship. This one floated too low in the water already. Garret sidled past people crying, holding wounds, shouting curses. At each other and at the Peekers. Should have been aiming them at the gods, Garret figured.

By some miracle he found Tunnel. One of them, anyway.

"Garret made it," the Peeker said.

"*You* made it," Garret replied in astonishment. "You're not turned then?"

Tunnel clicked, then slumped in what Garret took for sadness. "Sixteen made it. A twice-Paired Pair of Pairs."

"Thanks to the human." Another Peeker arrived with a wooden box on its antennae. "The Clasform box it gave this one holds off the Queen's influence."

The first Peeker shuddered. "Ignoring the Queen is...difficult. A powerful will emanates from the mountain."

"It's not her will anymore," Garret said. "Sixteen Peekers. Might be the only ones left in the world."

"There are more out there," the Peekers said, trembling. "There must be.

"Let's find out, then, shall we? The sooner the better. She'll get past the blockage in the Aerie soon enough." Garret grimaced thinking about all that meat in her way. The Queen would feast tonight.

"Where is Sentyx?" Tunnel asked.

Garret looked away. "You haven't turned. But he did."

"Then this vessel must flee," the Pair near Garret said. The rest crawled about the ship tending to humans and making preparations. "Where to?"

The score of human ships were sailing off mainly in two directions. They either angled north toward Canako to reach the canal to Liwokin, or to the east toward Paceeq. The same direction a ship would travel to reach Eko.

Garret yearned to return home. Prost and the Skardwarves might be heading there next. Peekers and Skardwarves would destroy the ecosystem Garret spent his whole life wishing to study. All that wildlife would go extinct without his intervention. He needed to rally the rangers to protect the stormjungles.

But what good would that do without an army to fight beside them? Against the infested Queen, he wasn't sure a big enough army existed. But if it did, it could only be in one place. Thinking of friends he hadn't seen in ages, Garret looked to the east and made his decision.

Then wondered whether he wasn't just opening himself up to another knife in the back.

CHAPTER FORTY-EIGHT

Resurgence

A shadow can cast no shadow
A torch can snuff no fire
Yet men can pretend that the house isn't burning
And kill a girl strumming her lyre

—Verse from False Light

"Are you sure you don't want me to carry you?"

Lorelay glared at the back of Vinlin's head. "The answer isn't going to change the fifth time you ask, Vinlin. Yes, I'm sure."

After being cooped up for an eternity unable to walk, she would force herself to do this. She was strong enough. She had insisted she was ready to Vinlin, and turning back would be foolish. Restless and frustrated with her body's slow healing, Lorelay had grown equally frustrated and anxious to learn Vinlin's supposedly worldview-shattering secret.

Now that their journey into depths unknown was underway, a voice nagged at her that she needed more time to prepare. But how could she have expected such a vast subterranean complex to exist beneath the Radiant Palace? Any farther down and they might fall out of the bottom of the world. Lorelay's muscles ached with fatigue, and the burns on her hands stung as sweat dripped down her arms.

"How much deeper are we going?" she asked, trying to stop herself from breathing too hard. One heaving breath and Vinlin would ask a sixth time, and she would grab that torch and crack him on the head with it.

"Not much farther, I promise." He turned and smiled, then continued down the gently sloping path, carrying the light away from her.

Lorelay hurried to catch up. This dingy cave stank of stale water, which she did *not* want to step in. There would be no handhold to grab if she fell. The walls were like river rock, carved smooth by ages of erosion. It was like this whole cave system was once submerged under water. Lorelay had lost track of the turns Vinlin was making through this dark labyrinth. That something like this cave system *existed* beneath the Radiant Palace defied belief.

They had passed the entrance to the dungeons at least a span ago, then crept through the crypts in silence Lorelay took to be reverence from the Kindling Emperor. No light save their own torch fire lit those catacombs. It was a domain of the Darkfather, lined with sarcophagi carved with the likenesses of Empresses long forgotten. Of all his ancestors, Vin stopped only to say a brief word to his mother.

Gemstones studded the walls in the nook surrounding Elzia's tomb, catching the dancing firelight and reflecting it in multicolored specks across Elzia's body. Inside the stone vessel, the last Empress' urn would be nestled among all the treasures Vinlin collected on his pilgrimage. Lorelay stepped close to check, but she would never know. It was sealed.

Vinlin was whispering something that sounded like an apology. When he noticed Lorelay standing beside him, he abruptly stopped. "Let's go," he said, and they continued yet farther down.

Lorelay was stretching the ache in her neck and wondering what Vinlin could possibly have to apologize for when he stopped at what looked suspiciously like a pillar carved into the cave wall. The way ahead opened up into an expansive cavern, but it was too dark to make out anything beyond Vinlin, who stood biting his lip as though nervous.

"I shouldn't be showing you this, but..." Vinlin sighed. "If not you, then who else?"

"What do you mean?"

"I have no heirs. My mother brought me to this place, though she never expected to. Me and my sister, we were the only ones..."

"I thought you had a brother," Lorelay said, and realized her mistake right away. Elzia never expected to show Vinlin...because he wasn't the heir. Lorelay's heart suddenly weighed as much as iron. "I'm sorry. How old were you when she..." Lorelay couldn't say it. If Vinlin's bond with his sister was a strong as her bond with Dunnax, she wouldn't say the words and tear open an old wound.

Vinlin shrugged. "Sixteen. Old enough to remember how her death tore apart our family."

He paused and seemed to weigh in his mind whether this was a story worth telling. Lorelay refused to push him one way or the other. If he was comfortable sharing, she would listen, and her heart would break for him. If not, she would understand.

"Really, it began the moment she was born. As soon as Mother had an heir, it felt like Elwin and I were completely forgotten. Father hired scholars from around the Empire, saw first-hand that she was educated to become an Empress. Mother was always busy handling matters of state and relations with the Church. The only time our parents ever noticed us was to scold us for our unprincely behavior."

Vinlin grinned wryly, and Lorelay couldn't help but smile back. She thought of the songs she had sung for him while escorting him to Canako. Lorelay had been trying to rile him up, but the Prince only complimented her singing voice.

"We were troublemakers," he said. "And Elzia was just a child. She hated being stuck in classes all day, learning manners and how to dance and stitch. We often snuck her out to play in the gardens while Father turned a blind eye. One time, we were swimming in the river.

Elwin was arguing with me—I don't know why I remember this—over whether the gardens contained too many red roses.

"Then we noticed Elzia's splashing and playful shouts, there in the background the entire time we bickered...they were gone. People think drowning is loud, but it's the quiet you have to listen for. I panicked, froze. Elwin saw her floating face down and rushed downriver, dragged her unconscious to the river bank." Vinlin trailed off, shook his head. "It was too late. Elzia was nine when she died."

Lorelay listened quietly, unable even to apologize past the tightness in her throat.

"Mother blamed my father for letting it happen. She was furious, exiled him from Paceeq. Elwin chose to go with him. I couldn't bring myself to leave. Not with the Church hounding my mother, forcing her to take additional suitors. But she never bore another child after my sister. And that's why I'm going to be Emperor. I would rather have my family back."

Vinlin sniffled and wiped a sleeve across his nose. Lorelay took a step toward him, wanted to comfort him, but he turned away.

"Do you want to...pay your respects when we go back?" Lorelay asked. "We can find her tomb."

"She was buried in the city. We never held a funeral, not like for my mother. I doubt most Paceeqi even remember there was once a true heir. The crypts are only for Empresses. And, I suppose, after I die, one Emperor. I'll be the first." He sighed. "The way things are going, maybe also the last."

"What?" Lorelay had never heard him in such a depressive state before. She was sorry she had led him to this dreadful reminiscence. "Don't say that."

"Why not? It's the truth. I have no heir. The Church would be happy to take over ruling the Bright Empire for what little time remains to us. I've a mind to let them. If the Benefactors are as dangerous as you fear, all of this political trouble will mean nothing anyway."

He gestured for her to follow. "We're on the cusp of another Dark Era."

The words stunned Lorelay into nearly being left behind in the darkness as Vinlin turned the corner with their only source of light. "Another *Dark Era?*" Where was this coming from? She caught up with Vinlin, her legs aching from their long descent, venturing deeper into the looming cavern. "You're poking fun at me, aren't you?"

"I don't expect you to believe me, not right away. Just as I didn't believe you about the Benefactors. Not until you showed me evidence."

"I *haven't* shown you evidence..." Lorelay grimaced. *This command would have been much easier if Grim had given me* anything *to convince a skeptic.* Then again, she had failed to ask for any. Not all the blame lay at Grim's feet.

"Oh, but you have. You practically threw yourself into my mother's funeral pyre to save a *plant.* A plant you claim will save us all. Ridiculous on the face of it, yet if you hold the belief so strongly you'd rather die than lose it, well... I believe you."

"You do?" Lorelay let out a sigh of relief. She had actually done it. Grim wanted an ally in the Bright Emperor, and he had it. "Then what are we doing here? We need to mobilize your armies.

She was no commander, so not exactly sure what that entailed, but she had heard Dunnax say something to that effect once. Both of them were drunk, granted, and the topic of Skardwarves had come up—always a touchy subject with her brother—but it still seemed a good idea.

"Do you know what the Dark Era was, Lorelay?"

A test of faith, was it? She had heard the Book of Light's warnings often enough from her mother's tongue. "An eon when the Lightmother had forsaken us and darkness enveloped all the land. The Brightdaughter no longer danced in the heavens. The Darkfather listened to our prayers only to laugh as his minions ravaged the world. We brought it upon ourselves because we let the fires of our faith die."

"You know your scripture."

Lorelay snorted. "Didn't have much choice in the matter. It's how the Church keeps us obedient. The Brightdaughter vanishing for centuries. Our ancestors being hunted by demons and Skardwarves in eternal night. Right. I've *met* a Skardwarf. He's really nice. They're just children's stories, meant to scare us because what *they're* afraid of is *us*. Rising against them."

Vinlin nodded slowly. "Metaphors, guides for proper behavior, a way to maintain Order. That's all the Book of Light is. Any adult will tell you that."

Lorelay's toe clipped a rock in their descent. She stumbled and caught herself on Vinlin's arm. It sounded like the future Bright Emperor was saying their holy book was a lie.

But he continued. "Only they're wrong. It's *true*. All of it." Vinlin came to a halt. He held aloft the torch and let his light flood the wide chamber.

Lorelay gasped. Here at the bottom of the world, she and Vinlin stood in a room constructed by human hands. Her feet guided her closer to the walls. They were scored with ancient carvings, worn away by time, hardly recognizable as symbols on most fragments of cracked, flat stone.

"What is this place?"

The words were a breathless whisper in the still air. How long had it been since humans built this place? Or was it built by something else? Some of the carvings depicted humans, but others... Their bodies were clearly human; their heads were anything but.

Lorelay traced the cool, smooth carvings of animal-headed people with her bandaged hands, ignoring the stinging sensation. A man with the head of a horse. Likenesses of foxes, birds, stergoderms, bulls, deer—many were animals she recognized. A few beggared Lorelay's imagination. Such bizarre creatures. Bulbous cheeks, huge jaws, raised nostrils on one. Another with reptilian scales, long snouts, countless teeth.

"This place," Vinlin said, "is the evidence."

A chill ran through Lorelay's body. "They're demons..."

The humans were depicted kneeling before them, almost as if worshiping them. Was this what the Book meant when it said they brought the Dark Era upon themselves? Or was this a depiction of subjugation? Men bowing before the servants of the Darkfather to avoid his wrath. No choice, only a matter of survival.

Her mind searched for some alternate way to interpret the evidence. The Bright Empire was wrong, she believed that her whole life. But these images disturbed Lorelay to her core. If Vinlin was right about what these ruins represented, then everything she believed was wrong.

Lightmother...how many years had she spent rebelling against the Church of Light? Rejecting their ways, convinced *their* actions were the true path to darkness. All that time, those traditions prevented their civilization from crumbling into *this*.

Her mother was right.

Dunnax was right.

Lorelay clenched her fists, angry with herself. She should have listened to them. Her knuckles cracked, she was squeezing so hard. Newly healed skin pulled tight. Then, she let out a deep breath.

She could still do right by her brother.

Lorelay had to believe that, or what purpose would she have?

"There's more." Vinlin beckoned from the next room, through a wide, low door.

Lorelay had to duck to reach him. She followed his gaze to the corner of the room, then screamed and fell backward. Vinlin caught her, and she let him hold her. She was staring at the perfectly preserved remains of...

"A Skardwarf?" Lorelay whispered. She leaned forward, approached the gray heap. "No, a...statue?" But how could that be? It was immaculate. Chiseled stone hardly touched by erosion. It had fallen over, and its arm was missing. If not for its missing eyes, Lorelay would have believed it was alive. "Why would there be a statue of a Skardwarf here?"

"I've asked myself the same question countless times. Mother knew as little as I did, and we couldn't bring it to the surface to let anyone else examine it." Vinlin grinned sheepishly. "I did try, once. I had to lie to the Archehealer about how I strained my back."

"Really, *no one* else knows about this? Not even the High Cleric?" Everything Lorelay knew about the Church of Light was caught in a maelstrom, and she had to pull the pieces out of the air and put them back together. It was like learning there was a new melody in the middle of *Reverie of the Brightdaughter,* discordant and out of time with the rest.

"I don't know for certain," Vinlin admitted. "But Mother insisted she had told no one but me and my sister. Namravi would have had to stumble across it on her own. Can you imagine the old lady exploring this deep into the caves?"

Lorelay would have laughed, but she was still in too great a shock. "Can't imagine him learning about this and not crowing to the whole world about the irrefutable proof of the truth of his faith."

Vinlin grunted in agreement, then sighed. "Finally telling someone else, it would almost be a relief if not for the fact that we're facing a resurgence of these demons."

"That's another thing I don't understand. Skardwarves as demons? I've met two Skardwarves, both Fingers of the Agency." Lorelay sensed Vinlin bristling and hurried to clarify lest he believe Grim some dark-lover. "Sentyx is a good person. He consoled me at my brother's funeral. I can't reconcile that with him being a demon."

The Kindling Emperor shrugged. "Has he ever used some sort of Dark magic?"

"Sentyx? I don't think I've ever seen him pick up a weapon, let alone..."

Dark magic? Lorelay had never heard of such a thing, but her mind was suddenly back in the hollow of the twisted tower where Ulken fell to Grim. Inac had done something she could not explain. The air had cooled, the light of the Brightdaughter fading. Lorelay had been so stricken with grief after that fight, the event had escaped her memory.

But Inac was a friend too. *Gah! None of this makes sense.* She tensed in frustration.

Vinlin regarded her through narrowed eyes. "You recall something?"

"Nothing." Lorelay shook her head. "You never answered my question."

"Hmm?"

"Another Dark Era? If anything, this just proves there was *one* Dark Era, long ago."

Vinlin nodded, then strode into another chamber. Lorelay followed close behind hoping for a good answer.

"There are too many signs to ignore." Vinlin held his torch near a wall carved with a mural. "Look at this. These are star charts. Maps of the sky."

To Lorelay, they appeared as no more than randomly placed dots on the wall. If Vinlin had not pointed them out, she surely would have only seen the mural on the lower half of the wall. Above each scene was a different collection of dots surrounding either one or two circles. "I don't understand."

"I hardly do myself. Only, it lines up with something the Mathemelodian Prime told me. The stars form different patterns depending on the Brightdaughter's movements. She hopes to use that to predict the length of the day but isn't optimistic. The calculations are too complex even for her."

Lorelay had no mind for numbers, only for music. "Is it, uh..." She was trying to be delicate. "Necessary to know this?" If so, her leap of faith would have to begin here. Lorelay would never piece together this puzzle. She would simply have to take Vinlin at his word.

"Only this." Vinlin gestured at the last panel, where two orbs decorated the sky above a crude depiction that looked like a faceless man controlling marionettes. Though, the strings were looping and wavy, not taut. "This big circle, that's the Brightdaughter. The smaller one, the Shadowson. Below him, the Darkfather commanding his demons across the ocean." Vinlin took a slow breath. "Lorelay, the mathemelodians have told me the Brightdaughter's light has been failing. The days are growing shorter, and they don't know why. Where else am I to look for answers than our faith?"

Lorelay bit her lip. "That's one sign. It could mean any—"

"We've got Skardwarves in the Empire. Citizens abroad return to seek refuge in the heart of Light. Prosecution of Archemages using Dark magic is up. And these Benefactors...everything you've told me about them. What if *they* are the demons our ancestors were warning us about."

Lorelay thought of the strange, animal-headed creatures on the walls. Unimaginable horrors—was that not what Ulken had called the Benefactors? Hard to disagree with that assessment. They were all writhing limbs and melted flesh, with Auras that claimed the minds of men. *Men, and Skardwarves.* Lorelay remembered how helpless Sentyx was in Reed's Woods.

So many contradictions. Grim *himself* was a Benefactor, and he was a friend. Was he not? Even now, was she doing a demon's bidding? She told herself that was ridiculous but searched the mural for any clues to help her figure out what to believe. "What's this?" Lorelay asked.

Below another sky with both Sibling Suns, the people were misshapen but clearly different than the way the ancients depicted Skardwarves. They gathered around something shaped like an egg.

"I'm not sure. Some sort of gem, maybe? A teardrop?"

"It looks like a Druid's Tear," Lorelay said, "but what's wrong with the people?"

Vinlin shook his head. "Lorelay, look at the last panel."

Lorelay looked, and her stomach dropped. She needed no explanation to understand what it showed. On the left side, buildings that reached into the sky. On the right, Skardwarves standing in their rubble among the dead.

"The Dark Era is approaching," the Kindling Emperor said. "This is what's at stake if we allow it to arrive."

The Bright Empire would come to an end. Everyone she loved would die. The world would burn. "How can we stop it?"

"Together," Vinlin declared. "The Bright Empire will join the Agency in their fight." More quietly, he added, "It's what my mother would have wanted."

Elation surged through Lorelay, even as doubt clouded her thoughts. This was what she had come for. Her mission was a success. But now she knew the true scale of what they were up against. The war was just beginning, and victory seemed more hopeless than ever.

"But I need your help in return," Vinlin said.

She took a deep breath. "Whatever you need, it's yours."

CHAPTER FORTY-NINE

Discernment

In timeless night the dance persists
After the music fades to silence
Sorrow born of broken love
Stillness below, chaos above

—Verse from Through Darkness Deep,
Third Song of Dusk

The carriage rattled to the sound of horses' clopping hooves, seat cushion doing little to save Lorelay's rear from the cobblestones. Vinlin sat beside her, waving and giving greetings to the Paceeqi they passed. They rode no ornate, covered carriage, but a common man's vehicle. They were even being pulled by shaggy mares, work horses brought in from the farmland west of the city. A political stunt, Lorelay knew, to gain her some favor with the people—but one that appeared to be working.

"The Lightmother's blessing upon you," Vinlin said to a mother holding her baby aloft. The mother was smiling, but the baby squirmed and wailed. The Kindling Emperor repeated the same blessing to the next dozen onlookers, then turned to whisper to Lorelay, "You should speak their praises too. They'll never forget it."

Lorelay bit her lip. That was what she feared. They would see her as someone who thought she was above them, a sentiment so far from the truth it galled. She wanted to do none of this parading about the city as though she were Vinlin's betrothed. But he had taken her promise in the palace depths literally, and she would make good on her word.

Whatever he needs. Though, she found herself wondering if she had it in her to provide it. She had suspected the man's desires from the moment she stepped into the city. They had repulsed her. They were positively repugnant. Looking at him now, seeing his confidence in the face of hopelessness, the idea seemed somehow less gloomy. Though the Dark Era was fast approaching, the Kindling Emperor resolved to be a source of light.

She raised her hand to wave from the seat beside him. The weight of responsibility Vinlin carried on his shoulders, perhaps it did place him above the average person in a way. If he failed, so many more than just his family would die. Lorelay and every other Paceeqi owed it to him to support his fight, to lift as much weight from him as they could. If a woman seated beside him made the Emperor appear more legitimate, Lorelay could pretend for a moment she occupied the same pedestal he did.

As long as she never let herself believe the lie, she could accomplish great things with Vinlin. Together they could save the Bright Empire.

Only if I don't snuff it up again.

Her burns had healed enough to go unbandaged, but both the pain in her hands and the pain of her remorse remained. She hoped no one noticed the scars that lined her palm and connected them to Elzia's pyre. Everything needed to go well this day, otherwise Vinlin's pledge of support meant nothing.

The carriage ride through Vos had gone well so far. Vinlin worried about how he would be perceived as Bright Emperor. Strong like his mother, or an incompetent man? He had nothing to worry about, in truth. He was a compassionate ruler, Lorelay saw that now. This ride might have been about managing public perceptions, but the look in his eyes when he greeted each of his subjects was genuine.

Word traveled faster than the horses, and before long the city streets were lined with onlookers crowding the sidewalks in front of myriad shops and houses. Lorelay never understood why Liwokin cordoned off each quarter of the city. In her home, Paceeqi worked in their houses and shopped at their friends' abodes. Everything was mixed together, wonderfully lively and diverse. Olive presses, bakeries, and fishmongers to feed the city; candy and toy makers for the children; Archemakers and blacksmiths, wheelwrights and lumberers, the fires of industry burned hot in Vos. Every shop emptied as the one-carriage parade passed by.

After overcoming her misgivings, Lorelay had fun waving to excited children, nearly forgetting the city faced a worsening refugee crisis. She even spotted Jenx in the crowd. Distracted from the line of homeless to whom he had been distributing food, he stared at Lorelay dumbstruck. She grinned and gave him a formal bow before the carriage moved on. The mood was so light she wanted to sing. Vinlin had encouraged her to leave his gifted lyre behind.

"Our destination requires reverence," he said, "not reverie."

As they neared the location, Lorelay understood how wise his words had been.

The tree-lined street gave way to the square before the Cathedral of the Light, where a huge crowd had gathered. A roar of sound washed over Lorelay as the city cheered their Kindling Emperor, but she had eyes only for the awe-inspiring structure straight ahead.

The cathedral reached heavenward, its facade a straight wall of golden pillars atop wide stairs. Beyond those pillars a carved lightwood door laboriously swung open. Flanking either side of the building were towering columns, Archemetal and marble spiraling upward to reach the golden domes at their pinnacles. Neither of the minor domes held a candle to the Mother's Dome atop the central spire. It soared high in front of the Brightdaughter, whose light shone through stained glass windows covering the walls.

Lorelay hardly had time to stop gawking before she and Vinlin passed through a line of Paladins and dismounted from the carriage. They climbed the steps and entered with one last wave to their people. The cheering of thousands was swallowed by the vast chamber she entered, and she was swept away by another wave of awe.

The cathedral's interior was one massive open space. Misty smoke trailed skyward from countless braziers and candles. Multi-hued rays hung in the smoky air that passed in front of stained-glass windows. Scenes from the Book of Light were depicted in glass, paint, and metal on every wall and pillar. Between those works flew crimson banners showing the Empire's golden sunburst flame. Lorelay spun about, admiring the sanctuary of religious and imperial power she had spent so many years fruitlessly fighting.

Throughout the vast expanse, only a few Clerics shuffled about. The important ones stationed themselves before the altar at the far end of the cathedral—a golden statue of the Lightmother bestowing her blessing to the first High Cleric. Vinlin's clicking heels echoed for the entire long walk toward that self-indulgent statue. If she were on anything less than her best behavior, she would have given the Clerics her honest thoughts about their iconography.

As the Clerics bowed before the Kindling Emperor—save one, of course. The High Cleric only bowed to a fully-fledged Bright Emperor. Lorelay and Vinlin held hands and made their required bows to Namravi, who then began the proceedings.

Poorly.

"You bring your wench to this holy site?"

Vinlin squeezed Lorelay's hand tighter, then calmed himself. Getting angry would do nothing to help their cause, and they had been expecting insults. "Brightness Lorelay comes to make amends."

The High Cleric stepped uncomfortably close to Lorelay. "So, you admit fault, do you?" She turned back to her cronies. "It appears there's no need for a trial after all."

A handful of the Clerics laughed, but fear stabbed through Lorelay. A trial? "I'm here to make a formal apology to the Church, Brightest One." It pained her to use the highest of honorifics with such a contemptible woman, but she promised Vinlin deference.

Lorelay's respect was not reciprocated. "An admission of guilt suits our needs even better," the High Cleric said with a grin.

Vinlin stepped forward. "There is no need for this, Namravi. Nothing you do to her can prevent what we know is coming."

Lorelay pretended she knew nothing of the Dark Era, information meant only for the heads of the three pillars of Vos—the Bright Emperor, the High Cleric, and the Mathemelodian Prime. "I have sworn my allegiance to the Bright Throne, Brightest One. You need not worry about further...lapses in judgment from me. We must all come together to support the Emperor in these times."

"Silence." The High Cleric waved a dismissive hand. "Do not deign to tell *me* what I must do. My word comes straight from the mouth of the Lightmother. Support the Emperor..." She scoffed. "No. It is the tenets of our faith we must adhere to when darkness is at its deepest."

"I agree. Which is why I feel obliged to mend the rifts I've caused between the Church and the throne. Two pillars upon which the foundation of this city rests."

Everything Lorelay said was a farce, but it mattered little *she* believed what she was saying was important. Only that the High Cleric must. And what better way to win the hand of a vain woman than by inflating her ego? Although the pompous way she looked down her nose at Lorelay, she doubted it was possible to puff it up any bigger.

"This city?" she continued. "No, the Bright Empire entire. Let not the misdeeds of one girl send the whole realm into chaos. The people of Paceeq, of Lawiko, Eko, Ayeir, and the Isles…they are all relying on both of you to work together. Anything I can do to help make that happen, consider it already done."

"Very well," the High Cleric said. "You can hang. Then I'll forgive everything. What say you, Your Radiance?"

Veins bulged in Vinlin's neck. He was squeezing her hand so hard it hurt. "Of course not. Lorelay will address the people from the cathedral's stairs. My Paladins have already constructed a podium." His words came through clenched teeth.

The High Cleric responded in kind, "Careful, boy. You are not Bright Emperor yet."

Lorelay gasped. Insulting *her*, that was expected. But insulting Vinlin? He could have the Namravi replaced on the day of his coronation. A day not far off.

The High Cleric had not finished. "I speak one word, and you and your whore will never sit on the throne." The woman's eyes widened raised as soon as her mouth shut, as though just realizing what she had said.

Vinlin refused to dignify the offense with a response. A verbal response, anyway. He drew back his arm to hit Namravi.

Lorelay caught him by the elbow, aghast. "Vinlin, no!"

He still tried to follow through with the motion, but Lorelay stopped the blow. "How dare you!" Spittle flung from his lips and landed on the High Cleric's face.

Namravi's eyes bulged further. "You are a disgrace to the Bright Empire! Your mother should have ended your life in the womb!"

The rest of the Clerics joined in hurling insults at Vinlin and Lorelay. The briefly civil meeting had dissolved into madness. Lorelay held Vinlin back from assaulting the head of his religion.

"What the snuff is going on?" she whimpered. She had never seen him act this way. Like he was drugged or—

The blood flushed from Lorelay's face.

Or there's a Benefactor.

She risked turning toward the distant entrance, assuming none of the Clerics brought a knife to this gathering. If they did, she might soon find it in her back. The people through the cathedral doors were small specks she could barely make out. Were they...writhing? Moving around more than simple impatience might bestow.

Suddenly there were Paladins between the pillars, and their swords were dripping red. Lorelay's gut sank. Her mind recalled an image of Dunnax's sword spattered with blood—the night he had killed his oath brother. Betrayal.

"Vinlin!" She pulled his gaze to the approaching men in gleaming silver. They crowded the doorway, preventing escape. And Lorelay understood. Another treachery had occurred. "Snuffing bastard!" she screamed at the High Cleric. "You're killing us!"

As the words left her mouth, they rang hollow. Not least because of the confused look on the Namravi's face. Ugly, but not dishonest. She tried remembering what was real. She wanted a public execution, not knives in the dark. The other Clerics were backing away in fear.

The Paladins entered the Cathedral of Light, and the sounds of clashing steel filled the air. Clashing steel, and shouting voices. Vinlin's army wasn't preventing escape. They were preventing the *entrance* of the crowd. One of the Paladins fell onto his back and was trampled by three bloodied people. They began sprinting across the cathedral.

Lorelay tugged Vinlin's arm. "What do we do?" Everyone had been jovial, cheering for her and the Kindling Emperor. Had a Benefactor Emerged in the middle of the cathedral square? They had no weapons, no hope of fighting it.

"Follow me." Vinlin led her and the Clerics to an eastern wing of the cathedral. An Archemetal carving of the swirling abyss spiraled outward from a darkwood door recessed into the wall. No stained-glass color splashed this wall. On a plaque read the words, '*In darkness, light. In light, darkness.*'

They escaped down a corridor of guttering flame and the faded tombs of High Clerics past. None of the procession argued as they fled, and Lorelay was left wondering if it was because they all discerned that the Darkfather's demons had just arrived in the capital of the Bright Empire.

CHAPTER FIFTY

Self-Deception

Empress Livarin's Paladins faced stout resistance from the combined militias of the Canako and Liwokin city-states. However, the heaviest tolls were exacted by the Outrush Canyon during the first campaign. The unpredictable waters turned back Imperial forces and necessitated a second campaign consisting of an overland march from the southernmost city-state of Sobiko. According to Liwo legend, an army of silver ghosts will one day flood Liwokin from the canyon and revenge themselves upon the city.

—Excerpt from All Her Light Touches:
Annals of Imperial Expansion

The weeks-long journey to Paceeq provided far too much time for self-reflection.

I had let my city fall, and it was nothing like what I'd imagined in my nightmares. It was far worse. Not mindless puppets like Reed dangled from his woods, or blood-starved monsters killing with no remorse. Just...people. Deceived by the Aura of a man who thought he was doing justice.

It was far harder to convince myself he was wrong. The Blight-dwellers had been trod upon for generations—I had always feared they'd rise up in rebellion. I never expected the leader of their uprising would be a mind-altering monster who stoked them all to fury.

I looked at myself in the polished metal of the steamship's pilot-house. The structure shuddered with the steam-turned wheel behind it, making my reflection appear to be shivering. The day provided little heat—the Brightdaughter shone behind my head, flickering through hair whipped by cold wind. Staring into my own eyes, unblinking, the details outside my narrow focus slowly fuzzed.

Hair vanished leaving wrinkled baldness. Black coat adorned with the Head's sigil became threadworn rags. My arms bulged with tightly knotted muscle. Bello and I were the same in so many regards. Two men of low status, risen to high ranks because of the monsters in our heads.

"Grim?" Inac approached from behind, boots clicking on the metal hull.

I turned, and he stopped short.

"You are...doing it again."

"Is it really so easy? All I do is imagine myself as Bello, and everyone on the ship believes I look like him."

One of the sailor's stared at me with suspicious eyes and confirmed my belief. I relaxed my mind, as Inac had been instructing me in our lessons. It helped to close my eyes and listen to my breath. When I opened them again, the sailor's face conveyed surprise.

Inac smiled. "It is for you getting easier."

"Controlling it? Yeah." I looked north at the distant coast of Lawiko. "But not everything."

I have not abandoned them. While I lived, the Benefactor that ravaged our city would be hunted.

"How about you?" I asked. The other Head had been helping me learn to control my Aura using the same techniques he taught me to control the Fire. Lately, however, my friend had taken to more solitude than usual.

Inac lifted his left hand and summoned a mote of Fire. His mouth twitched as he carefully danced the mote from fingertip to fingertip. The mage snuffed it out. "It is nice not to worry about burning the ship."

"I would prefer speed." While the rest of the fleet escaping Li-wokin had sailed the winds swiftly south, the steamships loped along at a steady pace, their metal bellies heavy in the water. Frustration boiled in my belly. "Can't we add more Fire to speed up the ship?"

A nearby sailor snorted. "Doesn't work that way."

I scoffed. "And what if I imagine a sail to catch the wind?"

As quickly as the words formed, so it was. A bright red sail instantly sprouted from amidships, billowing as the icy gale stung my skin. An Ekoan sailor dove to the ground as the rigging swung, but the vessel moved no faster.

"Of course not," I muttered. It was an illusion, with no real effect on the world except within the minds of men.

"The speed has for us given time to prepare," Inac said. "Have you considered what you will say to convince the Emperor?"

"I'm hoping I don't have to say anything. That Lorelay's swayed him, and we just have to tell him where to send his armies."

"And if that is not the case?"

I considered. In that case, Lorelay had either failed and turned him against us—not a likely option knowing the man's infatuation—or he just required more convincing. "It's his people who are dying. He'll help us."

He would. I had to believe that. The Benefactors threatened all of the Bright Empire. Vinlin would have to be suicidal to deny our request for aid.

Yet the possibility lingered. If he didn't do what was right...could I force him to? If I put the right thought in his mind, I could make him see things my way. Would I? To save my city, I would do anything.

A knot of regret stopped up my airway. My Aura was the reason Liwokin had fallen. To repeat that mistake here was to condemn Vos to the same fate. Some Emergent would arrive, and the people would have no chance to react. They would never see the signs, hidden as they were beneath my deception.

I forced myself to breathe calmly, wiping away the illusory sail from everyone's senses. It wasn't the wind that sent a chill through me.

It shouldn't be so easy.

Some part of me, deep down, knew what that meant. The Benefactor in my head was growing stronger. I needed to keep it suppressed.

I needed to rid myself of it.

But not yet. Not while other Emergents terrorized our cities. The power I wielded might be our only chance to survive.

When we approached the harbor of Vos two nights later, the waters were mobbed by countless ships. Approaching the docks would be dangerous. I spotted a ship's mast jutting from the choppy blue.

"Take us elsewhere," I commanded the captain of our vessel.

"Where, sir?"

I waved a hand. "Anywhere but this mess. We'll never reach the palace that way."

The pristine white building loomed over the scene of multicolored flags and sails. It rested atop a great plateau, as though built so the Empress could keep watch over all the workings of the city from her walls. Towers alike to the Gild's ruined that prospect, painting rooftops in shadow and blocking them from royal sight.

"We're going to the palace?" the Paceeqi captain asked, then grumbled in deliberation. "I might know of a way."

"You don't need to convince me. Just take us there."

Our ship kept well clear of the others, sidling around the island nation's Capital until it docked at a barnacle-covered jetty at the foot of a roaring waterfall. Directly overhead, the Radiant Palace's golden spires caught the sunlight and glowed as if ablaze.

"Old smuggler's pass, I'll wager," Oltrov yelled to be heard over the crashing water.

"Where's it take us?" I asked the captain.

He shrugged. "My old nan told tales of this place. Wasn't sure it'd even be here."

I fought down a flash of annoyance at the man. For a moment, the successful defense of the world was pinned on the truth of some old nan's tale.

"There." Inac pointed at an opening in the rock face.

"Yezna is in no condition to go spelunking," Arza said. "We will reach the palace by more conventional means."

It took some convincing that they'd be safe before I let them go. Arza assured me she could take care of herself and reach the Radiant Palace, but she wanted to check in first with the Paladins managing the influx of Liwo refugees. Her parents had fled Liwokin after the attack on the Market District, and she needed to know if they were safe.

Reaching into Yezna's mind, I found...resentment. She was weary of travel but yearned to be among people, away from me. After the botched summit, I couldn't blame her.

I sent all the Heels that were on the ship to escort her and Arza through the city—my worries wouldn't rest until they were in the safety of the palace with us. Vos might be a foreign city, but I knew cities. With so many desperate people crowding the streets, all it took was a spark to ignite a conflagration of violence.

With their party away in a skiff, I turned back to the cave. "What else did your nan say?"

She told her grandson of the cave and a harrowing descent, where rockfalls formed unsteady steps to make the way traversable. When she was a girl, she discovered the ruins of underground dwellers. We came to a stretch of flat-walled cave that gave an impression of a village street. It almost convinced me it *was,* with shop fronts ground down by time, and again I saw the truth in the old nan's account. She truly believed her account, at any rate.

The captain's nan had worked in the Radiant Palace. She and the other serving maids used to sneak off to play in the woods across the river. The girl hadn't been able to scramble back out after sliding down into the dark cave. She had to keep moving forward, farther from the Brightdaughter, delving down to some unknown depth. She lit the way with Archefire, and Inac did the same, following her path in reverse. Until sunlight appeared to guide us—right to the bottom of steep gravel slope.

When we emerged from the cave with burning legs and heaving chests, the Brightdaughter flew low. Again she guided us, this time west to the palace. Across the wide and swift river, the Radiant Palace was footed with green, a sprawling garden that covered the grounds down to the water's edge.

"And just how are we going to get over there?" Oltrov asked. "What did his old nan do, swim?"

The story hadn't said, but what other option was there? There were only three of us, and if we started upriver we could make it to the gardens. But Inac was missing a hand, and Oltrov carried the Benefactor cure in a case that would sink like an anchor. Even if we left our belongings behind, a span of water so wide might tire us out and sweep us downriver to the falls.

Torchlight flickered like fireflies across the river and caught my eye. They were moving—carried by guards. Something strange affected that light, as if it were obscured by a cloud of shadow.

"Do you see that, Grim?" Inac asked.

"I do." Closing my eyes, the darkness remained. "Incubating Benefactors."

Focusing on the Archedark disturbances, I searched the Paladin's mind for any way across the river.

There.

Through his eyes I saw the Paladin crossing the river by a rope ferry, working up a sweat with arms overhead. Night patrol, and he was grumbling to himself about it. Meant to keep away the wolves, but there were no snuffing wolves in these woods. Nothing but quail and foxes, and the Empress staged enough hunts to kill near all of those. For just *one* night, couldn't he take off? His loyalty to the throne squashed that question before it was seriously considered.

I released my grip on the man's mind. He was likely confused and feeling a headache, and I wanted him in a good mood when we met.

"Come on. I know where to go."

Oltrov and Inac followed, not once questioning how I came by an answer.

Easier for them not to think about it. Maybe it helps them forget what I am.

It scared me how easily *I* could help them forget what I had become. All I would need to do is deceive myself into thinking I was a normal man. Just like that, it would be true. No one would see me for anything else.

We reached the ferry and began working the rope to summon the raft. Hopefully no Paladins would spot their vessel moving and contest it. It arrived, and we boarded to begin the crossing. Halfway through, the craft started moving on its own, no rope work necessary.

That wasn't *entirely* true. The rope work was being done by the Paladins who'd arrived to begin their night patrol only to find their way across occupied.

Briefly I considered convincing the Paladins guarding the way to Vinlin we were brothers in arms. That was no way to greet the Emperor though, especially one with whom I had already misstepped before. Better to speak the truth and trust Lorelay had done her job.

One of the two Paladins, covered top to toe in polished silver plate, waved a sword to command us forward. "Armed mercenaries, are we?"

"If we were armed mercenaries," Oltrov said, "these three would already have burnt you to a cinder with Archefire."

"Refugees, then," the other Paladin said.

I grimaced. "In a way. We are official representatives of Liwokin. The city has fallen, and we've come to seek Emperor Vinlin's—"

"He's no Emperor. Not yet." The Paladin seemed displeased by the prospect.

"How'd you get to the Empress' Wood?" They both had their silver swords out now.

Thank the Lightmother none of my friend's hands were anywhere near their own weapons.

"What's important is we speak to the Emperor," I said. "We sent an envoy some time ago. Lorelay. Do you know her?"

The same Paladin who evidently still longed for the days of Elzia gave a sigh, then put up his weapon. "You sent that girl? What a mess she's caused," he muttered.

I suppressed a frown. What had she done?

The other Paladin kept his sword at the ready and regarded me with narrow eyes. "Describe her. Plenty of refugees have heard of her. Gossip of the whole city, she is. He may trust you," he said of his comrade, "but I don't."

"Easy, Cavendish. Use your eyes. This one's got Archemetal in his coat. That means money. The Kindling Emperor will want to meet them."

"Thank you," I said with relief. "For trusting us."

If the truth hadn't worked, I would have been tempted toward deceit.

"What mess for you did Lorelay cause?" Inac asked

Right out with it, then. He always kept his eye on the bigger picture, made me realize how stranded I would be if I had been doing this alone.

The Paladin's face twisted in disgust. "Ask her yourself."

Inac cast a look at me. "Not good," he whispered.

That must have been an understatement. We were shown to a suite of private rooms and told to await summons. Luxurious rooms, indeed, each with their own personal wash station, powered by the palace's employed Archemages. They were all located in a wing of the palace with access to a richly decorated library containing more books than I could read in all my days. The Emperor furnished his guests well.

The affront was that it took eleven days before we were finally summoned. While Inac simultaneously read and practiced controlling his Archefire uncomfortably close to the books, I failed to read a single page out of constant worry for what transpired in Liwokin. The only upside to the delay was that it gave time for Arza and Yezna to rejoin us, though the mortician remained in dark mood since failing to find her parents.

We waited, wasting time while people died.

At long last we found ourselves with one final wait—for the Emperor to arrive to the meeting he invited us to in the dead of night. We sat around a long marble table, silent but for Oltrov's fingers fidgeting on the stone.

The door opened on a squeaky hinge, and the Gildmember muttered, "'Bout time." He rose to his feet and flourished a bow with his Archemetal-trimmed coat. "Greetings, Kindling Emperor Vinlin. You look well, Your Radiance."

In truth, the Emperor looked nothing of the sort. Vinlin regarded Oltrov through bloodshot eyes. "Have we met?"

Inac cleared his throat, standing. "It has for us been some time, Your Radiance. I believe we last spoke to one another in the forest near the Pinegrave."

"Please, spare me the tedious formalities." The Kindling Emperor waved a hand as if to dismiss Inac's words. "The last time I saw you was outside Canako, where *he*"—Vinlin crooked a finger squarely at me—"accused me of being a smuggler."

I appreciated what my friends were doing, trying to be tactful. In fact, they were just trying to buff out the edges of history. Lightmother knew if the Gild was in the throne's good graces, but I certainly wasn't. I closed my eyes and breathed out, fighting the urge to tell Vinlin he *was* smuggling a branch of the Grieving Pine.

"You're right, and I'm sorry for that. It was a petty use of the Agency's authority. Now I own that authority, I see I was wrong." I met the Emperor's considering gaze, then took a risk. "Where's Lorelay?"

If she truly had caused such a big mess, her mention could send the conversation spiraling just as easily as airing old grievances.

Vinlin's eyes softened, but then he frowned. "I thought she might be with you."

"With us? She doesn't know we're here."

The Kindling Emperor groaned. "That girl, I swear to the Lightmother..."

"She was well?" Inac asked. "When last you saw her?"

"That depends on your definition of well." Vinlin sighed. "Well enough to run off from her rooms, anyway. She wasn't there when I checked on her."

Had he gone to invite her to the meeting, or was there some darker purpose? Could she be held under watch? What mess had she caused?

I shook my head to clear the fog of suspicion from my mind. "Wherever she is, she's tough. I'm sure she's fine."

The smile I hoped to see on Vinlin's lips failed to appear. "Or she's off getting herself into more trouble. If I listened to my advisors who suspect you of sending her as political espionage, you would be locked up below the palace by now. The same cell I found her in would be fitting."

Inac and I looked at one another. Both of us had agreed on the plan to send Lorelay to Paceeq. Had it been a mistake?

"We...apologize for any trouble to you our envoy has caused." Inac lowered his head toward the Kindling Emperor.

Again, Vinlin waved Inac's words off. "Think nothing of it. I didn't listen to those advisors. I listened to her. She's convinced me of the threat these so-called Benefactors pose."

My eyebrows jumped up, elated. Lorelay had done her duty. "She has! That's great news. There's hope, then. Arza, show him."

The mortician had been waiting patiently in the seat beside me. She shuffled to her feet and unlatched the Archemetal case containing the Benefactor cure. "We've discovered a method to defeat the organism. Benefactors only become Emergent monsters when their host dies. That is when they become the most deadly. With this," she said, holding up the cure, "we can kill them while they are Incubating."

Vinlin rubbed the bridge of his nose. "Lorelay only told me there were monsters at our gates."

"She's right, in a way," I said. "She's wrong in that they're not at your gates. They're already inside the palace."

"Indeed?" The Kindling Emperor seemed less surprised than I expected. Was he holding something back from us?

"Which means they're likely all throughout the city," Arza added. "Only Incubating. We'd know if there were an Emergent."

"And the refugees aren't helping," Oltrov said, a comment that was particularly unhelpful. If he started thinking of the situation in those terms, the Emperor would blame us for this disaster on his doorstep.

"It's not a problem," I said, "not yet. The city isn't under threat. As long as no one dies—"

"Someone is always dying in a city," Oltrov interrupted. Whose side was he on? Whichever was likely to result in him getting better paid, I wagered. "Made enough money betting on funerary records to know that for sure."

"Then let us hope the infestation has not spread itself to the old and infirm," Inac said, scoffing at the Gildmember.

Arza shook her head in disagreement. "Any Benefactors here are likely young. They won't be powerful when they Emerge. That gives us time."

"We can use our cure to make sure none of this ever becomes a problem," I assured Vinlin, hardly feeling sure myself. We had some time, but did we have enough?

"I've sat through enough of my mother's audiences to sense there's a catch coming."

None of the other three spoke up, even though to do so was within Inac's authority. It was up to me to deliver the bad news.

"Liwokin has fallen to a powerful Emergent Benefactor. We need your Paladins to take back the city."

"Fallen?" Vinlin gaped. "How many Paladins?"

"How many do you have?" Oltrov asked. "We'll pay whatever you need, of course. The funding won't be a problem."

The Kindling Emperor held up a hand, silencing them all to create a moment to think. The conversation was over, then. Trying to add more now was only like to hurt our case.

But I felt good, confident we had presented our case well. I had Inac to help with diplomacy, and he hadn't misstepped yet. While the Kindling Emperor thought, expectations roiled in my mind, perhaps subtly influencing the decision to be made. We would receive the help we need. We had to.

After a stretch of time that seemed never-ending, Vinlin pursed his lips and gave his answer.

"No, I think not. My Paladins are no private army. They must remain to defend Paceeq."

CHAPTER FIFTY-ONE

Collapse

Hoggens' discredited report remains the only primary account of the Peeker hive known to the Institute; however, the surge of Peeker vessels arriving in Liwokin in recent years provides hope to those seeking to understand these creatures and their uses. Unlike demons, they show no signs of warlike behavior—though that is no reason to throw caution to the wind. As with dogs and horses, we must remain wary when learning to train these animals.

—Page 51, Institute of Biotism Peeker Compendium, Vol. I

Garret's ship arrived under cover of night. He told Tunnel to await his return, received a chittering confirmation, then disembarked, one among many refugees streaming into the port. The Peekers' vessel was far from the first to arrive after sailing three nights and three days, but the situation was as orderly a crisis Garret had ever seen. Where they were stopped by Paladins at a checkpoint, Garret slipped away. He knew where Lorelay would be. Only place she could be. The palace.

Atop its hill, the golden spires flanking white walls reached higher than even the Mother Tree. They reminded him of the Gild towers in Liwokin, but far older. Ancient. Garret couldn't picture their ancestors building such a behemoth.

Luckily, the palace's size made finding his way trivial. Why did people think they needed maps for their cities? Garret shook his head. Never made a lick of sense.

The streets of Vos were quiet. People slept softly, unaware the world was ending. Their security was weak. Let him walk all the way up the switchback hills to reach the palace gates. Only there did two guards stop him, their silver plate dull under the black night sky. The Brightdaughter seemed to have abandoned the capital of her Empire. Like she knew what was coming.

"Palace is closed," the older of the two Paladins ordered. Grizzled and bearded with a bulbous nose where the other was young with a shaved, feminine jawline. That was all Garret could make out beneath their helmets' visors. The elder hocked up something nasty from deep in his throat and spat. "Go home."

Garret returned the gesture. "Would love to. Only problem is it's half an Empire away, and you'll all be dead before I get there."

Both guards drew gleaming silver blades. Even the youth hadn't mistaken an Ekoan ranger for some passing beggar. Knew their business, Garret would give them that.

"Are you threatening a Paladin, Ekoan?"

Garret showed his palms. "Me? Never. But aye, it's under threat. I need to speak to Lorelay. Know her? Tall girl. Much prettier than either of you. Here on Agency business."

The Paladins exchanged glances. "We know her."

Sounded like Peekers the way they said it together. Their tone put a smile on Garret's face. "What did she do this time?

"Vinlin nearly had us switched when he found out we turned her away," the younger grumbled.

The elder Paladin glared at the rookie. Shook his head and sighed. "She's not here. Go—"

"I'll wait inside." Garret strode forward. Only hesitated for a moment when the youngster's sword twitched. They made the wise decision to allow his entry. "Agency matters. Can't tell you what it's about. But tonight, if I were you..." Garret called back over his shoulder. "I'd be holding my loved ones close. Might be the last chance you get."

Fair's fair. They let him in, he warned them. He didn't expect them to go running off. Stubborn bastards, Paladins. Look what it took to make Dunnax turn against Ulken. The only thing that mattered more to him than rank was his sister. It had gotten him killed, but Garret couldn't summon any ill thoughts of the man.

Standing here under a building so old it seemed part of the land itself, he had only gratitude for the man. He lived thanks to Dunnax's love for Lorelay.

Hope she's been as successful inspiring loyalty in the Emperor.

Where would her rooms be? Garret took off in the direction his gut told him to follow. No idea where it would take him, but he would find his way. Explore, learn the territory. The palace grounds were huge, and this late the austere halls were empty.

Of people, anyway. Garret had no trouble marking landmarks in his mind. There seemed no end to the variety of decoration in each open room and stretching hall. Peeker tunnels possessed natural beauty in their winding, intricate structure. No two were alike, from the crevices of rock to the placement of fungi bulbs.

So it was in the palace.

A new portrait or depiction of history hung on every wall. Feasts with hundreds of attendees. Battles from ancient wars of expansion. If not rendered in paint, then in stone or metal. Painted statues of Empresses long dead. Golden statuettes adorned marble tables, molded into a depiction of the Brightdaughter, angelic and radiant.

The beauty of it saddened him. Every rendering was a fiction. This art showed the lies the Empire was built on. The stories they taught their children again and again until they forgot what really happened. Most remarkable was how long it had been effective. The Empire survived for generations by self-deception. But a house founded on false belief can only collapse.

The only truth is the dirt, and how we all go back to it.

All this beauty would burn. Human survival would end.

I couldn't stop it.

Garret's fist squeezed around an idol of the Brightdaughter he found himself holding. He had let this happen. He hadn't even learned anything of the Skardwarf's weaknesses for his efforts. The Brightdaughter was trembling in his hand.

Sentyx could have stopped it. He could have killed Prost and ended this. He could have smashed the Peeker Queen's skull and stopped her Emergence. The blood of everyone in the Aerie was on *his* hands.

If it was the last thing he did before being torn apart by Peeker jaws, he would see justice brought to the one who caused this. Vowing the oath calmed him. Garret had purpose again. One last duty to perform in the end of days.

A familiar voice drifted down the hallway and reached the ranger's ears. Vinlin. Garret's eyes widened, but he smiled as he pocketed the golden idol. This was a surprise, though not altogether unexpected. A ranger always found his way eventually.

Even if he didn't know what he'd found.

His footsteps slowed when a slimy voice chimed in.

"—of course. The funding won't be a problem."

He knew that man. Oltrov, Garret found a nearby corner to eavesdrop from. Used a shiny bit of metal he kept with him to glance at those in conversation. Five of them, sitting at a table beneath an Archemetal chandelier in a room flying banners of the Empire so large Garret was sure they were compensating for something. Appeared to be a meeting in a reception hall. None of the attendees were looking his way, so he risked a peek leaning out of cover. And gasped.

Grim and Inac were there. Talking to the Emperor. Had Lorelay won their armies already? But they looked haggard. Why were they with Oltrov, Ulken's money man? And who was that mortician? Take Inac away and those Grim surrounded himself with were no different from the first Head's cronies. Better to stay quiet until he knew he could still trust the man. So, he did. And he listened.

"No, I think not. My Paladins are no private army. They must remain to defend Paceeq."

"Do you think you can stop them without us?" That was Grim, frustrated. "Your borders are already overrun. More people are fleeing Liwokin, most of them infested. But they're not all going to get away. Too many will be trapped by the Emergent. They'll be *his*. And they'll come for us. Not refugees, but an army."

"I agree," the mortician said. "All of my samples showed the same thing. The organism spreads at an alarming rate. It's like it's driven by some will, always reaching outward."

"It might be too late to stop the infestation from spreading in Vos." Grim sighed. "I'll do my best to stop them before they become a problem, but I can't guarantee none slip through." The Head sounded bitter about that. "We'll need your Paladins to kill the Emergents."

"So you've said." Vinlin sounded weary. "And I need them to deal with this crisis you've brought to my shores."

Garret knew a conversation going nowhere when he heard one. Appeared Lorelay had failed. Sounded like Grim had too. An Emergent loose in Liwokin. Well, if the Emperor needed motivation to flee the city, Garret had just the thing.

He stepped through the doorway and announced himself. "How about I gi—"

"Darkfather!" Grim exclaimed. "Garret!? What are—" He turned to the Emperor. "Don't you have guards?"

"And who is this?" the Emperor calmly stood and leered down at Garret.

Inac had sprung from his chair when Garret barged in. He returned to his seat, extinguishing the fireball he'd prepared to sling. "A friend. You are to me a welcome sight, Garret."

"Ah, yes...the thief." Vinlin narrowed his eyes. "I remember you."

Garret pulled the Brightdaughter's statuette from his coat and laid it on the table. "Wasn't stealing it, only admiring the palace's fineries."

Vinlin's pursed lips looked like a puckered anus, and Garret had to suppress his laughter. Easy to do, remembering what was following him to Paceeq.

"Tell me you've brought good news." Grim was on the verge of pleading. He really needed a victory.

No can do, boss.

"That crisis he brought?" Garret thumbed the Head. "Nothing compared to the storm of shit I've got on my heels."

"Explain yourself," Vinlin demanded.

"Prost got away."

Grim clenched his fists, muttered something under his breath.

"And he killed the Peeker Queen."

Arza gave a choked cry. "No..."

"She's Emergent," Garret finished. "Every Peeker in the Colony is under her control."

The room fell silent, as if the weight of the situation pressed all the air out of the room. He considered adding the coming Skardwarf invasion to their list of ails, but chances were they'd all be dead before the legions arrived. Still didn't know how to kill a Skardwarf anyway. Trying to prepare for them was like lighting the cookfire before hunting the hare.

Garret spat to break the tension. "Aye. It's bad." He remembered what he had been going to say before he scared the piss out of Grim. "Head's right. We need to go back to Liwokin. Not to clean up whatever mess is going on over there. To escape what's coming."

"No," Grim said resolutely. "To *prepare* for what's coming."

Arza nodded, patting an engraved golden box on the table before her. "Everything we need to make more of this cure is in Lawiko."

Garret's attention snapped toward the woman. *Cure? We're supposed to be killing them.*

Vinlin slammed a fist on the table. His wine goblet spilled a drop and stained the gold-trimmed white tablecloth. "You would have me abandon my country?"

"I would have you save your Empire." Grim let the words hang. He closed his eyes and exhaled. "Let me show you the future that awaits every city your people call home if you don't."

A darkness rushed over Garret's senses. A hand of lightning gripped the back of his skull. Instantly he was transported elsewhere, to the Market District in Liwokin.

It was under attack. Feral people held smashed shop-front glass with signs that called for justice and resistance. 'Kill the Killer,' some read, but they were killing *each other*. Fires erupted from buildings and nearly engulfed me as I barreled through the streets in search of the Benefactor. This was my fault. I had let an Emergence happen in Liwokin, and Liwo were killing fellow Liwo. Their eyes were veiled by false reality, and the only thing keeping those around me safe was a false reality of my own. My Aura.

The Benefactor distorted the shops and stalls around us. Streets bent and curled in sickening ways. Its Aura was strong, an old infestation. From the Riot, no doubt. More of Ulken's handiwork. As we marched closer to the beast a crushing pressure built up in my mind. Agony, yet somehow I stayed on my feet. This was my *home*.

He will not *destroy my city.*

The Deluge winked out, and Grim was holding his head and rubbing the sunken cavity of his eye socket.

No wonder he looked like he'd crawled from the Darkfather's anus. Liwokin had gone to the abyss. No recovering from that.

"I'm sorry," Grim croaked. "I should have warned you. I thought I could show you more, but..."

"It is all right," Inac said.

Some of the sadness in Grim's memory remained with the mage, as it did with Garret. He'd failed his people. Garret grimaced.

And I failed the whole world.

"What was that?" Vinlin stared at Grim, stricken with fear.

Whether that fear was for the Benefactor in the vision or the Benefactor sitting before him, Garret couldn't tell. Knew which one he was more bothered by, though.

Resorting to Deluges to make your point now, are you?

"That carnage awaits the whole Bright Empire if these monsters aren't stopped." Grim's voice was ragged, bestial.

"We attempted ourselves to unite Liwokin," Inac added, "but it was a failure. The same Benefactor led an insurgency to stop it and burn to ash the Financial District."

"Still nothing compared to the Peeker Queen and the Skard-warves," Garret muttered.

"More demons? Then the Dark Era truly is here..." Vinlin tried to speak under his breath, but Garret's ears were better than a Skard-warf's. "We're running out of time. You saved as many as you could. And I must do the same for my people."

Grim's exasperation came out in a huff.

"This is pointless," Garret announced. Quick as an adder, Garret had a knife in his hand.

"By the abyss," Oltrov, sitting in the chair beside Garret, hissed.

Garret brought the tip of the blade to his temple. "There's only one cure for the Queen. And none of us are getting close enough to administer it." Shuddering, he shook his head. "You haven't seen what I have."

Grim fixed him with a strange look. "No, I haven't. Not yet."

CHAPTER FIFTY-TWO

Discordant Music

Kill the witch! Kill the witch!
But the girl is innocent
Her brother's blood! It slicks her hand!
Despair has fallen on this land

Her whistled tune! It sounds our doom!
You must remember what is true
Her brother's tears! They fill the air!
But they were never really there

—Verses from Aura of the Storm

Vinlin's Paladins had put the disruption at the Cathedral to order by nightfall. Bringing the weight of the Empire's army to bear seemed enough to take down a Benefactor, but none of the men reported any Deluge or indescribable monster. In fact, no one had found anything at all amiss. A few bodies had to be cleaned from the once-pristine steps, but the official story was that a pickpocket had set off a panic when his knife missed a coin pouch and slipped into the side of a noblewoman.

Pure fabrication, but who were the common folk to question a decree from the Church of Light?

Lorelay, on the other hand, had long since made it her mission to question all the Bright Empire's proclamations, and old habits died hard. What was more, in this case she *knew* the story was a lie. She hardly blamed Vinlin for assenting to the cover story—sometimes a lie was necessary—but if there *was* a Benefactor in Vos, she needed to know the truth.

They should have found something *awry*. They had been searching for days, supposedly. If not the monster itself, some signs of its passage. A clawmark wound on an unlucky victim. *Something.* Clearly, most Paladins possessed too few wits to do more than uphold a strict book of rules. As soon as Lorelay got the chance—thanks to an unusual nighttime meeting Vinlin had scheduled with foreign envoys—she slipped away to perform a *real* investigation.

The only thing strange now was the eerie quiet that had fallen over this part of the city despite the earlier fighting and festivities. The Brightdaughter dipped far below the horizon, plunging Vos into total darkness while its citizenry slept. It was a night for thieves, but most of Vinlin's Paladins had been directed to the port to handle the influx of refugee ships. As luck would have it, the Kindling Emperor's order included the Paladins guarding the supply room where he stored the Grieving Pine branch. Lorelay resisted its alluring numbness and collected a Druid's Tear for her encounter with the monster.

The Paladins knew nothing of the Benefactors, that was the problem. Lorelay, sneaking through an alleyway in black leathers en route to the Cathedral, had the opposite problem. She knew too snuffing much of Benefactors. Knew they were always changing, appearing in the most unexpected places, never repeating the same approach. It kept a Finger on her toes.

Or was she an Eye? An envoy? The Emperor's consort? Labels little mattered. All Lorelay wanted was to do right by Dunnax, and she knew exactly how he would react to a Benefactor appearing in Vos. There would be time to prepare for the Dark Era's worst only if they held the lines during the enemy's first volley. She was the only one in the city with experience fighting Emergents, so she disobeyed Vinlin's orders to remain in her chambers one last time.

He worries too much. She considered the war that faced them. *Worries too much about* me, *anyway.*

Running a thumb over the smooth glass bead in her pocket, Lorelay was confident. She had no intentions of fighting the monster, only of performing reconnaissance. Once she located it and discerned its Aura, Paladins could handle the dirty work.

Truth be told, she expected to see some Paladins who had remained behind to monitor the situation at the cathedral. However, she reached the open expanse and found it entirely devoid of torchlight. No guards. She padded forward.

Then froze.

Was it a trap?

Her breathing hastened, but she continued forward with vigilance. Though she made not a sound, every step increased her confidence someone would spring from the darkness and attack her. The night lay so heavy it was claustrophobic. Only the distant entrance to the Cathedral of Light served as a guiding star. Or was she a moth drawn to its flame?

She tripped over some piece of detritus and nearly blew her cover with a yelp. Even the sound of the wood she kicked skittering across the cobblestones could reveal her to someone close by. Lorelay froze, awaiting some sign she was no longer alone.

Her ears caught a faint sound behind her, like the whisper of skin scraping stone. A low, guttural growl put her in mind of a beast with gaping maw reaching forth to snatch her from behind. Lorelay stayed still...until clicking mandibles sounded in her ears.

Lorelay screamed and ran, positive she had to escape. The harder she ran, the more certain she grew that death was fast on her heels. She had no mind to fight it. Whatever it was that chased her, it was nothing she could handle alone. The last time she was in this scenario, Reed had just warned her Hand to run or die. A Benefactor trampled the ground flat in pursuit.

Nearing the safety of the Cathedral, Lorelay risked a look over her shoulders. Darkness obscured the monster, but...no pounding footsteps hounded her. Nor did any slavering beast's breath fall hot on her face. Her eyes widened, and she reached for the Druid's Tear in her pouch.

"Remember what's real," Lorelay told herself, jabbing the glass needle into her thumb. Blood welled and devoured the teardrop toxic. Calm washed over her, driving panic and fear to the recesses of her mind.

Tension draining from her body, Lorelay turned about and surveyed the empty square. The Cathedral's interior fires cast enough light through the wide doors to see by. Her fears were clearly unfounded, for she was entirely alone.

"Then where are you?" she mused aloud.

An Aura without a Benefactor. The creatures were ever-changing, but that stretched even Lorelay's understanding of the monsters. Was it invisible? Briefly she tensed, but no...that was the panic again. The Aura still touched her thoughts when she let it, but it was subdued behind the Druid's Tears like a musician playing in a room with thick stone walls. She could still hear the discordant music, only faintly.

An idea formed. Lorelay strode up the stairs of the cathedral. The music quieted. Returning to where she was, it grew louder. Paying attention to such an ephemeral thing proved difficult, but she circled the square looking like a madwoman until her efforts finally paid off.

The detritus she had kicked...it was no ordinary litter. It was a Clasform box, the same as she had in Reed's Woods. But those were meant to disrupt the Aura, as far as she remembered. What was wrong with this one?

Perhaps she let the Aura influence her once more, but her fears this time seemed rational. If something like this was in the city...what did that mean? Someone from the Agency was in the city, hunting a Benefactor? Lorelay turned the Clasform over in her hands, running through the implications in her mind.

But this was unlike the Clasform she knew from Reed's Woods. It gave off an Aura of panic, made Paladins kill Paceeqi. Lorelay tightened her grip around the box and looked at the blood that had yet to be scrubbed from the stone. If one of these wound up in the Radiant Palace, would the Paladins be able to save Vinlin from—

Lorelay's thoughts ground to a halt. Most Paladins had been sent to handle the refugee crisis.

Again, she ran, this time with no care for who spied her in the streets. She felt no fear, only desperation. Vinlin was in danger. She had to warn him.

Just as she reached the switchback leading to the Radiant Palace, a jolt of lightning crackled at the base of her skull, and Lorelay knew what the sensation meant. There was no mistaking it this time. A Deluge. A Benefactor was Emerging in Vos.

Before she knew it, the city burned around her.

CHAPTER FIFTY-THREE

Only a Man

Where there is bloodshed, the organism spreads most effectively. A lesson from the home I left behind.

—Excerpt from a stolen notebook

"No, I haven't," I said. "Not yet."

I needed to see for myself what happened in the Peeker Mounds. Memories conveyed what words could not. My head still ached from reliving Bello's mental assault in the Market. I meant to show them the burning Gild, to show the monster loose in my home, but couldn't even do that right. My control over my Benefactor was still amateur—what if I failed to see through Garret's eyes. Could I end up scrambling his mind, making him as mad as me?

While I considered the idea, Garret backed away like a rabbit cowering before a dog, affixing me with a suspicious look. What had gotten him so jumpy? In all my time spent with the Ekoan ranger, I had never seen him so afraid. His fear had a sense of urgency about it.

"How long do we have, Garret?"

The Ekoan sheathed his knife, then shrugged. "'Til those monsters finish eating all the meat left in the Aerie. With travel time, reckon that gives us five or six days to get out of here."

"We are not abandoning the city," the Kindling Emperor declared once more.

"I know, I know. We're not abandoning anything," I said, thinking of Liwokin. "But we don't have long to—"

"My *coronation* is in *two* days," Vinlin complained. "It will not be disrupted. If what you say is true, Ekoan, and a fight is coming, my people need a beacon of light. They need a leader."

Garret laughed. "Bright Emperor or big-titted wench in a whorehouse. Taste the same to a Peeker, I guarantee you. You can stay and sit in your fancy chair, or you can come with us and live."

The Kindling Emperor didn't hesitate. "I'm staying with my people."

Garret shook his head. "Your fool choice."

"No..." I said, eying Vinlin. He sat straight-backed in his chair, composed. Dignified. Face resolute. Despite myself, I admired the man, putting his peoples' lives before his own.

It was the choice I wished I had made. Jacquin might have valued my life above any other, but that wasn't a lie I could start believing. If I wasn't careful, it would start to become true. It would only be too easy.

"A brave choice," I said, then looked to my companions. "One we will match."

Oltrov started. "Shouldn't we talk about—"

Inac cut him off, nodding. "If we do not ourselves support the Capital, why should we expect from the throne any help?"

Garret scoffed. "Got no idea what you're talking about. None of you do. Stay here and die, fine. I'm leaving." He started for the door.

Anger surged through me. "When did you become such a coward?"

"Cowardice?" the Ekoan spat. "Aye, whatever you say. I'll be alive to mourn over your brave graves. You don't understand—"

"Then help me," I urged. "Help me understand."

Garret threw his hands up. "What do you think I've been trying to do?"

"No, not like that." I glanced at Vinlin. He hadn't reacted as strongly as I expected receiving my Deluge. Maybe he was demonstrating his fortitude in the face of ignorance. Hesitating, I decided it was better he knew the whole truth. "I can control my Benefactor... somewhat. View your memories with the Peekers."

"So it's true," Vinlin mused. "What Lorelay said. You're infested."

Garret returned a more skeptical look, but eventually relented. "Doubt I could stop you if I said no," he muttered. "But fine, if it'll convince you to get your asses out of here...do it."

Doubt crept in. "You're sure?"

Inac laid his hand on my shoulder. "It will for him be okay. Nothing happened to me."

"Oh good, so I'm not your first lab rat." Garret crossed his arms.

"Think of your time in the Mounds," I told him, then before he could make another wise remark I focused on the cloud of Archedark swirling about his head.

Tentatively, I reached in, until my Benefactor latched onto him. Memories surfaced and invited me to delve deeper. I did, following the currents wherever they took me.

I arrived in the harbor of Myrme with Tunnel and Sentyx. Watched through Garret's eyes as he investigated Prost, studied Peekers, and deceived Sentyx. Only one of the three were what I had commanded. After the Skardwarf rampaged in the Feeder Hollows, I found myself standing in the Queen's Grotto.

No...*I* wasn't there.

Garret was.

I had to keep him separate from myself. Again I struggled to maintain awareness of the situation. I was in the Radiant Palace. Siphoning Garret's memories, witnessing events as he perceived them.

What I saw terrified me.

Garret rushed forward through a crowd of tens of thousands after Sentyx rejoined his brother's side. His arrows missed, and Prost dealt the killing blow to the Peeker Queen. A Deluge took him, plunging me deeper into the depthless sea of memories. Hundreds were slaughtered as he escaped through the Human Aerie. Peekers surged forth in forms I had never seen before, stronger and faster than any man. My friend threw himself over a balcony rather than face one in combat.

So many were left to die, a feast of flesh to welcome the new Benefactor. But Garret survived. He always did.

I forced my Benefactor to release its grip. It did so unwillingly, and I opened my eyes.

Garret was rubbing his head. "Thought you said nothing happened to you."

"Nothing long term," Inac said. "I was unconscious when Grim did to me this thing."

Arza put a hand to her face to hide a smile.

A smile was the furthest thing from my lips. Garret was no coward. He was a realist. Now I saw what he was running from, my legs ached to start moving right away. "He's right...Vos will fall, Vinlin. We cannot save it."

I had to show them. None of our planning would pay off, not with an endless horde of Peekers bearing down on us. I began the Deluge—

The door slammed open against the wall.

"Vinlin!" Lorelay shouted. "You're safe." She stopped short. "Garret? Grim, Inac!" She clapped the Ekoan on his back on her way to me and Inac, then wrapped us both in a tight embrace. "Lightmother, it's good to see you. Have you brought more Fingers? A Benefactor just Emerged in the city."

Everyone sitting shot to their feet.

Everyone but Vinlin.

"Then...I'm too late," the Kindling Emperor said.

Lorelay went to his side, placed a palm on his red-stubbled cheek. "Oh, Linny...there was nothing you could have done."

Linny?

I looked at Inac, who shrugged. There would be time to figure out what sort of mess she'd caused later.

"That makes no sense," Arza muttered to herself. More loudly when I told her to speak up, she continued, "An Emergent in Vos already? They would have to be spreading an order of magnitude faster than my models predict."

"With so many refugees," Lorelay said, "it was a matter of time."

That was the same conclusion I had come to. With a sigh, I commiserated. "Seems our enemy is always one step ahead. The Benefactors. Prost and his Skardwarves..."

Garret spat. Had it really transpired as he remembered? Sentyx betrayed us. I felt the same pain Garret did but shoved it down. When the Benefactor Emerged in Vos, however, I felt...nothing.

"Where's the Benefactor, Lorelay? Are you sure?"

Lorelay slapped hands down on the table, frustrated. "I don't know. I found a Clasform box that gave off an Aura. Panic. I stored it somewhere safe before coming."

Garret produced a familiar box from beneath his cloak. "Like this?" Lorelay gasped. "Means Prost is already here. Found this in a stockpile in Myrme."

My eyes widened. "Those boxes were stolen by Cavern."

"A Skardwarf?" Lorelay shook her head. "But what about the Emergence? I came back to warn Vinlin, and that's when I got hit with the Deluge. It was horrible. People slaughtering each other in the streets. Buildings burning. I thought it was real."

I narrowed my eyes, then sucked in a sharp breath when I realized what happened.

Darkfather. How much of the city did I inflict that on?

"It's okay, Lorelay. That was me."

"You? But—"

"Tell me people were okay when it ended," I pleaded.

"I...I think so. They were shaken. Most just wanted to return to their homes."

Relief came in a small measure. What if I had shown the whole city the swarm that would soon descend on them? If I wasn't careful,

I might have the blood of another riot on my hands. And it would be a small mercy, for those who died by human hands and not Peeker jaws.

But I had done this properly before. When I intimidated the Council, no one outside their hall was affected. If I could repeat what I had done...

"I need to show you all what's coming," I said, focusing on five of the six storms of Archedark surrounding me. "You may want to sit."

Garret's memories were one with my own—in one small portion, at least. When I instructed my Benefactor to latch onto the heads of everyone in the room, those memories streamed into the minds of these unfortunate few who were now burdened by the truth. We were all in this together, and they witnessed every grizzly detail.

When the vision ended, Inac and Arza were crying. Vinlin had sicked up over his chair arm. Lorelay hadn't found a seat, and so sat on the floor holding her head, legs folded beneath her.

"You didn't get that, did you?" I asked Garret. He responded with a shake of his head. It worked, then. I controlled who saw the vision. "Figured I'd spare you reliving that nightmare."

Garret grunted. "We'll all be reliving it if we don't escape."

"No," Oltrov said, running two fingers through his mustache. He picked up the Clasform box to examine. "This is a good thing. You discovered Prost would travel to Eko or Paceeq after his time in Myrme. Would he come here if that monster he unleashed was on its way?"

For any normal person, that would have been a good point. But I knew a bit of Prost's mind. "Of course he would. He'll believe he's in control of them right up until the moment they kill him."

"Taktus often wrote of his master," Arza said, sniffling. "He admired the man's uncanny ability to predict events and his unwavering confidence in that ability even more so." She snorted. "He believed Prost saw visions of the future. Nonsense, of course, but he was thinking in the right direction. If Prost doesn't believe the Peekers will come here, perhaps he is correct."

Hearing this heartened the Kindling Emperor. "Well, then. If there is no Peeker threat, and there is no Benefactor...we're only dealing with a man."

Garret grinned wolfishly. The fight seemed to have returned to him. "Not just a man. Two Skardwarves as well, but I've just the thing for them." Between two fingers he toyed with the Peeker gem he'd stolen.

Arza nodded. "I think I know what you are suggesting. I can help with this."

Garret grunted. He'd picked up some habits from the Skardwarf. "The rest will be easy. I've seen how Prost works. The man doesn't run. He shows up exactly where you expect him to, only for you to find he's outmaneuvered you."

I smiled. "This time, he doesn't know we're here."

Garret had believed that in the Peeker Mounds as well, but this time, the man was halfway across the Empire when Liwokin fell. He couldn't have predicted I would travel to Vos. Nor my abilities with the Benefactor. I had to believe that, or I'd be mired down trying to predict his predictions of my predictions. If my mind went down that spiral, it seemed all of reality might collapse.

"Yes," Inac said. "It is to me obvious where he will strike."

"That's what most worries me," Lorelay said.

"My coronation." Vinlin sighed. "I don't suppose I can dissuade you from turning a nice event into a trap?"

CHAPTER FIFTY-FOUR

Sunset

The fields we sow will feed the world
When she returns to end our plight
Spread the word, haven't you heard?
About the coming of the Light

—Verse from Plant the Seed,
Second Song of Dawn

"You don't blame him for all this, do you?" Lorelay asked.

Vinlin had a sore spot for Grim, and as far as she could tell, it was entirely the Head's own doing. She sensed both men's agitation increasing as the meeting stretched into early dawn, discussing their plans for Prost. They were a bad match for one another—Grim resented Vinlin's royalty, and the Emperor viewed him as an upstart.

He *was* an upstart, Lorelay could not deny that, but the Benefactors and the Peeker Queen were not his fault.

The Kindling Emperor paused, the echoes of his footsteps fading in the spiral staircase. Lorelay silently thanked the Lightmother for the break. Her muscles had grown sore ceaselessly climbing step after step. She had hardly slept, with the Brightdaughter shining onto her pillow and their impending doom darkening her thoughts.

Those dark thoughts lingered, but witnessing Vinlin rise to his position found a way to brighten them when she most needed it. He had become so serious, as grave as their situation. Looking up at him, two steps above her in their climb to top a Fire Garden spire, flickering flame lighted his thoughtful face.

Thoughtful, but impossible to read. What was he thinking?

The Archefire mote Vinlin held aloft to light their way wavered, and he continued upward. "No, I don't blame him. I only grow annoyed with him. He is so swept up in his own priorities, he doesn't consider all the bigger picture."

Lorelay snorted. "Sounds like Grim. Single-minded. But he does try to do the right thing. That's more than you can say for the last Head. Snuffing man *welcomed* the Dark Era."

The Brightdaughter failing, cities falling, an infestation of Benefactors spreading. All of it was connected and would bring nothing but suffering. What could have possibly passed through Ulken's mind to convince him to hasten the world's demise?

Prost's words in his ears. Lorelay heard her thoughts in Garret's voice. The Eevoqian had something to gain from the chaos Ulken caused. Exactly what that was remained a mystery the ranger failed to solve. Garret sulked about that all night, almost as hard as he sulked over letting Prost escape.

Vinlin forgave Garret—which only seemed to make the Ekoan more uncomfortable. With a horde of Peekers approaching and Liwokin fallen, war had become inevitable, calling for the Paladins to be deployed. The Church of Light, however, failed to see it.

The Kindling Emperor wanted to deploy the royal navy to blockade the strait, a precaution in case they were wrong about the Peeker threat. Unfortunately, the power to command the armies would only be granted to Vinlin upon his coronation as Bright Emperor. Until then, they were vulnerable to the north.

All they could do was prepare for when their forces answered to Vinlin. Inac assisted with strategizing. The mage, surprisingly, had a mind for warfare and logistics, though he claimed it was all theoretical, stuff he had read in books.

None of their preparations fooled them into believing the fighting would fail to reach Vos. Lorelay and her allies would make their first stand here in her home. Prost had already struck the first blow, but they would soon strike the next.

If there was any bright spot in the pending calamity, it was that it had driven allies together. In darkness, light. The Agency joined with the throne. Garret would sail home to enlist the rangers. Even the High Cleric's stance against Vinlin had softened, once they explained what happened during the incident outside the Cathedral of Light. Not enough to take the appropriate measures to protect the city, but Namravi at least listened without protest when Lorelay explained the Clasform box.

The Dark Era might be near, but never had the union of those fighting for the Lightmother been stronger.

"Yes, well, Grim may not welcome the Dark Era," Vinlin said, "but he's only useful because of that parasite in his head. Lightmother knows the Agency is providing little in terms of manpower."

Lorelay huffed. "The Agency provided *me*." She smiled lopsidedly at Vinlin's back.

"I only meant—"

"Oh hush. I know what you meant. You're wrong, though. The Agency exists to fight these monsters. Grim may have been driven away, but don't think they'll give up Liwokin without a fight."

"I hope you're right."

"I am." Her optimism rose with her ascent up the spire. "And we can trust Grim. He..." She choked up as grief snuck up on her. "He buried my brother with me. *He* avenged Dunnax."

Vinlin stopped and turned around, his eyes showing compassion in the firelight. "I understand, Lorelay. If you say he's a good man, I trust you."

Her lopsided smile straightened out. "Thank you."

"Not that I have much choice in the matter, do I?" Vinlin sighed.

"Is that what you brought me up here for? To complain about how they're ruining your coronation?"

"That is precisely the last thing I want to talk about. No. I'll show you."

He sighed again, this time in relief, which Lorelay repeated as she joined him at the spire's pinnacle and stepped out into a refreshing breeze. She rushed to the railing, eyes wide but heedless of the several hundred pace drop she leaned over. From the top, the whole of the Empire seemed to surround her.

South and east the great seas stretched unending, and Lorelay swore she saw the Shadowson's faint blue light on the horizon. She ran northward around the circular spire until she gazed upon the fertile arm of Lawiko, a landmass too distant to discern details, but where she knew fields of golden wheat swayed in the cold wind. Further north the navy sailed, protecting the city from the Queen.

"Isn't this view amazing?" Lorelay turned back to Vinlin. He stood huddled near the spire's center, an Archemetal peak carved into the likeness of a flame frozen in time. "What's the matter, Linny?" she teased. "Scared of heights?"

Vinlin took a cautious step toward her, keeping his hand on the interior railing. "Yes...actually."

Warmth flushed through Lorelay's face. It took strength to admit weakness. She took his hand in hers. "Come on. I won't let you fall."

They circled west to where the Brightdaughter set, lowering toward the vineyards and orchards that covered the hills beyond the city walls. Rolling creeks reflected the deepening red of dusk. Crimson streaks in the landscape. Her lips drew down. Visions of blood-streaked streets in Liwokin haunted her mind. How easily they could become the streets of Vos, the blood of the Emperor.

"I...worried about you," Vinlin said. "Last night. When I found you missing from your chambers."

"You didn't read my note?"

"Hunting Benefactor, back soon?" Vinlin's face drooped. "Scared the light out of me. I'm just glad you returned safely."

"Funny," she said. His words were sunlight to a wilting flower for how they rose Lorelay's spirits.

"What is?"

"You. Scared for me?" Lorelay laughed. "I'm a Rank Four Finger."

"Is that high?"

"Means I've killed four Benefactors, so you've got nothing to worry about."

You worry too much.

Those had been Dunnax's last words to her. But he was wrong. She worried because she cared. About her brother.

And about Vinlin.

His arms wrapped around her in a hug. When did she start crying?

"Realizing the danger in the city, rushing back to protect you..." Her forehead dug into his shoulder. "I was so afraid." Her throat constricted so tightly, it took all the strength of her lungs to force out the quiet words. "I don't want to lose anyone else."

Vinlin shivered as he drew in a sharp breath. His fingers pressed into her back, pulling her into a tighter embrace. He held her there, then relaxed, drew back and looked her in the eyes. His were filled with tears, but he was smiling.

"All this," the Kindling Emperor said, looking out toward the setting sun. "Our country, our home. The Lightmother blessed us to live in such a world, did she not? She blessed us as well with the strength to overcome our trials. We will prevail over the darkness, as did our ancestors before us." Vinlin turned his smile back to Lorelay. "Don't lose hope. *'Think not of the night's deepest Darkness but remember the brightness of day.'*"

"Quoting the Book of Light at me? You don't know me at all."

His face held a self-satisfaction. "Then why are you smiling?"

Lorelay was smiling, she realized. "'*Who trusts not in Light is lost to a path of shadow, but the Fire of a fellow traveler can illuminate the way.*'"

"Ah, so you do know your verses."

"I'm a musician. I know more verses than you could dream of."

Vinlin smirked. "I can dream of quite a few. Take this one. '*When swords and bows fail, we're left only with song. There's no darkness or light in just singing along.*'"

Lorelay's mouth hung agape. His singing voice could use work, but his intonation was perfect. More importantly, he sang it with heart. "My song..."

"My favorite of yours is still the one about the lusty Peeker maid." He snorted. "Nearly drove the horses off the Canako road and into a ditch hearing that one."

"I can't believe you remember that." She flushed with embarrassment. She had sung *It Takes Two* to the Bright Prince? Oh, Lightmother.

"I'll never forget it," Vinlin said, taking her hands in his. "A day so bright, no darkness could ever tarnish it. The first day I spent with you."

She stared into Vinlin's glistening eyes, golden with the Brightdaughter's light. Her heart beat in her throat, stopped any words from getting through. She leaned forward. Closer, until their lips touched. Lorelay wrapped her arm around Vinlin's neck and kissed him.

For a moment, Vinlin failed to react, stunned, and Lorelay wondered if she misstepped. Then his arms wrapped around her waist, held her securely, and Vinlin's lips pressed more tightly against hers. His beard scratched her cheeks. There was no time to shave while Vinlin dealt with one crisis after another. He handled her as confidently as he handled his statecraft and knew when a gentleman should give a lady some air.

It was better than she expected from someone who once had no romantic prospects save for a marriage arranged by his mother.

When they disentangled, Lorelay felt dizzier than she had when struck by the heights. She kept ahold of the railing for safety.

"It's almost time." Vinlin was out of breath, she noticed.

"For what?"

"There." He pointed. "See the hillside with the rock formation?"

She nodded. Over the city, beyond a stretch of farmland, a boulder atop a hill cast a dark shadow on the valley.

"The Brightdaughter will set on that hill at the onset of dusk. A rare event, a good omen, the mathemelodians say. They say you should speak your intent to the Brightdaughter to make it so."

"What's so special about that hill?"

"It's not the hill that's special, but this view. Only on a day like today can it be seen. The Brightdaughter rose at true east and will set on this hill, where the obelisk marks true west. The longest possible day. The Lightmother blesses us with the time we need to prepare. Tomorrow, we will win our first battle against the darkness."

Hearing him say it, she could almost believe they would come through the ordeal alive. That she truly would lose no one else.

"Watch."

The sun's setting quickened as it approached the horizon. Lorelay and Vinlin held hands in silent anticipation to witness the end of a bright day.

When the shining disk of the Brightdaughter reached the stone obelisk, the shadow in the valley flared with light and revealed a radiant lake. Kaleidoscopic flames danced across the shimmering surface of the water, the Brightdaughter's light amplified to an eye-watering magnitude. Then, all at once, it disappeared, and dusk had begun. The Church of Light rang its arrival all throughout the city.

The effect the spectacle produced in Lorelay, she would not soon forget.

"The mathemelodians are a strange people," Vinlin said, "but smart. And they're right. This is a good omen. I've only seen two others in my lifetime, and I'm not sure how many more I'll see before my time ends. Until then, I can think of no better way to usher in the night than by refusing to dim my light. Lorelay."

Hearing her name drew her attention away from the spectacular lake. Its afterimage still danced in her eyes. She turned to Vinlin.

The Kindling Emperor was holding Elzia's crown on an unwrapped cloth. Lightmother, when had he gotten that?

"I love you, Lorelay. I want you to be my Bright Empress. Fight the darkness by my side. Together, our flames will burn with such light, the darkness will never overcome us."

CHAPTER FIFTY-FIVE

Coronation

*After Empress Alzenia's reign ended—cut short by lack of prudence—
the wounds of tragedy cut deeper still when her daughter's reign failed
to begin, cut even shorter by lack of practice.*

*—Excerpt from Rays of Light:
A Complete History of Vos' Royal Lineages*

The Kindling Emperor's coronation looked exactly like I expected it would.

The Radiant Palace throne room was resplendent in color. Stained glass used the Brightdaughter's light to paint the canvas of stark white walls and pillars. Crimson banners hung resolute and motionless, flying the Empire's starburst sigil. The same sigil that appeared on the coins changing hands between too many brightly garbed noblemen for my liking.

"Six hundred stars says he'll end up naught but a pile of ash."

Six hundred? Is he mad? There hasn't been an uncontrolled burn in centuries. "Is that all? You must not be so certain. Not worth my—"

"Twelve!"

Too much money and too little sense, as always, you dark-loving fool.

The nobles' thoughts confused me as I searched the sprawling chamber through their eyes. Momentary flashes of awareness from one person, then the next, continuously changing perspective as I jumped from one Incubating Benefactor to another. Long enough to seek any sign of Prost but brief enough not to cause the sudden onset of head pain.

The Kindling Emperor wanted his guests to enjoy the event.

I hoped they'd be able to as well, though the bets whether there would be a death this day sowed the seeds of doubt. What did they know that I didn't? Searching through their eyes was invasive enough. I wasn't about to siphon the memories of the entire Vos nobility, even if delving into their minds could provide vital information about Prost.

Some choices can't be unmade. The warning passed through my mind in Yezna's voice. She wanted nothing to do with this plan, and I couldn't blame her. Once you tread too far into the abyss, there's no returning. I was already on the brink of overstepping a line that would be all too easy to cross.

Most of the colorfully garbed men and women in the throne room were real nobility. They filled the stairways and corridors surrounding the already stuffed main hall, come to witness the highest of Bright Empire ceremonies. Cordoned-off balconies provided elevated viewing, and above those were entire sections reserved for the wealthiest of Vos's families. Outside the Radiant Palace, Vinlin's Paladins staved off crowds of infested beggars and refugees—and some of the city's poorest citizens.

If I had the mental faculties, I would have been monitoring that situation more closely. An Emergence in that crowd was all too likely. Sensing and suppressing it from afar would work. That was all I could manage while maintaining my Aura.

Most of the nobility were real. Likewise, I spent most of my concentration *avoiding* cloaking them with my Aura. Focusing only on the infested Paladins I hid from Prost proved difficult. The rest must have been infested too, only weakly, for no Archedark swirled around their heads.

I was meant only to remain unseen in a private suite, disguising the trap to spring on Prost. But the allure of seeing through their eyes was too great to resist. And all too easy. My Benefactor grew stronger. A problem for later. Until then, I would put my curse to good use.

Try to sneak in, Prost. Try it. I'll see you.

* * *

"Always feels good when you snare your prey," Garret said to the Paladin striding beside him, then sighed. "Today, we're going to catch the big one." Garret chuckled. "Literally."

The Paladin huffed. "Eyes up."

What did I say?

Surely, he'd been briefed on what Prost looked like. Then again, these were Paladins, not rangers. Garret marched beside the man, stiff-backed and square-jawed. A soldier in a religious army, as rigid as they came. Not like a ranger, flowing with the lay of the land. The Paladins posted guards at all the entrances, leaving one unguarded to tempt the man's entrance.

Stupid plan, but what do I know?

Besides, the plan wouldn't make a difference when the enemy arrived. All this patrolling was a waste. Garret's energy was better spent waiting for the trap to spring.

Won't be pretty, but survival rarely is.

Garret spat, and the Paladin scoffed and stomped off. "It's because I'm short, isn't it?"

Unusually short for a Paceeqi, but maybe no one would notice. If Grim's Aura was working, maybe he'd even be tall. He grimaced. On second thought, he preferred being short. Women seemed to like tall men, and he didn't want to encourage Arza any further.

Brilliant mind, that woman. As fine a biotist as he'd seen. *Mortician?* Terrible title. Whatever they called her in Liwokin, Arza had a deeper understanding of the interactions between Peeker and Skardwarf Patterns than even he could follow. As smart as she was beautiful, with that dark braided hair and the intense gaze in her hazel eyes. No, her looks didn't put Garret off her. She was just barking up the wrong tree.

More likely, she was just tired. Making bad decisions at the end of the world like they all were.

Stupid snuffing plan. Don't they realize how many people are going to get killed?

That was a best case scenario. How many ambushes from bandit nests ended up best case? Zero.

The list of ways this plan could go wrong was innumerable. Top of Garret's mind was Grim's role. He was playing with dangerous powers. If Ulken had those, none of Hand Sixty-Four would be left standing. And Grim wasn't so different from Ulken as he imagined.

Who's to say the wrong word from Prost doesn't end up in his ear, and he turns that power against us all?

One member of Hand Sixty-Four had already betrayed the rest. Only made sense more treachery was afoot. Hiding reality with the Benefactor's Aura? Abyss take him if that wasn't an abuse of his power. Made Grim untrustworthy at the least. Worst case, he was a monster.

Garret didn't change his stride. He was here to hunt monsters, after all.

* * *

Bright Empress of an empire at war. Was that who Lorelay wanted to be? Surrounded by many strangers and few friends, she had little to talk about and much to think about. Just as well, as she had little part to play in Vinlin's ceremony.

Like a rehearsed dance to a familiar tune, she told herself. *We're prepared. Vinlin will be fine.* Her words did little to soothe the butterflies in her stomach.

She had given Vinlin no answer, only asked whether they had to be married that night. A prospect more enticing than she ever would have guessed. But if she agreed, must she too be crowned on the morrow? That seemed to worry the Kindling Emperor, and he assured her she would not.

Lorelay played her part, small though it was. She stood closest in attendance to the throne, alongside Inac, dignified guests of the Kindling Emperor. The golden Archemetal chair's high back depicted the elongated sunburst of the Bright Empire, oriented toward a circular, east-facing window, looking out upon the dawn. The primary seat of power in the dominion of the Brightdaughter. Empty for too long, prepared for reclamation.

Vinlin had yet to appear for the proceedings, hence the din of chattering strangers. She knew not which of them were even real and which were cloaked by Grim's new powers. She recognized a fair few.

It can't be them, can it?

How could she be sure? They were treading unmarked territory. There had never been a Benefactor like Grim. There had never been a Bright Emperor. Vinlin was the first in history. The Bright Empress always took a husband, but the man never held true power. He was more of an official advisor, Vinlin explained, and responsible for raising the children.

Lorelay's stomach fluttered. *Children.* How to even begin untangling her thoughts surrounding heirs?

That was the old world. However the day proceeded, the Bright Empire would be forever changed. Was there time for love and children when fighting a war for survival? Somehow, it was better than the alternative. If Prost prevented the coronation, the Bright Empire would fall to the darkness without putting up a fight.

It won't happen.

Vinlin would be a beacon to guide them through shadow. She imagined him sitting the throne, Brightdaughter shining overhead. With a smile, she pictured herself standing beside the Bright Emperor, aglow. And she would be...what? Bright Empress with equal power? A glorified advisor? Mother of Vinlin's children?

Her lips curled down. It would be nothing like that, would it? The dawn window would remain dark. Tens of thousands would die fighting Peekers and Benefactors and Skardwarf demons. Every day would bring new trials, a life of constant bitter struggle. Only...she knew the weight Vinlin already bore. Adding more brought out ever more strength in the man. A verse from the Book of Light came to mind.

'If you must brave the darkness with one alone, seek she who brightest burns.'

As if the world acted to serve Lorelay, a door behind the throne opened, and musicians played a bombastic fanfare. Admittedly, a fine rendition of *The Daughter's Rise*, though it hardly fit the occasion, the ceremony being the ascendance of Elzia's son.

All attendees turned rapt attention to the dais where the High Cleric had been waiting to greet the Kindling Emperor. Vinlin hurriedly took his place before the Church's leader and knelt to receive his blessing. In the hush, Lorelay frowned when Vinlin whispered, "Let's get this over with, Namravi."

Vinlin's hands fidgeted beneath his overly long gold and red robes. He was more nervous than Lorelay was, and she felt like her lyre's strings had just snapped as she took the stage. Her nerves were only worsened by how helpless she felt. Lorelay had only to wait and pray nothing went wrong. Failing that, she wore boots under her dress rather than slippers, solely for the purpose of keeping her knives. If she spotted Prost before Grim, one of those would find its way to his eye socket, ceremony be damned.

The High Cleric opened with a prayer. "Lightmother, whose daughter art our guiding star, shield the Kindling Emperor from the Darkfather's will. Usher in the unfailing dawn, that thy daughter may witness her Bright Empire thrive."

Vinlin stood proudly looking out upon the quiet audience. "It heartens me to see you all here. I know a male Bright Emperor is nothing anybody expected, but I'm determined to make the best of it. Now, more than ever, we need to support each other. Whether I ascend to the throne this day or not, the most challenging of times lie ahead."

Lorelay kept her face stiff while Vinlin paused to take a slow breath. He should not have spoken of failure. It made the possibility all too real in her mind.

"'When the Son of the Father overhead doth roam, then shall the Daughter's Light guide us home.' Trust that her guidance has not forsaken us in these dark times. Indeed, it is ever when our need is greatest that our kindred light shines brightest." The Kindling Emperor looked right at Lorelay, and her stomach clenched when he recited a line from one of her songs, *In Darkness Come. "Together in light or in darkness come, the day is not over 'til say we done."* Vinlin returned his gaze to the wider nobility, and his voice boomed. "The will of the Lightmother shall never bend. The Bright Empire shall burn brighter than ever. The line of Elzia remains strong. Witness my flame!"

The gathered nobility must have expected more ceremony, for when Vinlin turned and strode to the throne their idle gossip redoubled. Some of it reached her ears.

"That's it? We closed our shops for this?"

"Think I'll have that wager after all. Four thousand says ash."

"Even his robes are mismatched. Oh, I do miss Elzia's fashion sense."

If Lorelay could hear them, she knew Vinlin could as well. Yet the words showed no effect in his body language or face. Stoic. He sat the throne as if it was meant for him from birth. The Kindling Emperor closed his eyes.

"Silence!" the High Cleric commanded.

The crowd hushed.

Vinlin breathed, slow and deep.

Lorelay's own breath caught in her throat. The entire world hinged on the next moments. Lorelay felt like she was about to break.

Glass shattered instead, then rained down on the screaming nobility. Stone cracked, and the floor shook. Lorelay whirled around, searching. Blood dripped in red streaks down white pillars. The collective nobility seemed to gasp all at once, as if too shocked to muster the proper reaction.

Terror flooded her veins when a Skardwarf stood in the center of a small crater atop a crushed body and unleashed its guttural, demonic roar.

CHAPTER FIFTY-SIX

The Way of Things

For all the pomp and pageantry, a coronation is considered a dull affair by many accounts. Empress Vothrai the Third's coronation, however, was tarnished by three deaths resulting from a brawl over an undocumented dispute. Scholars consider this the most eventful coronation in our history.

—Excerpt from Rays of Light:
A Complete History of Vos' Royal Lineages

Garret smiled as the Skardwarf howled. He dashed through a doorway into the main hall moments before the screaming and panicking nobility rushed the stairwells.

Right on cue.

That was Prost's problem. Too predictable. Cocky. Like a bearshark ignoring a tightening net when it senses blood in the water. Garret knew the Skardwarves would be sent in first. He had prepared for it. Not *strictly* in the way he'd told Grim he would be ready, but it ought to protect the Emperor just as well.

He eyed the Skardwarf who laid about with his stone fists, crushing noble bones and splashing rich blood. Sentyx or Cavern? Impossible to tell them apart, but did it matter? Both were Prost's lackeys. More importantly, he wasn't charging at Vinlin.

The Emperor looked furious his ceremony was disrupted. To his credit, he wasn't panicking like that sniveling High Cleric. He was ordering his Paladins to attack. Guised by Grim as ordinary nobles, Garret only spotted them because they carried swords and glaives glowing with imbued Archefire. They charged against the slow stampede, crying "Vinlin!" or "Lightmother!"

Fire swirled above the Skardwarf, then lanced down to strike it. Flames washed over stone with no effect. Archemagic slicked off the abyss-damned beast like it had the Archetempered daggerclaw outside Liwokin. One of the nobility was caught in the attack. Screamed and flailed trying to escape his burning robe. Drew too much attention to himself. The Skardwarf clapped the man's head with his stone palms, ending his wails with a crunch. Ignoring the Archefire, the Skardwarf roared and barreled into the backs of fleeing Paceeqi.

Garret's stomach turned. Bodies already piled up on the blood-stained floor. Some groaned and crawled over the fallen, dragging broken limbs and eviscerated friends. There were children in the audience.

Told Grim this was a dark-loving stupid plan.

At least his part in it was going right. Skardwarf wasn't going for the Emperor. He was charging toward the Aura emitter Garret and Arza had designed. He'd told Grim it would pacify the Skardwarf—though he'd left out that would only happen after the box was destroyed. Garret knew he wouldn't go along with enraging it, but they only had one gem from Prost's supplies. What was he supposed to do? *Not* use their best tool against the Skardwarves?

Garret only regretted that so many people were between the Skardwarf and that abyss-damned box.

He spat. "Time to get to work."

* * *

The strain of maintaining my Aura became too much. I released it and gasped for breath. Everything had gone wrong. Garret had assured me the emitter he and Arza designed would work. Instead, it had the same effect as Prost's did on Sentyx in the Peeker Mounds.

Lightmother, *was* that Sentyx down there? I couldn't imagine my quiet, caring friend committing such atrocities.

But then, I had seen what Garret had when he slaughtered all those Feeders.

Carnage.

I shook off the memory. The present was so much worse. Searching for Prost amidst the chaos became impossible, whether glimpsing through the eyes of Paladins fighting the demon or the men and women fleeing for their lives. As they fell, their Emergences began.

I squashed them all. So many. A cacophony of death, each one a hammer blow to my sanity. My mind withered beneath visions of terror-filled dying. In the brief respites between Deluges, I lost track of whose head I inhabited.

In a stairwell, people pushed against me in either direction.

A noblewoman died. Trampled.

At the entrance door now—someone had barred it. There was no way out. I struggled to draw breath.

Another death. Blood loss, slow and cold.

Charging the demon. It had its back turned. I swung with all my might. Struck its head...gasped. My blade deflected. It turned, its stone fist swinging.

Death. Instantaneous.

I couldn't take it. Somewhere, in a private suite cut off from the chaos, my body was screaming.

*　*　*

The Skardwarf bellowed, slaughtering people by the dozens. Lorelay watched in horror. Panic seeped into her blood, stopped her from moving. Lightmother, she was so afraid.

I can't lose him too.

Two Paladins urged the Kindling Emperor to flee, dragging him backward by the arms.

"I will not leave them!" Vinlin shouted. "Do your duty! Kill that demon!"

His words were nearly lost in the din. Screaming people, crying children, the demon's guttural rage.

The Kindling Emperor resisted his Paladins fruitlessly. They lifted him and carried him toward the door he entered by. At least a hundred people tried to squeeze through that door, the High Cleric included. Lorelay stood beside Inac on the dais and saw the same at every other entrance. Her stomach dropped.

"There is for us no escape," Inac muttered. The Archemage flinched. "Wait. The Archefields changed."

Lorelay felt it too. A pulse went through the air, squeezing her skull for an instant.

The Skardwarf's voice boomed again, turning to gravelly laughter. Then it spoke. "It seems you live after all, Ekoan! Clever trick, but we know you stole only one gem."

Ekoan? He was talking to Garret? Lorelay tensed up as the Skardwarf began striding toward the throne from the far side of the hall.

"What did you expect would happen?" Another laugh. "Rest assured, this is only a precursor of what awaits your homeland. But first..."

The Skardwarf broke into a run. Directly toward Vinlin.

"No!" Lorelay cried out in desperation. She found the will to move her legs. Before she had time to second-guess, she stood before Vinlin with both knives in her hands.

The two Paladins dropped the Kindling Emperor, then darted in front of Lorelay to provide a first line of defense. Inac stepped beside them and prepared Archefire in his hands.

"Lorelay..." Vinlin urged her to flee with a hand on her shoulder.

Her eyes filled with tears. She had no illusions she could stop the charging Skardwarf. But it was what her brother would have done. "I will protect the Bright Emperor. I will protect the man I love."

The Skardwarf's pounding footsteps shook the dais.

Vinlin's hand squeezed her shoulder tighter. "Please...don't..." His broken voice broke her heart, and her legs threatened to buckle.

Lorelay could lose no one else. She refused. She would rather die fighting for one shining star than live in a world of darkness. Lorelay squeezed the grips of her knives tighter.

The Skardwarf crashed through a flaming brazier, barreled through a marble pillar with a cluster of Clerics cowering behind it, then gathered speed to close on the Kindling Emperor. Blood coated the demon's stone fists and dripped down its torso. There was no hatred in its dark, passive eyes, only the certainty of death.

Movement caught the corner of Lorelay's eye. Out of nowhere, another Skardwarf sprinted from the other side of the dais toward Vinlin. All hope left her. She trembled at approaching death.

The second Skardwarf smashed into the first moments before it reached Vinlin's Paladins. The sound was a thunderclap that pushed her back a step. Lorelay's ears rang.

The two Skardwarves grappled, punched, and barked at each other in harsh tones, a song of demons. The trapped nobility kept a wary eye on the fight, keeping as far away as they could. But some could not escape. They were too hurt.

Lorelay pushed past the Paladins and rushed forward.

"No!" Vinlin called.

She looked over her shoulder as the guards restrained him. "Stay back!"

He had to survive. The Bright Emperor was too important. Lorelay was just a girl afraid of losing everything. The same as everyone else trapped here. She reached the Skardwarf's victims and began dragging the wounded away from the clash.

* * *

The two Skardwarves sounded like boulders crashing down a mountainside. Like the ground cracking open with ear-splitting rifts. Like ceaseless lightning in the stormjungle.

When their full legions fought, it would sound like the end of the world.

The raw power on display awed Garret. Wasn't sure even a dagger-claw could strike with such force. The Radiant Palace shook around them.

Hence, Garret stayed as far away as he bleeding could.

Lorelay and Inac had no such survival instincts. They ran *toward* the vicious combat. Even the Paladins kept a wide berth, weapons ablaze with Archefire. What was the point in keeping their blades imbued? Fire did nothing. Hadn't even chipped Cavern's skin.

Inac at least had the sense to save his energy for the injured. Mage set to work Archehealing those Lorelay dragged to some semblance of safety. To his surprise, even Vinlin joined in the efforts, breaking free from his Paladins. Once he began helping, the nobility followed.

The room thumped. Skardwarves hit the ground in a grapple. A seething lump of murderous rock. Less mobile than before. Not as immobile as he had planned, granted. Why hadn't the gem knocked the Skardwarves unconscious when it was destroyed? Didn't seem to rattle Garret's brains around as much either, come to think of it.

Whatever the case, Garret bounded toward Lorelay and Inac. Abyss take him, he would help too. Couldn't let these perfumed noblemen show him up.

* * *

Lorelay dragged a bleeding nobleman into the line of wounded that had formed in the recesses of the throne room. Too many were beyond saving. Even Inac's Archehealing could do nothing. Those he could help, he did, pouring more effort into his controls than Lorelay could imagine. He was sweating, standing near a large group of wounded and healing all of them at once. Golden glows faded, and Inac exhaled. He stumbled in exhaustion as he dragged himself to find more victims.

The Skardwarves had grown relatively quiet. Only the occasional grunting and thumping alerted her to their continued battle. The longer that went on, the more unnerved Lorelay grew. Despite that, the majority of what filled her ears were calls offering help or organizing the nobility.

Lorelay let herself smile for a moment. The people of the Bright Empire were rallying. Vinlin was leading them through the crisis.

"Take a break, man." Vinlin put a hand on Inac. The Archemage had no strength to resist and fell to his knees. "You'll burn yourself up if you keep that up."

"Archehealing is for me little effort," Inac said while taking deep breaths. "It is the running that tires me out."

Vinlin laughed in disbelief and pulled Inac's arm over his shoulder to help him walk to another group of bloodied nobles, near a door several men were attempting to break down to escape. "If I had half your skill, I wouldn't be a quarter as worried about today."

"Why?" Lorelay put in, wiping the sweat from her forehead. She tore a strip of fabric from her dress and knelt to fasten it as a tourniquet around a crying boy's arm. Why were they wagering whether Vinlin would survive? She needed to know.

"The ceremony." Vinlin straightened his crown and sighed. "It's only complete after my self-immolation."

Inac grunted. "A control to prove your strength in Archemagic." He shook his head. "Foolish. There is in this a serious danger of burning up. You must remain calm, entirely focusing your mind on the Archefields. If you feel on your skin the lick of flame and panic sets in...the Archefire will consume you entirely."

Lorelay gasped and unintentionally scared the boy she was tending to. His fear was a mirror of her own. *Four thousand says ash.* "They wouldn't let you *die* during the coronation!" Firm words, but doubt colored them with her worry. When had she ever believed the Bright Empire's traditions were kind?

Vinlin grimaced. "One Kindling Empress failed to achieve her coronation. The Church ruled until her heir came of age."

"Aye? Better calm things down in here, then."

Lorelay spun to find Garret leaning against a broken pillar, spinning an arrowhead on the tip of his finger.

"I've got an idea."

* * *

Mercifully, the Deluges ended.

I released control of my Benefactor and returned to seeing the world through my own eyes. Thank the Lightmother I was able to find my way back. I rubbed my head, half-expecting to find a knife planted in my skull. Pain throbbed behind my eye sockets. Squeezing shut my eyes, I listened.

The sound of the great hall had changed. Something had stopped the madness below. The Archedark swirling around the infested moved around more orderly in space. I seized one without thinking. A wary Paladin, wielding flaming glaive in trembling hands, daring not approach the grappling demons one step more.

I sucked in a breath and released the infested mind.

Sentyx?

Was Garret wrong about him? The fire kindling in my chest told me I desperately hoped so.

It renewed my vigor. Sentyx bought me time to continue searching for Prost. The exits around the throne room remained clogged with people, and in too many places...bodies.

I set my jaw in determination. If Prost was here, he was trapped with us.

We have you now.

* * *

"Hope you don't mind a bit of heresy, Your Radiance." Garret grinned when Vinlin didn't know how to respond. "Inac, those Archefire-imbued weapons. Can you do something like that with Archedark?"

The idea came to him as he rushed past all the corpses the Vinlin's citizen brigade left behind. No point wasting energy on the dead. Got him thinking about Benefactors and why none of them Emerged. That put his mind to thinking about Arza and the cure. She'd explained to him how they used the Dark to break the organism's defenses. If Archefire wasn't working against the Skardwarves...well, it was a crazy idea. Born of his mind wandering to escape the horrors of reality.

Get lots of ideas that way, don't I?

Well, that was the way of things. World's a nasty place.

Inac gave an abashed look at Vinlin, then nodded. "I believe I can do for you this control, yes."

"Just don't let the High Cleric see..." the Kindling Emperor muttered, though the Church's head looked as though she was losing her mind. Rambling to herself, shaking her head in denial. Clear to see who the real leader was here.

Garret smiled. "Knew I liked you."

Inac touched the arrowhead and closed his eyes. In moments, frost coated the steel-tipped arrow. The metal hissed, giving off a cold vapor. "Please hurry," the Archemage said. "This is nothing like Archefire. Fire wants to consume the weapon you imbue. Dark resists my touch."

"Say no more." Garret already had the arrow nocked when he started running for the Skardwarves. Weaving through volunteers, he reached the circle of Paladins surrounding the grapple.

He raised his bow and aimed. But at which one, Sentyx or Cavern? They were nearly identical, the fractal pattern of cracks across their stone skin their only distinctive feature. The blood of their victims smeared across both Skardwarves in the scuffle.

Garret drew the bowstring back. Did it matter who he hit? For all he knew, Sentyx was fighting Cavern to see who got the honor of killing Vinlin.

The thought tugged at the knot in his stomach. He remembered standing over Sentyx's motionless form, knife in hand. The tears filling his eyes...

He remembered the regret Sentyx felt for his destruction in the Feeder Hollows. The mutual pain he shared with the Skardwarf, twisting his insides.

Garret swore to bring justice to those responsible for the deaths in the Peeker Mounds. But a ranger listened to his body, and every fiber was saying Sentyx had a reason for doing what he did. That there was more to this story.

Now, as Garret determined how he should pass judgment, the Skardwarf was grappling with his brother to protect the Emperor. Wouldn't it be easier to believe Sentyx opposed Cavern?

To believe he's my friend...

The Skardwarf pinned on the ground suddenly got the upper hand. Their positions reversed, and the Paladins shuffled to keep them centered in the protective circle. All the good that would do.

"Garret," the pinned Skardwarf said. "Help."

Garret's eyes widened. He recognized that slow drawl. He knew what to do.

Lowering his aim, he loosed. The Dark-infused arrow shot forth. Skewered the pinned Skardwarf's neck. Sunk deep, and the Skardwarf's rock pattern pulsed with a brief flash of light.

Cavern bellowed, crying his pain louder than he had screamed his rage as he seized up on the ground.

"Sentyx would never ask for help," Garret said.

The Skardwarf standing over his brother responded with a grunt.

"Aye. That's the Sentyx I know."

The cracks in Cavern's body pulsed again, a bright, golden-red glow. His wails grew in intensity as the pulsing quickened.

Garret covered his ears. "What in the bleeding darkness is happening?" He couldn't hear the words in his own head. The Skardwarf's voice boomed at a stone-shattering volume.

Sentyx stood motionless, looking down at Cavern. He slowly raised his hand. Balled it into a fist, a stone mass that turned white, misting just like Garret's arrow had. With a yell that cut through even his brother's death throes, Sentyx hammered his fist down. Cavern's head shattered, and the world shook.

In the silence that followed, the dead Skardwarf's body crumbled into a formless pile of rock.

*   *   *

An inhuman roar dragged me cringing back into my own body. The sound shook my bones, rattled my teeth. Squeezing my eyes shut, chaotic patterns of Archefire swirled in the dark expanse. Was it Inac? I had never seen such a surge of power.

An even louder sound pierced the air, and I could hold back a scream no longer. Even clapping my hands over my ears, excruciating pain lanced my head. On the brink of my eardrums bursting, a thump resounded through the entire Radiant Palace. The sound and the vortex of Archemagic simultaneously died.

"Darkfather..." I muttered, rubbing my head. My ears rang and muffled my voice.

Peering over the balcony, Archefire weapons drew my eye to a Skardwarf. He stood hunched over the remains of his brother. Paladins charged in, but the Skardwarf lifted his hands. The silver soldiers skidded to a halt, fearful.

"I surrender." Sentyx's voice had never sounded so sweet. Garret stood, in his green cloak, aiming a nocked arrow at the Skardwarf, but Garret was wrong. Sentyx fought for *us*.

The Paladins and nobility weren't so sure. Angry shouts crested above the nervous chatter.

"Kill him!"

"Murderer!"

"Demon!"

One voice cut through the rest. "Enough!" Kindling Emperor Vinlin. The great hall silenced to hear his voice. "Let this madness end!"

"Your Radiance, that is a demon of the Dark!" a wizened woman in an Archemetal-trimmed crimson cloak spluttered. The High Cleric, if I had to guess. "It must be destroyed."

"How do you propose to do that, Brightest One?" Vinlin asked. "When one of these demons nearly brought down the seat of the Empire? Thank the Lightmother this one surrendered. It could end us all in an instant."

The High Cleric had the decency to hang her head in shame.

The Kindling Emperor stepped onto the dais to address the nobility. They had already started refilling the hall when Vinlin started speaking, though perhaps not so fully as before. I didn't blame anyone for fleeing when they had the chance. I only hoped Prost wasn't one of them.

"Our Light is failing us. It is not your imagina—"

Someone knocked on my viewing suite's door, tried the handle. I kept it locked, and for good reason. A Darkmetal pistol rested on my lap. I'd told myself I wouldn't use these weapons, but necessity called for the casting aside of morals. Taking the pistol in hand and creeping forward, I reached for the latch.

Opened the door and thrust the weapon forward.

"Garret?" I put up the pistol. "I thought you were down with Sentyx."

The ranger grinned. "Slipped out as soon as everyone took their eyes off me. Thinking now is exactly when Prost would make his move. Just when everyone believes it's over." Garret's grin slipped. "But this isn't over until Prost is in the ground."

CHAPTER FIFTY-SEVEN

To Burn All Belief

Like you, I've had my future stolen. But where I come from, we have a long memory. Work with me, and I assure you the name Ulken will never be forgotten.

—Request to meet a hopeful Liwo politician

"Our Light is failing us. It is not your imagination. The days are indeed becoming shorter, our mathemelodians confirm this."

The grand hall quieted. If not for the Prime Mathemelodian being bound by rites of anonymity, she could have stepped forward and confirmed Vinlin's statement. Were the people of the Bright Empire not yet ready to hear the truth?

While the rest of the nobility silently contemplated Vinlin's words, Lorelay gazed admirably at the Kindling Emperor upon his dais. She knew him well enough to understand what he was doing. Painting a picture of the coming darkness, that he might become a beacon of light in their mind's eye.

"Demons set foot in the Radiant Palace. Vos struggles to cope with the influx of our brothers and sisters fleeing their homes. Dark days are upon us, my friends, though none may be darker than today." He looked out upon the fallen with genuine sadness. It stirred the like in Lorelay. "Yet what does the Book of Light say of the Dark Era?"

The High Cleric stepped forward in answer, though her voice wavered. "'Fear not the Era when Light turns to Dark, for only from darkness can true Light emerge."

"Thank you, Brightest One. Only from darkness can true Light emerge..." Vinlin spoke softly, and the words were whispered behind Lorelay, a cascading prayer that reached the far end of the hall. "Remember that. When the darkness surrounds you and smothers your hope...that is the moment Fire will burn most brightly."

Despite the death all around her, hope stirred in Lorelay's chest. Benefactors, Skardwarves, whatever the Dark threw at them, they could survive it all if led by this man.

The Kindling Emperor clenched his fists, filled his words with fire. "Our home shall not wither beneath the darkness this day! I shall sit on her throne, and the Bright Empire shall burn brighter than ever. Witness my flame!"

Hope and fear formed a maelstrom inside Lorelay as Vinlin approached the throne to complete his coronation.

* * *

"Agreed," Grim said. "We're not letting anyone leave until we have him."

Until we have him?

Prost's bleeding head on a pike was the only outcome Garret would allow. He narrowed his eyes suspiciously at Grim.

Don't you back down on me now.

Grim huffed. "We don't have long."

"Aye, I know. I'm thinking." The bones in Garret's braided hair rattled when he shook his head. "If the Skardwarves are down there, Prost won't be. Too dangerous. He likes a personal touch, but not if it means risking himself."

"What then, an arrow from a balcony?"

"Or..." Garret nodded toward Grim's pistol.

"This? Useless at long range."

"Magic?"

"That's what Inac's there for. He'll be watching for signs of Archedark."

"But from where?" Garret considered his hunting blind. "Where would you hide if you wanted to stay out of sight in this kind of crowd?"

Grim gestured to the suite around them. "I *am* hiding there. Elevated. Dark. On the south side, away from the windows."

"Exactly where I'd expect to find Prost too. So." The ranger snarled. "Let's kick some fucking doors in."

* * *

Vinlin sat the throne with a confidence Lorelay knew he did not possess. Fear had won out over hope. She gripped her dress near tight enough to rip it. Her throat was parched.

You can do this, Vinlin.

He had taken Inac's advice to heart and assumed total calm. His eyes were closed, his breathing steady and deep. No one whispered over wagers or complained of inconvenience anymore.

The bells rang dusk outside the silent hall. The night had arrived, and they all needed a light to guide them.

Archefire formed around Vinlin's hands, then began spreading up his arms.

* * *

Bang.

I winced as Garret's boot connected with lightwood. Sturdy, unmoving. All the others had been unlocked, the suites behind them empty or filled with cowering families. We moved on, searching door to door until we had come to this one. Tucked away in shadow at the far end of the corridor, the nearby brazier contained cold ashes.

This had to be it. Behind the door, a cloud of Archedark stirred at the commotion Garret caused.

"Together," I said.

Garret grunted.

We both charged our shoulders into the door. It cracked but did not open. We reeled back for another go.

"Now!"

BANG.

The sound came from the other side of the door.

*   *   *

Garret and Grim put their full weight into the cracked lightwood door. It buckled, and Grim lost his balance, fell to a knee. Garret rushed forward through the cramped viewing suite.

Prost spun in alarm, raising his hand to attack with a blast of Archedark, light fading as a sphere of misting blackness gathered in his palm. Too slow. Garret already had a knife in hand. Threw it. The blade found its way to the Eevoqian's gut. Missing would have been like spitting and missing the ground.

Blood welled around the knife. Stained the man's nice white suit. What a shame.

Screaming, Prost dropped his cane clutched at his belly, daring not pull the weapon free.

"Here, let me help." Garret knocked the upraised cane aside. Grabbed the knife handle. *Pushed.*

The Eevoqian wailed.

"Garret, stop!" Grim commanded. "You can't kill him!"

Garret looked over his shoulder, watching Grim warily. The knife handle wiggled in Garret's hand.

Prost was laughing. "That's right, little Ekoan. My Benefactor is more ancient than any other. My Emergence will be immeasurably large." He looked at Grim, licked his lips. "And with the power you stole..."

Garret twisted the knife and drew out another scream. "Enough of that. Disgusting. Grim, we're gonna kill this guy, right? All those lives he took down there…" His fist quivered, and Prost cried out again. "Isn't enough, isn't even a start, but it's got to be done. Fair's fair."

Grim hesitated, mouth open but no words coming out. He got a hungry look in his eye…and that's when Garret knew.

The traitor in Hand Sixty-Four wasn't Sentyx.

The Head was no man. He was that monster inside of him. Wanted to steal Prost's memories like he had stolen Garret's own.

"You want *his* words in your head?" Garret demanded. "Have you lost your mind?"

The Head grew angry. "We need his—"

"No!" Garret barked. "No, no!" Betrayed by his commander again… Garret had *scalped* Kerren for raping those girls. Never forgot the sticky feel of that blood on his hands. He could do nothing to salve their pain. This time, he would stop it before it could happen. He wrenched the knife sideways and eviscerated Prost. Blood and guts poured onto his boots. The Eevoqian screamed wordlessly and gurgled as life swiftly left him.

"Garret!" Grim's eyes were wild. "What are you—"

"I'm not afraid of his Benefactor." He pulled the knife free.

Nor yours.

Garret spun the knife in his hand, then plunged it into Prost's skull.

* * *

"No!"

There was no Emergence to suppress. I didn't get a scrap of Prost's memories. No *hint* of what he was planning, why he was abyss-bent on causing chaos.

Nothing.

"What have you done?" My voice trembled.

Garret stood nonchalantly, about to wipe the blood from the blade on his cloak. He thought better of it and tossed the knife aside instead. "Delivered justice."

The ranger eyed me for a moment like he was considering killing me too, then pushed passed me and stomped through the door. His footsteps receded. I was too stunned to stop him. I fell to my knees, unblinking gaze on Prost's corpse.

My mind summoned thoughts of Tak, the Eevoqian's student. Dead before I could react. We needed their knowledge. Now, we were in the dark.

He'll have something on him. Some piece of information, some letter, something.

It was a desperate thought, but desperation had already gotten me this far. I started with Prost's strange metal cane, grabbed it near the end. Winced and pulled my hand back.

Hot. Why would—

I squeezed the pistol in my other hand, and my eyes slowly widened. It wasn't a cane. My ears picked out a solitary sound over the loud chatter below.

Screaming. Crying.

Lorelay.

Finding my feet, I stumbled to the balcony and looked downward. The nobles were...leaving?

"What?" I searched the room, eyes drawn toward the dais. Where my hope shattered.

Vinlin's brains were dashed across the throne.

* * *

Lorelay wailed, fighting Inac as he pulled her away from Vinlin's body. The moment played out in her mind, a vision that would plague her dreams and turn her days into waking nightmares.

The man she learned to love sat on his throne, and she looked on with enough admiration and pride to snuff out his nervousness. When his gaze met hers, his face calmed, and he smiled, then closed his eyes to begin. Archefire appeared first in his palms, slowly expanded to cover his hands, then snaked its way up his forearms. Lorelay's breath refused to come, her heart pounding in her chest.

Thump, thump, th—

A loud crack filled the silent space, and Vinlin's body jerked. His head snapped backward with enough force to splatter his blood across the high back of the throne. His body slumped, the Archefire wavered, and the scent of blood and burning filled Lorelay's nose, and that even that was not enough to snap her out of her stunned disbelief.

Her mind had gone blank as if she were struck in the head.

It didn't happen. It didn't happen.

But it had, and the truth seeped into the void left in her heart where she had let Vinlin take root, a blossoming flower cut at the stem before its colors brightened the garden. She began to scream.

The Kindling Emperor sagged on the gold and red throne, his hands and arms a burnt cinder.

She ran to him and smothered the fires when she held him and wept. Lorelay shook him, screaming his name. "Vinlin! Vinlin, please!" She pled with the Lightmother. She pled with Inac. "Save him! Save him!" She sobbed, but it was no use.

One look from the Archemage told her what she could not bear to accept.

Lorelay ran her fingers down his cheek, felt his blood slick on her fingers. His eyes were closed, eyes whose light she would never see again. Her stomach spasmed violently when her tearful gaze drifted upward.

Vinlin's forehead was caved in, his skull collapsed, bits of brain and streams of blood dripping over the throne's gold arm. She screamed in horror, closing her eyes.

No...no...no...

He was not gone. He was the light to guide them through the darkness. He was the Bright Emperor.

He loved her.

She failed him.

She failed the Bright Empire. The Lightmother.

And Dunnax.

Useless...so useless...

Everyone Lorelay loved, she lost. Her body gave out. Drained of strength and will, she gave up and let Inac drag her away.

* * *

Coldness rushed through me, as though all fire had been snuffed from the world.

Our alliance. The army of Paladins. Without Vinlin, all of it was lost. The Church was in ruin—the High Cleric stared at the dead emperor in shock, hands covering her mouth. Without a leader, the Empire itself would fall.

Everything I had fought for as Head of the Agency was crumbling.

We'll never save Liwokin. The Benefactors will kill us all.

The nobility shuffled out of the slow room in quiet conversation. Going home to set their affairs in order for what may come next. To them, the Bright Empire was absolute. It was eternal. The coronation may have failed, but that had happened before. Life went on.

They didn't know death lay just over the horizon.

Vinlin's proclamation of the Dark Era's approach would go unheard, resigned to the history books. There would be no books written if we didn't survive this. Of all those in the ceremonial hall, only my friends from Hand Sixty-Four knew the truth of our doom. Below, Inac consoled Lorelay, though he appeared to have little of himself left to give. Hope was dying in him as well.

I tightened my grip on the banister.

No. This has *to work.*

I promised myself I wouldn't warp the truth again, but this was a world I could not accept. One where monsters infested every man and woman, assimilated their flesh, toppled every city, wiped out humans, Peekers, and Skardwarves alike. Nothing could stop them. Nothing except the full might the Bright Empire.

Nothing except—

Me.

I *had* to ensure we survived. Had to use my Benefactor to the fullest extent. Even if that meant giving up on what little humanity remained to me. I would reach into the past, into the memories of everyone I could reach, to scour any evidence of this assassination.

To burn all belief in the truth and supplant it with my own.

The monster in my head writhed, sensing my intent. I unleashed it, let it do the only thing these creatures had ever wanted to do.

Expand.

It reached out, latching onto the minds of every person in the throne room, every person in the Radiant Palace, every person in Vos, extending into the countryside. Infested or not, it made no difference. The human mind produced patterns of Archefire—Benefactors fed on the field, expanding to take over the brain by reproducing the patterns with ones of Archedark. Controlling either pattern was the same to an Archemage, and Benefactors had abilities that would put even Inac to shame. They moved entirely in the Dark, and I lent the power of my Archefire.

Yezna's Pool existed alongside an ocean of others. She wouldn't stand for what I was doing, but her power was mine to control. I guided my Benefactor through it, imbuing my Aura with the emptiness of her Emergence. Where hers was tainted with her Ulken's rage, I subdued my anger to retain the purity of the effect. It emptied the minds of all who the organism touched, a dulling haze that stopped them in their tracks and brought the entire city to a standstill.

Between one moment and the next, there was *nothing.*

As my mind swam along the currents of countless Paceeqi, my body moved among their nobility. Time seemed to halt, an entire populace caught between moments of reality as if sleepwalking. I reached the corpse of Vinlin. I could allow myself to feel nothing, but deep down I knew this was a great shame. Another good man, dead.

Grief would come over me later if I wasn't careful. I had to believe he was unimportant. I pulled his body from the throne, dragged it and laid among the dead. Looking upon his face, I commanded my Benefactor to summon thoughts of him to the minds it controlled. With a squeeze of my fist, the man they knew as Vinlin became no more, every image of him, every mention of his name, fading from collective memory. Only his corpse remained, a stranger to all he knew him.

I reached Lorelay and Inac, kneeling on the ground leaning into each other, insensate like all the others. Fresh tears streamed down both their faces.

"I'm sorry I have to do this."

Reaching into their mind, I planted a new belief. A memory of a conversation that never happened. One in which they agreed Inac would take the place of the Bright Emperor, complete the coronation, and lead the war against the Benefactors. A contingency plan we discussed in secret.

In touching their thoughts, I siphoned Lorelay's and Inac's memories. Lorelay's threatened to break my control. I had sent her here to win an ally, dooming her to a broken heart. She had fallen in love with Vinlin, though she might not admit it to herself. She would want to do right by him, honor his memory as she honored her brother's. In the false memory she agreed to serve as the Bright Emperor's advisor. It would do nothing to salve her grief, but perhaps it would give her a purpose I sense she desperately lacked.

I crouched to look at Inac. His face flooded the minds of an entire people, a permanent change to their perception. His was the face of an emperor, stern and wise. They would follow him. They would be drawn to him as surely as if he were the trueborn son of Elzia.

When I relinquished control of the mind of a population, those in attendance flocked silently back to witness the end of the coronation. My Aura hid only the blood that marred the Archemetal throne.

Inac took his place on the dais and sat the throne without a word. He crossed his legs beneath him, whole body relaxed, forearms resting on his knees with his one palm turned upward. Slowly, golden flames formed around his skin and robes. In moments, smokeless Fire engulfed him. The Brightdaughter had set beyond the palace walls, but light filled the entire room.

The heat of Archefire bathed me as all watched the Bright Emperor complete his coronation, a shining star burning so bright it blinded them from the truth.

CHAPTER FIFTY-EIGHT

No Accident

They say the Head has eyes all around us. Thing is, that thought doesn't bother me so much anymore. Now I make sure to smile and wave when I drop trow to use the latrine.

—From the first oral history of Ekohold

"I trusted you."

Garret regarded Grim through narrowed eyes. *Can't say the same about you.*

Grim and Inac sat across the table from him in the Bright Emperor's solar. Light shined in on the two from an open window overlooking the Fire Gardens. The Head and Inac, the Bright Emperor, what a farce. Garret would have spat if he didn't think the Paladins scrutinizing him wouldn't object. No idea how the Head convinced whoever ran the Empire that the Agency's puppet should take over. Now that Inac was in charge, figured it didn't much matter. He'd been ordering the army and nobility around for a week, and they always did what he said. Good little followers. Garret rolled his eyes. Politics was so boring.

He shrugged. "Did what you tasked me with, didn't I?"

Grim pursed his lips. "I told you to *capture* Prost."

"Come on, Grim. You were a bounty hunter. You know how it works. Always a risk you'll come back with nothing but a body."

The Head was getting frustrated. Garret suppressed a smile of satisfaction. This monster was his enemy. Garret didn't know why Inac summoned him here, but he came with a purpose of his own.

"That was no *accident*." Grim's hands were balled into fists. "You murdered Prost. *After* I commanded you to stop."

"That? Thought it was more a suggestion than a command."

"You taunt him." Inac's face was puzzled. "Do you not realize for yourself the gravity of the situation."

"I never could tell what he's thinking," Grim said, "even when we were all Fingers. Dunnax was right. No morals at all..." His eyes were full of hurt. "And I trusted you."

Garret's lips curled down. "Aye, well...we've all made mistakes."

Grim rubbed his eyes. "Bring him in."

Inac nodded and relayed the order to his Paladins. The heavy footsteps that cut through the moments of tense quiet told Garret what to expect when those doors swung open. Two Paladins ushered Sentyx into the room, iron fetters around the Skardwarf's broad wrists.

Garret chuckled. "Think those will hold him?" The Paladins shared a worried glance.

"They belong on *you*," Grim growled.

Try it and you'll be a Head short one hand.

"Sentyx told to us all that happened in Myrme."

"And you trust *him?* A bleeding Skardwarf?"

"Demon..." A Paladin muttered, then withered under Inac's glare. With a flick of the Bright Emperor's hand, they left the room and shut the doors.

"I've made mistakes," Grim said softly. "Trusting Sentyx was not one of them. I've seen your memories. Seen how you sabotaged your hunt, investigated your *partner*. I thought you were best friends. It was all a lie..."

Sentyx gave a sad grunt.

Garret's stomach clenched. Seemed his cover had been *too* effective. "Aren't you at all curious why Sentyx and Cavern are here? Two Skardwarves. Just two." He shook his head, bones rattling. "Just the start, and you know it."

"We do want to know," Inac said. "But have you tried for yourself simply asking him?"

"Why?" He scoffed. "To hear lies?"

"*You* lie." Sentyx rumbled in anger. "Cannot read letter? Lie. Best friend? Lie."

Garret cringed inwardly. How was it *his* fault the Skardwarf thought Garret's time monitoring him meant they were best friends? "And what about you?" Garret shot back. The tangled knot in his stomach pulled tight. He'd been betrayed again. No room for forgiveness now. "Joining Cavern, letting Prost kill the Queen. You could have stopped him!"

Sentyx paused for a long time before whispering, "No choice... Must save Princess."

The egg? Thought they would have smashed that a while ago.

"Enough." Inac had taken quickly to his imperial authority. Like he knew he'd play that role and practiced. "Sentyx, free yourself."

The Skardwarf snapped the chain between his fetters with no effort.

"The way I see it, we owe to you a great debt. You saved countless lives by stopping Cavern."

"Your brother..." Grim added. "I'm sorry it came to that."

Sentyx grunted. "I face the wind."

Inac turned his stern gaze toward Garret. "One-hundred seventy-six people killed. Another three-hundred eleven wounded. Because you lied to us."

"You *knew* what the device you made would do to Skardwarves." Grim's face flushed with anger. "If you took the path to the Feeder Hollows you were supposed to, instead of following Sentyx, you could have captured Prost. Brought him to justice for all the Peekers he killed. Instead, you chose to *repeat* what Prost did on *us*. The *only* reason we're all standing here is because Sentyx salvaged the disaster you created."

Garret did regret the number of dead. But he couldn't be blamed for making the wrong decision in the Mounds. He was surrounded by enemies, working with what little information he had. No, that wasn't his fault. He crossed his arms. "Worked though, didn't it?"

Grim bolted upright, stood with fists on the table, glowering. "Unbelievable. I don't know how I so badly misjudged you." He closed his eyes, then stopped trembling. His voice was as cold as the Shadowson. "That ends now. Garret, you're discharged from the Agency."

Garret tensed. He'd expected this. Time to make his move.

"I also name you exiled from Vos," Inac said, "for what you did to my people. Leave the city by nightfall, or—"

He feigned outrage. "Discharged? Exiled? You bleeding hypocrites. Kicking me out because you don't trust me?" He clenched his teeth, found he didn't need to fake his anger after all. "How many peoples' minds did you invade? Betrayed the entire snuffing city! You're nothing but the monster in your skull." Garret prepared to move. "And I've already killed one of those this week."

He was on his feet in an eye blink. A knife flashed from his hand. Planted itself in Grim's shoulder. The Head cried out, but it wouldn't be fatal. Just a little something for a traitor to remember him by. Inac would set to healing Grim right away. Sentyx was the bigger concern. He regretted their friendship had to end this way, but Garret didn't see any way of convincing him the Head was unworthy of trust. By Grim's side, the Skardwarf was dangerous. Faster than he expected, but not as fast as an Ekoan ranger. No way to defend against him without Inac's help, but Garret knew the secret now. Archemages often burned by their own Fire. Archedark would fell the creatures of the Shadowson.

A sorrowful grunt was the Skardwarf's only reaction as Garret made for the window. A clean break. Garret grimaced anyway and didn't let them see his tears. That low, familiar rumble pulled at a wound inside him, filling him with an ache that threatened to consume him with if he didn't shove the pain away.

Betrayed again. Friendless. He'd be ready for his next encounter with the Hand. In fact, he was looking forward to it.

A chance to get even, and to save what little he loved that remained to him.

Wincing at the needles flaring behind his eyes, Garret vaulted through the window and escaped through the palace's royal gardens.

CHAPTER FIFTY-NINE

So Much Light

When lights go dark, the world grows cold
Memories fleeting, no more to make
Two fallen stars I yearn to hold
End this dark dreaming, a way to wake

—Verse from Fallen Stars

Empty. Lorelay felt so, so...empty.

A week passed, the pain not dulling but growing. Each time she saw Inac on the throne, the wounds on her heart bled anew. She spent her nights crying or screaming into her pillow. Throwing cups to shatter against white marble, raging at the injustice of it all. She had been right all along.

The Lightmother had no mercy.

Everyone I love dies.

She dared to open her heart to Vinlin, let herself believe she could live a life of happiness at his side. Consort to the Bright Emperor, mistress, mother of his children. She cared nothing for the title, only the future she had lost. In its place, a life serving as advisor to a forgery.

The day after Inac's successful coronation, Minny found her weeping in her chambers. Vinlin's aunt could not understand why she cried. After all, the Bright Emperor had just been crowned. Was Lorelay not elated?

"Inac always was a stubborn boy," Minny said of her nephew. "But looking at him now, I see his mother in him. Perhaps a mite too much," she joked.

Lorelay sent her away despite her protests. If something was wrong, Minny said, she would help. Something *was* wrong. Something beyond fixing. It had once been her dream, but its realization brought her only sorrow: the Bright Empire was crumbling.

All that held it up was an elaborate lie.

She still failed to comprehend how Grim ever convinced her to go along with his plan. His Benefactor scoured all memory of Vinlin. He survived only in her head and Inac's and Grim's. A precious memory. Perhaps that was why the pain had only grown. She refused to let go of her last scrap.

The only proof he ever existed at all.

Agonizing though it was, she held on. Vinlin was no longer the shining beacon in the darkness, but his memory was a candle whose flame she would tend.

The bell of the church rang dusk as Lorelay neared. She stepped through the lightwood doors, newly painted. The upkeep restored them to the condition Lorelay remembered when she was dragged here as a child. She found an empty pillow to sit upon—she had forgotten to bring her own. Flat and without cushion, it comforted her nonetheless.

A stillness hung in the church, fires burning low upon the altar. Dusk was the time for grieving, and hers were not the only sobs the filled the room.

'When darkness falls, seek solace in Lightmother's grace.'

The verse long meant little to Lorelay. There was always comfort to be found in song, and failing that, a strong drink. There was no song inside her now, yet her feet carried her not to a tavern but to a Church of Light. Song and drink had only gotten her here. Perhaps it was time to try something new.

Or rather, something old. As old as the Bright Empire itself.

Lorelay raised her eyes to the altar, an Archemetal statue of the Brightdaughter, lithe feminine figure with a halo of light overhead. Dancing fires in ornate sconces reflected off the goddess's skin. In her mind, she saw Vinlin's arms catching alight. She broke with a loud sob.

"Lorelay?" A hand fell gently on her heaving back.

She sloppily wiped her face and looked up. Her eyes widened. "Mother?"

Lorelay's mother hugged. Held her close while she wept and cried tears of her own for her daughter's grief. In truth, Lorelay cried in part for knowing her mother lived. Since the tragedy at the coronation, the city had been in a state of unrest that Grim and Inac barely kept under control.

When her tears ran temporarily dry, Lorelay straightened and calmed her breathing. "I thought you stopped practicing."

Her mother smiled. "I will always be a Lady of Ash, but I still come on occasion." She gestured to the rest of the congregation. "These are my friends. Who would I be if I was not here to grieve beside them?"

Lorelay swallowed against the tightness in her throat. "Does it..." She sniffled. "Does it help?"

"Nothing helps so much as time, little light. Helping them remember what the Lightmother has given them rather than what they have lost...that helps too."

"What if the person they lost had so much more to give, so much light left to shine upon the world..." Lorelay squeezed her eyes shut. "And instead it was snuffed out before they ever got a chance."

Her mother's smile grew sad. In the stretching quiet, Lorelay imagined she was about to hear a quote from the Book of Light. Something about how all people, young and old, have the Lightmother's blessing inside them. Her mother surprised her yet again.

"When you and Dunnax disappeared and your father was still deployed to Lumeeq... I had never been alone like that before. I questioned my faith, isolated myself from this community. Hid away in our house, closed the shutters, ignored the knocks at the door.

"The only thing that brought me out of the darkness was remembering you and Dunnax. Both of you so young, with so much light left to give. I imagined you looking down on me, wondering what had become of your mother, once so full of faith and hope. I read your songs, kept my heart open for you, and in return you opened my eyes.

"I decided then, if you couldn't live for yourselves, I would live for *you*. To make you proud to have me as a mother."

The tears in Lorelay's eyes matched her mother's. "Mother...I *am*—"

"Live for him, Lorelay. What happened to your brother wasn't your fault, but you can carry his fire. Honor his ideals."

The misconception that she was speaking of her brother jarred Lorelay, but the sentiment stuck. In fact, Dunnax would have told her the same thing, no? To serve the Bright Empire was his highest ambition. She could honor both of those she lost with the same actions.

The emptiness inside her seemed to shrink by some small amount. Small, but dense. Emptiness was heavy, and it felt like she had been freed from a great burden. Despite the pain it caused her to see Inac on the throne, she would serve him. She would ensure he accomplished what Vinlin no longer could.

She would keep the memory of Vinlin alive.

Live for him, and his light will never go out.

CHAPTER SIXTY

The Wind

Attention! Attention! Let it be known from this day forth that Inac, third son of Empress Elzia, has demonstrated the Lightmother's favor and his prowess with the sacred Fire at a coronation attended by all the nobility of Vos. Let all lands illuminated by the Brightdaughter bear witness to his ascension and swear fealty to Inac, first of his name. Long live the Bright Emperor!

—Heralded throughout the Bright Empire

"'Once you start down a bloody path, the only thing to do is keep walking.' You said to me this, long ago."

Ten thousand lifetimes ago. I pulled my eyes from the setting Brightdaughter, regarded Inac with a rueful look. "Was I wrong?"

Inac sighed. "I am for myself no longer so sure."

My stomach twisted with regret. Inac had always tried to keep me on the right path. Instead, he was stuck with me on the road I forged in blood and lies and broken promises. "I'm sorry. I wish it hadn't come to this."

Sentyx grunted. He'd been waiting quietly behind us, somber ever since Garret turned cloak and fled. "Cannot stop the wind."

"Not sure we can face it, either."

Refugees flooded the city, fleeing the Benefactor Queen to the northwest and the Emergent Bello to the north. But Garret's betrayal hurt most of all. I'd siphoned his memories as he fled, learned what he intended. Storm clouds roiled on every horizon. I feared the gale would be an unstoppable force.

"Do not lose hope, my friend." Inac turned away from the balcony overlooking Vos. The Bright Emperor brought me and Sentyx to this audience chamber across the palace for some reason. Perhaps to look out upon his citizens while we spoke of their fate. The darkening cityscape sprawled into the distance, fires alighting to ready for the night. "Do not let everything we have done for them become meaningless. We have for ourselves much to do to prepare."

Inac...always so practical. What would I have done without him? *Everything is easier with friends.* Remembering our shared drink in Li-wokin didn't bring the smile to my face that it should have. Was this how I treated my friends? Turned them into my pawns? Inac never truly agreed to become the Bright Emperor. I forced it upon him, heedless to the desires of his own will.

I pushed down the guilt before it threatened to escape my throat. No one could know the truth of what I had done, not even those closest to me. *I had no choice. I did what I must.* I had to believe that. Every choice I made was to unite the Bright Empire against the Benefactors. Though each step brought me closer to madness, if my belief in the path cracked, we would fail. Humanity would not survive.

Bolstering my resolve, I joined Inac and Sentyx. An icy wind blew at my back, a whistling cold that made the heavy curtains flap.

Sentyx grunted. "Not long."

"What is it you wished to tell to us?" Inac asked. "If my Paladins have not yet brought to us Lorelay, we must proceed without her."

Sentyx hesitated. "Garret was right. The Tyrant comes. Legions of Skardwarves."

The air became hard to breathe. A memory of Sentyx's returned to me, one I suddenly realized Garret had thought about often. The Skardwarf standing among legions, a burning hatred for humanity stoked in all of them by the Tyrant. *They will never see us coming.*

Why hadn't the ranger warned us? The memory made him obsessed with learning how to kill Sentyx, leading him to fail to stop the Queen's Emergence. Now, he fled to his homeland, a traitor to the Agency.

I asked the question Garret never had. "Why are you here, Sentyx?"

"To escape Tyrant's will. Is not mine."

It was the truth. We had spoken of this in the Fingers' quarters of the Agency, after our first command from Ulken. Sentyx was here because he wanted to help people. How could I have let Garret's thoughts make me believe otherwise? But there was another...

"What about Cavern?" I asked. "Why did he come?"

Sentyx let out a long rumble. "Believed in Tyrant. Prost used Cavern." After a pause, "Used us."

"To cause chaos," Inac said, considering. "He wished to disrupt the Bright Empire, yes?"

"But why?" I failed to keep the anger out of my voice. If Garret hadn't killed Prost, we would already know. "What does he gain from it?"

"Land. And revenge," Sentyx said. "Humans came here. Long ago. Left many behind. Forever, they hate you."

I wrinkled my brow in confusion. "How long ago?"

Sentyx grunted. "The last Dark Era."

Lightmother. That was generations upon generations in the past. A mythical time, one I would have thought was mere story were the present skies not so dark. All of our troubles, caused by an Eevoqian carrying out a blood feud thousands of years old...

I seethed. "How is that our fault?"

"Often, hatred of another is for a people all that holds them together," Inac said. "It gives to them something to strive for."

"For an entire Era of Light?"

"It was for them not so bright, I imagine, beneath the Shadowson."

Sentyx grunted his affirmation.

Outside, the Brightdaughter hid beneath the horizon. Still, the dusk bells did not ring. Inac returned to the balcony to gaze upon the city. "What choices of ours will our descendants curse us for, I wonder?"

"I'll welcome their curses," I said. "Means we lived through this."

"Yes," Sentyx said. "You must live. You must leave."

"Leave?" Inac asked over his shoulder. His hair whipped as a cold gale struck him, but he reacted as if he could not feel cold.

"All will burn," Sentyx intoned. "Cannot stop the wind. But you can survive."

How did he remain so confident? Arza and Oltrov were managing the logistics and preparations to administer the Benefactor cure, but we needed to retake Liwokin first for supplies beyond the Grieving Pine branch Lorelay saved. The Paladins were stuck in and around Vos, managing refugees or deployed on ships in the Lawiko strait anticipating the Queen's arrival. From the south a legion of Skardwarves approached, and we were completely defenseless.

A sonorous sound came from the city. Sentyx and I joined Inac outside in the cold. Over the howling wind, church bells tolled. Not for dusk but playing a melody outside the Rhythm of Time. It chilled me more than the winds ever could.

"The Mathemelodian Prime gave to me a warning of this song earlier today," Inac said. "A new Dark Era has arrived."

The three of us looked south, facing into the wind, where the Shadowson rose above the horizon. In his cold blue light, I imagined ships approaching, borne by the gale. Filled with demons of stone, flying sails of icy death.

Epilogue

The Tyrant followed the stars.

Nothing new to him existed beneath the wide expanse of darkness. Freezing sun and searing sun, the siblings shaped history in their eternal cosmic dance. Twin forces coalesced in him granting life, but not purpose. That, he shaped of his own will.

Existence. Consciousness.

The Tyrant took it upon himself to foster this state.

Creator. Destroyer.

There can be no Archefire without Archedark. There can be no consciousness without the void. Little evidence of the former existed before The Tyrant intervened. None ever remained in the wake of his passing. Yet without this tearing down, there can be no building anew.

Stronger. Greater. Spiraling upward into eternity.

But first the scouring of all to its foundations.

Only these tiny beings riding frozen vessels of his making possessed bodies hard enough to withstand his presence. They too required purpose. His Aura stoked them to the necessary hatred, though such manipulations of the primordial powers had no effect on him. Animosity guided his creations to distant lands, and only in these short moments at the beginning of each Turn reminded him he was alive.

Each day passed as an eye blink. An infinity of moments blended together into nothing. The drudgery of creation, pulling stone from the land. Preparations. Mundane. He did what he must for consciousness to thrive, yet none appreciated his sacrifice. For it they named him Tyrant. So be it.

The cycle would continue.

Each end was a mercy for the fruits of his creation. Each beginning, a mercy for him. A reprieve from monotony. As though awakened, the

Turn granted memories anew, each differing in minuscule ways. Two types of creatures have persisted for several iterations, providing proof of his grand designs.

In the previous Turn, a people were left behind. It had happened before, though this time they resisted extinction through the entire cycle. It mattered little. Their existence was the span of a breath to the Tyrant. When he exhaled, they would all blow away.

The cold sun sailed the ocean. The night sky turned.

And the Tyrant followed the stars.

* * *

END OF THE SECOND DANCE OF THE SIBLING SUNS

From the Author

Thank you so, so much for reading not one but now *two* of my stories. Readers like you make the many months of effort it takes to produce a book entirely worth it. I would write even if no one bought these things, but knowing someone is on the other end of the line fills me with a special warm-and-fuzziness.

If you enjoyed *To Burn All Belief*, I would love to hear your thoughts! Since you're reading an indie book, you probably hear this so often it risks becoming cliche, but leaving an honest Amazon or Goodreads review really does help us immensely. Whether you leave a full review, a simple star rating, or just tell a friend you enjoyed this story, I appreciate you and your support.

That's two books down, one to go! The story will continue in book three, *Last Dance of the Sibling Suns*. I very much hope it's the last of the series, though I have a lot of work ahead of me to bring the trilogy to a satisfactory close. As I did with this book, I'll be changing the POV characters once again. Next time, look forward to Inac and Sentyx chapters—though I have a feeling Lorelay and Garret won't let me stay out of their heads for too long. I hope you're looking forward to it as much as I am!

Face into the wind,
Joshua

Sign up for the
Archefire Newsletter

If you made it this far, consider signing up for my mailing list at:

joshse.com/signup

I send out the Archefire Newsletter once per month with writing updates, frequent giveaways, and lots of pictures of my pup, Nazgul. Having a direct line rather than relying on unreliable algorithms lets us keep in touch so you can be the first to hear any Sibling Suns news.

Acknowledgements

Major thanks to Stacey Kucharik, my editor, who gave me incredible feedback that helped me polish the heart of this story.

Felix Ortiz and Shawn T. King are two of the best in the industry and insanely hard-working. I'll always admire them for taking the time to work with a small-time indie author like me.

Thanks also to the team at Podium Audio, who took a chance on me and agreed to produce audiobooks for the Sibling Suns books. Danny Gavigan narrated the first book, and my dialogue in this book is infused with the voices he used to bring the cast of characters to life.

A special thank you to my alpha readers—Namravi, Nyna, Quinne, the Sugarman, and Paladin Cavendish. Er...sorry, that's Vinamra Tripathi, Nina, Quinn Guigere, Michael H. Sugarman, and Charlie Cavendish. This book benefited greatly from your feedback and kept me from embarrassing myself with continuity errors.

Tim, thank you for organizing a book club to read An Ocean of Others, and Alice, Jared, Justin, Alyssa, Cris, Chris, and Eric—thank you all for taking part. I immensely enjoyed hearing your theories. Some of them seeded ideas for this book and the next!

Of course, I can't forget mom and dad. Thirty-three years now, and their love and support is as strong as ever.

Finally, my love and thanks to my wife, Rachel, who graciously puts up with me spending way too much time in a fantasy land in front of my computer.

APPENDICES

Glossary

Note: Only the final section of this glossary contains information which would spoil events of the story. These are placed behind a spoiler warning so you can refer to the rest of the glossary at any point during your reading experience.

THE AGENCY

Head—Leader of the Agency.

Nerve—White-and-gold-uniformed couriers who relay messages directly from the Head.

Eye—Blue-uniformed reconnaissance officers who discern the abilities of Benefactors in reported areas

First Eye—Highest ranking Eye who oversees Hand operations.

Finger—Green-uniformed field agents who carry out the Head's commands.

Hand—A group of five Fingers often sent to hunt Benefactors.

Organ—Brass-uniformed administrator, typically responsible for one function within the Agency, such as Logistics or Personnel.

Heel—Gray-uniformed low-level workers assigned menial tasks.

Mortician—Studies Benefactors infesting the dead of the Agency's mortuary.

Technician—Crimson-uniformed assistant to the morticians.

MAGIC

Archemagic—Term encompassing all magic practiced throughout the Empire. The prefix Arche- is applied to many professions who use magic in their craft, e.g. Archeglaziers or Archemakers.

Archemage—Person capable of sensing and controlling Archemagic.

Archefire—Archemagic with the aspect of fire. Sometimes called the Fire.

Archedark—Archemagic with the aspect of dark. Sometimes called the Dark or Archedeath.

Archemetal—Metal imbued with Archefire. Exceedingly durable and cannot be burned.

Pattern—Archemagical configuration associated with the neural structure of a creature.

Seedling—Growth in human brain that regulates the human pattern.

Clasform—Box containing a seedling or other Aura-negating item.

Grieving Pine—Abnormal tree that gives off a soothing Aura.

Druid's Tears—Products of the Grieving Pine injected as a toxic to negate Benefactor Aura.

BENEFACTORS

Benefactor—Parasitic organism that infests the brain of a creature, turning them into a monster when they die through a process called Emergence.

Empath—Person with pattern similar to Benefactor host, who carries out the Benefactor's will.

Incubating—Someone infested by Benefactors who has not yet died.

Emergent—Benefactor whose host has died and transformed into a monster.

Aura—Archemagical field given off by Benefactor that induces sensory and emotional illusions to people within proximity.

Deluge—Memories of a Benefactor forced upon another person.

Pool—Collection of memories specific to one Benefactor.

Assimilate—Process by which a Benefactor combines its victims' flesh with its own.

Ocean of others—The combined Pools of over ten-thousand Benefactor victims, stored by Grim's Benefactor.

Death knell—Brief vision of the moment before an Incubating Benefactor dies.

LIWOKIN POLITICS

Liwokin Council—Traditional government of Liwokin.

Council Chair—Top-ranking official of the Liwokin Council selected by the citizenry.

Seats of the Hall—Members of the Liwokin Council appointed by the Chair.

Liwokin Militia—Citizen army of Liwokin. Disbanded shortly after the Agency was created.

The Gild—Cabal of wealthy financiers and rentiers often seen gallivanting in Liwokin's Financial District.

Archecloak—Guard employed by the Gild.

VOS POLITICS

Bright Empire—Hegemonic empire of the northern hemisphere.

Bright Empress—Leader of the Bright Empire who rules by religious mandate.

Bright Prince—Son of the Bright Empress, though not often heir to the throne.

Radiant Palace—Home to the royalty and nobility of Vos.

Paladin—Elite soldier that serves the Bright Empress.

The Order—Religous army of Paladins.

RELIGION

Church of Light—Dominant religion of the Bright Empire.

Book of Light—Holy book of the Church of Light.

Twelve Songs—Officially mandated songs and the only ones allowed to be performed in Paceeq.

Lightmother—Goddess of Light, associated with fire.

Darkfather—God of Dark, associated with ice.

Brightdaughter—Sibling Sun of the northern hemisphere with an unpredictable orbit leading to varying day lengths. Personified as the child of the Lightmother in the pantheon.

Shadowson—Sibling Sun of the southern hemisphere with a cold blue glow. Personified as the child of the Darkfather in the pantheon.

Rhythm of Time—Method of timekeeping in the Bright Empire, whereby bells are rung a dawn, half-noon, noon, half-dusk, and dusk.

Mathemelodian—Member of a secretive order that calculates to progression of the Brightdaughter to keep track of time.

Cleric—Religious figure in the Church of Light.

High Cleric—Holy figure who speaks with the voice of the Lightmother.

Lady of Ash—Widow who has ceased practicing her faith.

THE WORLD

Lawiko—Centrally situated country in the Bright Empire.

Paceeq—Island country southwest of Lawiko and home to the Bright Empire's Capital.

Vos—Capital city of Paceeq and the Bright Empire.

Eko—Country northeast of Lawiko covered by stormjungles and home to exotic wildlife.

Ayeir—Country east of Lawiko with sprawling deserts.

Stinbine Isles—Archipelago far east of Lawiko where Sea Pot Isle is located.

Old Country—Wind-beaten home of the Skardwarves in the southern hemisphere.

Peeker Mounds—Mountainous home of the Peekers west of Lawiko.

Lumeeq—Sparsely populated island country west of Paceeq, site of mines that produce majority of metal for Archemetal imbuement.

LAWIKO

Liwokin—Capital city of Lawiko, main trading hub of the Bright Empire, and home of the Agency.

Liwo—Citizen of Liwokin

Financial District—Wealthy district filled with luxury shops and attractions and Archemetal financial towers. Often called the Gild.

Residential District—Where many Liwo own homes or rent them from the Gild. Often called the Burg.

Market District—Where merchants and traders live and hawk their wares.

Artisans District—Where artists and craftspeople set up shop and display their works.

Old District—Dangerous and run-down section of Liwokin where the city began. Often called the Blight. Sometimes called the Old Hill.

Canako—City north of Liwokin where a canal provides easy passage to Paceeq and the Peeker Mounds.

Great Riot—Devastating outbreak of violence caused by the first Benefactor Emergence.

Brightcalm Bay—Liwokin's bay, often filled with merchants' vessels.

Outrush Canyon—Flooded canyon south of Liwokin that connects to Brightcalm Bay. Impassable by most ships.

PEEKER MOUNDS

Peekers—Enigmatic insect-like humanoids that communicate telepathically with one another and must form Pairs (or Pairs of Pairs, and so on) to function.

Colony—Common name for the population of Peekers living in the Peeker Mounds and abroad.

Collective—Peeker hivemind connected to the Queen.

Variant—Peeker with unusual morphology.

Worker—Most common Peeker seen throughout the Bright Empire.

Builder—Four-legged crawling Peeker variant that produces resin and maintains the Colony.

Soldier—Strong Peeker variant that guards the Colony from humans.

Cartographer—Peeker variant that maps tunnel complex and ensures it is navigable by all Peekers.

Gaoler—One of a mismatched Peeker Pair attending the Peeker prison.

Resin—Sticky substance secreted by Peekers and used for construction.

Peeker Gem—Growth in Peeker brain that regulates the Peeker pattern.

Myrme—Mountain that houses the primary tunnel complex of the Colony.

Human Aerie—Home of the humans living in the Peeker Mounds.

Nectar Hall—Common area where humans gather to eat within the Aerie.

Burner—Peeker term for Skardwarf.

Screamer—Peeker term for human.

EKO

Graln—Treetop capital city of Eko.

Institute of Biotism—Establishment producing the foremost knowledge of nature and its workings.

Biotist—One who studies nature.

Ranger—Revered citizen of Graln who proved their skills in the rite of endurance.

Brightwood giants—Old-growth trees mainly found in the storm-jungles of Eko.

OLD COUNTRY

Eevoq—Country in the southern hemisphere not occupied by Skardwarves.

Eevoqian—Large-bodied citizen of Eevoq.

Skardwarf—Stone-skinned resident of the Old Country.

The definitions in this section contain spoilers for events in To Burn All Belief.

* * *

Siphon—The ability for an Emergent Benefactor to see through the eyes of an Incubating Benefactor.

Darkmetal—Metal imbued with Archedark. Exceedingly durable.

The Resistance—Uprising of Blightdwellers against the ruling factions of Liwokin.

The Operator—Benefactor leader of the Resistance.

Kindling Emperor—Transitionary title between Bright Prince and Bright Emperor, granted when the previous Bright Empress is burned.

Demon—Skardwarf.

Queensguard—One of the eight incredibly strong Peekers who protect the Queen.

Feeder—Engorged Peeker that stores food for the Colony.

Feeder Hollow—Dark cavern in the depths of Myrme where Feeders await their fate.

Audience Chamber—Vast cavern where the Peeker Queen addresses all Peekers and humans within the Mounds.

Queen's Grotto—Peeker Queen's private cavern.

Princess Egg—Final egg birthed by the Peeker Queen containing her successor.

Mathemelodian Prime—Head of the Mathemelodians with a religious mandate to make long-term predictions about the arrival of the Dark Era.

Dark Era—Time when the Shadowson flies over the Bright Empire.

Character List

Note: Only the final section of this list contains information which would spoil events of the story. These are placed behind a spoiler warning so you can refer to the rest of the character list at any point during your reading experience.

LIWOKIN

Grim—Head of the Agency infested by a powerful Benefactor.

Inac—Archemage formerly with masterful control over Archefire and Archedark.

Arza—Ayeiri lead mortician tasked with finding Benefactor cure.

Jacquin—Ulken's First Eye with unwavering loyalty to the Head.

Oltrov—Gildmember who conspired with First Eye Reed.

Maise—Chair of the Liwokin Council.

Yezna—Ulken's wife and the first Benefactor whose Emergence caused the Great Riot.

Nill—Veteran Finger and Captain of a Hand that survived a daggerclaw attack with Hand Sixty-Four.

Cavern—Skardwarf Finger of Nill's Hand and Sentyx's brother.

Yesk—Archemage Finger of Nill's Hand who lost his leg to a daggerclaw in Reed's Woods.

Quinne—Finger of Hand Twenty-Eight, loyal to the Agency.

VOS

Lorelay—Blasphemous Paceeqi bard and envoy of the Agency in Vos.

Vinlin—Bright Prince and son of Elzia.

Minny—Lorelay's maidservant in the Radiant Palace.

Namravi—High Cleric of the Church of Light.

Jenx—Lorelay's childhood friend.

Lydia—Lorelay's mother and a Lady of Ash.

Gravis—Former proprietor of the Blueflame Tavern, imprisoned when Lorelay performed an unsanctioned song.

The Sugarman—Jailer in the Radiant Palace dungeons.

Ezebel—Servant in the Radiant Palace.

PEEKER MOUNDS

Garret—Ekoan ranger tasked with hunting Prost.

Sentyx—Skardwarf tasked with hunting Prost.

Tunnel—Peeker rescued from the Mental Ward by members of Hand Sixty-Four.

Half-Blind Eye—Deserter of the Agency investigating Auras in Myrme.

Helman—Eevoqian explorer.

THE DECEASED

Ulken—Former Head of the Agency killed by Grim.

Reed—Former First Eye who became the Chimera Benefactor and assimilated thousands of Liwo in the woods west of Liwokin.

Taktus—Lead mortician studying Benefactors under Ulken, killed by a Peeker's Emergence.

Elzia—Bright Empress.

Elwin—Vinlin's brother, who left with his father.

Elzia II—Vinlin's sister, heir to the throne who died young.

Dunnax—Lorelay's brother and an oathbreaking Paladin.

Wyran—Wick, Benefactor of Leppit village.

Andya—Benefactor of Canako Canal gate.

Pinch—Peeker Benefactor in Liwokin.

Lomin—The Hunter, Benefactor of the Shaded Grounds.

The characters listed in this section contain spoilers for events in To Burn All Belief.

* * *

Bello—Elevator operator from the Blight.

Raylen—Smuggler of Druid's Tears and emissary of the Resistance.

Counter—Member of the Resistance obsessed with numbers.

Peeker Queen—Ancient being who births all Peekers and controls the hivemind.

Aerienne—First and only friend of the Peeker Queen.

Prost—Eevoqian spreading Benefactors in the Bright Empire.

Tyrant—Eternal being who commands the Skardwarves.

Indie Book Recommendations

If you enjoyed To Burn All Belief, you may enjoy these other works by indie authors like myself. I've read each one and can vouch for their awesomeness!

Starlight Jewel by E.L. Lyons

A fresh take on dark fantasy with strong half-human, half-spryggan characters, compelling themes, and masterful worldbuilding.

Curse of the Fallen by H.C. Newell

Grimdark with a splash of humor that doesn't shy away from emotionally hard-hitting moments. Great for fans nostalgic for Skyrim and the Witcher games.

The Hand of God by Yuval Kordov

Old Testament gothic sci-fi/dark fantasy set in a world ravaged by two apocalypses with chilling horror elements.

Gunmetal Gods by Zamil Akhtar

A twisted and fast-paced dark epic fantasy inspired by the Crusades with Lovecraftian gods meddling in human affairs.

A Touch of Light by Thiago Abdalla

A book with heavy themes of death and madness, perfect for detail-oriented readers who love unraveling an intriguing mystery.

About the Author

Joshua Scott Edwards lives in Lansdale, PA with his wife, Rachel. He received an M.S. in Electrical and Computer Engineering from Rowan University, only afterward discovering that his true passion is for storytelling. Sadly, the topic was not covered in the engineering curriculum. By day, Joshua writes software to pay the bills. By night, he writes fantasy and science fiction stories, dreaming of a future in which those pay the bills as well.

You can find more of his writing at joshse.com, where you can sign up to the Archefire Newsletter for monthly updates about ongoing projects, discounts for books and merch, and more.